Loud Praise for C. E. Lawrence and SILENT SCREAMS

"Criminally compelling, *Silent Screams* by C. E. Lawrence nails you to your seat with a fascinating NYPD profiler who's hurled into the case of his lifetime. This journey into violence and the soul is unforgettable."
　　—**Gayle Lynds,** *New York Times* bestselling
　　　author of *The Coil* and *The Book of Spies*

"Pulse-racing, compelling, first rate. Lawrence knows how to build and hold suspense with the best of them. Once you get into this one, you can't get out."
　　—**John Lutz,** *New York Times*
　　　bestselling author of *Mister X*

"C. E. Lawrence delivers finely honed suspense, with unique twists, and accurately captures the logic and intuition of a profiler under pressure."
　　—**Katherine Ramsland,** professor of
　　　forensic psychology, and author of *The
　　　Forensic Psychology of Criminal Minds*

"C. E. Lawrence's *Silent Screams* is so compulsively readable, you won't just tear through the pages, you'll scream through them."
　　—**Chris Grabenstein,** Anthony and Agatha
　　　awards winner, and author of *Rolling Thunder*

ALSO BY C. E. LAWRENCE

Silent Screams

SILENT VICTIM

C. E. LAWRENCE

PINNACLE BOOKS
KENFSINGTON PUBLISHING CORP.
www.kensingtonbooks.com

ISBN-13: 978-0-7860-2149-9
ISBN-10: 0-7860-2149-7

First printing: December 2010

10   9   8   7   6   5   4   3   2

Printed in the United States of America

For Joan and Rusty,
who are so dear to me

ACKNOWLEDGMENTS

Once again, thanks first and foremost to my editor, Michaela Hamilton, a.k.a. Fearless Leader, whose continuing support, wisdom, and insight keep me going on cold winter nights— and thanks to Marvin Kaye for introducing me to her. Special thanks to my dear friend Gisela Rose, for her superb editing skills and invaluable perspective. Thanks also to my agent, Paige Wheeler, for her professional advice, good cheer, and support. Special thanks once again to Robert ("Beaubear") Murphy and Rachel Fallon for their generosity in providing ideal retreats in which to work—large parts of this book were written in Long Eddy, New York, and Toot Baldon, U.K. Thanks also to Bev and P. G. Gardner for their generosity in putting me up at "Chalet Gardner," where I worked out some key plot points with the help of delicious chocolates and the Vermont countryside. Also thanks to Kat Houghton and Coco for sharing their charming Chatham retreat with me, to Mike for pulling me out of the mud, and to Kathy Szaj for looking after the home fires for me. My deepest gratitude to the Byrdcliffe Arts Colony in Woodstock, New York, which has become my second home. Thanks too to Hawthornden Castle International Writers Retreat for providing a wonderful month in the most idyllic setting I can imagine—and to Martin, Angie, Mary, and Doris for letting me stay up late. Thanks to my mother, Margaret Simmons (a.k.a. Title Maven), and Joan Lawrence for their insightful feedback and continued support, to Anthony Moore for setting up my website, and to my sisters, Katie and Suzie, who are always in my heart.

Hell hath no fury like a woman scorned.

—WILLIAM CONGREVE, *The Mourning Bride,* 1697

PROLOGUE

There she is—just look at her with her chic little itsy-bitsy leather knapsack and her oh-so-hip camel coat and her CFM boots. Well, she wasn't so approachable as those boots might suggest, now, was she? Too bad—if she hadn't been so uppity and above it all, maybe she would live to see another day.

But it's too late for that. Even if she got down on those skinny, leather-clad knees and begged for mercy, we wouldn't listen, would we? No, because bad girls must be punished, and she has been a very naughty girl. Very naughty indeed. She couldn't be bothered with the likes of us—not even enough to be polite. Thought it was oh-so-funny that we would approach her, and wanted everyone around to know how amused she was by it.

She'll soon be laughing out the other side of her mouth— what's left of it. She has to be taught a lesson in manners, one she'll never forget.

CHAPTER ONE

The phone call was unexpected—unbidden and out of the blue. It took him so much by surprise that Lee Campbell found himself stumbling for words. The last thing he expected on a Friday night was a call from a former patient—and certainly not *this* former patient.

"Is this Dr. Lee Campbell?" The voice was high and breathy, petulance lurking underneath the seductiveness, like a bad Marilyn Monroe impersonator. He recognized it at once.

"Uh—yes." *Yes, Ana*, he wanted to say, but some part of him still hoped that it wasn't her.

But of course it was.

"This is Ana Watkins."

"Oh, yes—hello, Ana. How are you?" His professionalism clicked in automatically, keeping his tone steady and objective—or so he hoped.

"I'm downstairs—can I come up and see you?"

"Downstairs?"

"At McSorley's, actually."

How did she know where he lived?

As if reading his mind, she said, "You're in the directory."

Not true, but never mind. His explanation that he wasn't in private practice anymore didn't seem to put her off. She insisted that she wouldn't take up much of his time, but that it was very important to her.

"Please? I wouldn't ask, but—"

But what? he thought irritably. *You didn't cause enough trouble the first time around?*

"I'll come down and meet you at McSorley's."

"It's too loud in here," she said, and he could hear the din of clanking glasses and boisterous laughter in the background. McSorley's was always loud on a Friday night.

He glanced at the clock. It was just after six.

"I have a dinner meeting at seven."

"I won't take long—I promise."

He peered out the window down at the street. It was August, but as evening drew in a cold rain whipped the naked branches of the trees on East Seventh Street. They shivered in the chilly gusts, shaking like frightened skeletons. He caught a glimpse of his own ghostly image staring back at him—curly black hair, angular face, intense, deep-set eyes. He knew it was a face many women considered handsome, and wished that Ana Watkins weren't one of them.

Lee had an impulse to pour himself a Scotch, but decided against it—he needed his mind clear for the encounter. When the downstairs bell rang he took a deep breath and buzzed her into the building.

Her footsteps on the carpeted stairs were light and quick, the tread of a young person. He opened the door and fixed a smile on his face. She entered in a cloud of lilac perfume, and as soon as he breathed the aroma, he inhaled the memories of that time in his life along with it. It all felt so long ago.

She had changed very little—tall and thin and so pale that

she always reminded him of an albino. She wasn't an albino, she had told him in their first session together, but her pallid skin lacked the shade and depth of ordinary skin; it looked two dimensional, like paper. She wasn't exactly pretty—her nose was too big and her lips were too thin—but she was striking, and she knew it.

She took in the apartment with one nervous glance, probably noticing more than she appeared to. Lee remembered her IQ was 160, or so she had claimed. That could have been a fiction, of course—much of what she had told him was. She was one of his earliest patients, and he had not yet acquired the skill of seeing through the myriad lies and obfuscations of the narcissistic personality. Still, there was no doubt that Ana was bright—very bright. Her sessions may have been frustrating, but at least they were never dull.

She slipped off her gray raincoat and dangled it from her outstretched arm, as though she expected Lee to take it from her. That was so like her—her helplessness always had an aggressive quality, and she could turn even a small gesture like removing her coat into a demand. Evidently years of therapy had failed to change this. He suppressed a sigh and took the coat, hanging it on the antique bentwood coatrack his mother had found at an estate sale in Bucks County.

"Do you have any coffee?" she asked, rubbing her thin hands together and blowing on them.

Another demand. Lee was flooded with relief that they would not be continuing their sessions together. He had always done his best to disguise one of the uglier truths of the therapeutic relationship: there were some patients he just didn't like. If his enmity toward a patient ever threatened to compromise his effectiveness, he would find an excuse to suggest they seek out another therapist, but in the case of Ana Watkins, his dislike of her didn't become entirely apparent to him until after their last session together.

"I can make some coffee," he said in response to her question, though from the way her fingers twitched and her eyes roamed restlessly around the room, he thought coffee was the last thing she needed.

"Never mind—I'll be all right," she replied, the familiar tone of self-dramatization in her voice, as if instead of coffee, she were speaking of a rare and lifesaving drug.

"It's no trouble at all," Lee insisted. He wasn't going to let her win this first stab at manipulation—she had requested coffee, and coffee she would have.

Instead of thanking him, she tossed her tiny red leather knapsack on the nearest chair and flopped down on it as though this were her apartment, not his. It was, of course, his favorite chair—but that was probably why she had instinctively chosen it.

"Make yourself at home," he said, knowing she couldn't miss the sarcasm in his voice. He turned and went into the kitchen, glad for the opportunity to collect his thoughts and steel himself for what could be a very sticky conversation. Ana Watkins was, he felt, his first major failure as a therapist.

She was also the first patient who tried to seduce him.

And she had tried hard—very hard—and very nearly succeeded. And now she was sprawled out in his living room, in his favorite armchair, with God knows what in mind. He wasn't normally afraid of his patients—even the violent ones—but he was afraid of Ana Watkins. There was something about her, an undercurrent of needy malice, which had made it very difficult to be her therapist. Even her attempted seduction had been more of a conquest, like a declaration of war.

As the coffee beans rattled around in the Krups grinder, he wondered what had brought her here, and whether she would tell him the truth or only her version of it. When the coffee grinder stopped, the silence made him wonder what she was up to in the living room. He shoved the filter into the coffeemaker, dumped some water in, jabbed at the ON switch, and ducked back into the living room.

Sure enough, she was standing in front of his bookshelf, a thick volume of poetry in her hands. Like a lot of narcissists, she had boundary issues: what was yours was hers, as far as she was concerned. As he entered, she turned and smiled at him, one lock of blond hair falling artfully over her pale blue eyes. He wouldn't have put it past her to have planned that moment the whole time she was standing there. If she inclined her head just so, the hair would fall over her eyes, and then all she needed was to cap it with that sultry, come-hither smile.

"You have a lot of poetry here," she commented, still smiling.

"I like poetry." He tried to keep his voice neutral, to avoid showing his irritation.

"I guess so," she said, slipping the book back into its place on the shelf. Lee recognized the jacket—it was his *Anthology of English Verse*, from his days at Princeton. He knew its contents well: Wordsworth, Coleridge, Maxwell, William Blake, *Songs of Innocence and Experience.* The young woman before him could have been cast as Oothoon herself, with her wispy, waspish body—except that she was only pretending to be innocent. Experience had hardened her into something else entirely.

He poured them both generous mugs of steaming coffee and brought them out on a tray, along with the lead crystal cream pitcher and sugar bowl—more of his mother's estate sale coups.

"Nice crystal," Ana commented, helping herself to a heaping spoon of sugar and following it up with a lavish amount of cream.

"Thanks," Lee answered. To another guest, he might have mentioned the amusing anecdote of his mother's triumphal purchase, but with Ana he instinctively played his cards close. He sat on the couch opposite her and sipped his coffee.

Sticking her long nose deep into the mug, Ana slurped up the coffee greedily, and to his surprise, it did seem to calm her. Her bony shoulders relaxed, and her thin body seemed to soften. He realized only then how stiffly she had been holding herself. She shook herself, like a dog flinging excess water from its coat. Clutching the mug between her long fingers, she looked at him through lank blond bangs.

"You're probably dying to know why I'm here."

Lee noted the familiar, overly dramatic phrasing of the chronically narcissistic, but all he said was, "Yes, I am curious."

She looked around, gulped down some more coffee, and leaned in toward him.

"I've recently recovered memories of—being sexually abused."

A dozen questions darted through his mind, but all he said was, "Really?"

"At first I wasn't sure. It was just this one dream that kept repeating itself, you know, so I found a specialist in buried memories, and I've been working with him for about a year—and then one day I woke up sure of it."

Lee wasn't sure how to respond. He didn't entirely trust so-called recovered memories. Though repressed memory was a real, documented response to trauma, there was a subset of "specialists" in this field who, through a combination of subtle suggestion and hypnosis, could convince patients that they were the victims of anything from ritual satanic abuse to alien abduction.

In Ana's case, of course, it would explain a lot: her belligerent girlishness, her passive-aggressive attitude toward men, her childlike affect. But there were other things that would explain these traits as well—and the subject of abuse had never come up in their sessions together.

"When was this?" Lee said.

"I don't have all the details yet. I think it happened when I was a child, and that it was someone I knew."

"But you're not sure?"

She shook her head. "I haven't been able to make out his face. But Dr. Perkins—he's my therapist—says it's only a matter of time."

"Why did you come to me? It sounds like Dr. Perkins knows what he's doing." What exactly he was doing was another matter, but Lee wasn't going to dive headlong into that particular tar baby. Professional etiquette aside, he had no wish to challenge a colleague's competence or motives based upon so little information.

Ana tightened her fingers around the handle of her mug.

"I—I'm afraid."

"Of what?"

"Of everything. I just have this *feeling* that something's going to happen."

"Is there any particular reason you should feel this way? Could it be a response to"—he hesitated—"the memory of your abuse?"

She frowned at her mug, as though it contained vinegar instead of coffee.

"That's what Dr. Perkins thinks."

"And what do you think?"

She got up and began pacing the room, restlessness running through her like an electrical current.

"I don't know *what* to think. I'm jumpy, I can't sleep. I see potential attackers around every corner. And not only that, but I think—well, I think someone is stalking me."

"You're sure you're not just—"

"No, see, that's the thing—I really think I'm being watched."

"What makes you say that?"

She sat down again on the armchair and wrapped her long arms around her thin torso, swaying back and forth, her lips clenched. Lee really did feel sorry for her. She looked like a lost girl right now, and he felt the urge to make everything all right. But immediately the warning sounded in his head: *Steady on, Campbell. She's a first-class manipulator, and you know better.*

He leaned back and forced himself to take another sip of coffee.

She looked up at him, her pale eyes tragic. "There have been some things happening, you know? Scary things."

"Like what?"

"Like the phone ringing, but when I answer they hang up. And one time I know I left my car locked, but when I got out of the store it was unlocked."

"Was anything taken?"

"No, but I had the feeling someone had been in there."

"What about the phone calls—do you have caller ID?"

"Yes, but it always reads 'Unavailable.'"

"Do you still live in Jersey?"

"When my dad died last year I moved into his house."

"Oh, I'm so sorry for your loss." The words sounded like what they were—a stock phrase—but he hoped there was comfort in them anyway.

"Thanks." She looked down at her hand, the corners of her mouth twitching.

"He lived in Flemington, right?"

Flemington was in Hunterdon County, about ten miles

away from Stockton, the town Lee grew up in and where his mother still lived. When Ana was his patient, they were both New Jersey residents, but that felt like another lifetime now.

"Yeah," she answered. "When he—uh, got sick, I tried to be there for him, you know. . . ." She trailed off forlornly.

"So he left you the house?"

"Yeah. It's kind of big for me, but I don't think he wanted me to sell it."

"Is that what he said?"

She shook her head. "No, it's just that he loved that old house, and I feel like if I sold it he'd be sad."

Hunterdon County was full of charming old stone houses, some of them dating back to the eighteenth century. Lee imagined her father's house, tucked away among the green rolling hills of the southwestern Jersey landscape, with its fertile farmland, the rich black soil perfect for growing the famous Jersey tomatoes, and the sweet, sweet Silver Queen corn he loved so much as a child.

He looked back at Ana, who was chewing absently on the cuticle of her index finger.

"Is there anything else?"

"Yeah," she said, fishing around in the pocket of her green corduroy skirt. She had an unusual way of dressing that was all her own, Lee remembered—on her, even green corduroy looked stylish. Under the skirt she wore knee-high leather boots with sharp, pointy high heels.

"Here it is," she said, producing a crumpled piece of paper.

He took it and opened it up. It was a clumsy version of the kind of ransom note you might see on a cheaply produced television crime drama. The letters had all been cut from different parts of various magazines and pasted onto a plain sheet of white paper. RetrɪbuTɪoN is cOMɪnG, it read.

Prepare TO meEt Your FAte." His first thought was that she might have created it herself, a ploy for the attention she had been seeking all her life to fill the cavernous hole in her soul. But a look at the terror in her eyes banished that thought from his head. She was genuinely frightened.

"Have you gone to the police?" he asked.

She waved off his suggestion as though it were an annoying insect.

"Jersey cops," she said, rolling her eyes. "Let us know when someone tries to kill you, and then maybe we'll be interested. Better yet—give us a call if you are actually murdered."

"They said that?"

"More or less. They made it clear they didn't want to be bothered."

"So you came to me."

"I didn't know what else to do," she moaned, the old petulance creeping into her voice. "Raymond—that's my boyfriend—he's really nice, but he's just a restaurant manager. He didn't know what to do either."

At the mention of her boyfriend, Lee breathed a bit more freely.

"I mean, you work with the police, right?" she said, her blue eyes imploring.

"Well, yes, but we don't have jurisdiction in New Jersey."

"But can't you—I mean, couldn't you investigate this on your own or something, without telling them?"

"Well, I'm not a detective—"

"But you're a criminal profiler, right?"

"I'm a forensic psychologist."

"Right—but you profile criminals, don't you?"

"Among other things. What do you expect me to do?"

"Find out who's stalking me. Do a profile on him—or whatever it is you do."

"Do you have any idea who it might be?"

She bit her lip and shook her head. "I've been trying to think of someone. My boyfriend before Raymond broke up with me, so I don't think it's him. And he was really sweet and everything, anyway."

"Does Raymond know you came to see me?"

She looked at him and frowned. "Am I terrible to not tell him? It's just that I didn't want him to worry."

Or get jealous in case you decide to try to seduce me again, Lee thought, but he said, "You shouldn't be keeping secrets from him right now—not when your life could be in danger."

"So—so you think it is?" she said, her voice wavering between fear and hope.

"I think it's possible, and it's best not to take any chances. Anyone else it could be?"

"Well, I'm working as a waitress at the Swan Hotel in Lambertville, and I see a lot of people every day, but mostly it's wealthy, middle-aged people, and they're usually pretty nice." She fished around in her leather knapsack. "Look, money isn't a problem. I'll be glad to pay you whatever you—"

He shook his head. "I wouldn't even know what to charge you anyway."

"So can you—help me?" she said, her voice thick.

Lee was touched, in spite of their history together—or maybe because of it. She seemed so vulnerable—perhaps fear had humbled her. Without her usual arrogance, she was actually rather appealing.

"I don't see what I can possibly do," he said.

He glanced at his watch. It was after seven, and he was already late for his dinner meeting.

"I'm really sorry," he said, rising from the couch, "but I arranged to meet someone for dinner, and I'm late."

She jumped up from the chair as though she were on springs. "Oh, sorry—I didn't mean to take up so much of your time!"

"Please don't apologize. I'm just sorry I can't help," he said, fetching her coat from the rack and holding it open for her.

She slipped her arms into the sleeves and hugged the coat around her body, shivering, even though the room was quite warm.

"I—I wish you'd change your mind," she said, looking up at him with an expression that was part lost child, part seductress. That was her specialty, the woman/child in distress, guaranteed to reel in a certain percentage of the male population. His friend Chuck Morton would be helpless to resist her, he thought—if he weren't already tied up with his own personal Circe.

"I'm sorry," he said. "I just—"

"I've missed you, you know," she said, holding his gaze longer than necessary. He was afraid she was going to try to kiss him. But she just took his hand and pressed it between her own. Her hands were cold and smooth and dry, her grip surprisingly strong.

He disentangled his hands from hers and opened the door for her.

"I am sorry," he said. "I think you should take the note you showed me to the police in Flemington."

She gave a quick shrug and looked away.

"Well, I tried. If something happens to me—"

"Take the note to the police," he repeated, more firmly this time.

She gave a little laugh, like the tinkling of bells.

"Yeah—right."

And then she slipped out the door, leaving behind a trail of lilac perfume. He looked down at his hand and realized she had pressed a piece of paper into it containing her cell phone number. Hearing her quick, light step as she hurried down the stairs, he remembered from their days together in therapy that she always seemed to be in a hurry. He had a sharp, unexpected impulse to call after her—not because he was attracted to her, but because he was suddenly reluctant to let her venture out so unprotected into a wild and dangerous world.

Later, he would regret not heeding that impulse.

CHAPTER TWO

At first glance there seemed to be no connection between them.

A man in his twenties found floating in the Bronx River, cause of death: drowning. He was assumed initially to be a suicide.

Until the farewell note in his pocket was found to have been written by someone else.

A man in his forties found dead in his bathtub—a careless accident, perhaps. His hair dryer had fallen into the water, electrocuting him.

Except that he was bald.

It didn't add up, and whoever staged the bathtub "accident" had to know it didn't add up. Therefore, the clumsiness of the crime had to be taken as purposeful, and the manner of it as a challenge—no, a *taunt*—to the police. As for the floater—well, he wasn't necessarily linked to the baldy in the bathtub, but there was that suicide note scribbled on the mirror in lipstick—*lipstick?*—that made the whole thing as fishy as the corpse the boys had pulled out of the river only two days before they found Baldy.

Chuck Morton had already come to these conclusions by

the time he reached his office in the Bronx Major Case Unit on a warm morning in late August. He walked through the newly renovated lobby, across the polished marble floor to his cramped office in the back of the first floor. He plugged in his new automatic coffeemaker and added water and precisely six tablespoons of coffee, listening to the hum of the heating coil as it began to whir into life.

Charles Chesterfield Morton was a precise man. He liked his rituals at a certain time: black Kenyan coffee from Fairway first thing in the morning, with exactly one teaspoon of sugar and a dollop of cream.

His phone rang and he grabbed it.

"Morton here."

"Ah, yes, Chuck . . . how are you?"

Morton scowled. He recognized the voice at once—it was Deputy Chief Police Commissioner Steven Connelly, a man he despised. A call from him first thing on a Monday morning couldn't be anything good. And when Connelly called him by his first name, it was an especially bad sign.

Morton sank down in his chair.

"Fine, sir," he said, "and you?"

"Great, just great."

Morton ran a hand through his short blond hair. *Get to the point, for Christ's sake.* He knew from experience that the more Connelly stalled, the worse the news he could expect.

"And your lovely wife—how is she?"

Morton suppressed a groan.

"She's very well, sir—thank you for asking."

The deputy chief cleared his throat.

"Have you picked your team yet for this drowning business on Arthur Avenue?"

"Well, sir, I—"

"I'm sending someone your way, Chuck, and I want you to take her under your wing, so to speak."

"Yes, sir. Who is it?'

But before he asked the question, he already knew the answer.

"Elena Krieger. She just finished working undercover on the Strickley Affair, so I'm assigning her to you. She's a specialist in linguistic forensics—one of the best in the department. You need someone who can decipher those fake suicide notes, right?"

Chuck had never met Elena Krieger, but had heard enough to convince him they weren't going to get along.

But all he said was, "Yes, sir."

There was a pause on the other end of the line, as if the deputy chief was waiting for him to raise an objection.

"Okay, then," Connelly said finally, sounding surprised that Morton wasn't arguing with him. Chuck knew from experience that it wouldn't do any good. Connelly cleared his throat again. "Who's the primary on this one?"

"Detective Leonard Butts," Chuck said.

"Oh, yeah, that funny little guy who chews on cigars?"

"Right."

"Okay, Chuck, give me a full report as soon as you have anything, will you?"

"Yes, sir," he replied, and hung up.

Elena Krieger had risen quickly through the ranks to become sergeant, then lieutenant, and now detective. Oh, she was brilliant—and comely enough, so everyone said—tall and red haired and curvy and all the rest of it, but that didn't cheer him up one bit. Connelly's solicitous manner made Chuck suspect that he had slept with her. He pictured the deputy chief's skinny legs poking out from striped boxer briefs as he was straddled by a red-headed Amazon in a push-up bra. The image made him shudder.

There was a knock on the door.

"Come in," Morton barked, gazing with dismay at the mounting pile of paperwork on his desk.

Sergeant Ruggles poked his pink, bullet-shaped head through the door.

"Yes, Sergeant?"

"Message for you, sir—came in just as you arrived."

Ruggles had recently joined the NYPD after a stint as a beat cop in London. His accent was pure North Country, with the wide vowels and truncated consonants of that part of England. Chuck still hadn't gotten used to how polite he was.

"What is it?" he said.

"Detective Krieger called to say she's on her way and will be here in half an hour, sir."

Morton frowned.

"The Valkyrie rides again," he muttered. "Damn."

Ruggles's pink forehead crinkled. "Excuse me, sir?"

"That's what they called her at Brooklyn South."

"On account of her being German, sir?"

"That—and other things."

Ruggles coughed delicately.

"I've heard she's very . . . good looking, sir."

"Yeah, sure—a goddamn Teutonic goddess."

He looked up at Sergeant Ruggles, who was still lingering uncomfortably at the door, his thick fingers wrapped around the door handle.

"That's all, Sergeant," he said stiffly, and Ruggles withdrew, stumbling over his own feet as he backed out of the room.

Chuck frowned and opened the case file in front of him.

A lot of what he did as captain of the major cases squad was calculated to intimidate, impress, and control those under him. He kept the real Chuck Morton deeply hidden.

Squad commander was a role, and the script had been written long ago by people other than him. He knew that his success depended upon following it carefully: he must be strong, decisive, and, when necessary, intimidating.

For example, he liked Sergeant Ruggles, and had they met in a bar, might have asked him about his weekend, but as his superior officer he maintained a cool distance between them.

The coffeemaker on the windowsill, a recent gift from his wife, began to spit and pop, and the smell of freshly brewing coffee infiltrated the room. *Krieger*. How appropriate. He remembered enough from his college German to know it meant "warrior" in that language.

The phone on his desk rang. He picked it up and growled into the receiver.

"Morton here."

"Hiya, Chuck—it's Rob Murphy."

Rob Murphy had worked with Krieger at Brooklyn South, and had just about blown a gasket, according to Tanya Jackson, his ever competent and eavesdropping sergeant.

"What's up, Rob?"

"I hear the Valkyrie is headed your way."

"You heard right. Any advice?"

"Yeah. Play your cards close, and don't take any crap."

"I hear you worked with her on the Strickley Affair."

"Jesus Christ, Chuck, I never came so close in my life to hitting a woman."

The Strickley Affair was a delicate matter involving a corruption sting on a local union official. Krieger was working undercover, but had threatened to blow it all sky high when the official's son hit developed a crush on her and started following her around. He was beginning to get suspicious just as they finally collected enough evidence to round up the whole lot of crooks.

"Let's just say that Krieger wasn't exactly a team player," Murphy added.

"Thanks," said Chuck.

"Let me know how it goes," Murphy said.

"Okay," Chuck said, and hung up. The room suddenly felt overheated; he rolled his shirt sleeves up over his muscular forearms and opened his collar.

There were rumors that Krieger had been transferred because of Murphy's insistence he would never work with her again. And now Chuck was stuck with her just as he was about to investigate two very bogus-looking suicides.

He stared glumly at the full coffeepot on the windowsill. Normally he looked forward to this moment, when he could relax and enjoy a fresh cup of coffee after the long commute to the office. He had even splurged and bought some Jamaican Blue Mountain to mix with his Kenyan AA, but knowing he was about to meet the Valkyrie took away his enthusiasm.

Chuck poured himself a cup of coffee and took a sip, but it tasted bitter.

There was another knock on the door—sharper this time, brisk and businesslike. Chuck took a deep breath and squared his shoulders.

"Come in."

He smiled grimly. *Let the games begin.*

CHAPTER THREE

After Ana had gone, Lee pulled out his cell phone and hit the CONTACTS button, then selected the second name on the list and pushed the dial button. His party answered on the second ring.

"Butts here." The voice was a thick rumble, like a bulldog with a chest cold.

"Hi—sorry I'm late. I'll be there in five minutes."

"Oh, hiya, Doc. Well, I'll just have to order another beer."

Lee smiled as he put on his coat. He and Detective Leonard Butts were an unlikely pair, but the bond they had formed was a strong one. In the course of their relationship, he and Butts had gone from initial wariness and mistrust to a comfortable familiarity and mutual respect.

They didn't always see eye to eye, perhaps, but Lee had learned that Butts could be relied upon in a crisis. The squat detective's gruffness masked a deeply loyal, even passionate nature. The more Lee worked with the NYPD, the more he came to see beneath the masks that cops wore as protective covering. The city was not a soft place to live, and daily contact with criminals and creeps made it necessary to develop a thick outer shell. Otherwise, he imagined, you could be crushed by the harshness of police work in this town.

Virage, the restaurant where he was meeting Butts, was one long block away from his apartment. The rain had slurred to a steady drizzle, the air thick with a hazy mist. Shoving his hands into his pockets, he strode rapidly east on Seventh Street toward Second Avenue.

Sure enough, Butts sat at a corner table, a tall, thin glass of pilsner in front of him. Pockmarks littered his face like craters on the surface of the moon. A smile spread over the detective's homely face when he saw Lee.

"Hiya, Doc," he said, pulling up a chair for Lee to sit.

Physically they could not have been more different. Lee Campbell was tall and thin (overly so, according to his girlfriend, Kathy Azarian), with the clear, pale complexion and deep-set blue eyes of a true Celt. Butts was short and thick and swarthy, his face a minefield of pockmarks, his thinning sandy hair as straight as Lee's was dark and curly.

"Sorry to keep you waiting," Lee said as he settled into the chair Butts offered him.

"That's okay, Doc—gives me an excuse to have an extra beer. It's Belgian, I think they said—pretty good. You want one?"

"Sure."

Butts ordered them both a round and smiled at Lee's inquiring look.

"I'm takin' the train home tonight, so no worries."

"Muriel doesn't mind you being out on a Friday night?"

Butts grunted and downed the rest of his beer, wiping his rutted face with the back of his sleeve.

"Wife's taken up bridge. She belongs to this club—duplicate bridge, they call it. Some kind of a round-robin thingy, where the hands are dealt ahead of time, and each team gets a chance to play them."

"Sounds fun."

"I dunno, Doc—I'm not a card-playing man. All I know is they sit there playin' for hours, and at the end someone wins fifty bucks or somethin'. Seems like a waste of time to me, and they pretty much take over the living room for the evening."

"So you decided to be elsewhere tonight."

Butts threw his arms up in surrender. "I'm just in the way. I can't even go to the kitchen for a beer without havin' to pass by a dozen people or more."

"I understand. I felt that way sometimes when my parents had parties when I was a kid." Lee remembered with a pang what a handsome, glamorous couple they were—his tall, elegant father with his curly black hair and Italian suits, presiding over the arrival of smartly dressed guests, his mother hanging on his arm, her head thrown back, laughing—a hearty, full-throated sound Lee hadn't heard since the day his father walked out.

Butts took a swig of beer, wiped his mouth with his sleeve, and set the glass down on the table with a clunk. "Hey, listen, I'm glad the wife has her own thing, really I am. I just don't happen to share her love of cards, is all."

Lee rested one elbow on the white linen tablecloth and looked around the room. Virage had an easygoing East Village charm, elegant and casual at the same time, a relaxed atmosphere with seriously good food. The floor was done in the classic black-and-white Art Deco tiles used in so many building interiors in the twenties, and the décor reflected the French/Moroccan cuisine: comfortable green and white wicker chairs, white tablecloths, with French movie posters on the walls. With the slowly rotating ceiling fan and potted palms, the restaurant could have been a back room at Rick's in Casablanca.

Lee glanced at his watch. Kathy was late, but he knew the

rush-hour trains from Philadelphia often ran behind schedule.

"So what is this mysterious case you're working on?" he
asked.

Butts licked his lips and took another sip of beer.

"It's very weird, you know, Doc—very weird."

"How so? Who's the victim?"

Butts leaned forward and lowered his voice.

"Well, that's the thing. There's more than one."

"Yeah? Tell me more."

"Okay, but if they decide to call you in on this one, you
didn't hear this from me."

"Really? You think they might call me in?"

"Who knows? Alls I know is that we're not even sure yet
these are homicides."

"Is Chuck Morton involved yet?"

"Well, if we decide that these guys are vics and not suicides, he will be."

Besides being the head of Bronx Major Case Unit in the
Bronx, where Butts was a homicide detective, Chuck Morton was also Lee's college roommate and best friend—and
was largely responsible for his appointment as the only
criminal profiler in the NYPD.

Lee took a long swallow of beer. It was very fizzy and a
little sweet—it tasted yellow, like honey.

"Okay," he said, leaning forward, "tell me the whole thing
from the beginning."

CHAPTER FOUR

By the time Kathy showed up at the restaurant, Butts and Lee were well into their second round, hunched over the table deep in conversation, their heads almost touching. When he saw her, Lee leapt up from his chair and rushed over to her, his handsome face flushed with happiness. How different he was from the thin, pale, and worried-looking man Kathy had met five months ago. Though he still suffered from occasional bouts of depression, he was much more relaxed than he had been when they met. Of course, he told her it was because of her presence in his life, and as much as Kathy wanted to believe this, she suspected there were other factors as well.

"Hi! We were beginning to worry about you," he said, kissing her on the lips and putting his arm around her shoulders. She was much shorter than he was, so he had to bend down a little. Kathy was self-conscious about her height, but Lee Campbell made her feel good about the way she looked—one of the many reasons she loved him. She was dark-haired and small, and he claimed to prefer compact brunettes over the American stereotype of beauty—tall, leggy blondes. She didn't even need to believe him to feel grateful—it was enough that he said it. She was a successful scientist, brilliant and respected in her field, and a member of an old aristocratic Philadelphian family, but she was still a woman, with all the insecurities about her appearance of most American women, bombarded daily by impossible images of airbrushed physical perfection.

"What took you so long?" asked Detective Butts.

"Oh, you know, the whole rush-hour train thing," she said, slipping into the booth across from the homely detective. Kathy liked the plainspoken Butts—his lack of pretension was refreshing. Her father moved in elite circles in Philadelphia, and sometimes Kathy found his friends irritating, with their expensive wines and trendy restaurants—or at least as trendy as Philadelphia could claim to have. She enjoyed mentioning her frequent trips to New York, knowing that inside most Philadelphians is an envious would-be New Yorker.

Impulsively, she gave Butts a kiss on his pockmarked cheek, and his already florid face turned a deep cherry red.

"Let's get you a beer," he said, looking around for the waiter, though she suspected it was so she wouldn't notice his embarrassment. "You got a lot of catchin' up to do."

"What's everyone drinking?" she asked.

"There's a special on this Belgian brew," he said, signaling to the waiter for another round. "It's really not bad."

"Sounds good," Kathy said, looking around the room, which was beginning to fill up. Friday night was prime time for the East Village, but it didn't begin to really heat up until around ten. She and Lee always tried to be indoors by then, away from the roaming mobs of drunken bridge-and-tunnel teens.

"So," she said, turning to Lee, "what did I miss?"

There was an awkward pause as Lee looked to Butts, who said, "Nothin' much—we just been talkin' shop."

"I see," said Kathy. "I'm not allowed in on it."

"Well," Butts said, beginning to sweat, "see, technically speaking—"

"Technically speaking," Lee interrupted, "I'm not even officially in on it."

"Yeah," Butts said apologetically. "See, it's my case, but I probably shouldn't be talkin' about it."

"But if you're talking to him about it, why can't you talk to me?" she said.

Butts picked at the bumpy skin on his chin. "Yeah, well, I probably shouldn't' a even said anything."

"Well, you already have, so are you going to let me in, or am I just going to sit here all evening in suspense?"

Butts frowned and chewed on his lower lip. "Okay, okay—seein' as how you're a professional, too, I guess it couldn't hurt. But you can't tell anyone I told you," he added quickly, "or my ass is grass, you know?"

"Understood," Kathy replied. "Maybe I can be of some help."

"I dunno," Butts said. "It's not the science that's wacky on this one, it's the psychology."

"Ah," said Kathy. "So that's why you confided in Doc Campbell here."

Lee rolled his eyes. He was a PhD, not an MD, but Butts had insisted on calling him "Doc" ever since they first met. He wasn't sure whether Kathy was making fun of him or Butts—or both of them.

"We're not even sure there's a connection yet," Butts said, lowering his voice as the sleek young, white-aproned waiter delivered their drinks. "But there's a coupla pretty weird deaths within a week, both staged to look like suicides—but badly staged, y'know, suggesting they weren't no suicides."

"That's why you think they're linked?"

"Yeah, maybe—or maybe not. The two vics are real different, and as far as we can make out, there's no other connection between them. Didn't know each other—weren't even the same age or profession."

"What about race?" Lee asked. "You said they were both white."

"Yeah, sure, but that's not much to go on. We're still lookin' into their backgrounds, but so far we got bubkes."

"So what are the details?" Kathy said, gulping down a swallow of beer. It was delicious—cold, a little sweet but with a nice bitter edge.

Butts told her the puzzling particulars. Two men, both dead, one electrocuted and the other drowned—both clumsily staged suicides, "phony as a tuxedo on a rooster," as he put it. Kathy had no idea where he got his sayings—he had a gift for odd metaphors.

"Chuck Morton hasn't called you yet?" she asked Lee.

"Nope," he replied.

"That's odd," she said. "It's right up your alley."

"That's what I'm sayin'," Butts agreed. "Hey, I'm starvin'—you wanna order?"

They did. Butts ordered a steak, and Kathy got the same thing she always did—the Moroccan chicken. It was terrific as ever—tangy, spicy, and a little sweet, but the real winner was the spinach fettuccine in lemon caper sauce that Lee ordered. After trying one bite Kathy kept looking at it so longingly that Lee finally threw his hands up and pushed the plate toward her.

"Go ahead—have the rest. I can tell you want it." He turned to Butts and laughed. "She always does this. No matter what she orders, she always wants what I have."

"I do not!" Kathy protested, but she gobbled up the rest of the fettuccine greedily.

"Hmm," Butts remarked, chewing on his steak. "I guess you suffer from pasta envy."

"Touché," Lee said, poking Kathy in the ribs.

Butts smiled broadly, obviously pleased with himself. Kathy pretended to be irritated with both of them, but in truth she was feeling good—a little tipsy, full of excellent food, sitting in this charming restaurant with a man she loved. Happiness filled her like helium; she was buoyant as rising dough. She wished she could always feel the way she felt right now. Later, she would think back to that evening and wish she could have stopped the hands of the clock right then and there.

CHAPTER FIVE

As soon as Lee unlocked the dead bolt to his apartment door, the phone rang. He rushed through the living room to answer it, but he wasn't quick enough—by the time he reached it, the phone had stopped ringing.

"Damn," he muttered, throwing his coat on the couch. He looked at the caller ID, which read UNAVAILABLE. That meant someone was calling from a blocked number—or that they had dialed *69 before calling him to hide their identity. Either way, he wouldn't be able find out who it was and call them back.

Kathy trailed in behind him, closing the door after her.

"Just missed it?" she said, sinking down on the couch.

"Yeah," he said. "They blocked caller ID, too, so I don't know who it was."

"Who would be calling you at this hour?"

"My first thought would be my mother," he replied, "but she doesn't even know what caller ID is, let alone how to block it."

"Maybe they'll leave a message." She rubbed her stomach and grimaced. "Oh, I am so *full*. I can't believe I finished the rest of your fettuccine. I'm terrible, aren't I?"

Lee laughed. "One of these days I'm going to order something you really hate, like liver, so I can eat the whole thing myself."

She threw a couch pillow at him. "Sadist."

He dodged out of the way, then picked it up and threw it back. "Glutton."

She hurled it back at him. "Poseur."

He aimed at her head, then, as she ducked, threw it at her torso. "Nympho."

"Oof!" she said as the pillow hit her stomach. "Got me right where it hurts." She bent down to pick it up off the floor, then stopped. "What's that smell?"

"What smell?"

"Like lilacs," she said, sniffing their air. "It smells like lilac perfume."

"Oh, that," he said, feeling guilty, though he had done nothing wrong.

She threw the pillow back at him. "Do you have a mistress?"

He threw his hands up in surrender, letting it hit him. "Okay, you caught me."

"I *knew* it! What's her name?"

"Promise not to tell anyone?"

"Cross my heart and hope to die."

He sat down next to her and whispered in her ear. She hurled another pillow at him at close range.

"Ow!" he said. "That *hurt*!"

"Serves you right," she said. "Leading a girl on like that."

"Well, you *are* my mistress," he said. "Or my girlfriend, or whatever you want to call it."

"Seriously, though, was someone here wearing lilac perfume?"

"Yes," he said.

"Who was it?"

"Well, I guess since she wasn't here as a patient, it's all right to tell you."

He had known two things about Kathy Azarian soon after meeting her: that she was courageous and that she was willful, someone you would want nearby in a crisis. But it was as impossible for him to put a finger on what exactly he was drawn to as it was to pluck a single drop of water from a running stream. Her slim androgyny hid a femininity so profound that he felt in touching her, he was touching all women. It was as though his atoms had been perfectly formulated to resonate with hers.

He told her the story of Ana's visit, including her past as his patient—though he neglected to mention her attempt to seduce him years ago. Kathy didn't seem to be the jealous type, but he had no desire to test that theory.

Kathy listened, frowning. "Do you think she's telling the truth?"

"I don't know what to think. I was thinking that might be her calling when we came in."

"Maybe it was a wrong number. Why don't you see if they left a message?"

Lee went over to the phone, but as he reached for it, it rang again. He picked it up immediately.

"Hello?"

"Lee, it's Chuck."

"Hi, Chuck."

When she heard that, Kathy began waving vigorously from the couch.

"Kathy says hi," Lee said.

"Yeah, thanks—uh, listen, have you got a minute?"

His friend sounded disturbed, preoccupied—from the tightness in his voice, Lee could tell this call was all business.

"Sure, go ahead," he said.

"Okay. We got a really strange situation here, and if you're free, I'd like to have your input on it."

"Go ahead—shoot."

Chuck Morton proceeded to tell him about exactly the same case Butts had laid out before him over dinner, and Lee pretended to listen. Or rather, he pretended he had never heard any of this before, which was hard, since Butts had covered it quite thoroughly. Still, he managed to ask some leading questions, and thought he pulled it off pretty well. The last thing he wanted was to get Butts in trouble for spilling the beans about a case—even if it was to Lee, Butts could still catch hell for it, and even more since Kathy was there, too.

Strictly speaking, case details were to be spoken of only with the officers directly involved, lest something should leak out that would compromise the investigation. Of course, things were leaked all the time, and Lee suspected there was a fair amount of pillow talk that went unreported. He couldn't imagine a marriage of any substance without a few slips here and there. He thought of Chuck and Susan Morton in bed together. He had once shared a bed with her, and now . . . he forced the image out of his head.

"Okay," he said when Chuck had finished. "You're right—it does sound intriguing."

"It's damn perplexing, that's what it is," Chuck grumbled. "And that's why we need you on board. If you have time, that is."

"Sure," said Lee. "You clear it with brass, and I'll be in your office Monday morning."

"Great," said Chuck, sounding relieved. Lee could hear a woman's voice in the background, and Chuck called to her, "Just a second, all right? Okay, I will." Then, into the receiver, he said, "Susan sends her love."

"Thanks," Lee said, feeling his throat tighten. Whatever

Susan Morton was sending, it wasn't her love. Her lust, per-haps—maybe her desire, her need, which was bottomless—but hardly her love.

When it came to men, Susan Morton was a piranha—she ate them up. Junior year at Princeton she set her sights on Lee, after having chewed her way through most of the under-classmen on the rugby, soccer, and rowing teams (she favored those with brains and brawn, though not too much of either—she wouldn't touch football players or physics majors). Blessed with a body that needed little improvement on what nature had given her (or so she claimed), straight blond hair (Lee always suspected it was bleached), and bewitching green eyes, she only had to wiggle her pert little hips or flut-ter her expensive false eyelashes to have men drooling like doddering idiots.

Lee fell for her act for a while—then, after a particularly nasty fight over which restaurant they were going to (for her, the more expensive the better), he decided he'd had enough. Without even pausing to wipe the smudged lipstick off her pretty little mouth, she turned around and seduced his room-mate and best friend, Chuck Morton. If she felt awkward about the situation, she didn't show it. In fact, Lee thought it was the ultimate power play for her: *he* might reject her, but look!—she could have the very next man she set her sights on.

And she had him, all right. She tugged on every heart-string poor Chuck had, and since Susan gave him the false impression that she had left Lee—and not the other way around—he could hardly point out her flaws to his friend, who might think it was just sour grapes.

They dated all throughout junior year, and when Chuck left Princeton early to support his mother after his father's sudden death, they were married within a few months. And now there they were, with two children and a house in the tony suburbs of Essex County, in north Jersey. And Lee saw the look of disbelief on his friend's face when they were in public together—as if he still couldn't quite understand how he ended up with such a beautiful woman.

"Hey! What are you doing, standing there with that grim expression?"

Kathy's voice brought him out of his reverie. He set the remote receiver down on the phone charger. *Susan sends her love. Yeah, right,* as his niece would say. *As if.*

"Didn't Chuck just ask you to join the team?" Kathy said, now on her feet, plucking at his shirt sleeve.

"Yeah, he did."

"So what's with the long face, ya crazy mug?"

They both liked black-and-white movies from the thirties and forties, and enjoyed imitating the way the characters spoke. It was one of those little private jokes that keep happy couples from being all alike.

"Aw, cut it out, will ya, you crazy dame?" Lee responded, but his heart wasn't in it. His stomach was beginning to churn, and it wasn't just because of his close encounter with Susan Morton. He had a premonition that nothing good was about to happen.

On impulse, he pulled the slip of paper from his pocket with Ana's cell phone number on it and dialed. The call bounced immediately to voice mail. He frowned and tried a second time, with the same results. He folded the paper and put it carefully on top of the mantel. Of course, it could mean nothing—she could have turned off her phone. But he couldn't shake the feeling that something very bad was about to happen.

"You okay?" Kathy said, wrapping her arms around him.

"Yeah," he said. "Sure."

But even as he said it, he knew he didn't believe it.

CHAPTER SIX

In you go, nice and easy. That's it, slide right in. Don't be afraid—the water's fine. Don't struggle, now—there's no point. The drugs should make you feel all nice and sleepy, so this shouldn't hurt a bit. If you had been a better girl, there would have been no need for this, no need, but some women are just born bad. It's sad, but that's the way it is.

Caleb stood and watched as she floated away, looking so peaceful, her limbs spreading out from her still form, her white-blond hair blooming like water lilies around her head. His father would be so pleased. He could still hear his father's voice in his head, as if it were only yesterday.

"Your mother was born bad—wicked and evil and bad. So this is what you do to bad women. Watch, boy—no, don't turn away! And don't cry. Only sissy boys cry. No son of *mine* will turn out to be a sissy boy, not if I can help it. That's better—be a man, and take it like a man. Only women cry—don't you ever forget that. And women are bad—nasty, evil creatures. They have this thing between their legs that makes them bad—this bleeding, gaping thing *that will eat you up or bite off your manhood if you're not careful.*"

This one had nice hair—so pale and thick, like a white

halo around her head. Just like Ophelia, floating down the stream.

Oh, yes, Ophelia killed herself out of love, my dear, didn't she? Well, that was a bit of inspiration on my part, I must admit. A nice touch—I hope they like it when they find you. Of course, you won't look so pretty when they find you, will you? Not pretty at all—you'll be bloated like a watermelon, I should think, all white and ghastly and gruesome. Maybe some young policeman will even throw up when he sees you—some of them do, you know. I've seen them. That would be too bad, but you only have yourself to blame. I could have taught you some manners, but it's too late now, I'm afraid. Well, it's getting colder out, so I'm going to have to leave you. Bon voyage—sweet dreams.

CHAPTER SEVEN

Lee arrived at Chuck's office in the Bronx Major Case Unit a little before nine on Monday morning, feeling tired and worried. Tired because Kathy had spent the weekend—they were still in the early stages of their romance, and didn't want to waste time sleeping when they could be doing something together. For their first months together, that most often meant sex—Kathy had an unexpectedly voracious libido.

And he was worried because he had tried all weekend to reach Ana on her cell phone, with no luck. He even called the Swan in Lambertville to see if she had shown up for work, but was told she had requested that weekend off. That made him feel a little better—maybe she and her boyfriend had gone on vacation and she had turned off her phone. But she hadn't mentioned that when she came to see him, and under the circumstances, it seemed an odd omission.

He walked through the station house, which was unusually quiet for a Monday morning. The young desk sergeant tried vainly to stifle a yawn as he waved Lee through to Chuck's office, and the weary-looking policewoman talking to a thin young Latino man in purple rayon pants looked like she could use another night's sleep. Lee knocked on the door to his friend's office, and to his surprise, a woman's voice answered.

"Come in."

He paused a moment to register what he had just heard, then swung the door open cautiously. He didn't know what he expected to find, but he certainly didn't expect what he saw. Instead of Chuck was a woman, perched next to his desk, one hip resting on the windowsill behind his scarred old captain's chair.

There are some women who, for whatever reason, make men feel inadequate. There are other women who, for perhaps more obvious reasons, make men want them. And then there are those rare women who do both.

Elena Krieger was one of those women.

She was extremely tall—Lee estimated at least six feet—with absurdly long legs, as though the painter's brush had slipped when creating her, but he decided to keep going anyway. Her silky hair was a strawberry-blond color he associated with Swedish stewardesses and Hollywood starlets. Her body was pure Vegas: beside the long legs, she had the trim waist and solid round breasts of a showgirl. He didn't see how they could be real: they looked too sculpted, too firm—and the lemon-yellow silk blouse she wore didn't leave anything to the imagination. At the same time, there was something masculine about her body, the broad sweep of her shoulders, the big bones of her hands and feet. She gave off an impression of power and strength, so that her sexuality had an oddly androgynous appeal. He understood immediately how she got the nickname Valkyrie—she was the personification of a Wagnerian goddess.

Her face couldn't really be described as pretty. Everything was too big, too prominent: her mouth, her nose, her strong chin. And her eyes were rather small, light colored and deep set, so that they looked even smaller. Still, in the split second that Lee took in all these details, he also registered the fact that he couldn't think of a single man he had ever known who would kick her out of bed. The part of him that was pure animal instinct, the part that wasn't madly in love with Kathy, reacted to her as any other red-blooded heterosexual man would: he immediately imagined her naked, available, and interested.

And in that moment he also knew something else about her: she was dangerous. He wasn't sure who she was dangerous to—maybe herself, maybe the men she came in contact with, maybe other women—but there was no doubt she was dangerous.

In the moment or two it took for all of these thoughts to race across the landscape of his brain, Elena Krieger took the three steps required to cover the width of Chuck's small office and extended her hand.

"Hello," she said, with a light dusting of a German accent. "I'm Elena Krieger."

Lee wanted to say *Of course you are*, but instead he said, "Pleased to meet you," shaking her hand, which was firm, cool and strong, like a solid piece of oak, or cedar.

"And you are the famous Lee Campbell."

Lee laughed and felt his face go red.

"Well, if I'm famous, I'm the last to hear about it."

"Oh, but *of course* you are—everybody knows about you. What happened to your sister was terrible," she repeated, shaking her head so that her silky bangs swung back and forth like windshield wipers over her wide forehead.

Lee tried to avoid looking at her—frankly, it was distracting. He turned toward the door, which he had deliberately left open.

"Where's Chuck?" he said, pretending to search for him in the hall outside.

"He'll be back in a minute," she said. "That must have been so hard going through what you went through, the nervous breakdown and all. Are you *sure* you're well enough to work now?"

Stunned by this remark, he turned to look at her. His sister Laura's disappearance five years ago was the reason he turned from private practice as a psychologist to become a criminal profiler. And his recent nervous breakdown, though not a secret, was a private matter. It wasn't the kind of thing he talked about; clearly Elena Krieger had done some homework.

Her words were loaded with subtext—he just wasn't sure what it was. She certainly wasn't expressing concern for him. She didn't even know him, and from what he had heard about her, Elena Krieger cared about one thing: Elena Krieger. So there was definitely something else going on— was it a flirtation? Or perhaps she was trying to win him over with this appearance of sympathy, to get him on her side against Chuck. Or perhaps it was something even more subtle and sinister. Maybe she was trying to take him back to those awful days, to force him to relive them, thereby shaking his confidence.

He was pretty sure word had gotten around about his struggle with depression—which was definitely regarded as a weakness in the macho world of the NYPD. Any kind of mental health problem carried more of a stigma than say, having cancer, or any other physical illness. Most cops belittled psychiatry of any kind, so Lee's position as the force's only criminal profiler was tenuous to begin with. His own personal struggle with depression made it even more so.

He looked Elena Krieger up and down before answering. He wanted her to know that he was in control of the situation, not her.

"I'm fine now," he said calmly. "But thanks for asking."

Her plucked eyebrows arched upward as if she did not believe him, but at that moment Chuck Morton entered the room. He looked back and forth between Lee and Elena, then stated the obvious.

"I see you two have met."

"Ya-a-h," Elena Krieger replied, stretching the word out sensuously, like a cat sunning itself. But she was more lupine than feline, Lee thought—like a big redheaded wolf.

"Good," Chuck said briskly. "Let's get started, then."

Lee was startled. He'd had no idea that Elena Krieger was part of this investigation. He couldn't say that in front of her, so he just said, "Isn't Detective Butts the primary—"

Chuck cut him off. "Yes, he is, but Detective Krieger has recently been assigned to this station house, so she'll be working the case, too. Her specialty is forensic linguistics."

Lee thought two detectives was already one too many, but he said nothing. He could see from Chuck's discomfort that his friend didn't want her here any more than he did. It was clear she was here because of some bureaucratic game of musical chairs that neither of them had any control over.

"Where is Detective Butts, by the way?" Krieger asked. "Shouldn't he be here?"

"He should, and he is," said a voice behind them, and they all turned to see Detective Leonard Butts standing in the doorway, holding a cup of coffee and a bag of Krispy Kreme doughnuts.

"Glad you could make it after all," Chuck said. "Have a seat."

"Yeah," Butts said. "I told the wife that she'd just have to go to her uncle's funeral without me, and that I'd catch up with her at the reception. She didn't like it, but what can you do? Work is work. If you ask me, Monday morning's an odd time for a funeral anyways." He slurped happily at his coffee, took a big bite of a cream-filled doughnut, and leaned back in the chair with a satisfied sigh. "Man, these things are good."

"Have you met Detective Butts?" Chuck asked.

"I don't believe I've had the pleasure," Krieger replied. Lee couldn't tell whether she was being sarcastic or not.

"This is Detective Elena Krieger," Chuck said to Butts.

"Elena Krieger?" Butts said. "*The* Elena Krieger?"

She flushed from the base of her elegant neck to her cheeks, though Lee wasn't sure if it was from embarrassment or anger.

"Well, if there are others with my name in the police farce, I am unaware of it." Her mispronunciation of "force" took Lee by surprise, and he had to stifle an impulse to laugh.

"The pleasure's all mine," Butts said, shaking her hand vigorously before settling down to renew his attack on the bag of doughnuts. He seemed impervious to her charms—he was clearly more interested in the doughnuts. He munched away happily, hardly looking at her as Chuck went over the details of the case.

"Okay," said Chuck, taking out crime-scene photos and handing them around. "Now, the reason that there's some urgency on this is that if these two deaths *are* connected, then we may have a serial offender on our hands—one that's very difficult to catch. So far we haven't been able to find any links between these two men, other than they're both obviously phony suicides."

"Yeah," Butts agreed. "We talked to the families of both vics, and we get the same thing. No history of depression or mental illness. The floater is Nathan Ziegler, and he just got hired by Roosevelt Hospital as an anesthesiologist. Bathtub guy, Chris Malette, was doing just fine financially—he was divorced but very amicable with his ex."

"No history of mental problems?" Lee asked.

"Negative," Butts answered. "And before you ask, no, his ex does *not* wear that shade of lipstick," he added, pointing to the writing on the bathroom mirror in several of the photos. "She's been wearing the same lipstick for years, according to her girlfriends and sister—Passion Fruit Panache. Apparently she's a creature of habit. So if she did write that note, she bought or borrowed someone else's lipstick to do it before she killed Baldy here."

Elena Krieger stared at Butts. "I don't think you should speak of the dead so disrespectfully."

Butts stared back at her, then looked up at Chuck. "Is she always like this?"

"I always take our job seriously, if that's what you mean," she said iciliy. Lee noticed her accent thickened when she was upset.

"All right, knock it off, both of you!" Chuck said, running a hand through his blond crew cut.

"I beg your pardon," Butts said. "I mean *Mr. Malette*. The point is that his ex isn't a likely suspect. And we haven't found anyone who disliked the guy—at least enough to kill him."

Morton plucked another of the photos from the pile on his desk. "The writing in the suicide note found on the floa—Dr. Ziegler—is being analyzed by a handwriting expert, but there's no question it does *not* belong to him."

"That's an odd suicide note, in any case," Lee remarked.

Elena Krieger picked up the photo of the note and studied it. "*I'm sorry—I was wrong. I don't deserve to live,*" she read slowly. "It sounds more like a confession of guilt than a suicide note."

"Yeah," Chuck agreed, "but guilt about what?"

"If we can figure that out, we'll have a big piece of the puzzle," Butts remarked.

"Also, it's not addressed to anyone in particular, which is

odd. Most suicides who write notes address them to specific people in their lives," Krieger pointed out.

"Right," said Chuck. "And look at how carefully the note was wrapped in a Ziploc bag so the water wouldn't spoil it. Someone really wanted us to find it."

"You going to release it to the media?" Lee asked.

Chuck cocked his head to one side. "What do you think?"

"I wouldn't. It's not elaborate or long enough to give you a personality profile."

"That's what I was thinking," Chuck agreed. "I don't see someone seeing the note in the paper and calling us to say it reminds him of his brother."

"Yeah, right," Butts said. "This ain't no Unabomber."

He was referring to the capture of Ted Kaczynski, the infamous Unabomber. He was finally brought to justice when David Kaczynski recognized the ranting political polemic published by the *New York Times* and *Washington Post* as sounding very much like his brother Ted.

"No useable prints, I guess?" said Lee.

Butts shook his head. "The guy must have been wearing gloves."

"Or the *woman*," Krieger corrected him.

"Whatever," Butts said, rolling his eyes at Lee. "Anyway, we're doing a tox screen on all the vics, just in case."

"You think maybe the UNSUB drugged them first?" Lee asked. UNSUB was shorthand for "Unknown Subject." He didn't particularly like using cop jargon, but it was a way to sidestep the morass of gender issues that Krieger was clearly prickly about.

"Anything's possible—especially if it's a woman," Butts replied. "She'd probably have to drug them to control them, unless she's one strong bi—female," he said, with a nervous glance at Krieger.

If Krieger noticed the slip, she didn't react. "What about

the writing on the mirror?" she asked. "Any match to the other note?"

Chuck picked up the crime-scene photo and shook his head. "It's in block letters in lipstick, so our expert says she can't do much with it.

"But look at the wording," Krieger said.

Lee took the photo from Chuck and studied it. "*I am very bad. Sorry.*" He put the photo back down.

"They both say they're sorry," Krieger pointed out. "With most people who kill themselves, that would be an apology for the suicide itself. But this is different: they seem to be apologizing for being *bad.*"

Butts frowned. "So the same UNSUB wrote both notes?"

"It's extremely likely," Krieger replied.

"What do you make of the notes?" Chuck asked Lee.

"Well," he began, but Krieger intrrupted.

"Obviously the victims offended the killer in some way," she said.

"*Jawohl,*" Butts said.

Krieger glared at him, and then at Chuck, but he pretended not to notice.

Lee thought, not for the first time, that this was going to be a challenging investigation.

CHAPTER EIGHT

Lee arrived at his apartment a little after noon to find three messages on his answering machine. Unlike some of his friends, who were discarding their landlines, he kept his. He'd had the same number ever since he moved to the East Village, and he held on to it partly out of sentiment—but also because it was the coveted 212 area code, no longer available to newer residents of Manhattan. He was a little embarrassed that this meant something to him, but it did.

He pressed the button and listened to the first message. It was from Kathy, telling him she missed him. He missed her too, all the more so because he had been so preoccupied all weekend with Ana's plight. He felt he hadn't been truly present with Kathy. He was sure she noticed—but, true to form, she didn't reproach him with it.

He put the kettle on while listening to the second message. Fiona Campbell's voice was clear and cool as ever.

"Lee, it's your mother. Don't forget you're expected for dinner to celebrate Kylie's birthday on the weekend. She's really looking forward to seeing you. See you then— bye."

His niece Kylie would be turning seven in a week. She

had lived with her father, George Callahan, ever since Laura's disappearance, but spent weekends with her grandmother. There was the usual subtle playing of the guilt card in his mother's message. If you don't come, you'll disappoint your niece. Not her, Fiona; no, never her. She had renounced her own claim on personal emotions the day his father walked out.

It was also typical of her to remind him of social engagements, as if he were incapable of remembering them himself. His father's desertion left her with the overwhelming opinion that men were erratic, unreliable creatures who could not be counted on. And, of course, his father's abandonment had left its mark on Lee, and was probably the reason for his decision to become a therapist. If he couldn't mend his own family, at least he could help other people come to terms with theirs.

But when his sister disappeared, his need to help people traveled a darker road, driven by his need to *know*. And if he couldn't know who had killed his sister (unlike his mother, he was certain Laura was dead), then he would help other people find out who had killed their loved ones.

The kettle began its long, slow climb to a piercing whistle, and he ducked into the kitchen just as the third message began to play. He heard it as he was pouring the tea water into the cup, and what he heard stopped him cold, so that the hot water splashed all over the countertop.

The voice was cold, hard, and flat, almost reptilian.

"What about the red dress? You think no one knows anything, but I do. I know about the red dress."

There was a click as the line went dead, then a whirring sound as the answering machine began to automatically rewind. But Lee didn't hear any of that—all he heard, over and over in his head, was that reptilian monotone: "I know about the red dress." His sister Laura had been wearing a red dress the day she disappeared—a detail that had not been released to the press or the public. Stunned, he ignored the spilled water dripping from the counter onto the kitchen floor, and stumbled into the living room to look at the caller ID on his phone. He knew it was useless, but he had to look. To his surprise, there was a number there with a 212 area code—Manhattan! And the first three numbers were 533—which he recognized as an East Village exchange. His hand trembled as he picked up the receiver and dialed the number. It rang four times, then a man answered.

"Hello?" The voice was nothing like the one on his machine. This one had a thick Brooklyn accent, and was an octave lower.

"Hi—excuse me, but can you tell me what number I just dialed?"

"Well, there's no number on it, but you reached a pay phone on Third Avenue and Fifth Street. Who are you lookin' for, buddy?" The man sounded happily inebriated, eager to help.

"I'm sorry—I must have dialed wrong," Lee said, certain that he had dialed correctly.

"Hey, no problem, buddy—take it easy."

Lee hung up and sat down in the overstuffed armchair next to the phone. So the man had called from around the corner—from a pay phone, no less. *Who uses pay phones anymore, except to avoid being identified?* The questions swirled around his head. Did the caller pick a booth nearby on purpose, or does he live in the neighborhood? Or was it purely coincidence? Or was there an even darker explanation—what if he was stalking Lee, watching him? His number was unlisted—how did the man manage to get it? Would there be any point in dusting for prints? No crime had been committed—would Lee be able to convince anyone that it was even necessary?

Good Lord, Campbell, get a grip. His sister's disappearance was continual torture, a piece of unfinished business that would haunt him until the day he solved it—if he ever did. Maybe his mother was right about men after all. . . .

The swirling sensation began to transform into something darkly familiar and sinister, as he felt the evil fog of depression envelop him. The walls of the room seemed to close in around him, and his thoughts swarmed like angry bees in his head. He was losing focus, and knew he had to stop the fog before it could take hold. He had told Kathy and everyone else that he was feeling much better lately, and to an extent that was true. But depression was its own kind of minefield. Sometimes, if he stepped carefully enough, he could stay aboveground and keep from landing on the hidden entrances, secret traps covering gaping holes in the ground. But other times the ground gave way when he least expected it, and he sank down and was swallowed up before he knew it.

"No, goddamn it," he muttered. Staggering up from the chair, he reached for the phone again. Kathy was in Philadelphia, Chuck was still on duty, and his mother was useless, but there was one person he could turn to now—he just hoped she was available. He dialed the number and got a recording.

"You've reached the voice mail of Dr. Georgina Williams. Please leave a message and I'll get back to you as soon as possible. If this is an emergency, please call my beeper at 917-555-4368. Thank you."

Lee hesitated. Was this an emergency? He wasn't feeling suicidal—not yet, anyway. He decided to leave a message on her voice mail. If she was in the office, she would call him back soon.

"Hi, Dr. Williams, this is Lee Campbell. I wonder if you have any time at all today? I—I'm having sort of a bad day, so if you could give me a call I'd appreciate it—thanks."

He hung up the phone and looked around the apartment. This place, which he had worked so hard to make cozy and inviting, suddenly felt like a prison cell from which there was no escape. The familiar objects around him held no comfort—the carefully arranged bouquet of flowers on the piano might have been shards of straw stuck in a vase. He looked at the green Persian rug he loved so much, with the swirling patterns of light and dark that always reminded him of a forest at sunset. It might just as well have been cracked and dirty linoleum. He sat on the couch and put his head in his hands. *No,* he thought, *not today—please not now.*

The phone rang, and he jumped, his overstrung nerves rattled by the sound. He picked up the receiver.

"Hello?"

"Lee, it's Chuck."

He hesitated—should he tell his friend that this was not a good time, that he was having an episode? Or should he just tough out the phone call, jot down what Chuck said, and deal with it later? He could barely focus—his mind was being rapidly overtaken by the swiftly descending fog. He decided to tough it out.

"Hi, Chuck," he said, wondering if his voice sounded odd. "What's up?"

"There's been a development."

"What do you mean?"

"Looks like we have another victim. Can you come back up here?"

No, Lee wanted to scream, *no, I can't.* Instead he said, "Sure. Can you give me a little time?"

"As soon as you can make it, okay?"

"Okay."

"Thanks."

Lee hung up, his hand now shaking so hard that the receiver rattled as he replaced it. He headed for the bathroom and fumbled in the cupboard for the bottle of Xanax. It was going to be a long day.

CHAPTER NINE

By the time Lee reached the subway he was sweating and trembling almost uncontrollably. The darkness had closed in around him, and he was moving automatically, as if in a trance—sliding his Metro card through the slot at the entrance, going through the metal turnstile, walking down the concrete stairs to the train with the other passengers. The fog and confusion were bad enough, but today it felt as if his soul were on fire—a burning, searing pain that blotted out all memories of the past, any pleasures of the present, and any hope of the future. The only reality was the unrelenting pain. It had no beginning and no end, covering him like a thick blanket of concrete, crushing him.

He walked unsteadily to the far end of the platform and stared down at the subway tracks. A large gray rat poked its head out from under the near rail and scuttled across the wooden ties to a tiny hole in the subway wall, vanishing inside it. Lee wondered why the rats weren't electrocuted on the third rail—or, for all he knew, maybe some of them were. He wondered how much it would hurt and for how long, to be electrocuted. His stomach lurched and twisted as he contemplated the sensation of thousands of volts coursing through his body.

He wrenched his mind away from these thoughts and forced himself to take a deep breath. He tried to think of Kathy, to imagine her smiling face, but it only made him want to cry. This attack had taken him by surprise. In the past few months there had been a gradual improvement in his mental state. He was still having nightmares, but they had begun to subside recently.

And now this. He felt as if he were being dragged back to the first days of his affliction, which began five years ago after his sister disappeared and worsened after 9/11. Most New Yorkers were deeply affected by that terrible day, some of them so frightened that they couldn't sleep at night. Some left the city altogether. Others were angry, filled with a rage they had never felt. Lee didn't feel fear, or even anger—only a wrenching, leaden sadness that swept him up for weeks afterward.

He heard the rumble of the F train in the distance as it hurtled down the dark, musty corridors toward them. He imagined jumping onto the track just as it reached the station, the slamming of metal against skin. Would he be killed instantly, or just horribly maimed for life? There was no question of killing himself that way, though. In his darkest days, he had given it some thought, and concluded that he was unwilling to put the train conductor through the trauma and guilt of feeling responsible.

The train slid into the station and the doors opened. Lee composed his face into what he hoped was a mask of New York indifference and sat down, waiting for the Xanax to take effect. It wouldn't stop the pain entirely, but at least it would blunt the anxiety.

He changed for the uptown A train at West Fourth Street,

and by the time the train reached Penn Station and Thirty-fourth Street, the Xanax had begun to work. He felt blurry and light-headed, but at least the churning in his stomach had dissipated, and his hands were no longer shaking. Not for the first time, he silently blessed pharmaceuticals in general and benzodiazepines in particular.

When the train arrived at the Bronx station, he stood up, shook off a momentary spell of dizziness, and followed the rest of the passengers out into the burnished afternoon light of late August. Everyone had predicted an early fall this year, and the trees had a brittle, dusty look, their leaves beginning to dry out already in the soft air of the dying summer.

Chuck was in his office when Lee arrived, along with Detective Butts. There was no sign of Elena Krieger.

When Chuck saw Lee's questioning look, he said, "We tried to reach Detective Krieger, but without success."

Butts snickered. "We didn't try very hard."

"All right," said Chuck, ignoring him, "here's what's going on." He pulled a fresh stack of crime-scene photos from his desk and handed them to Lee. "This came in a couple of hours ago."

Lee took the photos and looked at the top picture. When he saw the face of the dead girl, his head began to spin, and the room swirled around him. He tried to speak, but before he could utter a word, blackness closed in around him and he lost consciousness.

CHAPTER TEN

He awoke to see Chuck and Butts standing over him, looking worried. He felt guilty when he saw the frightened expression on Chuck's face, his friend's pale skin even chalkier than usual. He struggled to get up, but Morton put a hand on his shoulder.

"Hey, hey—take it easy. There's no hurry. Take your time."

Butts's homely face crinkled with concern. "You just fainted," he said.

"I'm fine," Lee said, trying again to stand. He was sitting on the floor of the office. They had propped him up against the wall by the radiator.

"Here," said Chuck, rolling over his own chair, an old but comfortable wooden captain's chair.

"Thanks," said Lee, lifting himself into it shakily. "How long was I out?"

"A couple of minutes," Chuck said. "What happened?"

Lee suddenly remembered he had eaten nothing all day— black coffee in the morning, followed by the trip to the Bronx, and then once the depression seized hold of him, the thought of food was sickening. And then there was the Xanax—usually he took half of a one-milligram tablet, but today he had taken a whole one, spooked by the ferocity of the pain.

"It's stupid, really," he said sheepishly. "I haven't eaten, and I—". He hesitated, unsure whether or not to mention the Xanax. He decided against it. He picked up the photo from Chuck's desk and held it aloft.

There, her face washed of all color and life, was Ana Watkins.

"I know this girl," he said. "Her name is Ana Watkins, and she was my patient." He took a deep breath against the emotion rising in his throat, and continued. "She came to me a few days ago and said she thought she was in danger. I've been trying to reach her ever since, so when I saw this—" He clamped his jaw closed, determined not to surrender to his feelings. There would be time to mourn her later, but now what mattered was finding who did this to her.

"Jesus, Lee," Chuck said. "No wonder it was a shock for you."

"That's rough," Butts agreed. "What kind of danger?"

"She thought someone was following her."

"Looks like she was right," Chuck said.

"But what makes you think her death is connected with the first two victims?" Lee asked.

"That's what we were hoping you would help with," Butts replied. "We found the same kind of phony suicide note on her. Same thing as before—carefully wrapped so the water wouldn't ruin it." He fished around in the stack of photos, pulled one out, and handed it to Lee. It was neatly typed, on eight and a half by eleven paper, and it read, *I have been a very bad girl. Bad things happen to bad girls. I should have taken the advice to get thee to a nunnery. Please forgive me.*

Lee handed the photo back to Butts. "It's him, all right," he said, although up until this moment it had occurred to him that the killer might be a woman. But at the sight of that note, he felt with certainty that the perpetrator was a man.

"It doesn't make sense, though, does it?" said Butts. "I mean, don't these guys usually stick to one gender or another?"

"Usually," said Lee, "but not always. There have been cases of serial killers who killed both men and women— David Berkowitz, for example."

"Yes, but he killed couples," Chuck pointed out. "This is a different kind of thing."

"That's true," said Lee. "But he's just one example—there are others. I think one of the worst mistakes we can make is to try to categorize this offender as fitting one rigid type or another, rather than looking at the specifics of his crimes to see what they tell us about him."

Chuck rested his trim body against the windowsill and folded his arms, his taut muscles straining against the white cotton of his starched shirt. "Okay, so what do we know about him?"

"Where did they find . . . Ana?" Lee asked. Her name felt awkward, and he said it reluctantly.

"Up around Spuyten Duyvil," Chuck said. Spuyten Duyvil (Dutch for "Whirlpool of the Devil," named when New York was New Amsterdam, and under Dutch rule) was the thin slice of water between the mainland of the South Bronx and the island of Manhattan. The churning currents were notoriously treacherous there, as the waters of the Harlem River rushed to join the Hudson, already flowing south toward New York harbor.

"Who found her?" asked Butts, scratching his chin, where there was evidence of a five o'clock stubble, accentuating his already rumpled appearance.

"A couple of guys on the Columbia rowing crew," said

Chuck. "They were out practicing when they saw her floating in the water, snagged on some rocks."

The Columbia boathouse was perched on the bank of the slip of land jutting out into the eddies and fast-running currents of Spuyten Duyvil, clinging to the last thin strip of Manhattan Island before the river claimed it. Lee always thought it must be a hell of a place to row, but it was a beautiful setting for a boathouse. The view was spectacular—across the channel the Bronx mainland stretched out to the north as far as the eye could see, and to the west, the Palisades rose majestically along the Hudson. Lee thought of poor Ana, floating alone in those cold waters—it was never warm up there, not even in August.

"Well, at least they found her before she was swept out into the Hudson and out to sea," Lee said sadly.

"Yeah," Chuck agreed. "Not much comfort, but at least there's that."

"What do you know about the currents around there? Any idea where she might have been put in?"

Chuck shook his head. "I really don't know much—it seems to me she could have been put in as far south as the East River, and floated all the way up there."

"Allow me," Butts said, producing a nautical chart from his battered briefcase. "It just so happens my oldest kid is a sailor, and he lent me this."

Chuck raised an eyebrow and exchanged a look with Lee, but Butts continued, unperturbed. "I figured since we're dealing with floaters, this could come in handy, so I brought it along. Of course, we may need to consult with an expert in the field of currents and tides, but this should help for now."

He spread the map out on the desk. "Now, these arrows here," he said, pointing to little green arrows along the shoreline, "indicate the direction of the current at this spot."

"Okay," said Chuck. "So what does that tell us?"

Butts leaned over the chart, squinting, his face almost touching it. "I'm not a hundred percent sure, but I think what it tells us is that she had to have been put in somewhere between here, where we found the original floater," he said, pointing to a spot in the East River, "and here, where she was found." He placed a second stubby finger on the spot marked SPUYTEN DUYVIL.

"And Baldy was found here," he continued, poking his middle finger at the area of the South Bronx where Mr. Malette was found in his bathtub.

Lee and Chuck stared at the stretch of land that encompassed both the Upper East Side and, across the East River from it, Queens.

"So in all likelihood, he lives—or works—somewhere near here," Lee said.

"So that should narrow our search," Butts said triumphantly.

"Yeah," Chuck agreed, but none of them said what they were all thinking: Would it be enough to catch him before someone else died?

CHAPTER ELEVEN

When Lee got back to his apartment he found two messages from Dr. Williams: one on his landline and the other on his cell. He had neglected to take his cell phone with him uptown. It was all he could do to concentrate enough to lock the door behind him.

He called her back, and this time she picked up.

"Yes, Lee—you need to come in today?" Her voice was composed, but he heard the concern in it.

"Do you have any open time slots?"

"I can see you after my last patient—six o'clock okay?"

"Great. Thank you so much."

He hung up. Just hearing her voice—low, calm, and comforting—made him breathe easier. It was like the murmur of water over stones, a smooth, soothing sound.

He looked at the kitchen clock, a sunburst of bronzed Mexican pottery he had found at a yard sale upstate. It was just after six. He gazed at the piano, its polished wood gleaming in the slanting rays of the sun in the western sky. He looked down at his hands—they were shaking again.

He went to the kitchen, opened a can of chocolate protein shake, and forced himself to drink it. It tasted like chalk. He

chased it down with a glass of tap water, then went back to the living room. The piano waited for him—silent, watchful, the evening light lingering on the keyboard as the sun slipped northward and out of view behind the crowded buildings of Manhattan.

He sat down and dove into a Bach partita. No scales, no warm-up to get him in the mood—just Bach, straight up, no chaser. The sound washed over him, as primal and powerful as the first time he heard it. The notes twisted and danced on the page, in his fingers, on the keyboard. As he played, he experienced the piano as the percussion instrument it was—a great, resounding drum with eighty-eight voices, made up of tones and half-tones, a glorious creation of wood and metal and ivory, all melded together by engineering genius.

As he dug his fingers in deeper, pounding the keys in an ecstasy of fury and release, he was enveloped by a feeling of profound gratitude. He was able to participate in the grand dance of music, communing with great composers—a gift shared by even the lowliest musicians. It wasn't about ego, or showing off—there was a purity about this that existed nowhere else in his life.

It was only when he stopped that he felt the tears sliding down his face.

Afterward, he sat in the green stuffed armchair by the window and thought about Ana Watkins. What he didn't tell Chuck or Butts—what he had never told anyone—was that he had very nearly fallen for her. He had to admit, she was good—she pushed every button he had with such dexterity it left him breathless. She played the hapless victim, tossed aside by the men around her, a fragile waif orphaned by the storms of an unfortunate life. She drew out his need to protect and shield women, a need instilled in him by his mother long before his father walked out. His father's desertion only intensified his determination to make up for the sins of all

men, brutish and uncaring creatures. His mother had already decided, without realizing it consciously, that Lee's job—indeed, his duty—was to make up for the transgressions of thoughtless scoundrels like Duncan Campbell.

And so when Ana Watkins leaned into him, her thin body trembling with terror and desire, he met her halfway, pulled toward her with an inexorable magnetic force. Even as he felt himself falling into the sinkhole of self-disgust, he was helpless to stop, spinning like a top when he tried to pull back against the centrifugal force of their mutual desire. They shared a fervent and fumbling embrace in a rain-darkened alley one Friday night, soaked and sweating under a burned-out streetlamp. He managed to pull away after a prolonged and very wet kiss, but he felt himself weakening even as his forehead burned with shame and his ears rang with the sound of self-condemnation.

Fortunately for him, fate—or luck, or chance, or whatever it was—intervened before he betrayed his ethics and his profession. Ana came down with a serious case of bronchitis, and an elderly aunt swooped down from New England to nurse her back to health, breaking the forward momentum of their passion. Left standing alone, he took a shaky step backward before regaining his footing and his self-respect. When Ana recovered, he insisted on meeting only at the clinic in Flemington, and only on days when his accountant was sitting in the outside office.

Faced with this new reality, Ana discontinued her sessions and slunk away. He considered himself lucky that she didn't report his conduct to the state licensing board. Perhaps she had enough of a conscience to realize that would be less than honorable, since she had instigated the whole thing. He had not heard from her until she called two days ago.

And now she was dead. The only thing he could do for her now was to find her killer.

The walk to Dr. Williams's office on East Twelfth Street was less than fifteen minutes on average—he was there in less than ten. There was no one else in the waiting room when he arrived, and he sat listening to the murmur of voices coming from the rooms around him. Dr. Williams's office was on the fifth floor of a medical building and shared a waiting room with two other therapists. On the left was the office of a short, dapper man with spectacles and a goatee who could have been the young Freud himself. In the office to the right was a tall, willowy woman, an Upper West Side type with long silver-gray hair and owlish glasses. Lee found these women intriguing: they seemed to eschew conventional notions of fashion and beauty, and yet they had a natural quality and style that was its own kind of beauty.

Dr. Williams's door opened, and Lee's heart contracted. His throat felt dry and lumpy. He heard her familiar low, soothing voice, and then a male voice. Moments later a thin, intense-looking young man emerged from the office. He averted his eyes as he passed, focusing on the floor ahead of him. Lee had noticed, there was an elevated need for privacy in therapists' offices. People who might smile and make friendly eye contact in say, a dentist's office, studiously avoided noticing one another. He wondered if it was some vestigial feelings of shame or embarrassment, or perhaps the need to protect the tender ego, which could undergo quite a shredding process during the course of treatment. He knew this not only from his own experience, but from years of private practice as a therapist. It was a terrifying and wrenching journey, and sometimes it felt—as it did today—nearly unendurable.

Dr. Williams stepped out into the corridor and beckoned

to him. She was a very tall, elegant black woman with long limbs and a handsome, fine-featured face. Today she wore a long black skirt decorated with African motifs in earth tones, a yellow silk blouse under a short rust-colored jacket. He felt as though he could weep at the sight of her, but he just nodded meekly and followed her inside. She settled herself in her usual spot, a tall, ergonomic leather swivel chair, her back to the window. Lee sat opposite her, in a similar black leather chair with a matching footrest.

Dr. Georgina Williams had the most amazingly steady energy of anyone he had ever known. Of course, it was always possible he was projecting onto her the ideal personality for a therapist. They even joked about how he sometimes called her Yoda, but she really did seem to possess the perfect combination of calmness and intuition. She never pressed him with unwanted insights, and had an uncanny ability to come up with the perfect metaphor or key question most of the time.

The room was decorated in a style both comforting and relaxing. The walls were painted in earth tones, the lighting was muted, the prints on the wall were tasteful but not disturbing—a Monet haystack, a Matisse still life of a goldfish bowl, and a colorful Klee in cheerful primary colors. There were also a couple of original landscape paintings that looked to be Hudson Valley scenes. The bookshelf in the back of the room contained mostly works on psychology—classics by Jung, Freud, R. D. Laing, and Alice Miller, among others. There was also a small collection of poetry, in particular a book of poems by Rainer Maria Rilke. Wooden sculptures of African masks served as decorative bookends.

As always, she looked alert but relaxed. On the table next to her chair was a blue vase with white lilies of some kind.

"So," she said, studying him, "you're not doing well today."

"No," he replied. "I had . . . an episode."

"A bad one?"

"Pretty bad, yeah."

"How do you feel now?"

"Better, now that I'm here. But I always feel better here."

"You feel safe here."

"Yeah."

He looked at the potted palm in the corner next to her—was it his imagination or had it grown rapidly in the last few weeks? It suddenly looked much larger.

"But not out there," she said.

"No. Not out there."

She crossed her long legs at the ankle. He noticed she was wearing heeled sandals—in a heeled shoe, he imagined she would be taller than he was, and he was well over six feet. "Are you on a case?"

"Yeah."

"So is this episode related to that?"

"Partly, yeah."

"In what way?"

He told her about the visit from Ana, the shock of seeing her body, his fainting in the office.

"That's very upsetting," she said when he had finished.

"That's not all," he said, his palms beginning to sweat. "I had a—a phone call."

"What kind of phone call?"

He felt the old reluctance to talk, to drive a knife into old wounds, to feel its sharpness. He wished he could just sit here for a while, drinking in the calming atmosphere, but that wasn't the deal. And he knew perfectly well what the resistance was about, knew also that he had to overcome it. He took a deep breath.

"It was about the red dress. A man's voice—I didn't recognize it. He said he knew about the red dress."

"But I thought you never released that detail to the public."

"We didn't."

"So who is he, and how could he know?"

"That's what I'd like to know. It's bringing everything back again."

"Your sister's disappearance?"

"Yes." He almost wished she would say her *death*, because there was no doubt in his mind that Laura was dead.

"Anything else?"

He knew what she was hinting at, but he wasn't ready yet.

"I can't," he said. "I can't talk about it."

"Okay."

"That's it—*okay*?"

"I've never forced you to talk about anything—you know that." She uncrossed her legs and leaned back in her chair. "What, you were hoping I would? You want me to push you into dealing with it, so you don't have to make that decision?"

He looked out the window at the softly fading evening sun, a pink glow in the western sky. Now, in late August, the light was fading earlier every day, as the sun weakened in its journey across the heavens.

"Has it ever occurred to you that you might be suffering from post-traumatic stress disorder? All the symptoms fit."

He gave a wry smile. "A rose by any other name . . . oh, I don't know. When I'm like this I barely have enough will to make a cup of coffee."

"Do you think you're ready to talk about it?"

"You think I have to sooner or later." It wasn't a question—he knew the answer.

She shrugged, a tiny lift of her elegant shoulders. "Not necessarily. It depends on the person. Some people seem to do all right without processing their pain."

"Look," he said, looking her directly in the eyes, "you and I both went into this profession because we believed in the value of the therapeutic process. So why don't you just say what you really think and stop trying to give me an out?"

"Okay," she said after a moment. "I do think you have to deal with it, and that you're avoiding it, because when you finally do . . ."

He knew the rest. Sooner or later, he would have to confront his long-buried feelings about his father's abandonment. And then, he feared, his rage would rise up like a mythical beast, full and terrifying in its primitive fury, and swallow him up whole.

CHAPTER TWELVE

The visit to Dr. Williams had left Lee feeling somewhat better—still shaky, but better. He was able to sleep, and woke up early the next day to rent a car so he and Butts could drive out to New Jersey and interview Ana's coworkers at the Swan Hotel.

Ana Watkins had no family left. Her mother disappeared years ago, and, as she had told Lee, her father had died recently. He knew from their sessions together that she was an only child. He also planned to track down the boyfriend, hopefully, and speak with him—anything to shed some light on what might have led to her becoming the third victim of a very bizarre killer.

Butts met him at Enterprise Car Rental in Greenwich Village at nine o'clock, and within a half hour they were zooming west along Route 78.

"Sorry I couldn't drive today, Doc," Butts said as they headed west, the skyscrapers of Manhattan looming behind them in the rearview mirror. "The wife always does Meals on Wheels on Wednesdays. You know—brings food to the old folks and stuff. She's an RN, but gave it up when the kids were born. Still has that need to feel useful, I guess."

"Sure," Lee said. "I think we all have that."

He and Butts drove in silence for a while, lulled by the motion of the car and the soft morning light falling on the blacktop, damp from a rain the night before. The water evaporated in wispy threads of mist as the air heated up and the sun climbed higher in the sky. To his relief, Lee had not awakened with any symptoms from the previous day's attack, though his emotions were still close to the surface.

As they approached the exit for Route 202, Butts said, "What I'd like to know is why do we have to put up with that Krueger dame?"

"Krieger," Lee corrected him.

"Whatever." Butts stared moodily out the window, tracing waving lines with his finger in the thick mist of condensation on the interior of the glass.

"I don't know the story behind it, but I'll bet you Chuck Morton had nothing to do with it."

"Yeah, I know," said Butts. "He doesn't like her any more than I do. How about you—can you stand her?"

Lee thought about it for a moment. "She sort of reminds me of my mother."

Butts shivered. "Jeez. Some mother."

Lee smiled. "She's not so bad once you get used to her."

Butts reclined his seat a little and stretched his arms out over his head. "The scary part is that I just know my kids will be talkin' about me the same way some day—if they aren't already."

They said no more about Krieger, though Lee had a feeling this was not the last he would hear about her. A few miles from the Route 202 exit, Butts's cell phone rang, and he dug it out of his jacket pocket.

"Butts here." There was a pause as he listened. "Really? That puts a new spin on things. Thanks a lot, Russ, much appreciated. Yeah, right—thanks."

He closed the cell phone and whistled softly. "That was Russell Kim from the M.E.'s office—the tox screen on our first two vics just came back."

Lee knew Russell Kim—a quiet, dedicated Korean pathologist known for his thoroughness and reliability.

"Okay," he said impatiently, *"and*—?"

Butts paused for dramatic effect. "GBH."

"Jesus." GBH, or gamma-hydroxybutyrate, was well known to law enforcement as the "date rape drug." It was a soporific, and could be added to a mixed drink without the victim being aware of its presence.

"Yup, one and the same."

Neither of them said what they were both thinking—that Ana's tox screen results would be identical. Lee tried not to think about her last hours, but he couldn't help it—he could only hope that perhaps the barbiturate effect of the drug had made the ordeal less horrible, but he wasn't ready to bet on it.

"That still doesn't explain the lack of forced entry in the bathtub killing," Lee said.

"Right. Either the killer gives it to him somewhere else or follows him into the apartment and forces him to drink it there. Either way, we still have missing pieces."

Lee turned onto Route 202, leaving the interstate to cut straight southwest through the farm fields of central Jersey, heading down to the Delaware River town of Lambertville. His mother and his niece lived not far from where they were going, but he would be seeing them in a few days, and today's trip was not about pleasure.

"This part of Jersey is real pretty, isn't it?" Butts mused as they cruised past fields of grazing cows and horses. The sun sparkled on the damp meadows, the long grasses catching the yellow morning light in sprays of silver and gold.

"Yeah," Lee agreed. But his mind was not on the beauty

of the summer morning. He was thinking of the grim necessity of their task—to learn what they could about the life of a young woman whose time had ended far too soon.

The Swan Hotel was an eighteenth-century building tucked in between taller structures built a century later on Main Street in the former factory town of Lambertville, which hugged the valley between the Delaware to the west and the hills rising to the east. Lee knew the town well. When he was growing up it had the appearance of a hard-bitten working-class town gone to seed. Lambertville was originally a hub on the D&R canal, but with the advent of the trucking industry, canal and rail traffic slowed to a trickle, and the town dried up.

Just across the Delaware was the hamlet of New Hope, Pennsylvania, accessible by car or by a footbridge spanning the river. With its thriving gay community, boutiques, cute restaurants, and B & B's, many lodged in eighteenth-century buildings, it was a major tourist destination. Lambertville, its bulkier, lumpy cousin, watched from across the river as New Hope rapidly went from chic to gawdy, and then finally passé. Tourists still flocked to the overpriced boutiques and restaurants—Lee secretly continued to enjoy several of them himself—but the pronouncement among locals was that New Hope was hopelessly prettified, had been overrun by tourists, and—worst of all—had lost its *authenticity*.

Meanwhile, on the Delaware's eastern shore, Lambertville was discovering itself—but without the sense of excess that had doomed New Hope to the scorn of local residents. Young professional couples were buying the handsome, sturdy town houses and fixing them up. Local businesses popped up like mushrooms after a spring rain. The town was slowly shaking off its years of depression and realizing that ugly ducklings too could become swans—and with a minimum of fairy lights, purple shutters and lime-green window boxes. (Lee liked New Hope, complete with purple shutters and fairy lights, but never would have admitted this to his mother, who represented the mainstream, local conservative taste. She had not shied away from pronouncing the harshest possible verdict on New Hope: it was, that horror of horrors, so *tacky*.)

Central to Lambertville's renaissance was the Swan Hotel. A low wooden building dating from 1743, it had been built as a tavern, and, in the late 1950s, was returned to its original use. It quickly became a gathering place for groups of aging Yale graduates, whose rivalry with their fellow Ivy Leaguers from Princeton, just a few miles to the east, was well known. On any given night when Lee was a teenager, you could hear the inebriated strains of "The Whiffenpoof Song" coming from the piano bar at the back of the first floor.

Lee always thought it was an insipid melody with even worse lyrics, but those middle-aged Yalies loved it, and sang it, he suspected, just to encourage the inevitable rebuttal of the Princeton tiger song from their arch rivals, who also frequented the piano bar. The Princetonians never failed to take the bait: they would leap to their feet, red-faced from brandy and clogged arteries, and reciprocate just as unmelodiously, braying like the donkey from the Bremen Town Musicians.

The reason Lee came to the Swan was the piano player, a stocky local plumber who was a great favorite of the well-heeled clientele. A bulldog of a man with a face like Ernest Borgnine and sausages for fingers, he pounded the hell out of that baby grand piano. He could play anything—Rodgers and Hart, Gershwin, Bacharach, Beethoven. He could play by ear and he could play from sheet music—from Lee's boyhood perspective, there was no limit to the man's talent.

Now, as he swung the rented Saturn into a parking spot in

front of the hotel, he was gripped with nostalgia for those sweet days of youth when he was attending Princeton and would come home for holidays. He and Laura would go together with their mother to Lambertville to eat at Phil and Dan's Italian diner, then head over to the Swan for an hour or two of music. Laura had a pretty singing voice, and sometimes she would sing a solo, while Lee sat in the corner gripping his beer mug, silently urging her voice not to crack on the high notes, his chest full with pride in his pretty sister. He knew Fiona, too, was proud, though she was always sparing in her praise, true to her Scottish character.

Butts followed him into the building, grunting as he swung the heavy oak door closed behind him. The Swan was much as Lee remembered it, though the low ceilings and dimly lit rooms felt more claustrophobic than they had when he was a boy.

It was still an hour away from lunch, so the place was quiet. The maître d', a slim, dark, Middle Eastern man, led them to the atrium, a recent addition on the side of the building, to wait for the manager, who was expecting them. Lee was pleased to see that this part of New Jersey was finally acquiring a more multicultural look. When he lived there it had been very white—and very WASPy.

They settled themselves by the window, underneath a greenhouselike structure with potted plants on the inside and creeping vines along the outside of the glass. The sound of softly flowing water came from a stone fountain in the back of the room, and the effect was calming and peaceful.

They didn't have long to wait. The manager rushed in, a worried look on his face. Lee had told him over the phone that something had happened to Ana, but had not gone into specifics.

"Hello, I'm Sayeed El Naga," the manager said, shaking

their hands. He too was dark and, judging by his name and accented English, from the Middle East, but unlike the elegant maître d', he was small and balding, with a compact body and nervous, eager energy. He had a darkly handsome face, with large dark eyes, full lips, and very white teeth. He exuded personal warmth and goodwill.

He pulled up a chair and leaned forward, resting his elbows on the table, and looked Lee earnestly in the eyes. "You said you have something to tell me regarding Ana. So let's not waste time—what is it, please?" His tone was polite but firm, as though he expected something less than the truth from the encounter.

Lee met his gaze. There was no point in trying to soften the blow. El Naga had asked for the truth, and it would be a shock no matter how he said it. "Ana is dead. Her death has been classified as a homicide."

El Naga fell back in his chair as though he had been shot. He stared at Lee without speaking, his mouth open. Finally he said, "When—how? Who did it? Where did you find her?"

Butts stepped in. "They found her yesterday, in the river."

"The Delaware?"

"No," said Lee, "where the Harlem River meets the Hudson."

"What was she doing there?" said El Naga.

She was coming to see me, Lee wanted to say, but the time of death hadn't yet been conclusively determined. It was harder to pinpoint with victims who had been in the water for some time, as Ana had.

"We don't really know yet," said Butts. "I wish we could tell you more, but we're trying to figure it out ourselves."

"Ana hated the water," El Naga said. "She told me that once," he added apologetically.

"We'd like to ask you a few questions, if you don't mind," Lee said gently.

"Yes, yes, of course—anything."

"Did she have any enemies that you know of?" Butts asked. "Anybody who expressed a dislike for her, or who had a reason to harm her?"

"No, I can't think of anyone. She was a little strange, you know, had an odd way about her, but she was a good worker, and got on reasonably well with the rest of the staff."

"What about customers?" said Lee. "Was there anyone who acted suspicious or inappropriate with her recently?"

El Naga furrowed his thick black eyebrows and chewed on his lower lip. "Let me think. This is a pretty upscale clientele, you know," he said defensively, as if the restaurant itself were a suspect.

"Yes, I know," Lee reassured him. "I used to come here when I was a boy."

El Naga's face brightened momentarily. "Really?"

"Yes—I grew up not far from here."

"It's very nice here, isn't it?" El Naga said. "I like the countryside so very much. I still can't get used to snow, though—it is quite different where I come from."

"Yeah, and where's that?" Butts asked.

"Egypt—Cairo. Very noisy, very dirty, very polluted, don't you know? I much prefer it here—I have even bought the snow boots for this winter."

"So was there anyone you can think of who came here who might have acted strangely toward Ana?" Lee prompted.

El Naga's face grew serious again. "No . . . oh, wait, yes—there was someone, about a week ago. I remember Ana telling the maître d' that if he ever came again, would he please give him to another waitress."

"Did you get a look at the guy?" Butts said eagerly.

"Sadly, no. It was a very busy Sunday brunch, you see, and I was helping out in the kitchen. One of the cooks was away and we were short-staffed. I'm so very sorry I can't be more helpful," he added, looking dejected.

"No, thank you for what you've told us—it could be very helpful," Lee said. The man was so earnest and eager to please that Lee wanted to reassure him.

"Oh, one more thing," Butts said. "Do you happen to have the phone number of her boyfriend—what's his name again?" Lee had told him the boyfriend's name was Raymond, but Butts sometimes liked to get information out of people that he already had, just to see how they reacted to the question.

"Uh, it's Raymond, isn't it? Raymond Santiago. Yes, I think I do—I believe that's the number she gave me as an emergency contact."

"So you never met him?" said Lee.

"No. I believe he picked her up from work once or twice, but I don't know if he ever came inside the restaurant. He's the day manager at the Black Bass over in Lumberville—he might be working the lunch shift today."

El Naga arranged for them to talk to the rest of the staff, most of whom had been working last week's Sunday brunch. Apparently it was one of their busiest meals of the week. The only person who got a look at the customer in question was the maître d', whose name was Assaf Hussein.

"I wish I had gotten a better view of his face," he said, "but the man was sitting with his back to me. I can tell you this: he was rather tall, but slight of build, so I was surprised that Ana felt threatened by him at all. He was not an imposing-looking man, from behind, at any rate."

"What about hair color, race, that kind of thing?" Butts asked eagerly.

"Well, he was definitely Caucasian," Hussein said. "His

hair was quite straight and rather light in color—sort of a light mousy brown, I think. From the back he didn't seem to be at all the kind of man who stood out in a crowd. I meant to get a look at his face as he left, but he slipped out quietly while my back turned, I'm afraid. It was quite a busy day, even for a Sunday."

"Did she ever mention him again?" Lee asked.

"No, she didn't. She worked three shifts later that week but never mentioned him again to me. I'm sorry I can't be more helpful," he said. "I really liked Ana. She was troubled, you know, but I had a sense that her life was beginning to turn around, and I was glad for her. Terrible for a thing like this to happen to such a young person."

"Yeah," said Butts. "It's a bitch, ain't it?"

CHAPTER THIRTEEN

Lee and Butts decided to push on to Lumberville and drop in on Raymond Santiago at the Black Bass. They declined Sayeed El Naga's invitation to dine at the Swan as his guests. It seemed inappropriate to take advantage of his hospitality at a time like this, especially after interviewing the staff about their murdered colleague.

Butts had his regrets, though. As they climbed into the dark green Saturn sedan, he said, "It sure smelled great in there. Sorry we couldn't stay."

"It just didn't feel right to me," Lee said as he started the engine. "Don't you think it would have been uncomfortable?"

"Yeah," Butts sighed, buckling his seat belt. "But it sure smelled great."

Lee circled around the back of town before heading west over the bridge to Pennsylvania. Lambertville looked prosperous but relaxed on this Tuesday in late August. He saw children playing on the wide sidewalks, riding their bikes or Razor scooters, and others splashing in plastic pools on grassy side lawns. School would be starting in a week or so.

Lee remembered the feeling of wanting to fill the final glorious days of summer with as much activity as possible.

As he turned onto the bridge across the river, Butts said, "I wonder what that was we smelled cooking. God, it smelled great."

"Look, I'm sorry," Lee said. "But don't you think it would have been weird to stay?"

"Yeah, I guess you're right," Butts agreed, but he didn't sound convinced.

"I'll tell you what," Lee suggested. "If we can, we'll eat at the Black Bass, okay?"

Lee turned north on the River Road, which would take them to Lumberville, to the Black Bass Hotel.

Lumberville was a hamlet tucked along a narrow strip of land on a section of the Delaware where the river lay far below sheer rocky cliffs on one side, while on the other side the wooded hills rose abruptly and steeply from the town. Settlers in the eighteenth century had managed to carve out a bit of town, which consisted of little more than a general store, a few houses, and of course the legendary Black Bass Hotel.

The Black Bass, built in 1745, had a very different history than its New Jersey cousin, the Swan. It was a renowned Tory stronghold during the Revolution, and the dusty Union Jack over the bar was supposedly from that era—though it was admittedly hard to separate legend from reality in some of the claims that were made about the hotel. There were glass cases displaying scores of objects and artifacts, allegedly from the British Royal Family, all the way from Queen Victoria to the present.

Lee had worked there one summer as a teenager and remembered the owner well. His name was Mr. Shelton, and he was an odd, elderly gentleman with a halo of white hair, a pink face, and an alarming way of biting off his consonants when he spoke. He was inordinately fond of Boston bull terriers, and when Lee knew him, he kept three of them, the oldest and meanest of which was a female named Samantha—Sam for short—who had a vendetta against children. Lee still remembered the delight the old gentleman took in introducing him to the dogs, and the strange little smile he had when he said, "This is Sam. Sam doesn't like children." Even though he had yet to learn about the concept of projection, Lee had an instinctive understanding that the dog was Mr. Shelton's alter ego.

The front hall was deserted when they entered it. It smelled musty, of damp, ancient wood and slowly growing fungus. The wide floorboards creaked under their feet, and as always Lee had the feeling of being transported to the era when the building was constructed, over 250 years ago. He looked around. Not much had changed since his childhood—the entrance to the bar was still on the right, the narrow wooden stairs leading up to the rooms visible from the front entrance. The little sitting room where Mr. Shelton kept his dogs was on the left, covered by a thick brocade curtain with a blue-on-white design of fat naked angels cavorting, harps and roses in their plump little hands.

They heard a rustling sound from the sitting room and turned just as an exceptionally handsome young man emerged from it. He was of medium height, with thick, curly black hair, an olive complexion, and a face that was almost pretty, with a wide mouth and deep-set almond-shaped eyes. He wore a navy blazer over crisp white shirt and ironed blue jeans. His attitude was friendly but a little suspicious. He regarded them warily, while maintaining a courteous smile.

"I'm sorry, but we're closed for lunch. Can I help you?" he asked, crossing his arms and tilting his head to one side.

"Yeah, we're lookin' for Raymond Santiago," Butts said, swinging his large head around to peer through the partially opened curtains.

The young man smoothly closed the curtains behind him, and his smile relaxed a bit. "I'm Ray Santiago—can I help you?"

"Mr. Santiago," Lee said, "maybe you'd like to sit down. I'm afraid we have some bad news."

"I don't need to sit down," he replied. "What is it?"

"It concerns your girlfriend, Ana Watkins," Butts said, holding up his badge.

Santiago's face hardened when he saw the shield. "What about her? Is she okay?"

Butts glanced at Lee, so he took over. Once again, he thought it was best to get it over with quickly. As his mother used to say, tearing off a bandage slowly always hurt more than a single quick, firm pull.

Lee took a deep breath. "I'm very sorry to have to tell you this, but she's dead."

Santiago's reaction was unexpected. He stood for a moment staring at them, then abruptly burst out laughing. It was the strangest reaction to bad news Lee had ever seen. He and Butts stood watching uncomfortably as Santiago laughed.

Finally the laughter subsided, and he said, "Okay, you guys, well done—you really had me fooled. Tell Ana that was a good one. I like the whole thing with the badge—for a minute you totally had me."

"Mr. Santiago, this is not a joke," Butts said, looking irritated.

Santiago's eyes twinkled. "No, *of course* it's not. Hey, where did she *find* you guys? You're good, you really are."

He looked from Butts to Lee and back again. Lee saw the

instant the realization hit him. His face froze, then went slack. He took a step backward, as if he had been pushed. His breath caught in his throat and he said simply: "No."

"I'm so sorry—" Lee began, but Santiago grabbed him by the shoulders, looked deeply into his eyes, and said,

"No, don't. Just shut up—please?"

"Mr. Santiago—" Butts said, but Santiago waved him off.

"No, no, no! Stop it, please, just don't do this."

He looked as if he was about to crumple to the floor, so Lee grasped him firmly by the elbow and guided him through the foyer and into the empty restaurant. Butts trudged along behind, muttering to himself. Lee knew the detective hated delivering bad news. He didn't care much for it himself. He escorted Santiago to the nearest chair and gently sat him down. Santiago began to rock, hugging himself and whimpering softly.

"What happened?" he whispered. "How did she—I mean, was it—did she—?"

"No, she didn't take her own life," Lee said. "We think she was murdered."

"Oh, Jesus!" Santiago said, and began rocking again. "Who would—she didn't have any enemies, for Christ's sake! Who on earth—do you know who did it?" he asked imploringly.

"No, I'm afraid we don't," Butts said.

He looked as if he was about to lay a hand on Santiago's shoulder, then checked the impulse, and stared down miserably at his shoes, waiting for him to snap out of it. Both he and Lee seemed to sense that the moment couldn't be rushed, so Lee took a look around the restaurant while they waited, inhaling the familiar old building smell of moldering ancient secrets.

Little had changed since he was a boy. The dining area was surprisingly airy after the cramped entrance hall, with wooden tables and chairs scattered sparingly around a single large room. Tables lined the far wall of the restaurant, which was dominated by a row of windows overlooking the river. The oak tables and chairs were of eighteenth-century design, and the dark wood had been chosen to match the wide burnished floorboards, which were original. He remembered as a boy how he imagined centuries of feet treading those boards, the soft click and shuffle of shoe leather back and forth as people came and went. This building had been standing for over thirty years when the revolution began, and had sheltered Tories and patriots within its walls—brigands and bandits, lovers and murderers alike.

Santiago had stopped rocking and was staring off into space, a dazed expression on his handsome face. He exchanged a look with Butts, who frowned and raised his shaggy eyebrows.

"Mr. Santiago?" Lee said tentatively. "I'm so sorry for your loss, but we'd like to ask you a few questions, if you don't mind."

Santiago looked at up them with childlike vulnerability. His dark eyes were free of tears, but they were wild with grief. He gazed at Lee searchingly, as if he somehow held the power to release Santiago from this pain. Lee knew exactly how he felt and knew there was no release but time itself.

"Is that okay with you?" Butts said, and Santiago nodded. Lee wondered if they would get much out of him—he was still in a state of shock.

"How did she die?" he said, his voice trembling.

"She was drowned."

Santiago shivered. "She hated the water."

"When's the last time you saw her?" Butts asked.

"Friday. We had a fight, see, about this fear she had that she was being followed. I told her it was all in her head, and she got angry at me and stormed out." His voice was a shaky monotone, as if the power of his grief was blocking any expression of emotion. "She was always doing things like that—she was a real drama queen, you know. So when she didn't call over the weekend I figured she was just sulking and thought I'd let her chill out for a while. Her moods never lasted more than a couple of days. I called her this morning before I left for work and got her voice mail. I thought maybe she was studying. She is—was—taking a class at Rutgers."

Lee's calls to her had also bounced to her voice mail repeatedly. No cell phone was on the body when she was found. Lee knew Chuck had sent the CSI team over to her house at the same time he and Butts were heading out—they might even still be there, for all he knew. The cell phone, if found, might contain clues, but then again, it might not.

"You say she was worried about bein' followed," Butts said. "Who exactly did she think was following her?"

"Okay," Santiago said, rubbing his forehead with the tips of his fingers, as if trying to massage away the cobwebs in his brain. He was beginning to look more focused now—his eyes were clearer, and when he spoke his voice was less monotone and distant. "She was seeing this crazy shrink. I thought he was a total quack and told her so—"

"How did she react to that?" Lee interjected.

"Man, she did not like that at all," he said with a bitter little laugh. "Told me to go f—uh, screw myself. Said she had finally found someone who was going to help her unlock the secrets of her past, you know, and that I should just back off and let her do her thing. So I was like, all right, if that's what you need to do that's okay, just don't expect me to agree with it. 'Cause I really thought this guy was whacked, you know?"

"Dr. Perkins?" said Lee.

"Yeah, that's his name. Why, do you know him?"

"No," said Lee. "Did you ever meet him?"

"No, man, but I seen him once getting into his car when I picked her up there one time, and he had a look about him, you know?"

"What kinda look?" Butts said.

Santiago shrugged. "Just like, you know, the guy looked *evil*, man. I mean, he's all thin and gaunt with a little goatee and everything. Christ, he looks like the devil. I know you can't judge people from the way they look or anything, but this guy gave me the creeps."

Butts looked at Lee and then back at Santiago. "So you never spoke to him?"

"No. I wanted to, but Ana said I couldn't—that it would violate 'doctor–patient confidentiality,' or some bullshit like that, but I thought she was just trying to protect him. He had her under some kind of spell, if you ask me."

"Like a magic spell, you mean?" Butts said.

Santiago froze, his eyes wide. "God, you don't think—I mean, I know he's whacked, but do you think *he* could have—"

"It's very unlikely," Lee reassured him. "We think Ana was the victim of someone who has killed before."

"Really? So you might know who killed her?" Santiago searched their faces for a sign of hope.

"No. We don't have an actual suspect yet," Butts answered.

Santiago's whole body seemed to deflate. He slumped back down in his chair, and his vacant stare returned. "I don't know, man—maybe I could have done something to prevent this. I just don't believe it. How could this happen to her? What did she ever do to anybody?"

"You said before she thought she was being followed," Butts reminded him. "Did she say anything more about that, like who it might be?"

Santiago ran a hand through his curly black hair, which glistened in the afternoon sunlight streaming in through the row of windows. Outside, Lee could see the water of the Delaware sparkling silver in waves of reflected light.

"She was real secretive about that. She said she'd uncovered some kind of childhood abuse or trauma or something. I got the sense that the doc had spooked her so much that she believed whoever it was had come back to get her."

"So you didn't really believe her?" Lee asked.

"Naw, man, I just thought it was that crazy doctor, filling her head with all kinds of nonsense. That's the thing about Ana: she's—she *was* gullible, you know? She was always looking for answers, and when someone came along who looked like they had them, man, she was right there, first in line to get wisdom. The thing was, she wasn't always good at judging people, so she could get hurt." He shook his head sadly. "I tried to protect her—I always told her to question people's motives more, that kind of thing."

"Like with Dr. Perkins?" Lee asked.

"Yeah. That's why, when we had that fight on Friday, she was so angry at me—because I didn't believe her. Jesus," he said softly. "Do you think that's who killed her—whoever was following her? I mean, do you think there really *was* someone following her?"

"It's possible," Lee said, "but even if there was, it's also possible that her death was totally unrelated."

"Oh, man, I'd never forgive myself if it turned out her crazy fantasy was true. I just thought it was another one of Dr. Perkins's latest weirdo theories—and he had plenty of them, let me tell you."

"Like what?" Butts asked.

"Oh, man, you name it. He had this whole thing about past lives, and all kinds of mystical crap." He snorted in disgust. "I left that shit when I left California, man. I can't believe I ran back into it on the East Coast. There's irony for you, huh?"

"Yeah, real ironic," Butts replied. "Do you happen to have this guy's contact number?"

"Yeah, it's in my office. Just give me a second, okay?"

They followed him to the front of the building and waited in the foyer while he went into his office, emerging shortly with the number written on the back of an old menu.

"Here you go —he's in Stockton, just the other side of the river in Jersey."

"I know it," Lee said, taking the number, which was scribbled in between the tenderloin of pork with sage dressing and the salmon mousse with dill sauce. "Thanks a lot." He glanced at Butts. It was time to end this interview—they had what they came for.

"I—I guess I should talk to someone about a funeral," Santiago said, gazing off toward the river. A hazy mist had settled over the sluggishly flowing water. "She had no family, you know. A lot of friends, but . . . I guess we were her family."

"I think that would be a good idea, when you're up to it," Lee said.

They thanked Santiago and expressed their condolences again, leaving him a business card in case he remembered anything else. He followed them outside like a puppy, as if they were the last link to Ana and he was sorry to see them go. The last image Lee had in the rearview mirror was Santiago standing in front of the Black Bass, shielding his eyes from the sun with an upraised arm, looking after their car as it drove away.

CHAPTER FOURTEEN

Butts's stomach couldn't take any more fasting, so Lee drove to Dilly's Corner, a hamburger and ice cream stand along the River Road where it met Coldspring Road. It had been a favorite of his and Laura's when they were children, and was open all year round. It was very popular with tourists in the summer season, but also served as an after-school hangout for the local kids. As a boy Lee always thought it was cool being able to buy ice cream on a little country road in the middle of nowhere—the stand was several miles away from the nearest town.

As they sat at the wooden picnic table eating cheeseburgers and fries, Butts said, "You know, this place ain't half bad—this is actually a decent cheeseburger."

Butts happily stuffed a handful of fries in his mouth, picked up his chocolate milkshake, put the straw to his lips, and sucked deeply on it, his eyes half closed with pleasure. Lee shuddered and looked away. He had never understood chocolate milkshakes with cheeseburgers—it struck him as excessive and rather revolting. He glanced at his watch. It was half past three—they would be driving back to the city during rush hour. At least they would be going against the traffic, though that didn't always work out, as the middle lanes on both the Holland and Lincoln Tunnels would be switched over for the outbound commuters.

"Well," he said, tossing his sandwich wrapper into the metal trash can, "shall we pay Dr. Perkins a house call?"

Butts gave his milkshake a final mighty slurp and wiped his mouth with a satisfied flourish. "Now *that* was worth waitin' for!" he declared, and shuffled behind Lee to the car. As they arrived at the green Saturn, Lee caught a movement out of the side of his eye, over in the woods next to Dilly's Corner. Probably a deer, he thought—they were in abundance this time of year. In fact, they were hazardous to motorists, especially after dark—it was easy to hit one as it leapt out of the woods into the glare of headlights. He had a number of friends at school who had totaled their parents' cars that way.

"Whatchya lookin' at?" said Butts, noticing Lee peering into the thick green canopy of leaves.

"I saw something—probably just a deer," Lee said, climbing into the car.

"You sure?" Butts remarked sarcastically as he climbed into the Saturn. "You sure it wasn't an alien or something?"

"Very funny. We should remember to tell Dr. Perkins about it."

"Yeah. Maybe we'll get abducted if we're lucky." Butts stretched his seat belt across his body and patted his bulging belly. "Jeez, I shouldn't 'a had that second order of fries." He sighed. "I just know the wife is gonna put me on a diet this month—I can see it in her eyes. She's got that look, you know? Ah well, I might as well live it up while I can. It's broccoli and black beans from now on."

Lee smiled and started up the engine. Dr. Martin Perkins had an office in downtown Stockton—not that there was much of a downtown to speak of. It consisted of little more than a liquor store, a grocery store called Errico's Market, a gas station, and a couple of restaurants. One of the restaurants was the historic Stockton Inn, which contained the wishing well made famous in the Rodgers and Hart song "There's a Small Hotel." Lee's mother never tired of pointing this out to visitors. Lee had a job there one summer as a busboy when he was a teenager, riding his bike the mile and a half from his mother's house to get there.

Driving down the tiny main street pulled at his already raw emotions—it held so many memories of him and Laura. He thought about all the times they walked across the footbridge to Pennsylvania, or strolled along the canal towpath toward New Hope, or dipped into the Delaware for a quick swim. They loved doing errands for their mother, picking up groceries at Errico's, racing their bikes back along the towpath and up the hill to the stone house with its sweeping lawn and weeping willow trees.

Dr. Perkins's office was across from the gas station on the main street, next to the row of shops housing both the liquor store and the grocery store. It was a handsome turn-of-the-century Victorian, not too fussy. He had walked by it a hundred times as a boy, but in those days it was just a private home, with no business of any kind that he could remember.

Lee parked on the street in front of the building, and he and Butts walked up the steps to the spacious front porch. The sign underneath the buzzer read DR. MARTIN PERKINS, L.C.S.W.—BY APPOINTMENT and listed a phone number with a 609 area code. L.C.S.W. stood for licensed clinical social worker, which meant that even if Perkins was a crank, he was at least certified by the state. Lee knew from his own experience how much study and training was involved— enough so that anyone receiving certification had to at least do all the required reading and pass the courses. You had to have at least a master's degree to qualify. He wondered, though, what the "Dr." was for, and whether it was a degree in psychiatry.

He rang the bell next to the double French doors, and a single chime sounded deep inside the building. He and Butts both agreed it would be better to surprise the good doctor, to gauge his unprepared reactions and prevent him from concocting a story, should he prove to be involved in Ana's death.

There was a long pause, and they were about to turn and leave when they heard the sound of footsteps and a man's voice calling from within the house.

"Coming—just a moment!"

The long white lace curtains on the French doors fluttered. There was the sound of a lock being unlatched, and the door was flung open. On the other side of it stood a man of singular appearance. He was tall and thin, about fifty, Lee guessed, with slicked-back, jet-black hair and a goatee to match. He wore a black three-piece suit with tiny gray pinstripes so old fashioned that it looked like a costume from a Victorian-era drama. Dangling from his vest was a gold watch fob. His immaculate shoes were soft black leather and of a style and cut similar to shoes Lee had seen in period movies—they, too, appeared to be heirlooms. Everything about his appearance was so theatrical that his arrival at the door was like the entrance of a character in a stage play.

He greeted them with a cordial but formal smile.

"Hello, I'm Dr. Perkins. And who might you be?"

The voice was British, self-consciously posh, but with a suggestion of a regionalism—West Country, perhaps? Lee's knowledge of English dialects was fair—because of his Scottish ancestry he had traveled in the U.K. a fair amount.

"I'm Lee Campbell, and this is Detective Leonard Butts, NYPD."

"*Detective*, is it? Oh dear me, to what do I owe this honor?"

Perkins looked rather pleased, and his voice held a note of suppressed excitement. Lee waited a moment before responding, half-expecting Perkins to apologize for his odd attire and give some explanation about being an actor in a local production or something. But when no explanation was forthcoming, Lee said, "Could we have a few minutes of your time? It's about Ana Watkins."

"Is something the matter?" Perkins's face immediately assumed an expression of concern—so quickly that Lee didn't trust it.

"Can we come in?" Butts said, looking over his shoulder—or rather trying to, as he was at least half a foot shorter than Dr. Perkins.

"Oh, yes, yes—of course!" Perkins said, sweeping them into a spacious and graciously furnished drawing room. A grand piano covered with a cream-colored antimacassar, upon which sat a heavy blue vase filled with white tea roses, presided over the room. He motioned them to a pair of blue and white wing chairs in front of a marble fireplace. Butts complied slowly, taking in the room with some astonishment, judging by the expression on his face. Lee guessed that as a homicide detective in the Bronx, he seldom did interviews in dwellings like this one.

"Please, sit down," said Perkins.

"This is a very nice place you have here," Butts said, lowering his bulk into one of the armchairs carefully, as if afraid he might crush it.

"Thank you, but I really can't take any credit for it—it's all my sister's doing, you see," Perkins replied with a flip of an immaculately manicured hand. "She's the one with the artistic eye. I just live here." He pulled up a straight-backed chair in between the armchairs and settled himself in it.

Even his movements were theatrical. He looked not so much like a man at home in his drawing room as an actor playing the part of a man at home in his drawing room.

"Now then," he said, straightening his starched white cuffs, "what's this about Ana?"

"We understand Miss Watkins was a patient of yours," said Butts. It was a common interrogative technique to get as much information out of subjects as you could before giving them anything in return.

"You said she '*was*' a patient," Perkins observed. "Has something happened?"

"Was there anything in the course of her treatment that might lead you to believe she was suicidal?" Butts continued, ignoring the question. This too was standard operating procedure—never give away information to a potential suspect unless you find it necessary.

Perkins leaned back and crossed his arms. "I'm afraid that comes under doctor–patient confidentiality," he said primly. "In fact, I can't even confirm that Miss Watkins was—*is* my patient until you tell me what this is about."

Butts glanced at Lee, who said gently, "Dr. Perkins, I'm sorry to have to tell you this, but Ana Watkins was found dead yesterday."

Perkins sprang from his chair as though it were suddenly electrified. "Oh, dear me!" he cried, wringing his hands. "Oh, dear me—poor girl! What happened?"

"She was drowned," Butts replied bluntly.

Perkins stared at him, took one enormous gulp of air like a stranded fish, then paced in front of the fireplace, wringing his hands and muttering, "Dear me, oh dear me!" Once again, Lee was struck by the theatricality of his gestures. It was like watching an actor in a performance rather than a real human being in distress.

"Dr. Perkins," Butts said, "if you wouldn't mind, we'd like to ask you a few questions."

"Of course," Perkins said. "I'll do whatever I can to help—anything, I assure you."

"Right," Butts said, making a notation in the little notebook he always carried with him. Lee knew that sometimes the detective scribbled in it just to intimidate a suspect—often there was nothing on it but doodles. "Hey, is this an oil lamp?" Butts said, pointing to an old-fashioned-looking lantern in the foyer.

"Yes, it is," Perkins answered irritably. "And in answer to your question about whether she displayed suicidal ideation—no, not at all. In fact, I have rarely had a patient who was more *connected* to life. She had everything to live for, and was in fact making rapid improvement when she—" He stopped, but not out of grief so much as embarrassment, Lee thought. "How did she—I mean, do you think she took her own—?"

"She was found in the Harlem River yesterday morning," Butts replied. "There was evidence of foul play."

Perkins stopped pacing and looked at them in alarm. "Surely you don't think I—"

"No, no, it's nothing like that," Butts reassured him. "We're just talking to people she came in contact with to try and piece together enough about her to, you know, try and figure out what happened."

"Dear me," said Perkins, looking frightened. If he had an idea who killed Ana, Lee thought, he might be worried that person would come after him.

"Miss Watkins had expressed the fear that she was being followed," Butts continued. "Do you have any idea who might have been following her?"

Perkins put an elegant finger to his mouth and chewed on

it. "I suppose it can't do any harm, since she's dead. I may as well tell you that she had recently had a breakthrough in her therapy, and had come to realize that she was the victim of childhood abuse."

"Yeah?" Butts said, in a voice that said, *So tell me what else is new.*

"Yes," Perkins went on, completely missing Butts's sarcasm. "She had been struggling with demons in her past, until finally, under hypnosis, she recovered long-buried memories of sexual assault when she was a child."

Butts exchanged a glance with Lee, who kept his face impassive. He didn't want to spook Perkins. They were just closing in on the truth—assuming he would tell them the truth, of course. But Lee suspected that Perkins was as easy to read as a mediocre actor would be. If he was lying, he was sure to telegraph that to his audience.

"And who committed this sexual assault?" Butts asked him. Lee could tell he was doing his best to keep his voice even.

Perkins twisted the signet ring on his pinky finger. "Alas, I wish I could say, but we hadn't yet reached the point in therapy where she could make out the face of her assailant."

"Let me get this straight, Doc," Butts said, disdain leaking into his voice. "Under hypnosis, she gets a memory of being—assaulted—as a child, but somehow she can't see who's doing it?"

"Well, yes," Perkins said, his tone prickly. "These things are very complex, Detective. Sometimes the memories don't come all at once, and sometimes they don't ever come. We were just beginning to make progress, and I have no doubt that, after a few more sessions, poor Ana would have unlocked the door to her past and truly had a breakthrough in her therapeutic process."

"Ah, her 'therapeutic process'—I see," Butts said. Lee decided it was time to rescue this interview before Butts pushed Perkins into being totally uncooperative.

"So you don't have any idea who she thought might be following her?" he asked quickly.

Perkins raised his hands in a gesture of surrender. "I wish to God I did, truly I do. But she never actually saw anyone following her."

"Did you think it might be connected to this 'therapeutic breakthrough'?" Butts asked.

"Again, I can't say," Perkins replied. "Ana thought it was, but I think that just indicated her general level of paranoia, which was always quite high."

"What about your other patients?" Lee said. "Do you think any one of them might be violent?"

"I'm afraid that's confidential," Perkins said. "Though if I did think one of my patients was an imminent danger to himself or others, it would of course be my duty to report that to the proper authorities."

"And you made no such report?" Lee said.

"No. I don't think I have in the whole of my career. And in any case, my patients didn't have any contact with each other that I'm aware of."

At that moment a woman entered the room. She was a stork of a woman with a long, solemn face and soft brown hair piled up in a chignon on top of her head. Her face was not pretty, but it was striking, with large, mournful brown eyes, high cheekbones, and a full, serious mouth. She wore no makeup. Lee's first thought was that she didn't need any, and his second thought was that she was Perkins's sister.

Her attire was as old-fashioned as her brother's. She wore a long, high-necked white dress with flowered sleeves over high, laced-up leather boots; her clothes appeared to be aimed at downplaying any suggestion of sexuality, but in fact they had the opposite effect. Her presence had a restrained sensuality that was even more intriguing because of its understatement. She exuded coolness, reserve, and—or so Lee thought—restrained passion.

Everything about these two odd siblings and their house suggested an era of a hundred years ago. Lee had the feeling that when he and Butts stepped over the front stoop of the house they entered a time warp.

"Ah, gentlemen, allow me to present my younger sister, Miss Charlotte Perkins!" Perkins said, coming forward to take her by the hand. "Charlotte, my dear, this is Detective Butts and Mr. Campbell."

"How do you do?" said Butts, rising from his chair with a little bow. Lee was amused. He had never seen the burly detective behave like this, but he found himself bowing slightly as well. Something about Charlotte Perkins seemed to require it.

"How do you do?" she said, with the tiniest incline of her head.

"Charlotte, my dear, these gentlemen have come to see me about one of my patients. I'm afraid there's been an unfortunate"—he paused for the right choice of words—"uh, accident."

"I'm very sorry to hear it," Charlotte said. She had much the same upper-class British inflection as her brother.

"Did you know the young woman in question?" Lee asked, surprised at his own old-fashioned locution.

"Her name was—" Butts began, but Charlotte Perkins interrupted him.

"I never had any dealings with Martin's patients," she said. "I keep to my rooms when he is conducting his sessions."

Her choice of words made it sound like Perkins conducted séances instead of psychiatric counseling.

Charlotte turned to her brother, arms crossed in front of her thin chest.

"Martin, did you not offer these gentlemen something to eat or drink?"

"Oh, dear me, forgive me!" Perkins squeaked, bustling toward the door where his sister had just entered.

"No, really, we're almost finished here, and we have to be getting back," Butts said.

"It's no trouble, really," said Charlotte, but Lee and Butts were already backing out toward the door. For all its splendor and elegance, there was something about the house that made Lee want to leave it as soon as possible. He had a sticky sensation of being drawn into it, as though one could somehow get trapped there.

All of this flashed through his head in a fraction of a second as he and Butts sidled toward the door. Perkins and his sister took a step toward them, and it was all Lee could do to not turn around and run. He glanced at Butts to see if he was feeling the same way, but he couldn't read the expression on the stocky detective's face.

"Are you sure you wouldn't like to stay for tea?" Charlotte Perkins said pleasantly.

"No, thanks—we're expected back in the city," Lee answered, letting her know that other people knew where he and Butts were. It was irrational, it was crazy, but the creeping dread he felt was real.

"Give us a call if you think of anything else that might be useful," Butts said, placing a business card on the round rosewood table by the front door.

"I certainly will," Perkins responded cheerily.

"Nice meeting you," Lee said with another little bow. Perhaps following his lead, Butts did the same. Perkins bowed back, and his sister gave a tiny curtsy.

And then, with a push, they were out the door and standing on the front porch. The sun was sinking lower in the sky, and the town's quiet little main street was bathed in its golden light. It was like stepping from a bad dream into a painting. There was still a sense of unreality in the bucolic beauty of the setting, but the foreboding that had enveloped Lee melted the moment they set foot outside the house.

Lee looked at Butts, who was sweating—but then, Butts often sweated.

"Did you—?" he began.

"Yeah—what *was* that?" Butts said, loosening his tie.

"I don't know," Lee replied. "Something about those two—"

"And that *house*! No wonder Santiago thought Perkins was creepy."

Lee turned to glance behind them as they clattered noisily across the wooden porch. The lace curtains on the door fluttered, as though someone had been peering through them. Next to the door, he noticed something he had failed to see before. It was a statue of a Green Man, an ancient Celtic symbol of fertility that Lee had always found rather sinister. The image took many forms, but certain elements were always present—it was always the face of a laughing man, with vines and plants growing out of his mouth.

Green men had always struck him as grotesque and nightmarish, and this one was no exception. The eyes stared wildly over the lecherous grinning mouth, and the suppurating vines were reminiscent of the writhing snakes that sprouted from the head of the Medusa. It reminded Lee of a Green Man he had seen in Rosslyn Chapel, the famed church in the tiny village of Rosslyn, just outside Edinburgh.

"Whatchya lookin' at?" Butts asked.

"It's a Green Man."

"Yeah? What's that?" As they walked to the car, Lee explained the significance of the Green Man as a Celtic fertility symbol.

"You notice anything else weird about his place?" Butts said as they climbed into the Saturn.

"What?"

"There were no light switches on the walls."

"Really?"

"Yeah. I saw some—what do you call 'em?—sconces, but no switches. And that oil lamp I saw—I think they don't have any electricity there."

"You think?"

"Yep. I'm tellin' you, there's something weird about those two."

But as they drove up the tiny main street, Lee was struck by how normal and familiar his boyhood town looked, and how little it had changed. There were the same rambling clapboard houses with their leafy lawns and porch swings and hanging baskets of pink begonias swinging gently from the white wicker trellises. In the gentle afternoon sun of late August, the town resembled a Norman Rockwell painting. He half-expected to see a rosy-cheeked family through white lace curtains, sitting down to a meal of turkey and gravy and mashed potatoes, their faithful little black-and-white terrier sitting patiently at their feet.

He and Butts didn't speak as Lee drove the Saturn up the long hill leading out of the valley toward Route 202. They stayed silent as he passed the little churchyard and turned onto the long hilly road leading past Washington's Headquarters Road and Three Bridges. As he drove down roads he had driven a hundred times before, Lee forgot about the Perkins siblings and began to think about this river valley, steeped in Revolutionary War history. As a boy, he had thrilled to the stories of the patriots battling the British troops. It was hard to imagine this softly rolling countryside in the dead of winter. Even though he had seen it every year of his life, Lee always found it hard to remember these green and inviting hillsides in the stark, stony whiteness of late December. He thought of the cold, hard winter the soldiers endured before the heroic attack on Trenton, just a few miles up river.

The Matthew Arnold painting of that triumphal moment never lost its power to move him. It was not so much the heroism of Washington he admired, but the sheer raw courage of the men, cold and hungry and half-starved, trekking wearily across the winter landscape and across the half-frozen river in rickety wooden boats, moving horses and cannons to the other side in the dead of night. Not for the first time, he wondered, if faced with that kind of hardship, whether he would have stood the test.

Butts broke the silence.

"Where we goin' now?"

"To Flemington. It's on the way back."

Their last stop would be the most difficult—a visit to Ana's house. The crime-scene technicians already been called out to process the place for forensic evidence, but now Lee and Butts would follow suit and sift through what remained to see if they could find something—anything—that might lead them to her murderer. Maybe, just maybe, the key to her death lay somewhere among the detritus of a young life ended tragically and far too soon.

CHAPTER FIFTEEN

Ana Watkins's house was situated on about ten acres of land on the outskirts of Flemington—a name familiar to nonlocals for the renowned shopping malls and outlet stores on Route 202. Flemington itself was a handsome, decent-sized town with sturdy historic buildings and upscale, locally owned shops, including a few really good restaurants frequented by its comfortably upper-middle-class residents.

The village had a sleepy late-summer glow as they drove through it and turned east onto Duck Pond Lane, the country road leading to Ana's house. A few miles down the road, they saw it on their left. Perched on a slight rise, overlooking a few acres of pastureland, it looked like any other nineteenth-century farmhouse in the area—except for the bright yellow police tape stretching from the mailbox to the thick oak tree at the bottom of the broad, sloping front lawn.

Lee parked at the bottom of the driveway. He and Butts got out and walked up the long drive, which looked freshly graveled, the shiny black stones crunching sharply underfoot. A single officer stood guard at the door—a Jersey state trooper, looking snappy in his gray and black uniform. His patrol car was parked in front of the house, and he came halfway down the drive to meet them, shielding his eyes against the sun.

"Can I help you?" he said, striding rapidly toward them, carrying his hat in his right hand. The Jersey state trooper hats, with their stiff broad brims and crisply indented tops, always reminded Lee of Smokey the Bear—and the man's shiny black knee-high boots and matching wide leather belt did nothing to dispel the image.

"Detective Leonard Butts, NYPD," Butts said, flashing his badge. "This is my associate, Dr. Campbell."

Lee smiled—Butts still insisted on calling him "Doc." He supposed that the detective was trying to impress the state trooper, but it was unnecessary. He was very young—hardly more than a boy, with cheeks so smooth they looked untouched by the blade of a razor. His pale skin, and red hair and eyebrows over cornflower blue eyes added to his aura of innocence. He reminded Lee of a youthful Max von Sydow—he had the same exaggerated Nordic complexion.

The young trooper stumbled on the freshly laid gravel, blushing a deep scarlet as he hastily placed his hat upon his head.

"Lars Anderson, Jersey State Police," he said, extending a hand. "They told me you were coming."

Lee was relieved to see the friendly expression on the officer's face as they shook hands. These things could be tricky. Though there was a brotherhood between all cops, interstate rivalry was a fact, especially when jurisdictional issues were involved. He knew from experience that things could get prickly very fast. Law enforcement was not a profession that attracted Type B personalities. Typically, cops were quick to react, which was a good thing in the face of danger, but they were also equally quick to anger.

But Officer Anderson seemed genuinely glad to see them. Lee imagined this was a pretty lonely and boring assignment. He led them up the drive, the soles of his high leather boots grinding into the gravel with a crisp crunching sound.

"Your CSI team was here yesterday," he said as they mounted the three steps leading up to the porch. "I don't know if they found anything useful or not."

"Yeah, it's too early to tell," Butts replied as they walked across the wooden floorboards, their heels clicking sharply on the whitewashed porch floor. He and Lee each pulled on a pair of thin rubber gloves from the box Anderson offered them. The crime-scene techs had already processed the house, but you could never be too careful. The front door was unlocked, and its metal hinges creaked as Officer Anderson swung it open.

The front room was so bare that Lee's first impression was that no one lived there at all. Then personal little details began to emerge: the green pottery vase of dried flowers in the window, the child's wooden chair in the corner next to the fireplace. The room was clearly originally intended as the main living room of the house, but as Trooper Anderson led them through to the kitchen, it was clear that most of the living had gone on there. In contrast to the rather bleak spareness of the living room, the kitchen was a happy, untidy jumble. Bunches of dried herbs hung suspended from each of the three windows. Stained and spattered cookbooks lined one shelf of a battered built-in bookcase, and the shelves over the heavy, old-fashioned gas stove sagged with the weight of mismatched, obviously handmade ceramic plates and mugs.

A brightly colored hooked rug covered most of the floor, which was made of the same wide white-pine floorboards as the rest of the house. A wooden table painted turquoise blue snuggled up against the far corner of the room. The walls were painted a cheerful bumblebee yellow, with a mural of wildflowers on the north wall. The sun streaming in through white lace curtains fell on the riotous blossoms, turning it into a lifelike three-dimensional trompe l'oeil. An old pot-bellied stove against the far wall served as the heat source for the room, Lee suspected—a wooden crate full of firewood was nestled in the corner, next to the kitchen table. The two chairs on either side of it looked as though they had been recently and hastily vacated, and the sight made Lee's heart give a sad little skip until he realized that the room's most recent occupant was no doubt Officer Anderson.

"The crime-scene techs spent quite a lot of time in here," the trooper said. "Removed a few glasses and some silverware for fingerprinting." He looked around the room and shook his head. "Such a pity—someone was real happy here."

Butts stared at him. "How can you tell?"

Anderson waved a hand at a stack of unpainted ceramic mugs on the windowsill. "It's not hard to see—look here, see? She was in the middle of this project—and look here, too," he continued, indicating an open cookbook on the counter. Lee recognized it: *The Moosewood Cookbook*, an early pioneer of the natural food movement. The pages were stained and splattered—obviously the recipe was one she had loved, and made again and again.

"Okay," Butts muttered, "so she was happy here. Fat lot of good it did her."

The young trooper looked shocked at the detective's apparent callousness, but Lee knew Butts better—his disgust was an expression of his deep anger at the injustice of murder.

"Well, I'll leave you to it," Anderson said, with a disapproving glance at Butts. "Call me if there's anything you need."

"Thanks," Lee replied, and the young officer retreated quietly back to his post on the front porch. They heard the swing and slam of the screen door and the scraping of a chair across the floorboards, then silence.

Lee turned to Butts. "You know," he said softly, "not everyone knows you as well as I do. I think our friend has the wrong impression—"

"Yeah, whatever," Butts grunted, stomping over to the corner and sticking his face into a blue crockery bin. He immediately pulled it back and sneezed. "It's damn flour," he said with disgust, wiping the white powder from his nose.

"What did you think it was—cocaine?"

Butts ignored him and continued to poke around the kitchen, opening cupboards, lifting the lids off saucepans, rifling through drawers filled with silverware and kitchen utensils. Lee sat on one of the chairs and watched Butts for a while, then let his gaze fall idly upon the mural of wildflowers. It really was wonderfully painted—with the sun on it from this angle it was very lifelike. He wondered if Ana herself had taken up painting. As Anderson had observed, she had clearly taken up pottery, and was doing a pretty good job of it. The mugs drying on the windowsill were gracefully if imperfectly crafted, and the finished ones in the cupboard were creatively and gaily glazed. He wondered if she had a kiln somewhere on the property.

"Okay," Butts said finally, "I think I'm done in here."

"This doesn't look like the kitchen of someone who is suicidal," Lee remarked.

"Naw," Butts agreed. "Sure doesn't."

They wandered around the room for a few more minutes, and then, as they were about to leave, Lee noticed something hanging behind the potbellied stove. It was partially obscured by the black piping of the stove's chimney, so he stepped closer to have a better look.

He saw with a shock of recognition that it was a Green Man—the same Celtic symbol he had seen on the Perkinses' porch. This one was larger, of a different design, and even more threatening. The face was wilder, more primal, with an expansive, evil grin. A primeval tangle of thorns and vines spilled from its mouth, wrapping and twisting around its hoary head. It also had obviously been hand painted, in bold greens and blues—probably by the same person who had painted the handmade pottery in the cupboards. Lee looked around the kitchen for evidence of painting equipment, but saw none.

"Is that one 'a them Green Men?" Butts asked, coming up behind him.

"Yeah."

Butts leaned forward, studying it, his small eyes nearly disappearing under his heavy overhanging brows. "You think she made it?"

"Could be—especially if she made the mugs," Lee said. "Let's see if we can find a kiln somewhere on the property."

"Why? You think it's important?"

"Well, it's interesting that both she and Dr. Perkins have the same Celtic symbol in their homes. It's not all that common."

"Yeah," Butts said, trotting after him as they went back through the living room. "Maybe she made his and gave it to him as a present."

"That's one possibility."

They found the kiln in the basement, surrounded by pots and mugs and plates in various states of completion. The entire room had been turned into a pottery studio—there was a wheel and raw clay and a shelf of textbooks and instruction manuals on the craft of pottery and ceramics. Clearly Ana had dived into this recent passion with an energy and commitment Lee found touching. He imagined the comfort and satisfaction it must have given her, and pictured her sitting at the wheel, her thin hands wrapped around the spinning clay, a wisp of blond hair dangling from her forehead, as she turned raw materials from the earth into the graceful and useful household items he had seen upstairs.

He and Butts wandered slowly around the room for a while, but there was no sign of any more Green Men. There was, however, a mother and child figurine, the only one of its kind, on the table of white, as-yet-unfired pottery. Nestled among the mugs and plates, it was all curves, an impression- istic sculpture with a womblike roundness to the design. The mother's arms encased the child, as she cradled its head on her bosom, while staring down at its sleeping figure.

The symbolic significance to Ana's life struck Lee at once: she was playing the role of both mother and child, seeking her own "rebirth" in therapy. Perhaps that accounted for her susceptibility to someone like Perkins, whose past- lives theories were probably very attractive to someone who was never very comfortable in this life.

Butts picked up the figurine and examined it. "Looks like she was really into this stuff. Wonder if she sold any of it?"

"That's exactly what I was thinking," Lee mused. "And if so, who did she sell it to?"

"Here's somethin'," Butts said, plucking a piece of paper from the top bookshelf. Lee studied it over his shoulder. It looked like a ledger of some kind, with a list of about a dozen names and prices next to them, as well as a brief de- scription of the item sold.

"Looks like she did sell some of her work," Lee said. "Good job finding that."

"Some interesting names on here," Butts remarked. "Here's a funny one—Caleb. Like one 'a those old-fashioned New England names out of Hawthorne or somethin'." Butts scratched his head. "But what are the chances that one of her customers killed her?"

"I believe when we first met you pointed out to me that most murders are between people who know each other."

"Yeah," Butts said, "but we both know that the guy we're lookin' for is a whole different kettle of fish, right?"

"You're right," Lee said. "Serial offenders don't often kill people they know—but the suicide notes indicate that he may have had at least some contact with his victims."

"Right—so I'll hold on to this, for the time being," Butts said, dropping it carefully it into a blue evidence bag. "You never know."

The house yielded few more clues, only the sad feeling that here was a young woman working hard to put her life together, a life that was abruptly and cruelly cut short. The sun was low in the sky by the time they finished and bade Trooper Anderson good-bye. He seemed sorry to see them leave and stood watching as they walked down the long, sloping driveway back to their car. They drove in silence through the dusky summer evening, the smell of freshly mown hay mixing with the dark odor of cow manure as they drove past miles of pastures and farmland.

Just outside Somerville, the sky darkened, and big, fat drops of rain began to splash on the windshield. Just as Lee reached to turn on the windshield wipers, his cell phone rang. He fished it out of his jacket and tossed it to Butts, who put the phone to his ear.

"Hello? Oh, hi, Captain." He put the phone on speaker.

"Is Lee there?" It was Chuck, and he sounded anxious.

"Yeah—I'm driving," Lee called over the sound of the rain, which was escalating into a downpour. "We've got you on speakerphone."

"Hey, listen, are you guys about done out there?"

"Yes, we're about to head back—why, did something happen?" Lee asked, with a glance at Butts.

"Not exactly," Chuck said evasively. "It's—well, it's Krieger. She's mad as a nest of hornets and she's on her way over here later."

"Oh," said Lee. "And you don't want to face her alone, is that it?"

"How soon can you get here?" Chuck sounded miserable.

Chuck Morton's one weakness—if you could call it that—was his helplessness at the hands of strong women, especially when they were angry. Lee had seen his friend face down an entire station house of disgruntled cops and lead a group of riot police through an angry mob of protesters. At Princeton when there was a dorm fire it was Chuck who dashed into the building to see that everyone got out safely—against the orders of campus police. But women were another story. Lee didn't even ask what Krieger was upset about—they'd find out soon enough.

"Okay," he said. "We're on our way."

Butts turned the phone off as the sky let loose with a deluge of biblical proportions. The sound of the rain was deafening, as though someone were sitting on the roof pounding on tin buckets with sticks. Lee slowed the little sedan to a crawl and turned on the headlights.

Safety in numbers, he thought. That's what Chuck wanted. Well, they might outnumber Krieger, but they wouldn't necessarily outgun her—he could tell from their one meeting that she could be a formidable adversary. It was too bad that they were wasting precious time and energy in-fighting when there was a much more dangerous adversary out there taunting them to catch him—or her. With women like Krieger in the world, Lee thought, not for the first time, they couldn't necessarily assume their killer was a man.

CHAPTER SIXTEEN

"What are you standing there looking at, boy? Give me a hand! Come on, don't cry—remember, crying is for sissies and women. Do you want to be a woman, boy?"

His father's face was red, and there was sweat under the rim of his green John Deere tractor cap.

"Do you want me to cut off your little pecker so you can be a little crybaby girl? No? All right, then, stop crying—that's better. There's a little man for you. Now, give me a hand and open the door for me. Good—that's good. Now get the trunk for me—open it wide. Hurry up—this is heavy, you know. All right, now get in the car.

"We're going down to the river . . . because we have something to do there. Mommy has been bad—very, very bad, and you remember I told you what happens to bad women? Do you? Well, that's right—that's why we have to take her to the river."

She must have done something so awful to make Daddy so angry. I wonder what it was. Maybe she tried to cut off his pecker and make him like a girl, so he had to stop her. I would have to stop someone if they tried to do that to me. I would have to, because I'm just like Daddy. That's what he always tells me: you're my little man, just like me.

He bent down to pick up the heavy object, a dead weight inside the black plastic tarp. He remembered worrying that if they left the tarp down at the river, they would have to find something else to cover the tractor so it didn't get wet in the rain.

That night, lying in bed, he heard a freight train passing in the night. Its horn blared a harsh chord, mournful and plaintive and lonely. The whistle rose in pitch as it approached, then descended as the train sped by, the Doppler shift creating a feeling of mystery and loss. The wheels clanked and screeched sharply; he could picture the sparks flying as the train rounded the bend, metal grinding on metal. He imagined the engineer at his post, peering into the blackness as the mechanical beast churned through the night, spewing smoke and ash as it clattered through towns and fields and woods. He wished more than anything to be on that train, hurtling blindly into the night, alone with his thoughts, his future unfolding before him as smoothly and inevitably as railroad tracks.

CHAPTER SEVENTEEN

"No, I will *not* calm down until you explain to me what is going on!"

Elena Krieger was angry, and when she was angry, the world knew about it. By the time Lee and Butts showed up at Chuck's office, she had worked herself into a state and wasn't going to work herself out of it until everyone around her had a piece of her mind. Judging by the string of expletives she let loose, there were plenty of pieces to go around.

"Nothing's going on," Chuck explained patiently. "We tried to get hold of you yesterday, but we couldn't, so we met anyway."

Krieger threw her arms in the air and paced the small office. The men kept well out of her way—Lee and Butts hugging the wall on either side of the door, Chuck behind his desk. She was wearing a tight-fitting gray suit with a military cut, and as she harangued them, her long arms sliced the air like swords.

"You just *happened* to have a meeting when I was having my peer-review board, so that's what you are claiming?"

"We didn't know about your peer review," Chuck said. "How could we? You didn't say anything about it."

"It was easy enough to find out," she said, apparently determined to wring every last bit of drama out of this. "Is it because I'm a woman?" she demanded, looking at each of them in turn, as if daring them to answer yes.

Not so much, Lee wanted to say. Krieger was exuding more testosterone than the three of them put together.

"You know," she said, "I didn't ask to be on this investigation, but now that I am, you had better make me part of this team or there will be hell to pay, I can assure you!"

Chuck looked like he'd had about enough of this. His face was already the shade of overcooked salmon, and his hands were clenched in fists at his side. Lee decided it was his turn to take some of the heat.

"Look," he said, "it was an honest mistake, but I think we can avoid this happening again if we just touch base by phone or e-mail with each other every morning, and maybe again in the early afternoon. That way, if there are any more last-minute meetings, at least we'll have a system in place."

She opened her mouth to argue, but the reasonableness of his suggestion and his soothing tone of voice took the wind out of her sails. All she could do was make some sputtering sounds before collapsing into a chair, her energy spent. Lee felt almost sorry for her. He could only imagine what kind of battles Elena Krieger had already fought in her life.

"Okay," Chuck said, "so let's get on with it. What did you find out in Jersey?"

Lee and Butts exchanged a glance, unsure how much to say about their trip. They ended up reporting on all the interviews in detail, referring to Butts's notes when necessary, but they soft-pedaled the oddness of Perkins and his sister. Lee wasn't sure why—maybe because they were both a little embarrassed at the way it had affected them. Now, sitting in the prosaic surroundings of Chuck's office in the Bronx Major Case Unit, it seemed as though they were imagining it, and that Perkins was just a harmless eccentric with an equally odd sister.

"We got a roster of customers she seems to have sold pottery to," Butts said. "I'll see what I can find out about them. Might be hard—all I've got is a list of names so far."

"I'll see if Sergeant Ruggles can help you on that," Chuck said. "We're tracking down all calls made to and from her cell phone, and maybe that'll give us something."

"Any forensic evidence from the lab yet?" Krieger asked.

"Well, there is one interesting thing," Chuck answered.

"What's that?" said Lee.

"That threatening note she said she received, the one she gave you—"

"You know who wrote it?" Butts asked, helping himself to coffee.

"She did."

Butts did a double take just like an animated cartoon character. His jaw fell open and his eyes widened, giving him the expression of a startled bulldog.

"*What*?"

"The words pasted on the card came from a magazine found in her house—the pages were cut up in such a way that they were able to match it up in a few minutes. A child could have done it."

"But why would she fake that," Krieger mused, "if she really was being stalked?"

"Maybe so I would take her seriously," Lee suggested.

"Or," Butts offered, "maybe it was the boyfriend after all. He spent time in that house, too."

"But why wouldn't he cover his tracks more? Why leave the magazine in plain sight?" Chuck said.

"To freak her out?" Butts suggested. "I seen weirder things than that, believe me."

Krieger frowned. "But the manner of death—"

"Could it be a copycat crime?" Chuck asked.

"Highly unlikely," Lee said.

"But you said she was a crime buff," Butts pointed out. "She could have told the boyfriend about the other vics, or he could have read about them."

"It doesn't really make a lot of sense for the boyfriend to cast suspicion on himself by leaving the magazine around, though, does it?" Chuck said.

"No, not really." Butts looked disappointed. "But there's something about that guy I don't like."

"Unfortunately, we can't arrest people just because you don't take a shine to them," Krieger pointed out dryly. Butts glared at her. "May I ask what the magazine was?"

Chuck leafed through the evidence photos. "Uh, it was *Better Homes and Gardens.*"

Krieger frowned. "Does that seem like the kind of magazine a young girl like her would be likely to have lying around?"

"They dusted for prints," Chuck said. "Only hers were found on it."

"Well, if it was the boyfriend, he could have wiped off his—or used gloves," Butts pointed out.

"Any other evidence we should know about?" said Lee.

"Nope," said Chuck. "The crime scene didn't give us much. But that's not surprising. The water pretty much washes everything away."

"Very clever way to dispose of bodies," Krieger said. "Obvious but effective."

"That's not the only reason he does it," said Lee.

"What do you mean?" Krieger said, her eyes narrowing.

"Water is important to him—it's the only constant factor in every one of his crimes. I'm convinced it's part of his signature."

Krieger frowned. "Do you really believe in that whole 'signature' business?"

Lee stared at her.

Butts spoke up for him. "What kind of question is that?"

"I mean the notion of these killers needing to perform a certain ritual in order to get satisfaction. It's all a bit unscientific, isn't it?"

"It's not so much a question of ritual," Lee replied, determined not to lose his temper. "It's more that certain elements remain constant."

"But that's even more nebulous, isn't it? I mean, so we have a criminal who likes to leave his victims in water—what good does that do us if we have no forensic evidence?"

"It's an insight into his psychology, his personality," said Lee.

"So maybe he had a traumatic episode with water as a child," she scoffed. "I don't see how that helps us. And now you say that signatures can 'evolve' and change—which makes it even more useless, it seems to me."

"Not useless," Lee said, "just more complex."

"And what about all this terminology—psychopath, borderline personality disorder, and so on. I don't see what good that does us. So what if this man is a psychopath—how does that help us catch him?"

"Actually, the clinical term is sociopath," Lee corrected her.

Krieger rolled her eyes and opened her mouth to reply, but Butts beat her to it.

"Okay, we *done* here?" he said irritably. "Can we get on with this?"

Krieger stiffened, her spine even more rigid than usual. "I was just trying to save time by establishing what our working methods are going to be."

"Well, do us all a favor and don't, okay?" Butts snapped.

"All right, settle down, both of you!" Chuck said. He turned to Krieger. Lee could see from the tension in his shoulders he was making an effort to control himself. "Whether or not psychological analysis of a criminal is a flawless method—and I think we can admit that no method of crime analysis is perfect—it's all we have right now. So can we just agree to carry on until we have something more 'scientific'?"

Krieger smoothed her flawlessly coiffed hair. "I have no intention of hindering the investigation. I just thought it was appropriate to raise a few questions before getting too far into it."

"Look, lady," Butts interjected, "like it or not, we're already way further into it than any of us wants to be. The question is, how do we get out of it?"

"Okay, so what stands out about these killings so far?" Chuck asked Lee.

"Well, as I said, water plays an important part in the killer's fantasy. Although the one victim was electrocuted, it was still a death involving water, since he was in his bath-tub."

"It's weird, though, isn't it?" Butts remarked. "How often do you see these guys killing men *and* women?"

"That's an important part of the profile," Lee agreed. "But I don't know what it means yet. He's also going after relatively low-risk victims—"

"'Low-risk' victims?" Krieger interrupted.

"Yeah," Butts said. "In other words, he's not goin' after prostitutes and drug addicts—lowlifes who take risks."

"So that means he's bold—confident," Chuck added.

"Right," said Lee. "He's taking more chances by going after these kinds of victims."

Krieger frowned and crossed her long arms over her

ample chest. "How can you automatically assume the killer is a man?"

Butts rolled his eyes, but Chuck glared at him.

"Actually, that's a good question," Lee said, trying to maintain the delicate truce they had struck with Krieger. "Though there are female serial killers, they're very rare. Statistically the odds are against it being a woman."

Krieger made a little puffing sound with her lips and plopped down in the nearest chair with an air of dissatisfaction.

"Right," Butts said. "I'd say the odds of this being a woman are about as great as the odds that I'll develop an interest in playing bridge."

Lee had to smile at the irony of Butts defending the art of criminal profiling, considering his initial disdain when they first started working together. He suspected Butts was more interested in putting Elena Krieger in her place than he was in supporting Lee.

"I think Detective Krieger has an excellent point," he said. "At this point I think one of the worst mistakes we could make would be to close off possible options, just because they seem unlikely. I think keeping an open mind is really important in a case like this. There are already enough unusual factors to indicate to me that this is not a textbook example of any particular type of offender."

"Agreed," Chuck said. "So we keep an open mind, at least for now."

"What do you mean by 'not a textbook example'?" Krieger asked. "I didn't know there was such a thing in your field."

"Well, strictly speaking, there isn't," Lee replied. "No two criminals are exactly alike any more than any two people are identical. But there are greater and lesser degrees of conformity to certain—types, I guess you might say. We use terms like organized and disorganized, rage driven, sadistic, and controlling—but the truth is most offenders are some combination of those types."

"And this particular offender?" Krieger said.

"I would guess that he has some trauma in his past, probably early childhood, involving water. And in these killings he is playing out some version of that event—reliving it, so to speak."

"Why early childhood?" said Butts.

"Because that's when things tend to impact us most deeply. The brain is more fluid in young children, and it forms connections that are almost impossible to sever later on. So when Ted Bundy's aunt awoke from a nap one day to find five-year-old Teddy placing knives all around her as she lay in bed, she was witnessing the early deviant behavior of a serial killer in the making."

"Christ," Butts said. "That really happened?"

"Yes. It came out when his former friend Anne Rule wrote a book about him."

"I remember that book," Chuck said. "*The Stranger Beside Me,* wasn't it?"

"Right," said Lee.

Elena Krieger stood up and stretched her long body.

"All of this is quite fascinating, I'm sure," she said, "but shouldn't we focus on the matter at hand?"

Butts glared at her, his porous face reddening, as though it were about to sprout spores. He opened his mouth to say something, but Lee intervened.

"Have you been able to establish any link between the victims?" he asked Chuck.

"Not yet. The only link seems to be that they're dead."

"And the notes," Butts pointed out.

"Right. The notes indicate the killer had some interaction

with them before he decided to the kill them—but does that fit your usual situation in cases like this? Don't serial offenders usually prey on strangers?" Chuck asked.

"This case is odd in a lot of ways," Lee answered. "They do usually kill relative strangers, which helps them depersonalize their victims."

"And makes them harder to catch," Butts interjected.

"True," Lee agreed. "But guys like Gacy and Dahmer had some interaction with their victims before killing them, for example, so I think we should start with the idea that this UNSUB knew the victims—at least to an extent."

"He must have known the man he killed in the bathtub, no?" Krieger asked. "There was no sign of forced entry."

"I agree," Lee said. "A key element here is motive. Once we figure that out, it will help us to connect the victims. I'm convinced there is a link—we just haven't seen it yet."

"Maybe the killer is the only link," Butts suggested.

"Is there any chance the choice of victims was random?" Chuck asked.

Lee shook his head. "Highly unlikely. The notes all suggest a relationship of some kind—at least in the killer's mind."

"Okay, then we need to set up more interviews with people who knew the vics," Chuck said. "Detective Butts has done a few already, but I'm thinking we need to cast a wider net."

Lee nodded in agreement, but what he was thinking was that nets have holes, and their prey had already proven slippery enough to evade them so far. He was beginning to wonder if there was a net in the world big enough to catch him.

CHAPTER EIGHTEEN

When Lee arrived home, there was a message on his answering machine, and it wasn't entirely welcome. It was from Kay Shackleton, the head of the Psychology Department at John Jay College, asking him if he was interested in being a guest lecturer at the college. He sank down in the red leather armchair by the window and listened to the message a second time.

"We've been working on the list of visiting professors, and Tom thought of asking you," she said. Tom Mariella was a senior professor on the faculty and an excellent teacher—Lee had taken several of his courses.

". . . your position on the police force gives you a unique point of view, and we thought you might be interested in giving your perspective on the attack on the World Trade Center. It would be part of a series of lectures given by other faculty members as well. With the anniversary coming up, we just thought—" Lee hit the STOP button on the machine.

He had read somewhere—R. D. Laing, perhaps—that the primary emotion experienced by people in the presence of evil was confusion. He felt that now—as he did with every case he worked on. It was a familiar feeling, and yet one he never seemed to get used to . . . underneath the cold, hard fact of three dead victims lurked a whirlpool of bewilderment. *Spuyten Duyvil . . . Whirlpool of the Devil.*

He wandered into the kitchen and made himself a martini, shaking it in the sterling-silver decanter that once belonged to his father. He poured it into a V-shaped glass, added an olive, and took a swallow. The taste of gin was reassuring—sharp, medicinal, like drinking pine sap. He drank some more and wandered into the living room.

The anniversary is coming up. . . . He had lived through more than enough anniversaries already—his father's desertion, his sister's disappearance—and now this. His profession was about solving things, the puzzles and mysteries behind crime, and yet he could not solve the mysteries in his own heart. The questions gnawed at him, and they all seemed connected. How could his father have left his family behind, just walking out the door one rainy night, never to return? And how could his sister have disappeared without a trace, as though she had never existed? And how could someone slip through the crowded streets of the city, carrying the knowledge that he was a murderer, yet not betray that dark fact to anyone he met—until it was too late?

Dusk settled uneasily over Manhattan as Lee stared out his front window, martini in hand. The rays of the setting sun fell on the Ukrainian church across the street, caught in the vast circular design of the stained-glass window that took up most of the church's front façade. He imagined the light traveling forever in the circular whirl of saints and visions, caught in an endless trajectory of faith and belief. He was reminded that many of the stars whose distant light we see on clear nights are already dead, and that what we see is just the trail of ghosts, left behind long after their lives have ended.

Laura's trail still blazed brightly in Lee's mind, but he was afraid that her light was beginning to dim for others who knew her. His mother rarely mentioned her anymore, and Kylie had been too young when she disappeared to have any memories of her. He had taken up the torch to find her killer when he became a criminal profiler, but so far he had failed. His need to punish himself for this failure was intense, and it was only with an extreme effort that he could pull away from it.

The ringing of the phone snapped him out of his self-recriminations.

He grabbed the receiver.

"Hello?"

"Lee?"

The voice was deep, resonant, and cultivated. He recognized it at once.

"Hello, Diesel. How are you?"

"More to the point, how are you?"

"I'm okay."

"You don't sound it."

Lee smiled, in spite of the feelings raised by Diesel's voice. He had met the man through his late friend Eddie Pepitone. He missed Eddie, and he knew Diesel did, too.

"How's Rhino?" he asked, trying to steady his voice.

"Oh, he's very pleased with himself. He's lost five pounds this month and is unbearable to live with."

Diesel and Rhino (a.k.a. John Rhinehardt Jr.) were the most unlikely couple Lee had ever met. Diesel was a giant of a man, with shiny mahogany skin, whereas Rhino was tiny, muscular, and pale as a ghost. Lee was grateful for Diesel and Rhino's continued presence in his life. They were good men and all he had left of Eddie.

"Are you both still working at Bellevue?" he asked.

"Actually, I've had a promotion. I'm now in charge of all the other orderlies."

"Congratulations—that's great."

"Yes, it's great if you don't have to live with John K. Reinhardt Jr., I suppose. He's never forgiven me for it."

"You mean because now you're his boss?"

"Something like that," Diesel answered. "He said to say hi, by the way. But I actually called to see if you were investigating these bizarre killings."

Lee wasn't sure how to respond. His assignment to the case wasn't exactly a secret, but it wasn't something the NYPD would broadcast to the public. Luckily, Diesel saved him from having to answer.

"I can see by your hesitation that you are," Diesel continued smoothly. "I just called to offer our services. If there's anything we can do—anything at all—don't hesitate to ask. I think Eddie would have wanted . . ." Diesel began, but his voice trailed off, the silence on the line between them like a physical presence. "I'm sorry—I don't know what Eddie would have wanted. Maybe I'd just like to think I know."

"Yeah," Lee agreed. "I know."

"I think he would want us to keep in touch, anyway."

"I agree," Lee said. "I'm glad to hear from you. But this killer is dangerous, and I don't think—"

"Hey, look," said Diesel, "Rhino and I can take care of ourselves. I'm just saying that if you can use us as a resource, we're here for you."

"I appreciate that."

"There are some things Eddie didn't tell you about us. We have certain . . . *skills*, let's say, that might be of use to you at some point."

That was all very mysterious, and Lee was intrigued, but he heard the click of call waiting on the other line.

"Thanks," he said. "I'm sorry, but I have an incoming call."

"No problem. You know where to find us."

"Yes—give my best to Rhino," Lee said. "I'll talk to you soon." He clicked the receiver and picked up the other call.

The voice he heard had the same reptilian coldness as before.

"I know about the red dress."

Ripples of terror slithered across the surface of Lee's skin. He clutched the edge of the piano to steady himself.

"Who are you?"

"Does it matter?"

"If you know something," Lee said, trying to keep his voice from shaking, "why don't you go to the police?"

The caller chuckled—a low, unpleasant sound, like two rocks knocking together.

"What would be the fun in that?"

"Look," Lee said, but the line went dead. He immediately dialed *69, but a recording told him that the caller had blocked his number when he called.

He stood there for a moment, then picked up his martini glass and gulped down its contents. As he did, he made a grim vow. If this caller really did know something about his sister's murder, Lee swore to himself that he would hunt him down, no matter the cost.

CHAPTER NINETEEN

The largest of the five buildings comprising the campus of John Jay College of Criminal Justice is Haaren Hall, a handsome, imposing redbrick and gray-stone building on the west side of Tenth Avenue. The building spans the entire block between Fifty-fifth and Fifty-sixth Streets, the sidewalk outside busy with the comings and goings of students and faculty from early in the morning until well after dark. The building, originally the home of a public high school, houses a fully equipped theater, as well as a swimming pool and a gym.

Around twilight the next day, Lee stood across the street on Tenth Avenue staring at the entrance, thinking about all the times he had mounted the broad stone steps, on his way to class or, after graduating, to meet a friend or former classmate there. The building was backlit in the pink glow of the sun setting over the Hudson, the temperature of the windless air so perfectly matching the warmth of his skin that it felt as if there were no atmosphere at all. He could smell the fresh woodsy smell of the magnolia bushes in the little pocket park behind him.

He was still in a daze from the phone call of the night before, immersed in a deep, bitter fog of self-pity he couldn't seem to shake off.

Behind him, he heard a familiar voice.

"Hello, my friend!"

He turned to see the Greek hot dog vendor who worked that corner, a man who had sold him dozens of hot dogs over the years, pushing his cart along the sidewalk, on his way home. The man's weather-beaten face broke into a broad smile, displaying strong, yellow teeth.

"How are you, my friend? I no see you in long time!" he said, stopping his cart next to Lee and clapping a friendly hand on his shoulder. His hands were thick and brown, the skin mottled and cracked from the wind and sun. "Is good to see you!"

"Yes, it's good to see you, too," Lee replied, and in truth, it was. One of the sweet things about life in New York was the relationships you had with people like this man. The young Guatemalan immigrant who makes your breakfast sandwich so quickly and efficiently, the Cuban deli owner who knows just how you like your coffee in the morning, the Korean salad bar lady with the good sushi at the Essex Market, the Indian grocer who sells you your daily bagel or newspaper. You rarely know their names, and you may not know much about them, but the moment you share with them every day is a thread in the fabric of city life. Lee valued these relationships: they were not complex and layered and ambiguous like intimate relationships, but that was part of their charm. New York was so full of people who came from other places, and those moments where they briefly touched, exchanging a sandwich and a greeting, were something Lee clung to and valued greatly.

He turned to face his friend. "How have you been? How's business?"

The man wagged his head back and forth. "Now is so-so,

you know—not so good. When September come, is much better. Everyone back to class, everyone hungry!" He winked and let out a robust belly laugh. Lee was always impressed with the man's good spirits. After a hard day of standing outside in all kinds of weather, he still had good humor and a belly laugh. Lee didn't think he'd be up to a job like that—and this man probably had fifteen years on him.

"So, my friend, is good to see you—I see you again?" the man said, beginning to wheel his cart away.

"Yes," Lee replied. "You will definitely see me again."

He watched as the vendor pushed his cart uphill along the sidewalk, stooped over with the effort, favoring his right leg, his shoulders rounded from years of physical labor. Watching him, Lee's self-pity and indecision evaporated like steam from a hot dog bun. When the light changed, he strode out into the dusky street and toward John Jay College of Criminal Justice.

Little had changed since he was last there some five months ago. The building was quiet, in the break period between the end of summer classes and the beginning of the fall term. At the front security desk, the pretty black girl with the colorfully beaded hair was absorbed in her textbook and barely glanced at him as he flashed his ID card. She pressed the release button, and he went through the metal turnstile as he had a hundred times before. Lee wanted to get used to being in the building again, to acclimatize himself, as it were, before tackling a lecture hall full of students.

He started up the stairs to the third floor, where most of the faculty offices were, and pushed open the door to the familiar corridor. The hall was empty, which wasn't surprising—most of the professors and staff would be enjoying the last week of summer vacation. He walked slowly down the hall, his footsteps ringing hollow through the deserted corridor.

As he turned the corner, he heard the dreaded voice in his head, in all its reptilian coldness.

I know about the red dress.

His knees weakened and he began to sweat.

"Get a grip, Campbell," he muttered, and walked onward. But each step seemed to pound out the same three syllables, over and over. *The red dress . . . the red dress . . . the red dress.* His vision seemed to narrow, and the walls felt as though they were slowly beginning to press inward, closing in on him. He knew the warning signs of a panic attack, but fought the sensation by swinging his arms vigorously, concentrating on taking deep breaths.

He passed the familiar place where there was a water stain on the ceiling in the shape of Florida, and the janitor's closet two doors away. He headed for the big lecture hall at the end of the corridor, which was where he would probably be giving his talk. He thought he detected a faint, lingering aroma of clove cigarettes in the air.

He reached the lecture hall, but the door was closed and locked. He tried to peer in through the gray smoked-glass partition on the door, with no success—he could see nothing except the sheen of sunlight coming through the row of tall windows on the far wall. The interior of the room was foggy and indistinct. The numbers 303 were stenciled on the top of the glass in an old-fashioned, gold-colored typeface.

He thought he heard footsteps behind him and spun around, his heart pounding, but the hall was empty. He felt all of his senses were magnified, more acute, but especially his hearing. It was as though he had the ears of a bat, and every little sound gave him a start. He leaned against the wall and put his hand to his left side, throbbing and pulsing with each beat of his heart. *Steady on, Campbell.*

There, on the opposite wall, was a student bulletin board, and clinging to it was a tattered scrap of paper with the remnants of a photograph of a smiling young woman wearing a lopsided graduation cap. Underneath the picture he could still make out the words, *Please Help*. He recognized it at once as a picture of one of the thousands still missing from the attack on the World Trade Center—no doubt buried under the mounds of rubble still piled high in Lower Manhattan. In the months following the tragedy, these pictures were everywhere—plastered on bus stops, park benches, trees, fences—hundreds of them, perhaps thousands, and the message was always the same: *Missing—Please Help.* And there was always a phone number to call. The smiling faces in the photographs were a terrible irony, as if mocking the reality of their fate—the people were never found, the phone numbers never called.

The girl in this photo was about the same age his sister had been when she disappeared.

The irony was suffocating. He tried to intellectualize it: Here he was, in the halls of the largest school for criminal justice in the greatest city in the world, yet he was as helpless to find his sister as the family of the lost girl was to ever find her again.

He turned to go but was overcome with nausea and had to lean back against the wall again. Saliva spurted into his mouth. His stomach rolled and churned, but he fought it. "Damn," he muttered, "I'll be damned if I'm going to be sick." Even as he said the words, he was aware they were somewhat ridiculous, but he fought the nausea anyway, and after a couple of minutes he felt a little better. He took a few steps but was still shaking. and then realized what he really wanted, more than anything, was to scream until he was hoarse. That was impossible, as there were other people in the building.

Suddenly he wheeled around, his body filled with an intense, gathering rage. Hardly knowing what he was doing, he lunged back toward the door and swung at the glass partition with all his might, hitting it almost directly in the center with his right fist. The glass shuddered and held for a fraction of a second, then cracked and shattered, crashing to the floor in a waterfall of broken shards.

Lee stared at the broken pieces of glass at his feet, then at his hand, which was bleeding. He felt no pain yet—that would come later. His body was too full of adrenaline to register anything. It did occur to him with some irritation that it would be a while before he could play the piano again— some of the cuts were pretty deep. He watched with detachment as his blood dripped onto the polished tile floor. He thought of how a forensic investigation might classify it: *Blood spatter from a puncture wound, non-high-velocity impact, indicating no blunt-force trauma or femoral arterial spray. Not enough volume to indicate the death of the victim.* No, he wasn't dead—not yet.

But instead of feeling satisfaction or relief, he felt only a terrible, heavy sadness.

CHAPTER TWENTY

It began that day, the delight he took in wearing soft, fluffy fabrics and lacy undergarments—the kind of thing his mother wore when she was alive. It all started that day Caleb came back home with his father, and the house was so still. Instead of the sound of his mother preparing dinner in the kitchen, there was nothing—only the quiet scuttering of mice in the attic, the dripping of rain from the eaves. It had started raining when they left the river. His father drove without speaking as the drops grew in size, splashing onto the windshield as the wipers did their brisk business of flinging them off the car. He sat watching the wiper blades swoosh back and forth. *Foopah, foohpah, foo-PAH.* The sound they made was so soothing—they swung in front of his tired eyes like a pendulum, hypnotizing him. Their timing was off, so that one blade was always falling a little bit behind the other one. He remembered liking the syncopated rhythm they created—he found it comforting. *Foopah, FOOpah, foo-PAH.*

When they returned home, his father said nothing, retreating silently to his workshop in the basement. Caleb wandered the empty house, listening to the sound of rain on the roof. He didn't remember deciding to go there, but found himself in the little room off the master bedroom his mother used as a dressing room. There was her dressing table, with the brushes and combs laid out, as though she had just gone for a walk. He picked up a tortoiseshell brush and lifted a long brown hair that clung to the bristles. It was her hair, probably brushed from her head this morning, one of the last things she did while still alive. He rolled it up and tucked it carefully into his pocket.

The top drawer of her bureau was open—something black and shiny was poking out. Looking over his shoulder at the open bedroom door, he tiptoed to the dresser and pulled it out, running his hand over the silken material. It was a pair of black panties with lace trim. He put them to his face and caressed his cheek with the fabric as his father's words ran through his head. *Slut! Evil, whoring slut! She's just like all the rest of them—can't be trusted!* He inhaled deeply, the aroma of his mother's almond-scented body lotion filling his head. Perhaps this was the same pair she wore when she . . . *slut, whore, evil bitch.*

His hands trembled as he slid his own pants to the ground and pulled the panties on. He almost fainted as the cool silk glided up his bare legs. He pulled it snug around his crotch, his mouth dry with excitement and shame as his penis stiffened and grew at the touch of the fabric. *Slut! Whore! Bitch!* He imagined his mother pulling on the panties just like this, standing where he stood now.

He turned and went to her closet, where her dresses hung on their wooden hangers. His mother disliked wire hangers, because they were so easily twisted around each other. He reached for a yellow sleeveless summer dress and pulled it on over his shirt. It fell flat against his thin chest, so he rooted around in the bureau and found some panty hose, which he stuffed in the front of the dress. He had turned to admire himself in the mirror, when he heard his father's heavy tread on the stairs.

His heart hammered in his chest as he heard the movement of feet under the crack in the door frame, like the scurrying of gray mice, the flitting of far-off shadows—a brief, harried interruption in the thin band of yellow light that hugged the floor. He pulled off the dress, flung it into the closet, and pulled his pants back on. But he could still feel the silk panties on his skin. A satisfied smile crept across his face as he stepped out into the hall. Now he had a secret to keep from his father.

Chapter Twenty-one

"What happened to you?" Chuck's voice was weary, a combination of concern and irritation. He stood behind his desk, looking at Lee, arms crossed, his blond eyebrows knit in a frown, staring at his friend's heavily bandaged hand. Lee had come straight from the emergency room to the afternoon meeting in Chuck's office.

"I had a misunderstanding with a door," Lee said, avoiding eye contact.

"Yeah, very funny." Chuck didn't move. "What really happened?"

"Seriously, that's what happened."

"Okay—let me see, then."

"Look, I didn't try to kill myself, if that's what you're afraid of. If I'd done that, both wrists would be bandaged."

"Yeah? So let me see." Chuck was being unusually obstinate.

"I'll tell you the whole story, if you really insist on it."

"Okay."

Lee told him the whole episode of the visit to John Jay— and the sudden attack of rage that caused him to punch a hole through the glass top of the door.

Chuck listened warily, as if looking to catch him out in a lie, but when he was finished, said, "Okay. Well, maybe that's a healthier reaction than depression. Are you going to be okay?"

"I'm fine."

"Yeah—right." They both had to smile at that. It had become a little dance between them over the years: Chuck asking if Lee was okay when he obviously wasn't, and Lee responding that he was fine. Another inheritance of his stoic Celtic upbringing: to admit weakness was itself a sign of weakness.

"What did you tell the people at John Jay to explain their broken door?" Chuck asked.

"I just said that I slipped on some water in the hall and fell against it."

Chuck snorted. "And they believed you?"

"I guess so."

Morton rolled his eyes. "A place full of cops and forensic experts and you get away with a lie like that."

"I offered to pay for it, insisted actually, told them to take it out of my lecture pay, but they refused."

"Lecture pay?"

"Oh, yeah. They, uh, asked me if I could come talk about—you know." He didn't want to say the words, as if they would scorch the air and burn his skin if released into the atmosphere.

"Are you up to that?"

"Well, I wasn't sure until yesterday, but yes, I think I am."

Chuck heaved a deep, disbelieving sigh and put his hands up in a gesture of surrender. "If you say so."

"I got another call about the red dress."

"You want us to put a trace on your phone?"

"I don't know if it'll do any good, but you can try. He could be calling from anywhere—last time it was a public pay phone. This time I tried star sixty-nine, but the number was blocked."

"Okay, I'll see what I can do." Chuck put a hand on Lee's shoulder. "I hate to say it, but you're not looking all that good lately."

It was true that the return of the depression had caused the usual problems with his appetite. His sleep had been erratic since Ana's death, and gaunt circles had formed under his eyes.

"Yeah," Lee said. "I'll be all right once I get some rest."

"I don't know," Chuck said. "Maybe you should—"

"What?" Lee said, suddenly angry. "Give up my profession? Give up the search for my sister's killer?"

"God, Lee, I don't—"

"And what about this killer? Christ, Chuck, three people are dead already."

"I'm just saying—"

"If I walk away from this, it'll be worse—a lot worse. At least I'm *doing* something—"

"You know, Lee, sometimes you just have to walk away."

"Don't say that, Chuck—don't *ever* say that to me!"

He was surprised at the vehemence in his own voice. So was Chuck, by the look of it. He stared at Lee, then turned away and plucked a piece of paper from the pile on his desk.

"Fine," he said tersely. "Have a look at this."

It appeared to be a copy of a page from a diary. The feathery scrawl was elaborate, showy.

Must confront him, It read. The words were underlined twice. *Take courage—it's the only way.*

He looked at Chuck. "Ana's writing—from her diary?"

"It was in a secret drawer hidden in her bureau. The guys who processed her house the first time didn't find it, but the Jersey cop they posted to watch over the place got bored and started rooting around and discovered it."

Lee had an image of Trooper Anderson wandering through Ana's rambling farmhouse, sniffing around for clues.

"Okay," he said. "Where's the rest of it?"

"They're processing it for prints," Chuck said. "This was the last entry."

"This could be about almost anyone," Lee remarked.

"Maybe it refers to her abuser."

"If she really *was* abused."

"You think she lied about that?"

"Or was persuaded, or recovered false memories—anything's possible."

"Christ," Chuck said. "So that whole thing could be a red herring?"

"Yep. There are plenty of cases of patients 'recovering memories' of things that never happened—especially if the therapist eggs them on. It's like false confessions—people will say just about anything if you push them hard enough."

"Great," Chuck said. "So that's a possible false lead?"

"I'm afraid so. Unless we find something else more specific, I don't see what good it does us." He put the photocopy back on the desk. "When is everyone else getting here?"

"Any minute now—you're early."

Lee frowned. "I thought the meeting was at two."

"Two-thirty."

"Whatever." He sank down in one of the captain's chairs, carefully laying his injured hand on the armrest. He could feel it throbbing with each pulse of his heart.

There was a knock on the door. Chuck was standing next to it, and he flung the door open to admit Elena Krieger, who brushed past him as though she were visiting royalty. She glared at Lee.

"How long have you been here?"

"I just got here," he lied.

She narrowed her small blue eyes and looked around for a

place to sit down. She was wearing tight gray slacks and a white knit shirt with a V neck. She threw herself into the nearest chair, brandishing her cleavage. Lee tried not to stare as her breasts competed with each other to push through the top of her shirt.

"Okay," she said to Chuck, as if he were the servant and she the master. "What have we got?"

His reply was interrupted by the sound of wheezing. The door was flung open, and Detective Butts stumbled into the room, panting heavily.

"Sorry," he said. "Goddamn traffic on the GW Bridge. Am I late?"

"Nope," Chuck said. "Right on time."

Krieger raised her eyebrows and pursed her lips, as though Butts were the carrier of an incurable disease and she was determined not inhale the deadly spores.

"Okay," Butts said, pulling a chair up and sitting. His eyes fell on Lee's bandaged hand. "What the hell happened to you?"

"I put my hand through a glass partition in a door."

Butts shook his head. "This is the price you pay for breaking and entering in your spare time."

Krieger appeared to take his remark seriously. Her mouth fell open, and she turned to Chuck.

"He's kidding," Morton said.

Butts pulled a crumpled brown paper bag from his pocket and thrust it toward the others. It was smeared with splotches of grease. "Rugelach, anyone? My wife's sister made it. Left-over from the funeral."

Krieger scowled and crossed her arms. "Can we get back to business, please?"

Chuck held up the page with the diary entry. Before he could say anything, Krieger snatched it from him.

"This is from her diary?" she asked, studying it.

"Right," Chuck answered, with a glance at Butts, who didn't look at all put out by Krieger's behavior. It occurred to Lee that he might be deliberately ignoring her.

Krieger held up the diary entry. "So this could be referring to her killer."

"Unless she made up the whole thing," Lee remarked.

Krieger stared at him. "Why would she do that?"

Lee explained his history with Ana, and her narcissistic personality.

"She'd do that, then?" Butts asked.

"I think we can't discount that possibility. She might have even set it up so that her boyfriend would discover the diary."

"What about the warning note? You believe that is also fake?" Krieger asked.

"Well, it did come from the magazines in her house," Lee pointed out.

"But the boyfriend definitely could have done that," Butts said. "We need to have him in for a little chat."

"I think that's a good idea," Chuck agreed.

"Think about it, though," Lee said. "If he *did* create the warning note, then why doesn't he get rid of the magazines once Ana is dead? Why leave them in the house for us to find?"

"Criminals can be incredibly stupid," Krieger remarked.

"He didn't strike me as stupid—quite the opposite," Lee countered. "Did you think he was stupid?" he asked Butts.

"No," Butts admitted. "He's a sharp guy. And he seemed real shaken. Unless he's a terrific actor, the guy was definitely hit hard by her death. I still say we should bring him in, though. If for nothin' else, maybe he's thought of something that might help us find the real UNSUB."

"Agreed," Chuck said. "At this point, he's the one closest to the victim, so we can't eliminate him yet, and, in any case, he could prove useful."

"So you say this Ana Watkins was so desperate for attention that she faked being stalked?" Krieger asked.

"That's what I'm beginning to believe," Lee answered.

"Isn't that an odd coincidence that she was actually *being* stalked?"

"I'm not sure she was," Lee said. "I don't really know yet. But I can see her faking the whole thing to get attention."

"From who?" Butts asked. "You?"

"Yep," said Chuck.

Lee flushed and held his throbbing arm to his side.

"So she was that into you?" Butts asked.

"I'm sure she was getting attention from other people, too," Lee said. "Her boyfriend, probably coworkers—if she did invent the whole thing, you can bet she let everyone know about it." Then he thought about her face that night. "She really was scared—whether or not she had invented parts of it, there was no doubt she thought her life was in danger."

"You know," Krieger said, "this UNSUB needs attention, too. He isn't just punishing his victims—his crimes are also a ploy to be noticed."

Lee looked at her, surprised by her insight. For all her pooh-poohing the idea of profiling, he thought, she had good instincts.

"That's exactly right," he agreed. "This is someone who feels he can't attract attention unless he behaves in ways increasingly outside societal norms."

"Or, to put it another way," Chuck said, "he's displaying all the attributes of a sociopath. Right?"

"Exactly. There's another possibility, too. The diary entry could refer to her therapist. Maybe she was going to confront him about something."

"Or even her boss at the Swan," Butts suggested.

"Right," Lee agreed.

Krieger studied the note. "She wasn't faking it," she declared. "Her fear was real."

"How can you tell?" asked Chuck.

"If she was faking it, she would have been more elaborate. When people lie, they add unnecessary details—"

"You're right!" Butts cried, spewing rugelach crumbs into the air. "That's one 'a the ways you can tell if a perp is lying: too many details!"

Krieger gave a dignified sniff and turned to Chuck and Lee. "As I was saying, this note is too brief to be a ruse—it is succinct and to the point. She really is talking to herself, not to some imaginary audience. Look at the wording: 'Must confront him.' She doesn't say '*I* must confront him'—no, she leaves off the subject of the sentence altogether, because she already *knows* who the subject of the sentence is."

Butts apparently couldn't help himself. "That is goddamn brilliant, is what that is!"

Krieger's only reaction was a tiny upward curl of the left side of her mouth. "The real question that remains is who is the *object* of the sentence?"

There was a hesitant tap on the door.

"Come in," Chuck said.

The door opened just enough to admit Sergeant Ruggles's head. With his clean-shaven, shiny face, he looked like an anxious schoolboy.

"Beg pardon, sir," he said, "but DC Connelly is on the line."

Chuck rolled his eyes. "I'll take it outside. Keep going without me," he said to the rest of them as he brushed past Ruggles, who stood in the doorway staring at Krieger. With his thick neck, bald head, and short, muscular legs, he reminded Lee of a bull terrier.

"Is there anything else, Sergeant?" she said, returning his gaze.

"Uh, no, there isn't," he replied, still staring, as if she were the Medusa and he were rooted to the spot by the sight of the writhing snakes on her head.

Butts rescued him. "Rugelach?" he said, thrusting a crumbling fistful under the sergeant's nose.

"Uh, no thanks," Ruggles said. Retreating hastily, he closed the door behind him.

Lee thought he saw the corners of Krieger's mouth turn up in a smile as she watched him go.

"Now then," she said, turning back to him and Butts, "where were we?"

CHAPTER TWENTY-TWO

Lee Campbell looked out at the rows of upturned faces in the lecture hall. Most of them were thoughtful and attentive, hoping he would have answers for them—some kernel of wisdom to unlock the key to the darkest of human deeds. Not surprisingly, the room was packed. People stood along the walls, and he recognized a few professors in the rear seats. Word had gotten around that he was working on a serial-killer case. Very few details had been leaked to the press, though, and no doubt some people in the audience were hoping for some choice tidbits about the case.

"'Behavior reflects personality.' This statement was made by legendary FBI criminologist, one of the founders of profiling, John Douglas." He paused to let this sink in.

"'Behavior reflects personality.' What does this mean? Because a person's so-called 'personality' is comprised of so many things: upbringing, cultural background, religious beliefs, moral convictions—and the list goes on. So what can we take from Douglas's assertion, and how can we apply it to an active case?"

He took a breath. This was turning out to be even harder than he thought. It was one thing to prepare for this lecture—but now, in front of all of these people, he felt exposed and naked. His right hand throbbed, a dull ache like a steady drumbeat in the background of his mind. With his left hand, he took a drink of water from the bottle in front of him, then gripped the podium to steady himself.

"The writer Robert McKee has said that stories happen 'when you allow yourself to think the unthinkable.' As many of you know, I had a recent case where there were two offenders working together. Though not unknown, it is not what we usually would expect in a case like this. There are, of course, other examples—the most notorious being Charles Ng and his partner in crime. The pattern that operated there was similar to what was operating in this case: a dominant figure who plans and controls the actions of the more submissive partner. In both the Ng case and this one, if you look closely enough, you see the patterns of not one but two personalities at work.

"Profiling is especially useful when there is also little physical evidence—no blood, semen, DNA, hair, or even fibers—which often means a killer with both self-control and a sophisticated knowledge of crime scenes."

He paused and took a gulp of water, looking out across the sweep of faces. At this point in an elective lecture, you might expect a few people to have headed off for class. Since the events of 9/11 the whole city was jumpy, and this was nowhere more true than in centers of law enforcement, where there was an explosive combination of guilt, fear, and anger. He even heard rumors that enrollment had fallen off as a result. But no one had left the lecture room. In fact, a few more people had slipped into the room after he began his talk.

"I know there's been nearly a year of speculation about what went wrong on the morning of September 11," he said, looking out at the full auditorium, all eyes turned on him, the faces tense and expectant. "But there's really no other way to say it: We missed all the warning signs. We know now they were there—we just didn't see them. The men who did this lived and moved among us, and we blinded ourselves to the threat they posed, in part because our arrogance didn't allow us to see just how vulnerable we were."

He went on to talk about how the memorandum from the FBI agent was lost in the bureaucratic shuffle until it was too late. "It's important for all law enforcement professionals to take it upon themselves as individuals to fight the deadening effects of bureaucracy," he continued. "It's not a glass ceiling; it's a concrete one. And we have to make the effort to punch through it when necessary. It's too dangerous to do otherwise."

When he finished, the audience sat in silence for a few moments, the younger students wide-eyed, and then he took questions.

Several hands shot up at once, and he pointed to a thin, serious-looking young man in the third row with thick, round glasses. He looked more like a physics major than a future policeman.

"Did 9/11 make you question everything you learned?"

"I guess I'd say it made me question everything I thought I knew, but maybe that's not such a bad thing."

A pretty girl with caramel-colored skin in the back raised her hand.

"Are there any steps being taken in the class curriculum to make sure this doesn't happen again?"

"Since I'm not part of the administration of this school, I can't answer that question. I know there were support groups set up to help people deal with it."

"Did you attend one?" another student asked.

"No, I didn't."

"Why not?"

The real answer was too complicated, and too revealing: he had suffered a complete nervous breakdown, and was hospitalized at St. Vincent's for nearly a month.

"I was . . . laid up for a while. Also, I see someone privately."

There was an uncomfortable silence.

Someone shouted from the back of the hall, "What happened to your hand?"

Lee looked for the speaker, but couldn't see who it was.

"I had an accident."

There was a longer silence, as if the students sensed a line had been crossed, prying into what was personal for him.

"The important question is not what did we do wrong," he said, "but what can we learn from this? Because there's always something to be learned. Perhaps the greater the mistake, the more there is to be learned from it. Sometimes we are blinded because as human beings we don't allow ourselves to think the unthinkable. It is perhaps a failure of imagination, but it is even more a failure of courage. To face our darkest fear and fantasies is not easy, and it is not for everyone. But as members of the law enforcement community, it is the job we have chosen."

A chubby white kid in the third row raised a hand.

"Do you think the terrorists were psychopaths?"

Lee thought about it for a moment.

"No," he said. "I think they were misguided fanatics, but I don't think they entirely lacked the capacity for empathy."

"What about your current case?"

"I can't really comment on an ongoing investigation." Lee looked at Tom Mariella, sitting in the back row. He gave a tiny nod, and Lee continued. "Okay, one more question."

The thin physics major with the round glasses raised his hand.

"Yes?"

"Can we avoid—" He paused, flustered, his face reddening from the neck upward. "Yes?" Lee said.

"Can we avoid another attack like the one on September eleventh?"

Lee looked up, aware that they were all waiting for his answer. The room was dead quiet. He could hear the faint whoosh of traffic out on Tenth Avenue. In the back of the room, someone coughed.

"I think we can," he said, "if we can allow ourselves to think the unthinkable."

And as he said the words, he realized they applied not just to the tragic events of last September, but to this case as well. *Think the unthinkable.* Certainly the killer he was chasing was doing just that—and now Lee had to do the same.

CHAPTER TWENTY-THREE

Hush, little baby, don't you cry
Mama's gonna sing you a lullaby
And if that lullaby goes dry,
Mama's gonna bring you a nice big eye

The song had been running through Caleb's head for days now—he wasn't sure why. He didn't know whether his mother sang it to him or not. Maybe she did, but he didn't trust any memories of that time. He tried not to think about her, because when he did, he saw her face on that last day. As he shook his head to rid himself of the image, another song popped into his head.

Down in the valley, the valley so low
Hang your head over, hear the wind blow

He had been down in the valley that day, rummaging among the weeds and willows at the riverbank, spending all day outside so he wouldn't have to come home to his pa. Just the two of them in the house now, and his pa was almost always in an evil mood. Caleb tried to make himself inconspicuous, and he was pretty good at it, but sometimes his father had a few drinks and was feeling chatty. He hated it when Pa was feeling chatty, because then he would sit Caleb down at the kitchen table and lecture him on women and their evil ways, about how you could never trust them and they were all just a bunch of she-devils who would betray you the minute your back was turned.

Caleb would nod and pretend to listen, but it was the same thing over and over, and it made his head ache. He tried instead to hear the chirping of the frogs in the pond outside, or the soft scuttling of the mice upstairs in the attic—anything to drown out his father's voice. Perhaps his father was right that women really were wicked and evil, but he didn't want to hear about it night after night.

So that day he was down by the river playing with his pet frog, whom he had named Bogie, because the frog made a noise that sounded like "BO-gie." He was watching the frog swim over to a lily pad in the rushes, hoping he would climb up and eat some mosquitoes with his big gray tongue. Caleb loved watching that long tongue dart in and out of Bogie's mouth—he imagined what it must feel like to have a tongue like that, and be able to catch your dinner by swiping it from the air. It was nearly dusk, and a dense cloud of mosquitoes was swarming around the pond. Bogie had a great dinner ahead of him.

He knelt down to watch as Bogie struggled to get onto the lily pad, placing one splayed, padded foot on it and heaving up his fat green body. Caleb noticed something in the rushes softly bobbing up and down in the little ripples created by Bogie's swimming. It was gray and lumpy and looked like an old dress someone had thrown out. He rolled up his trousers and waded out to it, the water soft and warm on his bare legs, the river mud squishy under his feet. He reached down and tugged at it, but to his surprise, there was something inside the dress—something heavy and spongy and bloated.

His brain couldn't come up with the word or even the image of what might be inside a dress floating in the river, as if his mind rebelled against the thought itself. Odd as it was, it didn't occur to him until the moment he rolled it over and saw the dead, fish-white eyes of his mother staring up at him. Her face was hideously gray and swollen, as though someone had pumped air into it.

He stumbled backward in the shallow water, splashing violently in his attempt to get away from the horror he had just uncovered. Startled, Bogie leapt from his perch on the lily pad and dove down through the water to hide among the weeds along the shoreline.

Caleb heard a shrill, high-pitched sound. He realized it was his own voice, and that he was screaming. He scrambled back up the bank and plopped down amid the skunk cabbage and tree roots, panting heavily, river water running down his forehead and into his eyes. He wiped the water out of his eyes and put his head between his legs in an attempt to catch his breath.

He had developed a selective memory, and had buried deep within his psyche any recollection of the trip to the river with his father the week before—hidden it so well from his conscious brain that after his initial shock at seeing his mother's corpse, he felt puzzlement. It was only after sitting in the skunk cabbage along the riverbank, shivering in his wet clothes, that he remembered accompanying his father down to the river on that dark night.

It is a peculiarity of the mind, which seeks to protect itself from knowledge too terrible, that it was only at this moment Caleb linked the two events, realizing that what he had done the week before was to help his father dispose of his mother's body. It was only now he allowed himself the awareness that—in all probability—his father had murdered his mother.

Back in the river, Bogie the bullfrog settled himself on his lily pad and shot his swift, sticky tongue into the air, plucking an unsuspecting mosquito from the thick cloud of insects hovering above the water in the gentle evening air. But the boy on the shore did not notice. He was bent over in the tall weeds, crying and retching into the broad leaves of the skunk cabbage lining the river bank.

CHAPTER TWENTY-FOUR

After the lecture, Lee took the A train to the Bronx. The young desk sergeant nodded to him as he entered the Bronx Major Case Unit station house. An older policeman standing nearby with a clipboard made a joke, and the young sergeant laughed. Lee continued through the lobby, trying not to think they might be laughing at him. There was a bonhomie and camaraderie in the police force he had never really been part of. For one thing, he was a civilian, and had not attended the police academy. Plenty of other civilians worked for the NYPD, but his position as the only full-time profiler was unique. And then there was his educational and cultural background. Few New York City cops came from the kind of milieu he did, and fewer still had attended Princeton.

When he opened the door to Chuck's office, he was surprised to see Susan Morton sitting in the chair behind the desk.

"Hello, Lee," she said, smiling. "Long time, no see." She raised a finger to her mouth and smoothed away an imaginary smudge from her perfectly applied lipstick, then rose from the chair and swayed toward him, insinuation in the swing of her perfect hips. She moved with the sinuous grace of a large and dangerous jungle animal—a panther, perhaps. She was wearing a peach-colored Chanel suit, charcoal stockings, and black high heels. She looked like she was dressed for a board meeting.

"Where have you been keeping yourself?" she said, moving inappropriately close, looking up at him. Her eyes were oddly round—big and green and almost perfectly circular. Instead of finding this attractive, Lee now found it off-putting. He was reminded of the sad, big-eyed children in velvet paintings you might see in a tacky motel room.

"I'm working on a case with Chuck," he replied, careful to avoid eye contact with her.

"Yes, I heard about that," she purred. "What a terrible thing." From her tone of voice, she might have been talking about a bottle of overpriced wine or a stain on an expensive dress. "And you hurt yourself," she said, looking at his bandaged forearm.

"Yes," Lee said, moving carefully to the other side of the desk, putting it between the two of them. "I had an accident."

"Poor thing," she said. "Someone needs to kiss it and make it better."

"I was supposed to meet Chuck here—any idea where he is?"

She ran a finger slowly over the wooden desktop. It was suggestive, sexual, and Lee avoided the impression that he was watching her, though he couldn't entirely avoid it. She perched on the desk, her slim legs dangling back and forth. She was very lean—maybe even thinner than in college. Back then she had struggled with bulimia, and he imagined her weighing herself daily, measuring each gram of fat she ingested.

"I don't know where he is—they told me to wait in here," she said.

Lee glanced at his watch without registering what he saw. It was just something to do other than look at her.

"It's good to see you," she said.

"Yes," he answered, pretending to search for something in his pockets.

"Do you ever think about the old times we had together?" she asked, sounding wistful.

"I guess."

She twirled a strand of fat black pearls around her finger. He had no doubt they were real.

"Me too. Sometimes I think about them a lot."

Lee's hand closed around his cell phone in his pocket, and his heart gave a little leap—he saw his escape route.

"Excuse me," he said, heading for the door, "I have to make a phone call."

Sliding off the side of the desk, she blocked his way. "Why can't you make it in here?"

"I don't get good reception in here."

"Use Chuck's phone—I'm sure he won't mind."

He held his ground and looked down at her. "It's private."

Her face hardened. "Fine—have it your way," she snapped, stepping aside.

But as he reached for the doorknob, the door opened to reveal Chuck standing there.

"Sorry I kept you waiting," he said, brushing past Lee and into the room. "Oh—hello there," he said, seeing Susan.

"Hello yourself," she said, in her best Lauren Bacall voice.

"What brings you to the belly of the beast?" Chuck said, rifling through the papers on his desk, looking for something.

"Oh, does it have to be something in particular? Maybe I just miss my adorable, handsome husband," she replied, with a sidelong glance at Lee.

But Chuck continued his search, clearly preoccupied.

She watched him for a few moments, her face darkening, and then she said, "I can see you're busy. I don't want to interrupt you," in a voice that clearly indicated that was exactly what she wanted to do. "I can tell this isn't a good time."

But Chuck wasn't reading her signals. "Yeah—sorry about that," he said distractedly. "I'll see you tonight, okay?"

She stood there, hands at her sides, her thin body twitching with irritation—if she were a cat, Lee thought, she'd be flicking her tail. She was used to getting what she wanted, especially with men, and it must gall her no end to strike out twice in just a few minutes. She looked at Lee, displeasure that he saw her annoyance and knew what it was about showing on her perfectly painted face.

"Didn't you have a phone call to make?" she said, trying to sound solicitous, but it came out as a kind of snarl.

"It can wait," Lee replied cheerfully. Maybe he was enjoying her defeat a little too much, but he didn't care.

She examined her French-manicured nails. Then, seeing she had lost, she picked up her tiny red designer clutch bag and swished toward the door. "Fine," she said to Chuck in a tight voice. "See you tonight."

"Okay," Chuck mumbled, too involved in his search to notice her mood. Lee figured there would be hell to pay somewhere along the line—maybe for Chuck, maybe for him—but it was worth it to him to win even this small victory.

"You had something you wanted to show me?" Lee said after she had gone.

"Yeah," Chuck said, "some papers. I was sure I left them right here."

Lee had the unpleasant thought that Susan might have moved them, or even taken them, but he didn't suppose even she would do something like that. Chuck pressed a button on this intercom and said loudly, "Ruggles, can you come in here?"

The door opened to admit the sergeant, who stood meekly awaiting orders.

"Ruggles, did you see those papers I brought in earlier today?" Chuck asked.

Ruggles went over to the corner of the room, picked up a soft leather briefcase leaning against the wall, opened it, and pulled out a handful of papers.

"Is this what you're looking for, sir?" he asked. "I saw you stuff them in there before you were called away."

"Ah—well done!" Chuck crowed, taking them. "What would I do without you, Ruggles?"

"I expect you'd get along just fine, sir," Ruggles said modestly. "Will that be all, then?"

"Yes—thanks very much," Chuck said, and Ruggles disappeared as quietly as he had come.

"Amazing man," Chuck said, looking after him. "He's always there when you need him—sort of spooky, really."

"Like Judith Anderson in *Rebecca*—whenever Joan Fontaine looks up, she's standing there, but we never see her enter the room."

Morton smiled. "Well, Ruggles isn't *that* creepy, I hope."

"No," said Lee. "What was it you were going to show me?"

"This," Chuck replied, thrusting the papers at him.

It was an arrest record of one George Favreau, a Peeping Tom who had finally been caught stealing women's underwear from laundry lines.

"Could this be our guy?" Chuck asked.

Lee studied the arrest report. Favreau's escapades read more like a Ben Stiller comedy than the exploits of a serial killer.

According to his file, George Lamont Favreau was a

Peeping Tom who liked to steal women's underwear from laundry lines in his suburban Jersey neighborhood. He had the misfortune to be caught when a sprinkler system had gone off, frightening him so much that he tripped on it and sprained his ankle. The occupants of the house had spotted him writhing on their lawn and called the police. The man of the house held a .45 to his head while the police were on their way, frightening poor Favreau so much that he peed in his pants. To add to his humiliation, several pairs of women's panties were found tucked into his coat pockets, still damp from the laundry line. He was then linked to a series of underwear thefts when a search warrant revealed the missing items neatly folded in the bottom of his dresser drawer.

Lee handed the report back to Chuck. "It wouldn't hurt to interview him, I guess."

"But you don't think it's him."

"Not really."

Chuck looked disappointed. There was another knock on the door.

"Yes?" he said.

Sergeant Ruggles poked his head in.

"Detectives Butts and Krieger have just arrived, sir."

"Send them in," Morton said.

Chuck and Lee exchanged a look. He wasn't sure what Chuck was thinking, but Lee was thinking that at least they hadn't killed each other in the lobby.

CHAPTER TWENTY-FIVE

Chuck Morton poured himself a cup of coffee from the pot on the windowsill. A fat black fly buzzed sluggishly against the windowpane in a halfhearted attempt to escape into the steamy August air. The atmosphere was muggy and oppressive, the air heavy with rain that refused to fall.

"Okay, what do we know about this guy?" he said, slinging himself into his chair. He was feeling antsy, and more coffee probably wasn't a good idea, but he didn't care. Elena Krieger was at the far end of the room, putting as much distance between her and Detective Butts as possible.

Lee Campbell rested his lean body against the doorframe. Chuck thought his friend looked tired—there was a gray pallor to his face, and he cradled his injured arm in his left hand.

"There's evidence of some confusion as to sexual preference or gender identity," he said.

Detective Leonard Butts settled his broad backside into one of the chairs across from Chuck's desk.

"In English, Doc?" he said, scratching his ear. His ears were large, with long, pendulous lobes, and reminded Chuck of the ears of his childhood beagle, Charlie.

"He kills men as well as women," Lee said. "And since these probably are sexually motivated crimes, it points to an offender who is either attracted to both men and women, or is confused about where he belongs in the gender spectrum."

"How do you know he is sexually motivated?" Krieger challenged.

"Postmortem mutilation almost always has a sexual element," Lee replied.

"So he's one kinky bastard," Butts said, throwing a glance at Krieger, who stiffened. Chuck opened his mouth to reprimand Butts, but realized with a quiver of guilt that he enjoyed watching the detective bait Krieger. He turned and poured himself more coffee.

"Would that mean we're looking for someone who is . . . effeminate?" Krieger asked.

More effeminate than you, Chuck wanted to say, but he took a sip of coffee instead.

"Not necessarily," Lee replied. "He's conflicted, but he might appear completely normal to the casual observer."

"Let me get this straight," Morton said. "Are we talking about a bisexual?"

"It's not as clear cut as that," Lee answered. "I'd say that he's primarily heterosexual, but displays some form of feminine identification—maybe rooted in a childhood trauma of some kind."

Butts frowned. "We talkin' about a tranny?"

Krieger stared at him. "A trann-ee?"

"A transsexual," Chuck explained.

Krieger flushed, color spreading from her elegant neck to her forehead. "Oh, yes—of course."

"Very possibly," Lee replied. "Or a transvestite. There are plenty of men who like to dress in women's clothing, but are primarily or even solely attracted to women."

Butts leaned forward in his chair, elbows on his knees,

frowning so that his bushy eyebrows nearly touched. "Let me get this straight. You're talkin' about a guy who's a hetero but who likes to wear panty hose?"

"That's one possibility," Lee answered.

They all paused to consider this idea. Chuck listened to the sound of daily life in the station house. Footsteps came and went, office doors opened and closed with a click, snippets of conversation drifted into the room. Out in the lobby, someone laughed—a short, percussive sound, like a dog barking. He found the everyday ordinariness of it comforting. After the horrors of 9/11, which swept them all up the flood of disaster and its aftermath, there was something reassuring about the gradual return of daily routine.

"Is there a chance this—person—could be a woman who had an operation to become a man?" Krieger asked.

"Sexual murders of this sort are almost entirely committed by men. I don't see it as likely—it's not just the physical size and strength required, it's also the amount of testosterone in the system. This killer linked violence and sex early in life. Women aren't likely to act as sadistic sexual predators. They're much more likely to become victims, not offenders."

This seemed to displease Krieger. She frowned and bit her lip, but said nothing.

"Some of 'em become sidekicks to killers," Butts said. "They work with their boyfriends."

"That's true," Lee admitted, "but I'm fairly certain this offender is working alone."

There was an awkward silence; then Butts said, "Well, what are we waitin' for? Let's get out there and track down some leads."

"I have an idea of where we might start," Lee suggested.

"What?" Chuck asked. He recognized the look on his

friend's face—the narrowing of the deep-set eyes, the pursed lips. Lee Campbell was coming up with a plan.

"I'd like to look through old police reports of missing persons."

"How come?" Butts asked.

"I'll explain on the way. Let's go down to records."

The NYPD was in the process of converting old case records into computer files, which was—predictably—taking forever. There were miles of dusty stacks of manila folders containing all that was left of people's lives. It was ironic, Morton thought, that if you were a crime victim you stood a good chance at having the details of your life recorded—even if it was in a smudged file folder in the basement of a police precinct.

"Shall I come?" Krieger asked.

"Many hands make light work," Lee said, opening the door for her. He looked back at Chuck. "I'll check in with you later."

"Right," Chuck said.

When they had all gone, Chuck sat down at his desk with the crime-scene photos. He stared down at the bloated bodies of the victims, grotesque and swollen beyond recognition. He rubbed his eyes, red from lack of sleep and bad city air. Murder was a nasty, dirty business. Sure, you could glamorize it in books and films and tidy little stories where the bad guys always got caught and crime never paid, but the truth was that crime *did* pay, far more often than anyone in law enforcement wanted to admit.

He knew all this, and tried not to let it keep him up at night. But when it came down to it, there was no one left to speak for the victims except people like himself who were willing to do whatever it took to track down their killer. The responsibility he felt was oppressive—and instead of growing lighter over the years, it had become heavier. He looked back down at the crime-scene photos, forcing himself to think of each lifeless body as a former person—with a soul, if you like, a living flame snuffed out by a ruthless murderer who was just getting started.

There was a knock on the door, and Sergeant Ruggles stuck his head through the door.

"Beg pardon, sir."

"Yes?"

"Your wife's on the phone."

"Thanks, Ruggles."

"Not at all, sir." He cleared his throat. "I was wondering, sir, about—" He paused, blinking rapidly.

"Yes, Ruggles?"

"It's about Detective Krieger, sir."

"What about her?"

"Is she—I mean, she's not—" He cleared his throat again. "I mean, do you know if—"

"If she's married?"

"Not that it's any of my business, of course," Ruggles added quickly, frowning. He looked like a condemned prisoner facing a firing squad.

"No, she's not."

Ruggles's eyes widened. His neck muscles tightened, and he swallowed hard, his Adam's apple bobbing, like a turkey gulping for air.

"Right—thanks."

"She's trouble, Ruggles. I wouldn't, if I were you."

"I'll keep that in mind, sir," he said, but Chuck knew the sergeant was lost already. Krieger would eat him up and spit out the bones, not even pausing to pick her perfect teeth as she searched for her next victim.

But Ruggles was glowing. Sweat darkened his collar, and his hands trembled, but the man was grinning all over. If the brass buttons on his uniform could smile, Chuck thought, they would have.

"I'm off now, sir, if you don't mind."

"Sure—see you tomorrow, Ruggles."

"Yes, sir—thank you, sir."

Ruggles withdrew and closed the door. Chuck wondered if he should be more sociable with his desk sergeant. Maybe it wouldn't be such a bad idea after all to ask Ruggles to join him for a drink sometime. The cops under him socialized with each other all the time—why couldn't he join them once in a while? And maybe he could warn him off Krieger. That woman was a Venus flytrap; he had no wish to see poor Ruggles caught in the sticky sap, wriggling and struggling to escape as she slowly digested him.

He looked down at the phone on his desk, the console blinking red. He sighed and picked up the receiver, but as he did, his eye caught one of the crime-scene photos. He leaned over and flipped it facedown, then cradled the phone to his ear.

"Morton here."

His wife's voice stroked his ear like a cool caress.

"Hi there. Will you be home for dinner tonight?"

He glanced at his Rolex, a Christmas present from Susan. He didn't give a fig about expensive trinkets, but she did. It was after six—he was officially off duty over an hour ago. The meeting had lasted well over two hours.

"I'm on my way," he said.

"The kids want to wait to have dinner with you."

"I'm leaving now."

As he put on his jacket, Chuck thought about the photos of the victims on his desk. No one would be waiting for them to come home ever again, he reflected as he flicked off the lights and closed the door behind him.

CHAPTER TWENTY-SIX

Lee had been promising Kathy he would go with her to a Café Philosoph, an informal monthly meeting of people to talk about philosophy. There were apparently quite a few of them in Europe, especially France, and she had been going to one in Philadelphia. When she found one that met not far from him in New York, she begged Lee to join her, and he agreed.

It was Friday, so she came in by train after work, meeting him at his apartment before heading off for the meeting.

When she saw his bandaged arm, he spoke before she could ask about it.

"I had a run-in with a door."

"Yeah?" she said, raising an eyebrow. "And wait till I see what the door looks like?"

"Very funny."

"Seriously, how do you have a—"

"I was angry and I punched out a glass door." He went into the kitchen.

She followed him. "Angry about what?"

"Everything." He began unloading the dishwasher, just so he didn't have to look at her.

"I can see you've given this some serious thought," she replied sarcastically as he slid a steak knife into the wooden rack on the counter. He kept unloading dishes as she stood, arms crossed, leaning on the wall next to the Italian spice cabinet he had bought for a song at the Eleventh Street Flea Market.

"Okay, I get the picture—you don't want to talk about it," she said, and went back into the living room. This time he followed her.

She sat down on the couch and put her feet up, kicking off her sandals. She had nice feet—small, well-formed, with high arches. Her nail polish was the color of dried blood.

"Was this before or after the lecture?" she said, plucking a grape from the ceramic bowl of fruit on the coffee table.

"Before."

"You could have mentioned it."

"I thought you had enough on your hands."

"Oh." She had been asked to join the team of specialists identifying the remains found at Ground Zero. There was little left of the victims, so what was left was that much more precious.

"How's that going?" he said.

She reached down for another grape, but changed her mind and leaned back against the couch. "I guess I have mixed feelings about it. On the one hand, I'm glad to help, but on the other . . . it's so hard."

"Yeah," he said, feeling the inadequacy of words in this situation.

"The whole thing is so . . . overwhelming."

"Are you sure you can handle it?"

"Oh, yeah, you know—I didn't go into this line of work expecting it to always be easy. It's just that this feels different, you know? The sheer scale of the disaster . . . it's hard not to feel a crushing sadness about it all."

"Yeah, I know." In the weeks afterward, he was down near Ground Zero meeting up with some friends—going downtown as often as possible, to spend money in the restaurants and shops, following the mayor's urging, to try and stave off some of the economic devastation that was just one of the many by-products of the tragedy. Suddenly, without warning, he was seized by a fit of sobbing so intense that he had to lean against the side of a building. A middle-aged woman with a kind face stopped and laid a hand on his shoulder, asking him if he was all right. He remembered nodding, helpless to stop the heaving sobs racking his body. The look on her face told him that she was aware of the reason for his weeping—no one in the city in those days remained untouched by what had happened.

Kathy got up from the couch, slipped her sandals back on, and stretched. "Well," she said, "we should get going."

Minutes later, strolling down Elizabeth Street, he thought that some semblance of peace was beginning to return to the city, though it was a jittery kind of normalcy. They walked through the burgeoning neighborhood that had recently been dubbed NoLita (North of Little Italy), where art students, Asian fashionistas, and would-be screenwriters mixed with the Italian and Latino working-class families who had lived there for generations. The night was balmy, and the trees along Ludlow Street swayed and rippled in the gentle breezes of late summer.

"No-lit-a?" Kathy said, when Lee told her where they were. "What is it with New York? Does every neighborhood have to have a trendy name?"

"I remember TriBeCa before it was called TriBeCa," Lee said. "It was just a jumble of industrial buildings, not anyplace you'd want to live."

"Wow," Kathy said. "And now no one can afford to live there—it's worse than Chelsea."

"So are you saying that in Phillie you don't name your neighborhoods?"

"Well, some of them, sure. But I don't think we have quite the same rabid zest for it you do."

"I see."

"Don't get me wrong," she said quickly. "This is a great town. It's just that everything is so—so *intense*, you know? People here are so self-conscious, so aware of the impression they're making."

"I know," he said, smiling as they passed an artsy couple all in black, very thin, perfectly Euro-chic. The woman's black heels clicked sharply on the pavement, and the man's pants were so tight that Lee wondered if he had to hold his breath when he sat down.

"Is your arm bothering you?" Kathy asked, glancing at the way he carried his bandaged forearm.

"No, it's fine," he lied. Even with the ibuprofen, it still throbbed insistently, but he wanted to get off the subject as quickly as possible.

The meeting was held at Le Poéme, a French/Corsican restaurant owned by a family who lived in the back of the building but seemed to do a lot of their living in the actual restaurant—there were always a couple of kids underfoot, as well as assorted dogs and cats.

When they arrived at La Poéme they were escorted to the rear of the restaurant by the owner, a tall, long-faced Gaul with rumpled gray hair, slumped shoulders, and a weary, benign expression. The back room was kind of a cross between a living room and a restaurant—the décor was an eclectic mix of objets trouvés, secondhand furniture, discarded children's toys, and dusty spider plants. Furniture and knick-knacks from various cultures and time periods lined the wall—blue and white Quimper pottery hung on the wall above a Regency-style couch complete with silk tassels, next to which sat a sturdy French country oak coffee table. Lee would have called it East Village chic, but since this was NoLita he supposed it would have to be called NoLita chic.

The philosophers straggled in one by one, looking very much like what you might expect. A tall, seedy Frenchman with baggy eyes wearing a tattered gray pullover arrived with his petite, sharp-eyed wife, chicly dressed in black spike-heeled boots and a miniskirt over black leggings.

A bearded Russian with tobacco-stained teeth strode in carrying a large leather-bound volume—Dostoevsky? Pushkin? Tolstoy? Lee couldn't make out the embossed lettering on the front, but it looked old and well worn. Perhaps the Russian had brought it to back up his points with quotes. A nervous-looking young man with an unforgiving crew cut and little round glasses looked as if he was either emulating the dissident German writer Bertolt Brecht or auditioning for the role of Motel the Tailor in *Fiddler on the Roof*. There were others, arriving alone and in groups of two or three. By the time they were ready to start, a dozen or so people had gathered at the tables and couches along the wall.

Even for New York, it was a strikingly European-looking crowd. Philosophy just wasn't an American pastime—it didn't drive fast or shoot or take its clothes off in public.

The moderator was a charismatic, soft-spoken man who taught philosophy at Baruch College, Bernard Elias. His skin was olive, but his accent suggested Paris rather than Cairo. His face and manner were charming, gracious, and kindly.

"We have a rather good turnout tonight," he observed, looking around the room. "I see a few new faces."

Lee stiffened, hoping he wouldn't ask them to introduce themselves, but to his relief, Elias continued.

"Those of you who are new, just a few quick ground rules. To avoid confusion or cross talk, we ask that you raise your hand to be recognized by the moderator before speaking. This week I'll be the moderator, though we often take turns—if other people volunteer to moderate, it's fine with me."

"You're still the best," the sharp-faced Frenchwoman said, and several other people nodded.

"Well, thank you, but my job is mostly just to keep things moving," Elias replied with a modest smile. Lee didn't doubt the Frenchwoman was right—Elias exuded warmth, and had a quiet self-confidence.

"Now then," he continued, "this week's topic was suggested by Jonathan." He nodded in the direction of the young man with the round glasses, who nodded back stiffly. "So it is our tradition to have him begin with the first comment—perhaps telling us why he chose this topic."

Jonathan removed his glasses and wiped them with his napkin.

"Well," he said, replacing them on his nose, "I have always been interested in the relationship between culture and language. The Japanese, for example, have no word for 'no'—only an elaborately polite way of avoiding saying yes. This tells you something about the way their culture operates."

Several people nodded and smiled. Jonathan was younger than most of them, and it appeared he functioned as a kind of mascot, or pet, of the group.

"So I was wondering what it says about our culture that we seem to place a lot of value on this word 'evil'—especially in the current political climate."

"Very timely, Jonathan," Elias said with a fatherly smile. "Would anyone care to comment?"

They discussed the connotation of the word as it relates to religion and sin, and whether or not the concept of evil existed at all outside religion. Most of the group agreed it did—and also that it seemed to exist as a concept in most cultures. Then they began to investigate where evil comes from, and whether it exists in the animal kingdom outside the realm of humans.

"It seems to me that animals have no moral sensibility," the chic Frenchwoman said. "Therefore their actions, no matter how vicious or cruel, could not be said to be evil."

"All right," said Elias. "So would you also say that a knowledge of right and wrong as defined by society is necessary in order to call an action—or, indeed, an individual—evil?"

As the others contemplated the question, Elias looked around the room, and his eyes fell on Lee and Kathy. She had offered one or two comments, but Lee had not yet spoken. Elias smiled at Lee.

"What do you think, Mr.—"

"Campbell," said Lee. "Call me Lee."

"Lee, then—what do you think?" Elias repeated.

Lee squirmed in his chair. He didn't want to throw the cold, hard light of criminal psychology into the discussion, but it was exactly what was needed.

"Well, in my profession I deal with criminals—"

"Oh, how *interesting*," the Frenchwoman said, leaning toward him, hands clasped in her lap. Her husband frowned and crossed his arms. "What's the difference between a sociopath and a psychopath?" she asked.

"It's subtle," Lee said, and went on to explain what a psychopath is. The group listened silently, a few people nodding when he gave examples of psychopathic behavior, and how it seemed to reflect an inability to feel compassion or empathy.

"So if they can't feel empathy, how can they know their actions are wrong?" the Russian asked, pouring himself more tea. He had a large pot of black tea on his table, and he held little bites of sugar cubes between his teeth as he drank.

"They know their actions are wrong," Lee answered. "They just don't care."

"Ah!" said the Russian, brandishing his book like a weapon. "But if they can't empathize with how their actions affect others, then how can they have a real sense of morality?"

"How do they . . . get like that?" asked Jonathan, the serious young man with the glasses.

"There's some indication this kind of hardwiring takes place when they are young," Lee said.

"How young?" said the Russian, concentrating so hard his bushy eyebrows almost touched.

Lee told the story of Ted Bundy's aunt waking up with the knives all around her bed, and everyone was suitably impressed.

"My God," said the Frenchwoman with a gasp. "How can you blame a five-year-old boy?"

"So does that mean evil exists but we're not responsible for its existence?" asked her husband.

"How old does someone have to be before their actions can be considered evil?" said Jonathan.

"Can they be . . . helped?" asked the Frenchwoman.

"We don't know for sure," Lee said, "but there is evidence to suggest that once this psychopathic personality is in place, no amount of therapy can change it."

The Russian slurped down some tea and wiped his mouth with his sleeve. "It sounds as though these people lack a key component of what it means to be human."

"That's very tragic," said the Frenchwoman.

"So you're saying that this kind of monster can be created—through no fault of their own?" Elias asked Lee.

"And they can't be fixed?" the Frenchman added.

"There is some indication that once those neural pathways have been laid down, there's no going back," Lee said.

A pall fell over the group.

They went on to discuss the difference between evil deeds and evil people, and concluded that while no one was totally good, it was likely that no one was totally evil either. They did not revisit the issue of psychopathic personalities, perhaps because it was too depressing—Lee had the feeling his comments had upset them. Kathy added few more remarks, but he kept silent. No one invited him to comment further, which was just as well, he thought.

They ended on an upbeat note, with the agreement that if evil does exist, it is overshadowed by good more often than not. They took a vote on next week's topic of discussion, and "Is Happiness Attainable?" won.

The formal discussion over, they broke into small groups. Heads bent over their wineglasses, they continued their earnest discussion. Lee found it profoundly comforting that these people were willing to gather twice a month to tackle the Big Questions—wine or no wine, they clearly took their philosophy seriously.

He and Kathy stood next to a life-sized statue of Apollo and sipped their wine. Someone had covered his private parts with a yellow polka-dot bikini.

The French couple approached them, smiling; the serious young man they called Jonathan lingered just behind them, as if he wanted to be a part of the discussion, too, but was too shy to come forward.

"We found most interesting what you had to say," the Frenchman said.

"Yes," his sharp-faced wife agreed. Her accent was thicker than his, though Lee could tell from her English that she was educated in British schools. "*Mon Dieu*," she said with a little laugh, "how do you ever catch zese criminals?"

"Well, sometimes we don't."

The French couple nodded and murmured something polite Lee didn't quite catch. Jonathan stepped forward at that moment, blushing.

"But when you do catch them, how do you do it?"

By this time anyone in the group who hadn't yet left the restaurant had gathered around to listen to what Lee had to say. The Russian stood at the back, clutching his thick volumes and pulling at his beard.

"Sometimes they make mistakes," Lee said. "They get sloppy or careless."

"Because zey wish to be caught?" the Frenchwoman said.

"Like Raskolnikov?" the Russian added hopefully.

"Not really. That would be nice, but most of the time these guys are eaten up in the end not by their crimes, but by the pressure of being on the run, having to look over their shoulder all the time."

The Frenchman nodded. "It is very stressful, being pursued, *n'est-ce pas?* Like your Raskolnikov," he added with a glance at the Russian.

The Russian scowled and clasped his books to his chest.

"So zey feel no remorse for what zey do?" the Frenchwoman asked.

Lee shook his head. "Remorse doesn't seem to be part of the equation with most of these killers. They never really see their victims as people."

"You mean people like Ted Bundy, for example?" Jonathan said.

"He's a good example," Lee said. "It's amazing they didn't catch him earlier. By skipping state to state, he managed to duck under every net they attempted to throw over him. Then, when they did finally collar him, he used his charm and skill to escape not once—but twice."

"So he was charming—but he was a monster," the Frenchman remarked.

"If anyone was, Bundy was. Like most serial predators, he dehumanized his victims in order to consummate his crimes—it's a switch he turns to the off position before he can continue. For most of us, that switch doesn't even exist. For the serial killer, it's part of what makes him who he is."

Lee was aware of a tugging on his sleeve and turned to see Kathy looking at him. The expression in her eyes was clear: she wanted to leave.

"Okay," he murmured, irritated that, having dragged him here, she now wanted to go.

Though he usually attempted to keep any memories of his father at bay, he heard Duncan Campbell's deep, sardonic baritone say, *Isn't that just like a woman?*

CHAPTER TWENTY-SEVEN

It was all a lark, really—they were a couple of Jersey boys on a Friday-night spree, hitting the bars on the Upper East Side, trawling for some action. But these *Sex and the City* chicks were so stuck up—thought they were all that, with their designer shoes and their two-hundred-dollar haircuts and expensive boob jobs. They weren't going to mess with a couple of dagos from Bayonne, so Joe and Bobby figured they'd go down to the Village just for a gag and see what the faggots were up to.

Bobby said he knew about this place on Christopher over by the river where the trannies hung out, so they headed down there to see the freaks. They'd go in and pretend to pick one up, then give him—or was it her? Ha!—the slip, maybe even mess her up a bit. They had plenty of time and plenty of rage.

When they got to the place it was dark and crowded and smelled like a cross between a locker room and the perfume counter at Bloomingdale's. It also smelled like sex. There was music, if you could call it that—house music with the repetitive chords and insistent drumbeat. Joe hated house music. In high school he organized a band in his parents' garage and wrote all the songs himself. They broke up eventually, after playing a few local gigs, but Joe still thought of himself as a musician, and no self-respecting musician likes house music. He wanted to leave, but Bobby wanted to stay for a while, so they ordered drinks and looked around. The place was packed with freaks—Joe had to admit some of them looked pretty good, in their high heels and short skirts. With their shaved legs and wigs they looked like tall chicks from a distance—it's downright creepy, he said to Bobby. But Bobby said what you have to look at is the Adam's apple—that's the giveaway. And the hands—the hands are bigger than a chick's hands. There were also guys dressed regular like Bobby and Joe, but Bobby said they were all faggots.

They wandered around for a while until this one tranny started eyeing Joe. He wasn't too tall, and had on this long, dark wig and really long legs under a little black leather skirt. A lot of the freaks were black or Hispanic or Asian, but this was a white guy—his face was actually kind of girlish, Joe thought. He wasn't really attracted—no, that was too weird—but if the he/she had been a chick he definitely would have looked twice.

They were on about their sixth round when finally this freak caught Joe's eye and winked, and just for a lark Joe winked back. And then this tranny was all in his face, and asking if he can buy them a round, and when had Joe ever turned down a free drink, so he said sure, why not? The tranny bought a round and Bobby bought a round, and then they were totally plastered and laughing, and the freak said her name was Violet, and Bobby said is that like the color or the flower, and she said whatever you want it to be, and they laughed and laughed.

Bobby had to go take a piss, so Joe and Violet were alone at the bar, and Violet put her hand on Joe's knee and said she'd like to show him something, so Joe figured why the hell not—he wasn't getting any other action tonight—so he went with her out the back door into this little alley, where there were garbage cans and those blue recycling bins. It wasn't really dirty, though—it had been swept and was pretty tidy. You had to hand it to faggots for being clean. Violet said she forgot something and went back into the bar for a minute. Joe leaned against the brick wall of the building because he had a lot to drink. He could hear a dog barking from one of the nearby apartments, one of those fluffy little dogs that faggots like.

The air was warm, and he could hear the music from inside the bar. It was still that damn house music, and he was starting to feel not so good. He was ready to go in and tell Bobby it was time to leave when Violet came back out and said she had something for him, and she pulled a condom out of her brassiere (her tits were pretty big—probably falsies) and said they should get it on there in the alley, and suddenly Joe felt terrible, like he was going to be sick, but she was still all up in his face, pawing at him and purring, and it was disgusting, and he just wanted to go home.

He tried to push her away, but she wouldn't listen, so he finally got fed up and started punching her—not to mess her up too much, just to get her to leave him alone. She went down easy. After just a few blows she staggered back against the brick wall and slid to the ground and just sort of sat there, staring. Joe wanted to ask her if she was okay, and help her up or something, but just then Bobby came out of the bar and saw them.

He grabbed Joe and said they had to leave *now* before they got in trouble. Joe was feeling really sick, so he didn't argue and stumbled after Bobby, through the alley and around to the front of the building where they parked their car. When they got there Joe told Bobby to wait because he was going to be sick. After he finished throwing up on the curb, he looked around before getting in the car, just in time to see Violet staggering out of the alley toward them. He felt bad about having to hit her, but he didn't hit her that hard, and he was more scared about getting into trouble. So he climbed in Bobby's car and they drove away. He couldn't help turning back to look out the back window one last time, and saw Violet standing there in the street. She looked sad, and he felt kind of bad, but Bobby was snickering and punching him in the shoulder and saying what a close call that was with that faggot, and wait till they tell their friends. So Joe laughed and reached into his jacket for a cigarette, and they headed toward the Holland Tunnel, driving down Varick Street, with all the windows open to let in the steamy summer air.

CHAPTER TWENTY-EIGHT

Tanika Jackson looked at the clock above her on the wall. It read 11:32 P.M., which meant she had been manning the 911 line for almost ten hours. This was the second Friday in a row she had worked overtime—her shift was almost over, thank God. She was thinking about those new slinky three-inch heels she was going to buy with her overtime pay. They were gold with little teensy straps, and they were going to drive Kevin wild with desire when he saw her in them.

She couldn't wait for Shirley to see them, too—the bi-atch. That would teach her to hang around someone else's man—like she even *had* a chance with Kevin to start with, with her big-ass booty and fleshy upper arms. Good Lord, that girl was a walking tub of lard. In her cheap leopard-print shirts from Target she looked like a fat hooker. Tanika prided herself on her slim figure, which she kept trim by running, working out three times a week, and watching her diet.

Tanika looked down at her sociology textbook, trying to concentrate, but her mind kept wandering to those sandals. It had been a slow night for a weekend. No stabbings or shoot-ings or anything like that, which is how she liked it. Unlike some of the other 911 operators, who worked the lines because they enjoyed the drama and excitement, Tanika was only here for the money. She just wanted an uneventful shift so she could study for her classes at Mercy College, where she only had six months before getting her degree as a social worker. She didn't like to think of people hurting one another. She had lost a cousin to a gang shooting, and she knew firsthand the toll violence takes on people.

She looked down at her textbook, rubbed her eyes, and yawned. Damn, she was tired. Her line rang. She picked up, and, trying not to let her voice betray her fatigue, she said the words she had said a thousand times:

"911—what's your emergency?"

The voice was soft, almost breathy. "I'd like to report a drunk driver."

Tanika thought it was a man's voice, but she wasn't entirely sure. She could hear music playing in the background. She adjusted her earphones and moved the microphone closer to her mouth. "What is the location?"

"Christopher and Greenwich."

"Has anyone been injured?"

"Not yet, but the driver was very drunk."

"Do you have a description of the car?"

"I have better than that—I can give you the license plate."

"Go ahead."

He described the car and gave a New Jersey tag. She asked him to repeat it, writing it down both times just to be sure.

"I'll alert officers in the area. Do you wish to give your name?"

"No, thank you."

"Thank you for your call."

"Thank you," he said politely, and hung up.

Tanika immediately dispatched a call to the Eleventh

Precinct, in the West Village, alerting them of the complaint. She didn't know what they would do from there, but she hoped they nailed the bastard—she hated drunk drivers. In her neighborhood a sweet little girl had been killed a few months ago by a hit-and-run they never caught. She walked past the girl's shrine every day. Sometimes Tanika bought flowers and laid them next to the yellowing photographs and stuffed animals and packages of Gummi bears. She had a little sister, and she didn't know what she'd do if anything ever happened to her.

She looked back down at her textbook, *Sociology for the 21st Century,* and stifled another yawn. She looked back up at the wall clock: it was 11:37 P.M.

CHAPTER TWENTY-NINE

The night was so dark that Lee could barely see where he was going. He stumbled through a thicket of vines and branches tripping and clutching at him like skeletal hands, digging their cold, dead fingers into his flesh until it shivered with the dread and disgust of their touch.

And then he saw it in front of him—the Ansonia Hotel, with its ornate balustrades and rococo masonry. It beckoned to him, rising out of the mist like a stone leviathan, lights blazing in all the windows—and brightest of all in the penthouse apartment.

He struggled on through the forest, keeping his eyes on the grand old building, perched atop a stony hill, like a fortress. He sensed that this was not the usual look of Broadway and Seventy-third Street, but couldn't quite remember what it was supposed to look like. So he dragged himself on through the thick, clinging vines and underbrush, vaguely aware that it was odd to see such forestation on the Upper West Side. It occurred to him that maybe he was lost, but there was the Ansonia, so how could he be lost?

He wasn't sure why he was there, though—did he know someone who lived there? He didn't think so, but then suddenly he was out of the forest and riding up in the elevator, the button that said PENTHOUSE lit.

When he rang the apartment bell, the door swung open and there was his father, looking just as he had the last time Lee saw him: young, handsome, and dashing, his curly black hair just a bit shaggy, suggesting the poet/philosopher that he was in life. Without a word, Duncan Campbell beckoned his son inside and closed the door behind him.

The room was elegant, tasteful, and old-fashioned looking, with expensive Art Deco furnishings. His father had always gravitated toward the elegance of that era, whereas his mother preferred the heavier Victorian designs.

He sat on a sleek satin sofa, admiring the silky fabric as he looked around the room. In the middle of a black-and-white throw rug, his childhood beagle slept peacefully. The dog's paws jerked convulsively, as he chased rabbits in his dreams. Lee was about to ask his father why their dog was here in New York, but when he turned to ask, his father ducked behind a curtain. Moments later he came out carrying a long, sharp spear, which he plunged into Lee's side. Shocked, Lee cried out in pain as the cold metal ripped through his flesh.

He awoke with the sound of his own voice in his ears. He knew he had cried out in his sleep—but Kathy lay next to him sleeping soundly. She slept like the dead, he thought, even without the earplugs she always wore. Fearing he had disturbed the neighbors, he listened for sounds upstairs. Hearing none, he threw off the blankets and sat up on the edge of the bed. He was sweating and panting, the gash in his hand throbbing. He looked out the window at the mimosa tree swaying in the wind, its branches hitting his window softly, rat-a-tat-a-tat. To his frayed nerves the sound was like machine-gun bursts.

He took a deep breath and went into the kitchen for a

glass of water, passing the piano. It sat silent in the corner of the living room, moonlight reflecting off its shiny black veneer, a reminder that it would be a long while before he would be able to play again. He poured himself a glass of water.

So the demons still raged in his soul. He took a drink, cursing his father for leaving him with nothing but memories and bad dreams.

CHAPTER THIRTY

George Favreau was an ashen-faced, nondescript little man, neatly dressed in gray trousers and a pinstriped blue blazer. Quiet, cooperative, and well mannered, he was the very essence of inoffensiveness—unassuming, well spoken, with a light, gentle voice.

As they waited for Chuck to finish with a phone call, Lee watched Favreau through the one-way glass partition. He sat patiently, studying his immaculate nails and playing with a St. Christopher's medal around his neck. His eyes moved nervously around the room, then fixed on the door. He stared at it hungrily, like a dog waiting to be let out for a walk.

Chuck came down the hall, Butts trotting behind him, his short legs pumping to keep up with Morton's long stride. They both carried mugs of fresh coffee.

"Come on—let's get this over with," Morton said. It was Saturday, and Lee knew he hated working on weekends. But they all knew they couldn't afford to waste time on this investigation. They had flagged the Favreau house because he occasionally went to the Swan—and because he was a convicted sex offender. His name turned up on a list of credit card receipts—and on VICAP—so they figured he was worth a closer look.

The three of them entered the room, Lee carrying a cup of coffee for Favreau. Butts winked at him, expecting the coffee to be a setup for the good-cop/bad-cop routine, but actually Lee felt sorry for the poor little guy. He had studied his file: Favreau had done his time, attended every counseling session set up by the court, and his parole officer said he seemed truly contrite for what he'd done. Lee didn't doubt it—the man had a sincere, self-effacing manner, without the underlying arrogance of a true psychopath. This guy might be sick, Lee thought, but he was no killer.

Lee knew it wasn't unusual for Peeping Toms to graduate to more hardcore crime, but this guy—he just didn't think so. Detective Butts sat directly in front of Favreau, with Lee to his right and Chuck on his left side.

As the three of them took their places in the room, Favreau studied his hands. They were small and delicate, the nails pink and well cared for. Lee had trouble imagining those hands killing a woman—or a man, for that matter. Favreau had been a math professor at Rutgers before his arrest and prosecution for sex crimes. Maybe it was a coincidence that Ana was taking classes there—but maybe not.

"So, Mr. Fav-reau," Butts said, "do you know why you've been brought in here?"

Favreau looked up at the detective and pursed his lips, as though he had just eaten a lemon. "I can only assume you have orders to beat the bushes a little to flush out this notorious murderer. A useless and ineffective gesture, of course, but something to placate the public thirst for vengeance."

Lee looked at Chuck, who sat back in his chair, arms crossed. He had evidently decided to let Butts take the lead on this one. Lee wondered how Butts would deal with this guy—and to his surprise, the detective backed off a little.

"Look, Mr. Fav-reau, only you know whether or not you have anything to do with these crimes, okay? So let's just say that even if you're innocent, the easier you make my job, the sooner we can both get outta this dump, right?"

"Sounds reasonable," Favreau responded, flicking a speck of something from the table. *Meticulous, orderly, outwardly calm,* Lee thought. *Like the killer.*

Butts took a gulp of coffee. "Okay, good—good. So it's pretty basic stuff, really—where were you on the night of so and so, this and that. Okay?"

"Fire away, Detective," Favreau replied smoothly, giving Lee a little smile. "Thanks for the coffee, by the way."

"You're welcome."

Butts consulted his notes, though Lee knew it was purely for show. He had a nearly photographic memory, and no doubt had each date memorized. "Do you remember your whereabouts on August—"

"Twentieth?" Favreau finished for him. "You see, Detective," he said with a wry smile, "I know exactly why I'm here. And believe me, when I read in the papers about that poor girl's death, I made sure to take an exact accounting of my actions, because I knew sooner or later, unless it was solved quickly, someone would try to put my head on the chopping block. Not that it's your fault." He took a sip of his coffee. "I mean, you're only doing your job, right?"

"Okay, fine," Chuck said, "We're only doing our jobs. Big of you to give us that. So would you mind telling us where you were that night?"

Favreau placed his manicured fingertips together. "At the movies. I am an avid fan—I see nearly everything the moment it comes out. Ask anyone. Helps keep my mind off things."

"Okay," Morton replied slowly. "And was anyone with you?"

Favreau smiled. "I'm afraid not. I was forced to enjoy Julia Roberts's manifold charms by myself that night—except for the other people in the theater, of course. And of course I saved my ticket stub. Under the right circumstances, it can be tax deductible—did you know that?" He took a neatly folded yellow ticket stub from his breast pocket and handed it to Chuck. "You'll find my fingerprints on it, too. If I'm not mistaken, you already have a set of my prints on file."

Chuck studied the ticket. "Well, it's the right day, but you could have gotten this in any number of ways. Did anyone see you at the cinema that night?"

"I'm not really sure. I'm not exactly someone who stands out in a crowd, as you may have noticed."

Butts leaned forward. "You were seen on the campus of Rutgers prior to the victim's death. What business did you have there?"

"No business at all, really. I was just wandering around the campus, reflecting on better days, when I taught there. Mathematics. Oh, but you probably already know that—no doubt you read my file. But did you also know that I have an IQ of 165? Genius level, so they tell me. I'm afraid it hasn't done me all that much good."

"So you were just wandering around?" Butts said. "Did you speak to anyone?"

Favreau shook his head. "No. I recognized some of the security guards, but I was too embarrassed to say hello. Sort of puts a crimp in your self-confidence, being convicted as a sex offender, don't you think?"

"I wouldn't know," Butts replied acidly. "So how long were you wandering around campus?"

"Oh, for at least an hour. I *am* allowed to do that, you know—it's a free country, or at least until our Republican administration has its way. Then, look out—pretty soon civil liberties will be just a fond memory. Sort of like my career, actually," he added thoughtfully.

Lee wasn't sure how much of what Favreau was saying was an act—he seemed to be playing with them, enjoying the self-pitying ruminations and wisecracks. He liked having an audience. That wasn't surprising—good teachers were part actor, part scholar. According to his file, Favreau's reputation as a professor before his fall from grace had been very good—he was popular among both students and faculty. He had a dry way of saying things that made you wonder how sincere he was.

Lee was beginning to change his mind about Favreau. He no longer seemed so pathetic or downtrodden. In fact, he was downright self-possessed, even arrogant, in his professorial way. *Arrogant*—maybe the contrition routine had been for the benefit of his parole officer, or maybe it too was just an act. He decided to tell Chuck later that they should watch this guy.

In the end, nothing constructive came of the interview. Favreau claimed to have been at the movies, but couldn't produce anyone who had actually seen him there. It also struck all three of them that there was something a little tidy about his alibi—he happened to be at a movie during the time frame in which the murder was committed, but if he was setting up a fake alibi, why not do a better job? But then, with an IQ of 165, he may have already anticipated all of these questions, and, if he was the killer, be several steps ahead of them.

CHAPTER THIRTY-ONE

Caleb pushed back the French lace curtains and looked out the window. Soon twilight would come, and he would venture out. He loved the city at night. When the sun went down, he owned the streets. He loved to roam around when he knew everyone else was asleep. His favorite time of night was 3 A.M.—the Witching Hour, or, as his Gran had called it, Dead Time. The time when the bridge between the living and the dead is thinnest, when spirits can be seen by those who have the Gift.

He had the Gift—he'd known it since earliest childhood. He saw his first spirit at the age of five, only he didn't know it was a spirit. He just thought it was the old man who lived across the bridge in the woods. But when his father mentioned the brutal murder that had taken place there many years ago, he knew—knew that the old man was dead and had been for many years before Caleb saw him.

He didn't tell anyone except his Gran, and only then on her deathbed. He touched the cream-colored lace curtains fondly. She had made them, years ago, and he had taken them with him when he left. He missed his Gran. She alone understood him. She alone had kindness in her heart for him, and when she was gone, terrible things began to happen—terrible, unspeakable things. He covered his eyes with his hands to make the images go away, but that only made them burn brighter in his head. They came to him at night. But if he stayed up all night, catching catnaps during the day, that would sometimes keep the memories from swirling through his dreams, shadowy visitors looming over him as he slept.

Now he saw spirits all the time—especially the ones he killed. They came to him at night, reaching toward him with their dead, white fingers, their faces strewn with seaweed and water lilies and other flora of the rivers and streams. They looked so wistful, so lost, and sometimes they seemed puzzled, as if they couldn't understand why they no longer walked the earth among the living. He tried to explain to them, tried to tell them why he had to do it, but the words never came. He was as mute as the lovely mermaids whose murky faces haunted his dreams.

Slowly, he let fall the curtain his Gran had made with her own dear, beloved old hands. He picked up one of the syringes from the table in front of him. His father wouldn't mind if he borrowed one or two from time to time—the people at the hospital had given him so many. The familiar thrill threaded its way through his bowels as he watched the sun slink its way out of the sky. It was time.

CHAPTER THIRTY-TWO

On Sunday, Lee left early to get to his mother's house for Kylie's birthday dinner. He took the Holland Tunnel as usual, heading west on Route 78, but when he reached the turnoff to Route 202 he took local roads the rest of the way, winding through the towns of Morris, Sussex, and Hunterdon Counties. He watched pastures give way to villages, winding through narrow main streets before emerging back out and past the sweet-smelling farm fields of the central portion of the state.

Most people thought of Jersey as an ugly jumble of industrial wasteland wrapped around Newark and Jersey City. That's what you saw when you came in from the south: miles of polluted swamplands crisscrossed by major highways and crammed with factories and spewing smokestacks. Visitors to New York flying into Newark Airport would go rattling and jouncing along poorly kept roads with signs that looked as if they'd been there since the 1930s—and that would remain their only impression of the much-maligned neighboring state.

But the vast majority of New Jersey was fertile farm fields, orchards, and pastures. Driving through the soft late-summer countryside, it was hard to imagine that there was anything harsh or wicked in the world.

But of course, Lee knew better He was nine and Laura just six when their secure and cozy existence was shattered, like a plastic Christmas village picked up by an unseen hand and shaken, the familiar scene obscured by the snowflakes falling all around. There had been increasing tension between their parents for some time. They had few arguments, but there was a growing distance between them that both children noticed. Long silences at the dinner table were becoming more common, their mother serving the meal, then wordlessly slipping into her chair without even saying grace, something that had been unthinkable in the past. She had always insisted in maintaining certain social rituals, regardless of belief. But lately she had become a grim creature, going about her daily tasks with a dour determination that was unlike her, her high spirits dampened by some unseen sorrow. It seemed to Lee that she was laughing less and less, and he often saw her staring out the window after his father's car as he drove off to work in the morning.

His father, too, had changed: gone were the evenings when he would come up behind her in the kitchen and tickle her neck. She would turn just as he slipped his arm around her waist, hugging her to him, tucking his head into the nape of her neck. Neither of them was given to public display of affection, so this was a ritual the children especially enjoyed. But now they seemed to be moving around the house like strangers, talking only when necessary, acknowledging each other's presence with no affection or intimacy. There were no fights, but there was such a coldness between them that the air itself seemed to shiver. Lee longed to ask about it, but important matters such as that were rarely spoken about in their family.

It was a Friday evening in September, and their father had

come home late, missing dinner that night, whiskey on his breath, his mood unusually volatile. The children were up- stairs getting ready for bed, and they heard his footsteps on the stairs, slower and heavier than usual. They were both in Lee's room. Laura was sitting cross-legged on the floor read- ing a book of Grimm's fairy tales, and Lee was mending a piece of track on his model train. Their father came into the room and greeted the children with unusually affectionate hugs for such a normally reserved man, squeezing both of them until they pulled away, puzzled at his odd behavior.

Lee remembered his words on that night, because they were some of the last words he ever heard his father say.

"I love you both very much—you know that, don't you?" he said, holding each of them by the shoulder. Lee remem- bered the feel of that strong hand pressing down on him, a kind of desperation in the touch. He could smell the musty aroma of malt whiskey on his father's breath, and looked at his sister, who seemed as perplexed as he was. She was wearing her pink pajamas with the fluffy white bunny tail, and next to her was her beloved Pooh bear with the missing orange glass eye, whom she always slept with. Both of the children were taken aback by this emotional declaration of affection in a man who believed in spareness in all things— except perhaps single-malt Scotch.

Duncan Campbell stood gazing at them, and Lee was startled to see his eyes brimming with tears. "Whatever may come," he said huskily in a voice throaty from emotion and whiskey, "always remember that I love you." The children were too surprised to say anything. They sensed from their father's mood something important and solemn was about to happen, but they had no idea what it was.

Their father opened his mouth as if he was going to say something more, then, changing his mind, turned and left the room. Laura started to cry softly. As always, feeling that it was his job as the older brother to comfort and take care of her, Lee patted her head as though she were a puppy and said, "Don't cry—it's all right." But even as he said the words, he did not believe them. He knew that something was very wrong.

The sound of conversation rose from downstairs, and he and Laura crept out to the landing overlooking the living room, peering down through the wooden slats to listen to the unfolding drama. Their parents were in the kitchen, but the door was open, and their voices carried through the house to where the children sat listening intently.

"Don't lay all of this on my doorstep," their father was saying, his voice tight and angry, the words a little slurred at the edges.

"That's exactly where I'm laying it!" their mother replied, shrill and almost hysterical. Lee's stomach twisted as he listened—this was so unlike his mother, normally so calm and in control of her emotions. Laura grasped his hand in hers, crying harder now, the tears spilling onto the front of her pink pajamas. Lee squeezed her hand and put his other arm around her shoulders.

"None of this would ever have happened," his father said, "if it weren't for—"

"Don't you *dare* bring that up!" his mother cried savagely. "I swear, Duncan Campbell, if you *ever* dare mention that again—"

Now it was his father who interrupted. "Fine, I won't. But you know as well as I do if we'd only been able to talk about it, none of this would have—"

"Doesn't that sound all tidy and virtuous?" his mother sneered. "All we have to do is *talk* about it, is that it, and everything will be all right?"

There was a pause, and his father said slowly, "You blame me. You have always blamed me, and you will always blame me. There's nothing I can do with that, Fiona, and I have tried these past three years—God knows I've tried. I thought I could earn your forgiveness, but I see now I was wrong."

"Forgiveness!" his mother hissed. "After what you've done, you can talk about *forgiveness*?"

There was a long pause, and then the sound of footsteps coming out of the kitchen and toward the living room. The children ducked back from the stairwell landing, but their father crossed to the front door without a glance in their direction. He was wearing his coat and hat and carrying a suitcase. Their mother came running after him, crying hysterically.

"Fine, then!" she shouted, her voice choking and wavering with emotion. "Go—just go, will you? We don't need you around here—we're better off without you! Just go, damn you!"

Their father turned around, his hand on the doorknob, and looked at her sadly. "Good-bye, Fiona," he said, and left the house, closing the door behind him.

It was the last time the children ever saw their father. Fiona collapsed onto the living room couch, weeping uncontrollably. It was a horrible sound—strange, strangled sobs, like the agony of a wild animal. Caught between the need to care for his sister and comfort his mother, Lee crept downstairs and cradled his mother in his arms.

CHAPTER THIRTY-THREE

As he drove through the gently sloping farm fields, Lee thought about each victim, and what they had in common. On the surface, they had very little in common, but there was some thread connecting them. There had to be—there always was. Once you saw the pattern, and how the pieces connected, you had a clearer insight into the killer's personality.

But this murderer might as well be a ghost. He was hiding his pattern, his victimology, so well . . . but what if the lack of a pattern was *in itself* a pattern? What if they could somehow connect the seeming randomness of the crimes to a particular type of person?

As he pulled into the driveway of his mother's house, Lee saw purple and white balloons festooned on the lamppost at the end of the drive. He smiled—purple was Kylie's new favorite color. She had given up pink as "too girlie" a few months ago. As he pulled up onto the patch of lawn that served as a parking space, the front door of the house was flung open and his niece came rushing out, trailed by two other little girls.

"Uncle Leeeee!" she cried as he opened the car door, throwing herself at him.

Her two friends followed suit. "Uncle Leeee!" they yelled gleefully, wrapping their arms around his legs. He pretended not to notice and tried to walk, a girl clinging to each leg, as Kylie peeled off and hopped up and down alongside him.

"You look so funny!" she hooted as he pretended to be unaware of the clinging girls, struggling to move his legs forward. After a couple of minutes of this, all three of the children dissolved into laughter, and the two hanging onto him were forced to let go.

"You're *funny*!" the smaller one said. She was a pixie with olive skin and straight jet black hair cut short with long bangs over large dark eyes.

"Aren't you going to introduce me?" Lee asked Kylie as they all headed toward the house.

"This is Angelica," said Kylie, stroking the pixie's shiny black hair, "and this is Meredith."

Meredith was not a pretty child—much taller than Angelica and Kylie, she was very pale with bushy red hair, deepset blue eyes, and a long, serious face. "Hello," she said, studying Lee as though he were a laboratory specimen or object d'art. "You're the criminal profiler, right?

Lee thought Meredith was entirely too precocious for her age.

"I'm in law enforcement, that's right."

Meredith walked backward so she could look up at him, as Kylie and Angelica skipped hand in hand alongside them, humming.

"I've read about the kind of work you do. It's very interesting," Meredith said, trying to skip backward. It was an awkward gait, and she was an ungainly child. "Is that how you hurt your arm?"

"Kind of."

"I think I want to do what you do when I grow up."

Lee smiled. "Well, you're young—there's plenty of time to change your mind."

Meredith shook her head. "No, I'm very focused—I know that's what I want to do." She looked at him, her face serious. "I have a very high IQ, you know."

"Well, that's great," he said as they reached the house.

"Don't pay any attention to her," Kylie said, taking Meredith by the hand and pulling her down the grassy slope toward the springhouse. "She thinks she's all that."

"No, I don't," said Meredith, "I just—" But at that moment Kylie threw herself onto the ground and began rolling down the grassy hillside. Angelica quickly followed suit, giggling all the way. Meredith stood for a moment with her hands at her sides, then said, "Oh, what the heck," and rolled down after them.

Watching them, Lee remembered all the times he and Laura had rolled down that same hill—or, in winter, sledded down it and across the frozen stream at the bottom. He looked at his mother's house: there were a good number of old stone houses in this river valley, and some of them had connections to the Revolutionary War, but his mother's house practically oozed history. The massive gray river stones were bulky and uneven and looked as if they had been hewn from the sides of mountains by giants. When Lee was a child he thought they were the most wonderful thing he had ever seen.

The sound of giggling bubbled up from the bottom of the hill, where the three girls lay on their backs, breathless and laughing, their hair and clothes covered with grass and bits of twigs. The lazy August sun fell on the girls' hair—blond, black, and red—and Lee was reminded of seeing a herd of horses in a field when he was a child, and how pleasing he found the different-colored manes.

Looking at them, it was hard once again to imagine anything was wrong in the world, or ever would be.

He heard the familiar sound of the front screen door slamming and turned his head toward the house. For one painful instant, he expected his sister to be coming out onto the stone porch to wave at him. He had to blink to clear his eyes when he realized that it was, of course, his mother.

"Hi," she called, shielding her eyes from the sun. "Where's the birthday girl?"

Lee pointed to the bottom of the hill, where the girls had gotten up and were brushing the grass from their clothes, still laughing. He didn't want to disturb the sweetness of the moment, so he turned and joined his mother on the front porch.

Fiona Campbell greeted her only son with a quick, firm kiss on the cheek, then held him at arm's length, grasping his shoulders with her long, strong hands.

"So glad you could make it," she said. "It means a lot to Kylie." She would never say it meant something to her, too—that was not her style. "What on earth did you do to your arm?" she said, frowning.

"I ran into a door."

She raised a single eyebrow, but didn't say anything more about it. That was typical of her—the less said about unpleasantries, the better.

His mother was tall and straight, as lean as the day she was married to Lee's father. Her salt-and-pepper hair was cut in a businesslike sweep of bangs, short in the back, just reaching the nape of her neck. Her cheekbones were high, her eyes a clear, piercing blue, and she walked with the unyielding step of a woman who has never known a moment's self-doubt.

Loss was the touchstone of his family's life, and his

mother was both ridiculous and rather heroic in her refusal to bow down to it—indeed, to recognize its existence. The straightness of her spine, the clearness of her gaze in the face of disaster were both vexing and full of an odd grandeur, like a Greek tragic heroine.

Lee turned to see George Callahan emerge from the house. He was Kylie's father, and Lee believed that a kinder, more patient man had never walked the earth.

"Hi, George," he said, extending his left hand.

"Hey there, fella," George replied, grasping Lee's hand in his enormous paw, holding a beer in the other. George was big and blond and bluff, with a touching awkwardness around other people. When there was work to be done, he was your man—hardworking, honest, reliable—but in social situations he always seemed to be struggling to overcome his natural shyness. Big and broad-shouldered, he never really looked at home at the kind of cocktail parties Lee's parents had favored. He was much more comfortable in front of a grill, flipping steaks, spatula in one hand and beer in the other. He was wearing blue jeans and a freshly ironed white shirt on his generous frame, and wore his straight sandy hair slicked back. His square face was shiny and pink, as though he had spent the day in the sun.

"What'd chya do, get in a fight?" George asked, indicating Lee's injured arm.

"Yeah—but you should see the other guy."

George laughed. "Yeah, I'll bet!" He jerked a thumb in the direction of the kitchen. "Can I get you a beer?"

"Sure."

"Comin' right up," George said happily, lumbering back into the house. He loved waiting on people—it was talking to them that presented problems.

"So it'll just be the three of us and the three girls," Lee's mother said, sitting in one of the chaise longues on the porch. "Kylie will have another birthday party at school on Monday with all her classmates. George has already taken the morning off to bake cupcakes."

"He's a great dad," Lee said.

"Yes, he is," she replied.

A silence hung heavy in the air between them. What neither of them were saying, but Lee was sure they were both thinking, was how much they missed Laura and how they wished she were here now to see her daughter turn seven.

George reemerged from the house just as Kylie and her friends came up from the bottom of the hill. Kylie and Meredith walked side by side, carrying an enormous watermelon between them, as Angelica skipped along behind.

"Look what we found in the springhouse!" Kylie exclaimed.

"That's for after dinner," Fiona said sternly. "For dessert."

"But we have birthday cake for dessert," Kylie pointed out. "Why can't we have the watermelon now?"

Fiona started to answer, but George Callahan stepped in. "It's your birthday, right?" he said to his daughter.

"Right!" she said, grinning.

Angelica wiped some grass from her forehead and looked at them all wide-eyed. Meredith crossed her arms and did her best to regard the adults with an ironic gaze, but she just looked as though she had indigestion.

"Then I think you should have the watermelon whenever you want it," he said, with a challenging look at Fiona, who shook her head.

"George Callahan, you're going to spoil her," she said.

"Then she'll be spoiled. But it's her birthday and I say she should have the watermelon when she wants it."

"Yea!" the girls cried. They hopped up and down, chanting, "Wa-ter-me-lon! Wa-ter-me-lon!"

The three adults couldn't help laughing at the sight, though Fiona still shook her head, clicking her tongue in disapproval. Such things as watermelon on demand didn't exist in her world—but then, in her world, her only daughter was alive somewhere, not an undiscovered corpse slowly rotting in some lonely and abandoned corner of the world.

CHAPTER THIRTY-FOUR

Bad boy! You're a bad, bad boy, and you deserve to be punished for it. Did you really think you could humiliate me and get away with it? Well, you're about to learn your lesson. All bad boys learn their lesson sooner or later.

Caleb turned the dial on his police scanner until he picked up the call from Patrol Unit 85. He smiled as he heard the officer's voice—the familiar, flat intonation of a cop reporting a routine stop.

"Suspect in drunk driving apprehended, white male, being taken to Tombs for booking. His companion is also inebriated, so car is being impounded following suspect's release."

He leaned back in his seat, letting his head fall back onto the headrest. They would take Joe to spend the night at the Tombs, then release him in the morning. He would emerge into the bright daylight, hungover, disgusted with himself and the world, and Caleb would be waiting.

CHAPTER THIRTY-FIVE

It was a wonderful summer meal, the kind Laura would have loved. George outdid himself on the grill, the salad was mixed greens and juicy tomatoes from local farms, and the sweet corn was tender and perfectly cooked. Lee's mother had something of a corn fetish. She would set the timer for precisely one minute once the water came to a boil, standing over the pot to pluck out the ears with her tongs, her face red and sweating as the rising steam slowly enveloped her.

They sat at the oblong oak table in the tiny dining room with the burnished maple-wood paneling. They had planned to eat outside at the picnic table, but a plague of mosquitoes plummeted down like tiny dive bombers when dusk fell. They grabbed their plates and scurried inside, abandoning the bucolic splendor of the front lawn for the comfort of the small but elegant eighteenth-century dining room, with its smell of apples and ancient wood.

As a great concession to her granddaughter, Fiona had agreed to serve—*horrors*—hamburgers and French fries along with the corn and salad. In the Campbell family the birthday child always chose the menu for the birthday dinner. Fiona favored fish and chicken and vegetables. Born in

Scotland and forced to endure Scottish cuisine as a child, she had a horror of what she called "stodgy food," but tonight Kylie would have her way. This pleased George Callahan no end, as he was the appointed chef—he loved to stand at the grill, a cold beer at his side, inhaling charcoal smoke and wielding the specially fashioned grill tools he had designed himself. It was his dream to someday have enough to invest in a small business and make outdoor grilling equipment. The one concession made to Fiona was that the meat was pure grass-fed Angus beef, ninety-seven percent lean, organic, and hormone free.

They all sat around Fiona's long oak table, halfway through Kylie's birthday dinner. "Great burgers, George," Lee said, as he finished his, medium rare, dripping with caramelized onions. George had cooked each one to order, and seasoned them with a special sauce he made himself, guarding the recipe as carefully as if it were a state secret.

"Thanks," George replied, snapping open another Rolling Rock and taking a long swig. He wiped his mouth with his sleeve, then looked sheepishly at Fiona, but fortunately for him she wasn't watching.

The girls chatted and giggled all throughout dinner, and though Fiona shot her granddaughter looks from time to time, Kylie ignored her and continued enjoying her friends.

The subject at the moment was Ouija boards—the girls had discovered the one Lee and Laura used to play with in the upstairs guest bedroom closet. When he explained what they were for, Meredith immediately scoffed at the idea, but Kylie and Angelica were intrigued and wanted to play with the board after dinner.

"There's no such thing as foretelling the future!" Meredith declared, spreading a liberal amount of butter on her ear of corn.

"How do you know?" said Kylie. "What if there is?"

"Well, even if there is, you wouldn't be able to do it with a wooden board with a few letters painted on it!"

"My granny says that she can tell the future from the scratches our chickens leave in their feed on the ground," Angelica said, her chin shiny from beef fat and butter.

"You have chickens?" Kylie said. "That's cool!"

Angelica lowered her eyes and glanced at Fiona, who sat stiff as ever in her chair, delicately nibbling on an ear of corn. Her fastidiousness extended to her eating habits. Though she enjoyed her food, she was never one to throw herself into any activity too vigorously, as if an excess of enthusiasm was itself a character flaw.

"Why do people want to believe they can foretell the future?" Meredith grumbled. "Why can't they just live their lives without this . . . *need* to believe in things that can't be proven?"

"Speaking of the future, you sound like a future scientist," George remarked, helping himself to more steak and salad.

Meredith set her fork down with a clank. "Yes," she said portentously. "I intend to be a forensic specialist."

"What's for-ensics?" asked Angelica.

"The study of evidence in crime scenes," Meredith replied, popping a cherry tomato into her mouth. The juice squirted out through her teeth and hit Fiona square in the forehead.

"Less chatter and more attention to what we're doing, please," she said sternly.

"I think the reason people want to believe in the unproven is because we all want to be able to touch the past and the future," George said. "We don't want to think that this is all there is."

Meredith snorted and rolled her eyes.

"You're too young to understand," George continued, "but

by the time you're our age, you will. We're all afraid of death, and we've all lost someone we love. So if we can believe that maybe—just maybe—there's something else, then we feel better."

"Well, *I* think it's silly!" Meredith scoffed, stuffing a piece of bread in her mouth.

Lee looked at George, taken aback by his uncharacteristically serious response. He knew that George was referring to Laura, but he was surprised that he would allude to her in front of the children—especially his daughter. But Kylie appeared to miss the reference, and was happily dipping her bread into a little pool of melted butter on her plate.

"In Scotland, some people were said to have what we called the Second Sight," Fiona said.

Lee stared at his mother. This was the first he'd ever heard her mention anything like this.

"Really?" said Kylie, her fork stopped in midair.

Fiona's expression didn't change, but her tone was low and mysterious. "When I was a child there was a woman, Mary McFarland, who could see things that had yet to happen."

"Like what?" Angelica said, leaning so far over the table she nearly upset the salad dressing.

"Gareth McKinney came to her in a dream, and the next day he was dead."

"Wow," said Kylie. "That's cool."

"How did he die?" Angelica asked.

"He fell off the roof trying to mend it."

Meredith sniffed officiously. "Probably just a coincidence."

"Then one time she told Kerry McClelland not to take the ferry to the mainland, and the next day the ferry sank."

"*Wow*," Kylie said.

"How come you never told me any of this?" Lee asked.

Fiona leaned forward and plucked another ear of corn from the platter. "The subject never came up."

Kylie and Angelica could hardly wait to finish dinner so they could get out the Ouija board, over Meredith's objections.

Lee joined his mother in the kitchen, where she was busily cleaning up after dinner. Fiona was an exacting housekeeper, and often seemed so eager to begin the "tidying up" process that Lee was worried someday she would snatch a half-finished dish from under her guest's nose.

He found her rinsing and stacking dishes—she owned a dishwasher, but a dish rarely entered it in anything less than pristine condition.

"Do you really believe those things you told the girls?" Lee asked his mother.

"I am neither a believer nor an unbeliever," she replied, scraping corncobs into the compost bin. A fanatic gardener, she was intractable when it came to composting, believing that artificial fertilizers were the devil's work.

"But you told them that story," he protested. "Why did you tell them if you don't—"

She stopped working and turned to face him. "Where are you headed with this? Because I won't talk about—*you know what*," she finished, her voice low.

"That's not why I was asking," Lee said. "But since you mention it, why *can't* we ever talk about it? For God's sake, she was—"

His mother abruptly dropped the compost bin onto the floor with such a loud bang that it made him jump. "*Don't* you say she '*was*' anything!" she hissed, her eyes narrowed in fury. "Don't you *dare* give up on her!"

"Oh, for God's sake—I'm not 'giving up' on anything!"

he shot back. "When will *you* accept the fact that she's gone? She's not coming back—she's *dead*, and all the wishing in the world isn't going to change that!"

When he saw the look in his mother's eyes, he immediately regretted his words. She stared at him, her face frozen in an expression of horror and reproach, then turned sharply, whipping her dish towel onto the counter like a punctuation mark, and stalked out of the room.

Lee stood there for a few moments, his head spinning with remorse and anger—anger because this was such predictable behavior on her part, and remorse because he should have known better than to bring it up—and on Kylie's birthday, of all times.

He heard a sound behind him and turned to see his niece standing in the doorway, a stricken expression on her face.

"What's the matter? Why are you angry at Grandmother?" she said, her chin beginning to pucker, her lower lip trembling.

"I'm not angry at her, honey," Lee said, bending to take her in his arms.

"Is it about my mommy coming back? Will she be coming soon?"

"Maybe, honey," he lied. "I hope so."

CHAPTER THIRTY-SIX

It was just another Sunday night for Roberto Rivera—like all the countless other Sundays he checked into work, thermos under his arm, to work his way through the Midtown office building to clean up the detritus of the past week before everyone arrived back at work Monday morning. It wasn't a bad job—union pay plus benefits, and he could turn his mind off while he worked, dreaming of his native Guatemala, of the fishing boat he was going to buy in a couple of years. He imagined Carlita's face when he showed her all the money he earned in New York—nothing like this kind of job existed in his country. He did odd jobs around the building, too, and they sometimes paid him under the table for those—he was handy with mechanical things, and proud of his ability to learn to fix almost anything with a motor.

He plugged his earphones into his iPod—a Christmas gift from his eldest son, who was doing very well working at a fancy Upper East Side restaurant—slung his mop and cleaning utensils into the metal bucket on wheels, and took the elevator to the second floor. He liked to work his way up the building, starting on the lower floors and finishing in the office suites in the sky, where he would pause to look at the lights of the city below. It was sweet: his work finished, he would sit in one of the fancy chairs in the big corner office, and lean back with his feet up on the desk. Carefully he would unscrew the lid of his thermos and pour himself a steaming cup of café con leche, sweet and dark and hot, and sip it dreaming of the green forests and sandy white beaches of Guatemala.

He always started with the men's room in the back of the second floor, and he flipped through the songs on his iPod trying to find the right one to get him in the mood. He pushed open the door, pulled the bucket in after him, and stood, head down, fiddling with the dials.

Then he looked up. He could see a pair of legs protruding from one of the stalls—it looked as though someone was praying in front of the commode. His first thought was that it was a man being sick in one of the toilets.

"Hey, mister, you okay?" he called out, removing the earplugs from his ears.

His voice echoed through the tiled chamber and came back to him, and then there was nothing—nothing but utter stillness, complete silence.

The quality of the silence told Roberto something was very wrong. As he turned to go get help, his eye was caught by something on the bathroom mirror. Trembling now, he took a step into the room for a closer look. What he saw made him drop the mop handle. Leaving the bucket where it stood, he backed out of the doorway, his legs carrying him out of the room and down the hall as if they had a will of their own. Later, he had trouble even remembering making the phone call to 911 from the security desk in the lobby.

CHAPTER THIRTY-SEVEN

"*I* think *all* crime is *fascinating*," Meredith declared, stuffing another French fry into her mouth as the girls helped to clear the table.

"*I* think crime is *scary*," Angelica said.

Kylie rolled her eyes and looked at Lee, as if to say, *See, these are the idiots I have to endure.* Already she was acquiring some of her grandmother's disdain for the common run of humanity.

"Can we please be excused?" Kylie said. "I want to play with the Ouija board."

Even though dinner was over, no one had been formally "excused," a ritual Fiona still insisted on.

"Ooh, yes, can we please be excused?" Angelica repeated, jumping up and down.

Meredith rolled her eyes. "Those things aren't *real*, you know."

Kylie made a face at her. "What*ever*."

"Yeah," Angelica chimed in. "What-*ever*!"

"Yes, you may," said Fiona as she brushed crumbs off the linen tablecloth. Even in the summer, she set a proper table: linen cloth and napkins to match, candles, polished silverware—as if by clinging to these proprieties she could stave off disaster and loss.

Kylie dashed off to the living room, followed by Angelica. Meredith strolled after them, careful not to appear the least bit eager or interested.

"I had one of those when I was a kid," George said. "Where'd you get it?"

Fiona dabbed at the edges of her mouth with her napkin. "Kylie found it in the attic. It belonged to . . ." She looked away, chewing on her lip.

"It was Laura's," Lee finished for her. "I remember playing with it when we were kids."

"Uncle Lee, do you want to play?" Kylie called to him from the living room.

He looked at his mother, who had gained control of herself, and was calmly finishing clearing the table.

"Let me give you a hand," he said.

"No, go ahead and play with her—George can help me," she answered.

George rose hurriedly from his chair, almost knocking it over, and grabbed a couple of plates, sending a fork clattering to the floor.

"Go on," he said, bending down to pick it up. "I'll give her a hand."

Lee took his wine and went into the living room, where the girls had set up the Ouija board on a low coffee table in front of the wide stone fireplace.

He sat on the floor next to Angelica, who was perched on a couch cushion. She leaned over the board, her dark hair falling over one eye. Her hair was just a shade darker than Laura's, and the way it fell across her forehead reminded him of Ana, on her last visit to him. . . . *Christ,* he thought, *does everything have to remind me of death?*

"Okay," Kylie said, "everyone ready?"

Angelica nodded eagerly, squirming on her cushion, her dark eyes shining with excitement. Meredith compressed her lips and gave a little shrug, but Lee noticed that she too rested her fingertips on the pointer.

"Come on, Uncle Lee!" Kylie said, and he placed his fingers next to theirs. It was an odd feeling—he was propelled back to his childhood as though he had been sucked through a time warp. He looked down at the pointer, at the delicate young fingers resting beside his much larger hands, which looked crude and rough next to theirs.

"Okay," Kylie said. "I'm the birthday girl, so I'll ask the first question."

"Okay," Angelica agreed, her voice tight with anticipation.

"Are—you—real?" Kylie said, with a look at Meredith, who rolled her eyes.

The pointer shot off to the far side of the board so quickly Lee could barely keep his fingers on it.

It stopped at the word YES.

Kylie gave Meredith a superior shake of her head, but Meredith ignored her.

"Are you *sure*?" she asked.

Once again the pointer took off and began spelling out words so quickly Lee could barely keep his fingers from slipping off it. He looked at the three girls to see who was controlling the pointer, but couldn't figure out who it could be. They all looked equally surprised when the pointer finished spelling out a brief sentence.

Q-U-I-T S-T-A-L-L-I-NG.

"Quit stalling?" Meredith murmured. "What the hell does that mean?"

"You said a bad word," Angelica said, her eyes wide.

"Oh, get over it," Meredith muttered.

George Callahan wandered into the room.

"Whatchya doing?" he asked, peering down at them.

"Come join us, Daddy," Kylie said. Lee winced at the sound of the word—he had noticed she rarely called him that, and had several theories as to why. George and Laura had never been married—George wanted it, but Laura didn't—and while Kylie did share his last name, he knew that Fiona thought of her as a Campbell through and through. He had experienced his mother's subtle but relentless propaganda all his life, and knew that when Fiona wanted something, she usually got in the end.

"Yeah, Mr. Callahan, come on!" Angelica said, sliding over to make room for him.

"Okay," George said, lowering his bulky body down to the floor. He sat cross-legged between Angelica and Meredith, sweat gathering on the back of his neck as he settled down. He folded his thick legs stiffly under his body, joints creaking, hunching awkwardly over the table. He reminded Lee of a bull elephant trying to hatch an egg.

"All set," George said. "Now, what shall we ask it?"

He had barely placed his fingertips on the pointer when it flew off across the board again, even faster than before.

Lee stared at it as it zipped from letter to letter.

A-S-K A-B-O-U-T T-H-E R-E-D D-R-E-S-S

The walls of the room began to close in on him, and he didn't hear the phone ringing in the other room. When his mother appeared at the doorway, phone in her hand, she had to call his name twice.

"Lee!" she said, holding out the phone. "It's Chuck Morton. They need you right away. There's been"—she hesitated, looking at the girls—"a development."

CHAPTER THIRTY-EIGHT

Miguel Rodriguez, the man on the front security desk at 545 Sixth Avenue, really did want to help. It was clear from his body language that he had nothing to hide. Sitting in the lobby chairs opposite Lee and Butts, he leaned into them, his face expressing a willingness—even eagerness—to cooperate. He was fidgety, but Lee knew no one is completely at ease when being questioned by the police, no matter how innocent they are.

Butts had already asked him who came into the building around the time of the crime, and so far, he hadn't come up with much. After all, most of the offices were closed, though he did say people came and went even on the weekends.

"Now, Mr. Rodriguez, can you think of anyone unusual who came *into* the building in the past twenty-four hours?"

Rodriguez clenched his hands tightly and leaned forward even more, rocking a little in his chair. He was young—maybe late twenties, with an earnest, open manner and a light Puerto Rican accent. He wore a gold wedding ring and a tiny gold cross around his suntanned neck.

"Wait! We did get a UPS delivery around six on Saturday." He seemed pleased to have thought of this, and looked at Butts like a schoolboy who has done well.

"Is that unusual?" Butts asked.

"Not really. We usually get a few UPS deliveries on weekends—it's easier to find parking, for one thing. Sometimes they even come twice a day—once in the morning and once in the late afternoon."

"Was the delivery guy someone you'd seen before?"

He pursued his lips and twisted the gold wedding band around his finger. "No, I don't think so."

"Did you get a look at him?"

"No, not really. He wasn't the usual guy, though—I know that."

"How come?"

"Most often it's Jimmy—he's from Jamaica," he said, with a glance at Lee.

"Yeah?"

"Jimmy's black. This was a white guy."

Butts looked at Lee and raised his left eyebrow just a bit.

"You sure about that?"

"Oh, yeah—definitely." Again Rodriguez looked pleased with himself, and glanced at them for signs of approval.

"Can you describe him at all?"

"Well, it's kind of hard, because he's not the kind of guy who would stand out in a crowd. I didn't really study him or nothin', you know?"

"Height, weight?"

"Average. Maybe five-ten, not built big, but not skinny either. Just average."

"Can you tell me anything else about him?"

He chewed on his lower lip, his face set in concentration. Finally he shook his head. "Naw, sorry, man. Oh, wait, yeah: he had a real soft voice—that was kind of unusual, I thought."

"Unusual how?"

"Breathy, like . . . well, this is silly, but—"

"But what?"

"Well, it kinda reminded me of Marilyn Monroe. I mean, it was definitely a dude, no question about that, but the voice . . . it was kinda weird, now that I think of it."

"Do you think you'd recognize it if you heard it again?"

"I don't know—maybe."

"Okay, thank you, Mr. Rodriguez—you've been very helpful," Butts said, closing his notebook and standing up.

Rodriguez looked at them. "If there's anything I can do," he said, lowering his voice, "anything at all, just let me know, okay?"

"We will," Lee replied. "Thanks again."

He leapt up and accompanied them out, shaking both their hands before they headed through the revolving glass doors.

"Man, I wish every interview was like that one," Butts said when they were outside on the street.

"As the song says, wouldn't it be nice?" Lee agreed.

"What song's that?" Butts said, starting to walk down Sixth Avenue toward the subway entrance.

"The Beach Boys."

"You like that stuff?"

"Some people think Brian Wilson is a genius."

"I don't know about genius, but I do know those guys sing like girls."

"What's wrong with that?"

Butts looked at him, frowning. "C'mon, Doc, you pullin' my leg?"

"I'm just asking."

Butts stopped walking and pointed to a street vendor selling Middle Eastern specialties. "I'm starving—want a sandwich?"

"Sure." He followed Butts over to the vendor's cart,

which had a sign that read HALAL FOOD. That was the Islamic version of kosher—it meant there was no pork and the food was prepared according to religious standards, though exactly what those were he wasn't sure.

The vendor was Middle Eastern, slight, and very dark-skinned, and wore a white smock and a simple white turban. Not all the vendors of halal food were orthodox, or even religious, Lee suspected, but in the wake of 9/11 he worried about anyone who looked as though he might be an Arab, or—God forbid—a Muslim. He hadn't seen any ugly instances of racism directed against them in New York, but he had heard of it elsewhere. Although the city was a place where most people got along with people from other cultures, there was no predicting the emotional fallout from something like this. It had shaken them all deeply, though in different ways.

The vendor gave them a shy but friendly smile, and Lee smiled broadly back at him. Maybe he was overreacting to the political tension in the air, but he felt protective of these people. They too were citizens of this city, and probably as horrified by the events of that terrible day as everyone else—or so he liked to think.

They ordered chicken sandwiches on pita bread, and sat down in front of the fountain at 666 Sixth Avenue to eat them. People dressed in summer clothes strolled past them in the mild August evening. The sidewalks still held the heat of the day, but the air blowing in from the river was cooler now. Yellow cabs rattled uptown, their transmissions taking a beating from potholes that pockmarked the broad avenue.

"Oh, man, this is good, isn't it?" Butts slurped, his mouth half stuffed with food.

The sandwich was delicious—hot, spicy, with grilled onions, a suggestion of cardamon, and some kind of curry powder.

"Oh, man," Butts said, wiping sauce from his mouth. "What do they put on these things? It's amazing. I gotta get the wife to try and make somethin' like this sometime."

"What does she usually make?" Lee asked.

"Corned beef, potatoes, and cabbage—that kinda thing. She's Irish," he said apologetically.

"I like a good Irish breakfast," Lee said.

"Yeah, but it's all downhill after that." Butts looked at his sandwich and sighed. "Man, sometimes I think she's allergic to spices, you know?"

"Hey, listen, my family is Scottish, and that's even worse."

Butts stared at him, a piece of grilled onion clinging to his chin. "Really?"

"They say that all Scottish cuisine is based on a dare."

"'Zat so?" Butts murmured, plunging his face deeper into his sandwich.

Lee thought the detective's unself-conscious enjoyment of food was a way of keeping his sanity amid the constant barrage of death and destruction he dealt with in his line of work.

"We're meeting first thing tomorrow in Chuck Morton's office to report on what we have."

"Okay," Butts said, licking sauce from his fingers.

"Shall I call Krieger and tell her, or do you want to?"

Butts snorted. "Oh, be my guest, by all means. I got a few leads of my own to track down tonight."

"Great," Lee said. "Thanks a lot.

"You asked," Butts said, wolfing down the rest of his sandwich. He got up stiffly, stretched his pudgy body, and brushed crumbs from his clothes. "Okay, I'm off—see you tomorrow."

"Right," Lee said, and watched the detective shoulder his way through the crowd of people swarming up Sixth Avenue. But his mind was not on them, nor on the unfinished sandwich in his hand. He kept turning the words over and over in his brain:

Ask about the red dress.

If only there was someone to ask, he thought. Of course his unconscious mind must have been controlling the pointer—that was the obvious explanation for what happened. But he was so tormented by the idea that he found himself wishing the answer were somehow buried in the wistful promise of a children's game.

CHAPTER THIRTY-NINE

"Okay," Butts said, slapping a bag of doughnuts onto Chuck's desk. "Here's what I found out. Vic Number One liked to get all lacy and decked out as a girl—pretty in pink. Wigs, makeup, heels—the whole nine yards."

It was just after nine o'clock Monday morning, and they were all there—Butts, Lee, Chuck, and Krieger. She was looking more sulky and sultry than usual, in a gray silk blouse and tight black skirt.

Butts flipped open the lid of his coffee cup and slurped loudly. "So assumin' this is the same perp, sounds like you were right on target, Doc," he told Lee.

"Good work," said Chuck. "That may shed some light on the victim profile."

"It took some digging," Butts said, gulping down more coffee.

Krieger frowned. "Why didn't a search of his apartment turn up the women's clothing?"

"Because he didn't keep them *in* his apartment," Butts announced triumphantly. "Apparently he was worried his wife would find out, so he had a little storage unit Midtown where he kept all his fancy dresses. But you figure he had to wear them somewhere, otherwise—"

"He'd be all dressed up and nowhere to go," Lee said.

"Exactly!" Butts said, raising his coffee cup as though it were a glass of champagne. "His sister finally spilled the beans, after a little persuasion that it would help find his killer."

"Well done, Detective," said Morton.

"Wait—there's more," Butts said, setting down his coffee. He was clearly enjoying himself. "Get this: Vic Number Two liked to hang out in tranny bars." He looked at them, awaiting their response.

"Wow," Lee said. "How did you get that information?"

"Let's just say that it involved a trip to Christopher Street and about a day's salary in tips to a certain bartender."

"How did you know where to go?" Krieger asked.

Butts shrugged. "I got friends in vice downtown—they know all the tranny hookers. Some of them work outta this place."

Lee always found it ironic that "vice" in law enforcement referred to illegal sex and drugs, as though those were the only offenses deserving that description.

"Do we have an ID on yesterday's victim yet?" Krieger asked.

"Yep," said Chuck. "Name's Joe Grieco, twenty-four years old, contractor working in his dad's business in Nutley, New Jersey. He was arrested for drunk driving on Friday, held overnight in the Tombs, then disappeared until he turned up yesterday with his head buried in a men's room toilet. He was ID'd by his friend he'd been out partying with on Friday."

"We should interview the friend as soon as possible," Lee said.

"As soon as we're done here," Chuck said. "I've got his cell number and address in Jersey."

"I'll do it," Butts said. "I live just down the road."

"Okay," Chuck said, picking up a manila envelope from his desk. "Now, this is what we're *not* going to release to the media." He fished out an eight-by-ten glossy crime-scene photo and pinned it up on the bulletin board next to the others.

Krieger put her hand to her mouth.

"Jesus," Butts murmured, staring at it.

The crime-scene photo showed a young man with his eyes neatly cut out of their sockets.

"That's Joe—the latest vic?" Butts asked.

"Yeah," said Chuck.

They all looked at Lee.

"What do you think it means?" Chuck asked.

Lee stared at the photo, thinking of Ana—at least he didn't have to see her face this way. A shiver wormed its way down his back.

"It could be something specific to this victim. Or—"

Krieger looked intently at him. "Or what?"

"His signature is evolving."

"That's not good," Butts said.

"In either case, it means *some*thing—the question is what?" Chuck asked.

"With the eyes, my first thought is there's an association with watching or being watched," Lee answered.

Krieger cocked her elegant head to one side and crossed her arms. "You mean he doesn't want the victim looking at him?"

"Or he *does* want to be looked at, which is why he took the eyes as trophies."

"Or maybe he's conflicted about that, too," Chuck offered.

"Either way, it's a good bet that it's linked to a specific trauma in his past," Lee said.

"Perhaps someone he loved went blind," Krieger suggested.

Lee rubbed his left temple, which was beginning to throb. "Could be. But whatever happened, it became sexualized for him—and filled him with rage."

"You really know all that from what he did?" Krieger asked. Like her smile, her tone was half challenge and half flirtation.

"There are certain constants you learn to recognize," Lee said.

"Such as?" Krieger leaned on the windowsill so that the afternoon sun fell on her upswept hair, bringing out the gold highlights. Lee wondered whether the move was conscious or not—he still was undecided about some aspects of Elena Krieger's personality.

"Mutilation of a corpse almost always has a sexual element," he replied.

"The mutilations are postmortem," Chuck pointed out. "What does that tell you?"

"That he wasn't driven by sadism—otherwise he would have done it when they were alive."

"Assuming he could control them that well," Butts pointed out, digging through his jacket pockets, looking for something. "What was the cause of death?"

"Strangulation," Chuck said.

"So he's strong," Krieger mused.

"Or he takes his victims by surprise," Lee added.

"So he didn't want them looking at him *after* they were dead," Krieger said.

"That don't make sense," Butts said, taking a bite of a powdered doughnut. "They *can't* see him once they're dead."

"Exactly," Lee agreed. "Or hear him."

"I don't understand," said Chuck.

"Hey, I think I know what you're gettin' at," Butts said. "When I was a kid, I had to go to my uncle's funeral, which was open casket. It freaked me out, lookin' at this dead guy lyin' there, and I kept waiting for his eyes to open. It was creepy—I had nightmares about it for weeks."

"So maybe something like that happened to him when he was a child?" Krieger suggested. She looked really engaged now, and had dropped her confrontational manner.

"Whatever it was," Lee said, "it filled him with a rage so deep that he has to kill over and over." He looked at the picture of poor Joe, his empty eye sockets blind as Justice herself.

"And the note?" he said.

Chuck handed him a photocopy of a handwritten note, in the same block letters as the others.

Next time I'll look twice before being such a bad
boy – <u>not.</u>

"So now he's a comedian," Butts remarked with disgust.

"It's time for some undercover work," Krieger said to Chuck.

He frowned at her, then scratched the back of his neck.

"I don't know. It sounds too dangerous, especially—"

"For a *woman*?" she said, challenging him.

"I was going to say especially after so many deaths in so short a time. We're dealing with either a particularly driven or desperate killer."

"I'm not afraid," Krieger snorted.

"You may not be," Chuck said, "but—"

Krieger wheeled around to face Lee. "Do you agree?" she demanded.

"I guess I do," he said. "Some serial killers wait weeks or

months between victims, but this one is working very fast. That could indicate he's very confident or becoming more and more enraged, and heading for a breakdown. Either way, it means he's extremely dangerous."

Krieger snorted and whipped around to focus her attention on Butts, who was calmly munching on a Bavarian crème doughnut.

"And what do you think?"

Butts held up the doughnut and inspected it as if it were a precious gem.

"I say if that's what you want, go for it."

Krieger turned to the others triumphantly. "Well?"

Chuck shook his head.

"I don't like it."

"But that's what I *do*," she protested, her voice sharp with impatience.

"I thought you were a linguistic forensic specialist," Butts said.

"That, too," she snapped back.

"Okay," Chuck said reluctantly. "But you carry a cell phone and you have a uniformed and plainclothes officer on your tail every second. See Sergeant Ruggles and he'll arrange it."

Krieger's face broke into a broad smile, showing large, somewhat horsy teeth. Lee realized this was the first time he had seen her really smile. He hoped it wasn't going to be the last.

CHAPTER FORTY

"I was wondering," Dr. Williams said, "if it's ever occurred to you that you may never find your sister's killer?"

It was early evening, and the sun snaking through the yellow curtains threw thin fingers of light onto the vase of white carnations on the table next to her. She sat with her long legs crossed at the ankles, her hands folded calmly in her lap.

Lee felt his throat constricting at her words, and the heat of shame rising from his neck.

"What makes you say that?" he asked in a tight voice.

"Well, it's a possibility you may have to face at some point, and I was just wondering if it was something you've considered." Her voice was mild and nonconfrontational, but his neck hairs bristled at the remark.

"That's a rather punitive question, isn't it?" he replied, not bothering to hide his irritation.

"Why would I want to punish you?"

"You would know that better than I would."

She leaned back in her chair, the tips of her long fingers touching.

"Actually, I was wondering if your continued search for Laura's killer could be a form of self-punishment."

He stared at her. "Why on earth would you say that?"

"Well, it is keeping open a wound, isn't it?"

"I don't see any way that would change until her killer is found."

"Other people might have decided to move on by now, that's all."

"They haven't even found her body, for God's sake! How am I supposed to 'move on'?" The blood vessels in his head were pulsating. The headache he'd been fighting all day was getting worse.

"It's interesting you're having such a strong reaction—"

"Oh, Jesus Christ!" he exploded. "What kind of reaction do you *expect*? We're talking about my sister's death—how am I *supposed* to react?"

"It's your reaction to my suggestion I'm talking about. You could have just said that was an interesting observation, and moved on. But you didn't—you saw it as an attack."

The light was directly behind her now, surrounding her head like a gauzy halo. He blinked and rubbed his temple. The light seemed to pulsate at the same speed as the throbbing in his head.

"Okay," he said, "I know where you're going with this— it's Therapy 101. The force of my reaction means that you struck a nerve, which means that the more I protest, the more you have a point. Ergo, I am using my sister's death to serve my own masochistic need to punish myself because I feel responsible somehow."

His words hung in the air, the harshness of his voice echoing in his ears. But Dr. Williams merely smiled.

"All right," she said. "Shall I write you a check this week?"

"Touché," he said, ashamed of his outburst. "But why do you always have to be so goddamn *right* all the time?"

"I'll take that as a compliment," she said, taking a sip

from her sports bottle, which was usually filled with iced tea. He was wondering if she sometimes wished it were filled with whiskey. She opened her mouth to say something, but he spoke first.

"Please don't say that my anger at you is all about my mother."

"Actually, I was going to observe that your anger at your mother is somewhat ironic," she said, crossing her legs.

"How so?"

"Well, you're mad at her because she refuses to believe your sister is dead."

"And?"

"Hasn't it ever struck you that your profession is in some ways an attempt to keep your sister alive?"

He took a deep breath.

"I don't see it that way. I know she's dead—I've accepted that. I just want to find out who killed her. And if I can't do that, then I can at least catch the people who are out there killing other people's sisters."

"Or wives, or husbands—"

"Right."

"So we're back to my first point."

"That I may never catch him."

"Or her."

Or her. Funny, but he had assumed from the first that Laura's killer would be a man—even now the idea of it being a woman struck him as odd and unlikely. Not that he believed women were incapable of great violence and evil deeds—he had too much experience for that—but he felt Laura would never have fallen victim to anyone unless she was vastly overmatched in size and physical strength.

He looked at Dr. Williams, who was smoothing her long maroon skirt as she rose from her chair.

"I'm afraid our time is up."

Later, on the walk home, as he calmed down, he realized that—as usual—there was something to what she said. He remembered as a child the feeling of worrying a scab, and the perverse satisfaction at the sight of his own blood as he pulled it away from his skin. He recalled the summer after his father left, when he had skinned his elbow jumping from the tree house next door on a dare from Drew Apthorp. She was a slim girl with smooth, straight-as-a-stick sandy hair and freckle-mottled skin who came to spend summers with her grandparents, and he had a crush on her.

He would lie in bed at night thinking of Drew, picking at his scab while listening to the buzzing of moths as they hurtled their hairy bodies against the window screens. He wondered why they were so desperate to get into the lighted room that they were willing to risk self-destruction. He remembered his fascination with the gathering globule of bright blood on his arm, and his odd enjoyment of the stinging sensation as he pulled back the scab.

He was irritated with the fact that once again Dr. Williams was right, but he was even more irritated at his own reaction. For God's sake, it *was* Therapy 101. Hit a nerve, and the patient will respond emotionally. Good Lord, he'd done it scores of times with his own patients, and knew all the signs, but when it came to his own unconscious . . . *Physician heal thyself*, indeed.

It was only now that he made the connection between his father's disappearance and the odd satisfaction he took inflicting pain on himself—as though the physical pain lightened the heaviness inside him. It was exactly the same mechanism with the "cutters"—teenagers who nicked their skin with knives or razors until the blood flowed. They too were suffering, whether from garden-variety adolescent angst or something more sinister. But somehow physical pain was preferable to the emotional kind and served as a distraction—the cutters had figured this out, and, bizarre as it looked, were actually self-medicating.

He passed the Cooper Union building, its square, red-brick facade stately and solid against the dimming evening sky. He felt a drop of rain on his cheek as he rounded the corner and swung out onto the Bowery. As he headed toward Seventh Street, he felt another drop, and then another. This was no misty autumn rain—the droplets were fat and full, falling faster and faster as he hurried toward his apartment.

A stooped old Asian woman scurried along the sidewalk, trailing a garbage bag full of plastic bottles and soda cans behind her in a rickety shopping cart. He wondered how many hours she had spent rooting through trash bins and Dumpsters in search of bottles and cans to recycle at five cents each. Her face was weathered, wizened, worried looking. Her thin brows were drawn together in a frown as she bent her head under the rapidly increasing rain.

So much misery in the world, he thought, *so much suffering.* He looked at the woman's retreating figure, her thin chicken legs and scrawny body, her feet stuffed into cheap shoes. She stopped to fish a battered green raincoat out of her shopping cart before continuing on her way. As he trudged through the rain to his building, he wondered what she was going home to. What kind of life did she have? What twists of fate had brought her to collecting discarded cans and bottles on the Bowery in the rain on a Friday night?

Later that night he sat at the piano struggling with the left hand of a Bach prelude. His right hand lay useless in his lap, and the notes winding around each other on the page made his head ache. Normally he found Bach profoundly illuminating, but tonight the scramble of black notes on the page reminded him of raindrops—and of the unending, inscrutable suffering that was mankind's lot. He forced himself to grapple a while longer, but gave up just as a clap of thunder shook the skies, as the storm settled in, rattling the windowpanes in its fury.

He got up and looked out the window. The droplets hurtled themselves at the panes just as the moths had that childhood summer so many years ago, with equal determination to get inside, it seemed. He thought about Drew Apthorp, and wondered what had become of her. *So many people who touch our lives and who we never see again.* He didn't like loose ends. He knew that life is full of them, but he still didn't like it. His sister's death was just another kind of loose end, and he ached to solve the gnawing question in his soul.

He and Drew had shared a kiss out in her grandmother's summerhouse, at the end of the long narrow lawn, on the edge of the woods. They sat on the marble bench until their legs stiffened and their bare feet got cold, as the sun settled over the tree line and the mourning doves cooed softly to each other from beneath the honeysuckle bush. The air was full of its fragrance, and the night began to come alive with the twittering and hoots of woodland creatures. Lee tasted the faint flavor of strawberries on Drew's lips as she inclined her freckled face toward him, her sandy hair brushing his cheek. It was his first kiss—he never did find out if it was hers or not. He knew even then that life would never be sweeter than it was sitting in the summerhouse kissing a girl he might never see again, but whose straight hair and freckles had become, for him, a template of beauty itself.

A gust of wind drove a sheet of rain at the window—the droplets rapped against the panes like bullets, startling him. He peered out at the Ukrainian church across the street, its huge rosary window dark and cold against the stormy sky. He thought of the window as though it looked into the mind of the killer. What source of illumination would he need to see inside that mind—to finally glimpse, and perhaps understand, the darkness within?

CHAPTER FORTY-ONE

"Look what I brought you," Caleb said, closing the door behind him as he entered the darkened room. He raised the window shade to let sunlight stream in through the grimy windows. "Why do you stay here in the dark? It's such a nice day outside—you should really get out more."

But his pa just lay there, unmoving except for his hands, which twitched spasmodically at his sides. Caleb moved closer, holding out his prize. They were still wet and dripping onto the floor, so he fished a Kleenex out of his pocket and dried them off.

"Good, aren't they?" he said, bending down so his father could see. "I like blue eyes, don't you?"

There was no reply, but he was used to that. His pa didn't talk much anymore. Caleb preferred it that way—when his father used to talk all the time, his words were so hard and cold they hurt Caleb's ears. No, it was much better like this, much easier. He could take care of his pa, and bring him what he needed—even clean him up when he soiled himself, which he was doing more often now. It was the least he could do, after all his father had done for him—brought him up all by himself, and looked after him, keeping Caleb away from wicked women and their influence. No, it was no trouble at all to look after his pa now, Caleb told himself—a good son does that when his father gets old and feeble.

He turned and put his prize in the jar with the others, then took a moment to admire them as they bobbed gently up and down in the formaldehyde. This was his first pair from a human, which was very exciting, but the others were nice, too. So many different shades of brown and blue, and one pair that was even a little bit green—hazel, his mother would have called them. Those belonged to a golden retriever who lived next door to them a few years ago, and had the unfortunate habit of waking Caleb up late at night with his barking. No one had even suspected him when the dog disappeared.

The dog's eyes were hazel, like his mother's, with little flecks of caramel brown. Even now his mother's eyes floated through his dreams at night, the brown flecks spinning and whirling like the kernels in the air popper she used to make them popcorn on Sunday night. That's when Caleb's favorite show was on—*The Wonderful World of Disney*. He liked to watch Tinker Bell fly around waving her wand as the fireworks exploded behind her—the sight always made his stomach tingle. He thought Tinker Bell looked cute in her little green outfit, and wondered if she had a fairy boyfriend who was as tiny as she was. He imagined what it would be like to be that small, and imagined himself kissing Tinker Bell. He always thought she would taste lemony, like his mother's dishwashing liquid.

When his mother was still around, she watched his show with him. They would eat popcorn together, sitting side by side on the big green sofa, their faces lit by the glow from the television screen. He still had that air popper, and now he made popcorn for himself and his father on Sunday nights. That show was no longer on the air, so he and his pa watched football, or *60 Minutes*, or whatever was on. It's too bad his mother turned out to be wicked in the end—even so, sometimes he wished she were here so she could sit with them and eat popcorn in front of the television on Sunday nights.

He put the jar back in the closet by the bed, and looked down at his father. He was working his jaw, trying to say something, but all that came out was a high squeaking sound, like a frightened mouse.

Caleb smiled indulgently. "What is it—what are you trying to say? Concentrate now," he said, bending lower so that their faces almost touched. His father's breath smelled rusty, like old coffee grounds. "Remember what I said about concentrating on each word," Caleb said with a tolerant smile.

His father struggled to speak, his face growing redder until it was a mottled scarlet. Caleb smiled down at him. He would be patient until his pa got the words out. He didn't mind waiting—he had all the time in the world.

CHAPTER FORTY-TWO

The next day Lee and Butts dropped by the Jack Hammer, after finding out from Bobby Vangetti that was where he and Joe partied the night before Joe was killed. It was a Monday, though, and the place was closed, locked, and bolted. The owner was out of town, so rather than try to get a search warrant on short notice, they planned to return when it was open, figuring the clientele would offer more leads than an empty room. Technically speaking, it wasn't a crime scene—though both Lee and Butts thought it likely Joe had met his murderer that night.

Bobby had been so stoned that night he remembered little about the evening. They failed to get much out of him during their interview, other than that he and Joe "weren't faggots," and were just there "on a kick," a phrase he repeated over and over. They suspected he had been on other things besides alcohol, but it hardly mattered; whatever altered state he was in, he couldn't remember much.

In the meantime, they decided to pay another visit to Dr. Martin Perkins. The Honorable Deborah Weinstein, the judge they approached for a warrant to search his patient files, turned out to be a stickler for civil liberties and didn't feel they had enough cause to go rifling through people's private lives.

"You're persuasive," she said, gazing up at them over bifocals while munching on a ham sandwich. "Use your charm—get the good doctor to surrender them voluntarily." She added a few choice comments about the Bush Administration's recent rollbacks on civil liberties—her refusal felt like a backlash reaction to the excesses of the White House.

They left early, driving in the opposite direction from the commuters headed into Manhattan, and arrived in Stockton in about ninety minutes. They had not warned Perkins of their visit, and they parked down the street in front of the liquor store, hoping to catch him off guard. The chances of getting something out of an interview with a potential suspect increased exponentially when you added the element of surprise.

When they knocked on the front door, it opened almost immediately to reveal Martin Perkins, immaculately dressed in a cream-colored flannel suit and Italian leather shoes. A striped blue and ivory cravat was wrapped tightly around his neck; he looked like something out of an Oscar Wilde play. A pair of old-fashioned bifocals perched precariously on his thin nose. The wire rims looked handcrafted, and the lenses had an uneven quality, the glass thicker in some places than others.

"Hello there," he said, trying unsuccessfully to sound friendly. "To what do I owe the pleasure of a return visit?"

"We just had a few follow-up questions for you," Butts replied.

"I see," Perkins said, stepping out onto the porch and closing the door behind him. "This is about poor Ana, then? I don't know what I'll be able to add, but I'm always glad to assist the law in any way I can."

"I noticed your Green Man," Lee remarked with a glance

in the direction of the statue. The stony eyes glared down at them, vines gushing out of its sculpted mouth.

"Ah, yes," Perkins said, squinting up at it. "An excellent specimen, isn't it? I found it in a wonderful antique store in Tewkesbury."

"England?" Lee asked.

"Yes, indeed. Have you ever been?"

"I have—my mother is Scottish."

"Ah, yes," Perkins said, giving Lee an appraising look over the rim of his bifocals. "You do look rather Celtic. So you know of the Green Man?"

"Yes, I do."

"Sort of like the Medusa," Butts remarked, "except it's got vines instead of snakes. It's kinda creepy."

"I see—so that is your verdict," Perkins replied with an extravagant sigh. "I'm sorry you don't appreciate my little souvenir. Shall we go inside?" He turned to open the door.

"Well, *I* think it's just the right touch for your porch," Lee said, trying to make eye contact with Butts, who was studying the statue.

"I'm glad," Perkins said, not sounding at all placated. "Come in and I'll make you some tea. That is, if that meets your approval, Detective," he added with an sardonic smile at Butts.

"Sounds good to me," Butts muttered, trundling after him.

The living room was as pristine a showroom as before—everything was in immaculate order, as though it had been prepared for a photo shoot. The tasseled pillows were perfectly plumped on the chaise longue in the corner, and the gold drapes over the French windows were swept back, displaying their expensive elegance. The brass on the fireplace tools gleamed, reflecting the cut glass on the ceiling chandelier, which sparkled like diamonds.

"Now then, I'll just fetch the tea," said Perkins.

"Please don't go to any trouble," Lee answered, but Perkins dismissed him with a wave of his elegant hand.

"I was just about to have tea myself—all I have to do is add two cups. I'll just be a minute," he said, withdrawing from the room, leaving Lee and Butts alone.

"What are you trying to do, alienate him?" Lee whispered fiercely to Butts when Perkins had gone.

Butts sank into one of the armchairs in front of the fireplace. "He gets on my nerves," he replied in a sulky voice.

"Look," Lee scolded, "as long as he's a suspect, we can't afford—"

"Yeah, I *know*," Butts said irritably. "I been doin' this a lot longer than you, Doc, so cut me some slack, will ya? He just gets my goat, is all. I'll get over it. Hey," he continued, waving a hand at the room, "I was right—no electricity."

Lee looked around at the elegant lamps in wall sconces. Butts was right—they did resemble old-fashioned gaslights. The morning sun streamed in through the French windows, so there was no way to test their theory except by coming back at night.

Hearing the sound of approaching footsteps, he cleared his throat and sat down opposite Butts. Perkins entered the room carrying an enormous silver tea tray. Lee had no doubt it was solid sterling, and couldn't help staring at it.

"Here we are," Perkins said, setting it down on the rosewood sideboard. "I hope you like Indian tea, Detective?"

"Fine with me," Butts mumbled, flicking an imaginary piece of lint from his trousers.

"I cannot abide Chinese blends," Perkins continued, setting out a plate of shortbread. "No body at all, and they have an unattractive grayish color. No, give me a good Darjeeling or an Orange Pckoe any day," he said, but Lee wasn't listening. He was trying to figure out how many hours it took to keep that tea tray polished, where Perkins and his sister got their servants, how much they paid them, and where all the money came from.

"Your house is very impressive," Lee remarked. "And your decorating style is quite—unique."

"Ah, yes," Perkins replied. "You might have said old-fashioned, but you are too polite for that. You see," he continued smoothly as he poured steaming tea from a blue chintz china pot, "my sister and I are the reincarnated spirits of a husband and wife who lived—and died—in the nineteenth century."

"Really?" said Lee, keeping his voice neutral. He glared at Butts, who was rolling his eyes.

"So," Butts asked, "are those gas lamps?"

"Yes, they are," Perkins replied smoothly. "You wouldn't believe how much more attractive they are—they cast such a soft, relaxing glow."

Perkins handed him tea in a delicate blue cup, so thin it was almost translucent. The porcelain was a creamy white, and the blue glaze was the color of a Mediterranean sky. Lee knew enough about ceramics to know that it was bone china, and very expensive. The glaze was cracked around the edges, which meant that it was also very old.

"It's Spode," Perkins said, handing Butts a cup, "in case you're interested. Blue Italian, circa 1860."

Lee raised an eyebrow and studied the cup.

"I see you've heard of him," Perkins said with a smile.

"Well, I haven't," Butts interjected. "I've got no idea what you're talkin' about."

"Josiah Spode perfected blue glazing in the late eighteenth century in England. And as if that weren't enough, he also invented bone china by adding bone ash to the formula for porcelain, which had been perfected by the Chinese centuries earlier," Perkins explained, stirring sugar into his tea. "It's the finest quality of English china, delicate but strong."

"Oh," said Butts. He looked unimpressed.

"Are you a fancier of antiques, Dr. Campbell?" Perkins asked, settling down on a blue and gold flowered love seat with matching tassels.

"My mother is," Lee answered.

"Ah, then you must bring her around sometime. I would be happy to give her a tour of my humble abode. There may be some items of interest to her, and I'm always happy to meet a fellow aficionado."

"Thanks, but she lives in Texas," Lee lied.

He avoided looking at Butts to see his reaction to the lie.

The detective cleared his throat. "So, you and your sister are . . . reincarnated, you said?"

"I don't expect you to understand," Perkins said with another dismissive wave of his hand. "In fact, I wouldn't even have mentioned it if not for the fact that you noticed the Green Man."

Butts's brow furrowed, increasing his resemblance to a pockmarked bulldog. "What's that got to do with the Green Man?"

"It's a long story," Perkins answered. "Perhaps another time."

"Where is your sister?" Butts asked, looking around. Except for the sound of their voices and the rattling of teacups, the house was still and silent.

"Oh, Charlotte was called out suddenly," Perkins said. "She's a midwife by vocation, and one of her patients found herself unexpectedly in labor, a week or so early."

Lee couldn't help thinking there were midwives in the nineteenth century, though he knew there were plenty in the present day as well.

"That's what happened when my son was born," Butts said. "He popped out ahead of schedule. Surprised the hell out of my wife—she was in the housewares aisle at the IGA."

"How very interesting," Perkins murmured. Lee couldn't tell if he was mocking Butts or being sincere, since his voice always had an edge. "Do you have any hobbies, Detective?" he asked, leaning back in the love seat and putting his feet up. A casual observer might think he was the picture of relaxation and ease, but a vein in his neck twitched, and he was blinking frequently. Lee suspected that the languorous pose was just that—a pose.

"I leave that to the wife," Butts replied, slurping his tea. "She's the one with the spare time. I spend most of my time chasin' down bad guys, and that keeps me pretty busy," he added with a significant look at Perkins.

"Yes, I can imagine," Perkins replied, raising his teacup to his lips and sipping delicately, his lips barely grazing the lip of the cup. Once again, Lee was reminded of an actor playing a role. Everything about Perkins was theatrical, as though done for effect, from the crisp striped cravat around his neck to the precise, archaic phrasing of his speech. There was something odd going on here—he just didn't know what it was yet.

"Not to press the point," he ventured, "but have you always known you were—uh, reincarnated?"

"No," Perkins said, setting down his teacup. "You see, Charlotte and I are neo-pagans—it's the modern version of the ancient Celtic religion. Hence the Green Man on the porch—it's a symbol that is particularly meaningful to people of our faith."

Lee looked at Butts, but the detective was showing admirable discipline. His face betrayed no sign of disbelief or disdain.

"Yes," Lee said. "Go on."

"The pagan faith has in common with Buddhism the belief in reincarnation," Perkins continued, "though there are differences in the way we believe it manifests. Well, when we became members of the Old Religion, as we call it, we discovered that we in fact were reincarnated souls from the nineteenth century—husband and wife, to be exact. No doubt you observed a certain old-fashioned style in our manner of dress," he added.

"Now that you mention it," Lee said, "I did."

Perkins indicated a pair of portraits hanging over the parlor grand piano.

"That's us," he said casually. "Or rather, that *was* us about a hundred and fifty years ago."

Lee rose to study the portraits. One was of a handsome man of middle years, with thick black hair, high cheekbones, deep-set eyes, and a full mouth. The hair was oiled and slicked back, but from the rogue curls around his temples, it was clear that had taken some effort. The likeness was so remarkable that Lee could have been looking at a painting of himself. Taken aback, he turned to look at the woman. To his relief, she looked like no one he knew. She had a sweet, heart-shaped face, full lips and large, intelligent gray eyes.

He turned back to Perkins, who smiled. "No doubt you are struck by the resemblance between Mr. McLean and yourself. I too noticed it when we first met. Perhaps that accounts for the certain . . . simpatico between us."

Lee felt no such thing, but he nodded. He wanted to keep Perkins talking.

"That's your ancestor?" Butts said. Lee thought he was being deliberately dense.

"Not my *ancestor*, Detective," Perkins corrected him. "That is the man whose soul I now possess."

Butts stared at him, then muttered, "Oh, yeah—right."

"I don't expect you to believe me," Perkins said, pouring himself more tea. "Few people outside of the Old Religion do, of course. But those of us who know better—well, let's just say our number is small, but our membership is growing."

"And was Ana Watkins one of your new members?" Butts asked.

Well done, Lee thought, *catch him off guard.*

But Perkins didn't answer immediately, no doubt giving himself time to formulate a response that wouldn't let slip anything he didn't want revealed. He rose and took the plate of shortbread from the tray, offering it to Butts.

"Would you care for a lemon cream tea biscuit?"

"Thanks," Butts said. Taking one, he settled his stocky body back in the armchair. Without taking his eyes off Perkins, he waited for his answer.

Lee relaxed. Butts was back on form, playing his hand like the pro he was. It was a mistake to ever let your feelings toward a suspect get in the way of the job you had to do, which was to get information.

Perkins took a piece of shortbread and sat back down on the chaise longue.

"Ana Watkins," he declared, "was a very confused young woman. At least, she was when she came to me. She was making progress, though—real progress," he added, shaking his head sadly. "That's what makes her death a double tragedy—not only did she have her entire life in front of her but she was beginning to take control of it."

"So was she a member of—the 'Old Religion?'" Butts persisted.

Perkins bit his cookie in half and chewed thoughtfully. "Ana was an interesting case. She had repressed memories, you know—terrible things had happened in her past, and I was using hypnosis to free up those memories. And while she was under hypnosis, she began having other memories as well—recollections of a past life."

"So you helped her to 'remember' this past life?" Butts said.

"Well, yes. Once she started having these experiences, naturally I was there to facilitate anything that came up."

"I see. And what form did this 'facilitating' take?"

"Nothing dramatic, Detective, if that's what you're getting at," Perkins replied. "I merely wrote down what she said under hypnosis so she could read it later. Like a lot of people, she had almost complete amnesia regarding what went on during her sessions, once she came out of them."

"Oh, really?" Butts said. "That must be pretty tempting for you with an attractive young woman like that. I mean, if she didn't remember what went on while she was being hypnotized, then you could pretty much do whatever you wanted, I guess."

Perkins regarded him with a mixture of disappointment and pity. "I fear you've been chasing criminals too long, Detective. Your mind seems to be stuck permanently in the gutter."

Unperturbed, Butts took a bite of his cookie, crumbs tumbling onto his trousers; a few of them fell onto the carpet. As Perkins watched, Lee saw his hands twitch and jerk. It occurred to him that Perkins might have OCD, or obsessive compulsive disorder, in which case it would be very difficult for him to watch crumbs falling on his carpet. The twitching might be his impulse to scoop them up.

"It's my job to consider all the angles," Butts said placidly. "So you're saying you never laid a hand on her?"

"Even if I had been tempted—which I wasn't, by the way—I would never betray my profession or my patients like that. I merely assisted in guiding her thoughts where they were headed and recorded what she said. Why?" he said, his eyes narrowing. "Was her murder a sex crime?"

Lee intervened. He wanted to give Perkins as little information as possible.

"No," he said, "but with an attractive young woman we have to consider all the possibilities."

"I see," Perkins said, giving him a searching look. Lee thought Perkins was clever enough to sense he might be lying, but kept his face blank as a poker champion—or so he hoped.

"I hope you will appreciate the delicacy of our task," Lee added, realizing once again that he was beginning to sound like Perkins, adopting his quaint and archaic manner of speech.

Perkins smiled. "As to the answer to your question, Detective, Ana wasn't a member of our faith. But she was becoming interested in it, especially as she found herself repeatedly recollecting a past life. She was beginning to think we were on to something."

"And what about you?" Butts asked. "Did you encourage her belief?"

"I neither encouraged nor discouraged it. As her therapist, it is—was—my job not to tell her what to believe, but to support her in the search for truth."

"And how was that going—her search for truth?"

"As I indicated, I felt she was on the verge of a real breakthrough."

"Does it usually happen like that?" Butts asked, leaning forward so the small pile of crumbs on his trouser leg tumbled to the floor. "I mean, that's kind of strange to know you were abused but not who did it?"

"It's not all that unusual, Detective," Perkins replied with a dismayed glance at the crumbs scattered on the expensive wool carpet. "When things are deeply buried in the unconscious mind, you'd be surprised. They can emerge any which way, years or even decades later, in bits and pieces, all higgledy-piggledy sometimes. As a therapist, you have to be flexible—and ready for whatever emerges."

"Well, I guess that's where your job and mine are alike," Butts remarked. "We both have to be ready for whatever emerges."

Butts had a friendly smile on his face, but Perkins frowned at him, perhaps suspicious he was now the one being mocked. Lee had to hand it to the stubby detective for turning the tables so neatly—in spite of his rumpled appearance and unsophisticated manner, Butts was a crafty investigator with a keen mind. He used his homely ways to mislead suspects into a sense of false superiority, catching them off guard, as he had just done with Perkins.

Their host rose from his chair and pulled his gold watch from his vest pocket.

"Oh, dear," he said, "you'll have to forgive me. I am chairman of the Neighborhood Watch committee, and I have a meeting in twenty minutes." He smiled at Butts. "You were right, Detective—our jobs are not dissimilar at all."

"One more thing," Lee said as they walked toward the door. "I don't suppose you'd let us have a look at your patient files, just in case Ana's killer was—"

"One of my patients?" Perkins replied. "Oh, dear me, no—that's highly unlikely. And I'm afraid I couldn't violate doctor–patient confidentiality—not without a warrant, of course. What a pity you couldn't get a judge to give you one. Better luck next time," he said, patting Lee on the back as though he were a child going off to school. Lee glanced at Butts, who looked as though he were about to explode. He hustled the detective out to the car before he say anything—no sense in alienating Perkins when he might still prove useful to them.

As they walked through the foyer on the way to the front door, Lee glanced at a table of magazines in the hallway. On top of the pile was a copy of *Better Homes and Gardens*—the same magazine from which Ana's threatening note had been constructed. But Chuck had said only her prints had been found on it. And yet . . . he couldn't help wonder if there was a connection.

As Lee and Butts drove up the hill toward Fiona Campbell's house, Lee reflected upon how neatly Perkins had managed to gain the upper hand once again. Just when they were closing in on him, he wriggled out of the net. It was frustrating, though Lee suspected Butts had plenty of experience with slippery suspects. But without more forensic evidence, their hands were tied.

He glanced over at Butts, who was slumped down in the seat staring out the window. His body language said it all: Perkins had managed to evade them twice now. From the determined set of the detective's jaw, though, Lee knew it would not happen a third time.

CHAPTER FORTY-THREE

Lee had promised his mother he would stop by briefly, and it was a short drive up the hill to her house. When Lee and Butts stepped out of the car, they were greeted by a chorus of giggles. But when they looked around, they couldn't see the source of all the merriment. The woods lay lush around them, in shameless summer fullness, with the deep green decadence of late August. The leaves clung to the trees as if they knew that in just a few weeks they would be parting forever, in the eternal seasonal cycle of death and renewal.

The giggles sounded again, and Lee heard rustling in the bushes next to the toolshed. There was no garage on the property, only an old wooden toolshed at the foot of the driveway. Fiona always claimed to like it that way, saying that she didn't see any reason cars had to be "put to bed at night, as though they were children." Lee suspected she just didn't want to spend the money. Cars meant nothing to her—she drove a battered old blue Pontiac. She preferred to lavish her time and money on antiques and expensive home furnishings. Her house looked like something out of an upscale decorating magazine, with English hunting prints, medieval armoires, and handwoven Persian carpets.

Lee peered into the thicket surrounding the shed and saw a flash of yellow hair, then red. "I see two little birds hiding in the bushes," he said, coming closer.

The giggles resumed again, growing more hysterical, as two small figures tumbled out of the bushes onto the lawn—his niece Kylie and her friend Meredith. The girls rolled around on their backs, laughing and clutching at each other, until Kylie got to her knees, panting.

"Did we scare you, Uncle Lee?"

"Well, I was certainly surprised," he said.

Meredith got to her feet and brushed the grass from her clothes. She wore green pedal pushers and a yellow T-shirt, while Kylie had on a white cotton dress with purple flowers. Meredith's bright red hair was in a thick braid down her back, and if not exactly pretty, at least she looked less odd than she had on Kylie's birthday.

"Who's that?" Meredith said, squinting up at Detective Butts, who was fishing a cigar out of his jacket pocket.

"That's Detective Butts," Lee replied.

"No way!" Meredith said. "That is so *cool*!"

"Uncle Lee works with detectives all the time," Kylie said airily, pulling twigs and leaves from her hair. Her bare knees had grass stains, and her fingertips were stained purple.

"You're a real detective?" Meredith said, walking over to Butts. She was only a few inches shorter than he was.

"Yup," he said, placing the cigar between his teeth. "For instance, I know you've been berry picking."

"Hey," said Kylie. "How can you know that?"

Meredith laughed and grabbed Kylie's hand, holding up her stained fingertips.

"*Duh*," she snorted. "That's an easy one."

"You want me to do something harder?" Butts asked, regarding her through half-closed eyes.

"Uh—sure," Meredith answered, and Kylie nodded.

"Then stick around," Butts said. "I'll come up with something when you least expect it."

"Okay," Meredith said. "Can I be your assistant?"

"I don't see why not," Butts replied.

"Me too!" Kylie chimed in. "Can I be your second assistant?"

"Okay. You can both be my assistants."

Lee was pleased to see how sweet the burly detective was with the girls. He would not have guessed Butts had a soft spot for kids, but he had learned that people are often surprising.

"Okay," Lee said. "Shall we go find Fiona?"

"Oh, she's with *Stan*," Meredith said, poking Kylie in the ribs.

Stan Paloggia was Fiona's boyfriend, or, as she called him, "my ha-ha boyfriend," insisting she was too old to be dating anyone. Stan didn't share her view—he was doggedly faithful, following her around like a trained seal. Fiona took frequent breaks from his devoted companionship, and refused to marry him, though he had had asked her half a dozen times. For instance, she hadn't invited him to Kylie's birthday dinner, which was typical of how she treated him.

"Is he your grandmother's boyfriend?" Butts asked.

Meredith lopped off the top of a honeysuckle bush and waved the plucked sprig under her nose, inhaling deeply. "Stan *loves* her."

Kylie grabbed a honeysuckle branch of her own and yanked, but it was too thick and wouldn't come off. Lee leaned down and broke it off for her. The honeysuckle this year was wild, rampant, growing everywhere with heedless promiscuity. He loved the smell, but Fiona hated it—she waged a continuous war against "those cheeky weeds," as she called them. Fiona wasn't enamored of flowers of any kind. As far as she was concerned, if you couldn't eat it, it wasn't worth growing.

When they arrived at the house, Fiona insisted they stay for iced tea and lemon cake. Lee was about to protest, but when he saw Butts's eyes light up at the mention of lemon cake, he acquiesced. They went out to the front porch, where the girls volunteered to set the table.

Fiona pointed to a round wrought-iron table with a glass cover.

"My latest estate sale acquisition. How do you like it?"

"Very nice," Butts remarked, settling his bulk into the nearest chair.

"It's late nineteenth century," she said, flicking away a few stray twigs from its polished surface. "I don't want to scratch it. . . . Let's see, what can I use? Oh, yes!" She turned to Lee. "Last week I came across straw place mats I'd completely forgotten about. . . . Where did I see them?" she said. "Oh, I remember—they're in the closet where I keep the Christmas ornaments."

"I'll get them," he said.

He went inside and climbed the stairs to the second-floor landing, where there was a built-in closet in the hallway. He opened it and began to look among the boxes of ornaments, wrapped in crumpled bits of tissue paper, faded and brittle with age. Fiona never could stand to throw anything away if it could be at all useful. That included old tissue paper, so the ornaments were carefully wrapped in the same ragged, yellowed bits of paper year after year.

At the back of the closet, he saw the edge of what looked like a green leather book of some kind. He pulled it out carefully—he had never seen it before. On the front, in gold script, the word SCRAPBOOK was embossed. He opened the cover and carefully leafed through the yellowing pages. There were many photos of himself and Laura as children— playing with cousins, opening Christmas presents, dressing their fat yellow tabby cat in baby clothes, squinting into the sun in front of their aunt's swimming pool. There were even a few photos of Fiona herself, though none of his father. Lee didn't know what she had done with all the pictures of him after he left—perhaps she had burned them.

As he reached the middle of the album, a piece of paper fell out. He bent down to pick it up and saw that it was a birth certificate. It was dated two years after Laura was born.

State of New Jersey

BORN TO: *Duncan and Fiona Campbell*

Adrian Campbell, baby boy

And underneath it, one word: *Stillborn.*

He stared at it. This was the first time he had any inkling that he and Laura had very nearly had a baby brother. His mother had never spoken of it. And yet, in a flash, it explained everything.

"So that's what happened," he murmured.

He slipped the document back where he had found it and replaced the book. He didn't know why his mother had kept this secret from them all these years. Maybe she didn't want their pity, maybe she didn't want to relive that horrible day, or maybe it was too linked with their father's desertion. Whatever her reason, the subject was clearly taboo. And yet she had saved his birth certificate—which, sadly, was also his death certificate. He wondered if she was even aware she still had it. But knowing how obsessively organized Fiona was, he thought it more likely that she had sent him to find the place mats because, on some unconscious level, she wanted him to find it.

But at last Lee understood his mother's need to suppress her emotions. If she ever fully unleashed her grief and rage, he thought, she must imagine the resulting torrent would drown her. He found the place mats, closed the closet door, and went back downstairs. The irony didn't escape him— now he and his mother each had a secret to keep from each other.

CHAPTER FORTY-FOUR

Hildegard Elena Krieger von Boehm leaned over and scrutinized her makeup in the beveled mirror over the antique mahogany vanity. The dressing table, imported from Hamburg, was a birthday gift from her father. Squinting, she rubbed a stray smear of mascara from her smooth pink cheekbone and brushed on some rouge ("Afterglow" by Max Factor, a good Polish Jew, as her Vati would say). Turning her head this way and that, she flipped her thick red hair from her muscular shoulders and shook her head to make it appear fuller and a bit disheveled. She knew that men liked the tousled, just-from-the-bedroom look. Though she hated having a single hair out of place, she was willing to do whatever the job required. That was one of the secrets to her rapid rise within the ranks of the NYPD.

Hildegard Elena Krieger von Boehm—or Elena Krieger, as she was known—was not as hard as she appeared on the outside. For instance, she had made the decision upon entering the New York City police force to use her middle name instead of her Wagnerian-sounding first name. She also dropped the "von Boehm," an indication in Germany of her family's noble blood (Beethoven, for instance, hoped the "van" in his name would give the appearance of nobility). It was all well and fine to have a "von" in front of your name when you were in Düsseldorf, but in America, she feared, it would simply conjure up images of Nazi storm troopers. Krieger was her mother's maiden name, whereas "von Boehm"—her paternal family name—meant "from Bohemia."

She regarded most Americans as pitifully unaware of their heritage. Germanic blood still ranked as their most common ancestral lineage—more ubiquitous than English or Dutch. A large number of Hessian mercenaries settled in states such as Pennsylvania after the Revolution and were given land in exchange for their promise to never take up arms against the United States again. This fact troubled Hildegard Krieger not a bit. She regarded practicality—which might manifest on occasion as discreet opportunism—as a virtue. Though the irony of the situation was not lost on her, she thought her ancestral cousins had made a good investment. Why travel back across a treacherous sea to a crowded, contentious continent scarred by centuries of squabbling when you could start afresh in a new, relatively unsettled land of unrivaled abundance and beauty?

She lifted the crimson feather boa from its box, peeling away layers of crumbling tissue paper, and wound it around her neck. She had worn it only once before, in a cabaret show back in Germany, where her talent and taste for acting were already apparent. She wasn't sure why she had saved it, but now she thought it was the perfect touch to her costume: over the top but classy, made of the finest peacock feathers Deutsche Marks could buy.

She puckered her lips and swiveled her hips back and forth, tilting her chin forward in a come-hither look. She opened her mouth in a wide smile, trying to imitate the famous portrait of Marilyn Monroe in which the actress looks as if she is about to gobble up the camera in one ravenous bite. Regarding her reflection in the mirror, Hildegard heaved a sigh and plopped down on the green satin cushioned chair. There was no denying it—she was more Dietrich than Monroe, with an aggressive masculine edge no amount of makeup or feather boas could disguise. Maybe that accounted for her talent at undercover work. She seemed to be born with an urge to slip into another persona, something more socially acceptable.

Not that Elena Krieger felt any shame or guilt over her heritage—she was proud of her background, and identified closely with her Germanic forefathers, who included (on her mother's side) Johann Wolfgang von Goethe, the great poet and playwright.

She plucked a tissue from the box on her vanity and dabbed at her lips, blotting the thick layer of lipstick. Why, she had even read Goethe—in German, of course—at school, and rather enjoyed his play *Faust.* What a great story, what an archetypal struggle! She certainly possessed the Germanic passion for heroic stories—she also admired the Ring cycle, even though she found operatic singing distasteful. She loved the staging and was always thrilled by the entrance of the Rhinemaidens and their *Ho-jo-to-hos.*

Hildegard Krieger was a something of a Rhinemaiden herself. A woman with energy, flair, and ambition in a world still largely populated and controlled by men, she sometimes had the urge to mount a white steed and soar over the wild, mountainous landscape of her ancestors—all the while quite conscious of the ridiculousness of her taste for self-dramatization.

Still, life at the NYPD had never been easy for her, so she donned a hard, brittle shell that was only part acting. As a woman, a German, and a lesbian, she knew what it to be an outsider. To her delight—if hardly her surprise—she found the ranks of lesbians within the force were strong.

Some of them were mannish like her, while others were softer and more "femme." She had a certain cachet and popularity among the other dykes, because of her exotic looks and accent. Some women found that alluring, especially if they were into sadomasochistic role playing.

But Hildegard had no wish to squander her time and energy on sexual peccadilloes. There would be time for that later. What she wanted more than anything was to rise within the ranks—she longed someday to be a station commander. She watched very carefully every move Chuck Morton made. She knew that as head of the Bronx Major Case Unit he was one of the most respected and successful members of the NYPD brass.

She looked into the mirror, drew the wine-colored feather boa across her bare shoulders, and shivered. Captain Morton was quite attractive, too, she had to admit—those bluer-than-blue eyes and tight, muscular body. A smile crept across her face as she thought about what it would be like to throw him across that big oak desk and . . . *What was she thinking?* First of all, he was her boss. Second, he was married, and third, she was a lesbian.

Actually, her sexual identity was not that clear cut. The truth was that sometimes she liked women, and sometimes she liked men. She had had both, and was aware of the advantages of each. Men were exciting, primal, commanding—and, like a lot of strong women, Hildegard Krieger enjoyed being dominated sexually. She liked the way they smelled, of aftershave and cigars and saltwater. On the other hand, women were beautiful and soft and took their time. In general she found them to be more considerate lovers. She was attracted to quite feminine lesbians, women whose "secret" was not readily apparent—that was part of their allure. Men could undress them with their eyes as they walked across a room, but she was the one they went home with at the end of the night.

She picked up her tiny leather purse and took one final look in the mirror. She liked what she saw. Her lanky body was clad in a short black leather miniskirt that hugged her narrow hips. Over that she wore a red silk bodice drawn tightly in to slim her waist, which she thought was too thick. Over it she wore a short black leather jacket, and around her neck she had flung the red boa. Her heels were at least three inches high, and her slender legs looked even longer in black fishnet stockings.

Still, it wasn't quite right—something was missing. On impulse, she jabbed a long red fingernail at the fabric and tugged, ripping a small, ragged hole in the diamond-patterned weave. She surveyed the results with satisfaction. That was it, she thought: now she looked like a proper slut. She felt the familiar shiver of pleasure in her intestines in the presence of danger. The fact that she had told no one about her plan heightened the excitement.

The hunt was on, and she was the bait. It was time to go trap a murderer.

CHAPTER FORTY-FIVE

The scene at the Jack Hammer was just starting to heat up on this steamy Friday night. It was early yet—not even nine o'clock—and most of the action usually took place after midnight. But the heat had brought people out into the night to escape the confines of their stuffy apartments. Like cockroaches skittering out from beneath the refrigerator, they ventured in swarms into the darkness in search of adventure and sex.

The bar scene around Christopher Street had never fully recovered from the AIDS crisis, but widespread use of condoms and the advent of more effective antiretroviral medication had revived the scene in the last few years. Although still not what it used to be, it was the place to go if you wanted a drink, a dance, and a date with some husky young stranger who would go to bed with you and disappear the next morning, no questions asked. The Jack Hammer was not an upscale place like The Townhouse, a piano bar on East Fifty-eighth Street where older gentlemen of means went to meet younger men. It catered to rough trade, and the atmosphere of danger added to the thrill of the chase for many of the customers.

At the Jack Hammer, gym rats mingled with bikers, and cross-dressers of all races and ages rubbed shoulders with trannies and personal trainers. Beer was sold behind the bar, but sex was the main entrée on the menu. Testosterone swirled in the air along with the cigarette smoke that curled in blue clouds under the hot colored lights on the dance floor—red, pink, and blue, just enough light to illuminate the sweating bodies, but not quite enough to make out the faces.

It was into this atmosphere Hildegard Elena Krieger stepped, clad in her red bustier, boa, and torn fishnet stockings. This was where Joe had gone with his friend the night before he died, she knew, so this is where she must be.

She had played many roles in her time, but had never impersonated a man dressed as a woman. Excitement and fear wormed their way through her gut as she pranced down the narrow steps to the entrance, balancing precariously on her three-inch heels. She felt like she was going to be sick, she was terrified, and she had never felt so alive. Like many people who take up careers in law enforcement, Elena Krieger was addicted to danger, and her adrenal gland was working overtime tonight.

She had ignored Chuck Morton's advice—she didn't really think of it as an order—to have backup. She felt it would interfere with her cover identity; she knew from experience that an undercover role was only effective if the mark, or target, couldn't smell a rat—and some of them had a very well-developed sense of smell. If the killer came to this bar, she would find him—before he found her.

The pounding of percussion made her head vibrate as she tossed her boa over her shoulder and stepped into the darkened room. She was instantly swallowed up by the crush of bodies twisting in a fog of swirling blue smoke.

CHAPTER FORTY-SIX

Lee sat at the cafe at the Eighty-second Street Barnes & Noble, playing the table upgrade game. Customers perched on the edges of their chairs, waiting for someone to vacate a better table than the one they occupied. Downstairs, people glided dreamily between shelves of books, roving planets in a shifting constellation of bodies.

He and Kathy were meeting there, but he had come early to be alone for a while, to think about the case somewhere outside his apartment or Chuck's office. Sometimes a change scenery helped him think about things in a new way, and he liked bookstores. He inhaled the musty, comforting aroma of paper, book bindings, and steaming espresso. It was the smell of thought, of learning, of culture and commerce coming together in a calming cacophony of cookbooks and coffee. The voices all blended into one, a smooth overlay of sound soothing as raindrops.

We seek each other, he thought, looking around. These people weren't here for the coffee or the books or the pastries—they were there for the nearness of other human bodies.

And now he was seeking someone in a different kind of

way. He yearned for this man's capture almost as one might yearn for a lover—as his killer might yearn for the victims he killed seemingly so heartlessly. These crimes were anything but heartless, of course. Some murders were heartless—people who killed for money or property—but not this murderer. He was full of repressed rage, and though his choice of victims might seem impersonal to the untrained observer, they were very personal to him.

Lee sensed something else behind the brutality, a motif running like an underground stream beneath the carnage: loss, longing, and disappointment.

The bearded man next to him was playing with his PalmPilot. Lee wondered whether all these gadgets were really useful time-saving devices or merely sophisticated toys. And did it even matter? Toy or time-saver, what was the difference as long as people were enjoying themselves? His killer was enjoying himself—that was for certain. Or, at least, in whatever way a tortured soul like him could be said to be enjoying anything. Was a compulsive act an enjoyment, or merely the scratching of an unbearable itch?

He looked up to see Kathy headed his way, slipping in between the rows of tables, cheeks flushed, her dark hair tousled. The sight of her made his stomach do a little flip.

"Hi—am I late?" she said, seeing his half-empty coffee cup.

"No, I got here early," he said, pulling up a chair for her.

"The train was a nightmare," she said, setting her cloth briefcase next to her. "What are you drinking?"

"Just coffee."

She frowned and twisted around in her chair to squint at the menu over the counter.

"Hmm. I think I'll go for something stronger. Be right back."

She slipped between the crowded tables to the coffee bar and returned balancing a cup of espresso and a piece of carrot cake.

"Help yourself," she said, putting out two forks.

"Thanks."

Kathy took a sip of espresso, a little bit of foam clinging to her upper lip. He wanted to lean forward and lick it off. She flicked her little pink tongue over it and it was gone.

"Working on the case?" she asked, seeing his notes spread out on the table.

"Yeah."

"Making any progress?"

"Hard to say . . . it's a tough one."

"Do you ever think what that would be like?" she said in a low voice.

"What?"

"To totally lack compassion or remorse."

"I've tried—it's nearly impossible. It's like trying to imagine being an alcoholic if you're not one."

She leaned over the table, her breasts brushing the table-top.

"And if these people really are lacking these qualities, is it their fault?"

"Probably not. But does that matter? They have to be stopped, they have to be caught, and they have to be imprisoned. There's no other solution."

He had been through all this in his head, many times—but he wasn't going to tell Kathy that. He wondered if she was aware that the woman sitting at the next table was listening to them. Her untouched tea sat in front of her, and she had been staring at the same page in her book for the past five minutes. She was doughy and middle-aged, with heavily mascaraed eyes and a bad dye job, her hair the color of a shiny new penny. An oversized leather bag lay at her feet, and when Lee and Kathy paused in their conversation, she pretended to fumble around in it, but she never pulled anything out. Lee put her down as a fan of mystery novels, the kind where the heroine has lots of cats and solves crimes while holding down a job as the local librarian.

"What kind of creatures *are* we?" Kathy said, running her fingers lightly over the lip of her coffee cup.

"Creatures of extremes," Lee replied. "We seem to be capable of the worst and the best that Nature has to offer."

"Or is that just our egocentric view of things?" Kathy mused. "Are we really all that—from Auschwitz to the Sistine Chapel? And is it all because we happen to have opposable thumbs?"

Lee smiled. "You're the scientist. Don't forget our enormous brain . . . and the capacity for speech. I suppose orangutans would build cities if they could."

"Do you think they'd also build concentration camps?"

"Even dolphins engage in 'criminal activity'—according to the Science Channel."

"Wise guy, eh?" she said, imitating a thirties movie mobster. "Bringing dolphins into it?"

He did his best to imitate her accent.

"Yeah, sure—you gonna do something about it?"

She made a fist. "Why, I oughta—"

Lee glanced at the eavesdropping woman, who quickly pretended to be reading. He looked back at Kathy. "You know, I keep feeling I failed Ana."

"What do you mean?"

"I'm afraid that if she had been any other patient—any other person—I might have taken it more seriously and she might not have died."

As he said this he could feel the lady at the next table leaning in to listen.

Kathy frowned. "What do you mean 'any other patient'?"

Suddenly he felt an impulse to tell her everything—he hated having secrets from her.

"What is it?" she asked, seeing the look on his face.

He rubbed his eyes and looked away. "There's more to it than I told you before." He proceeded to tell her about the way Ana tried to seduce him. He left out nothing, including the fact that she almost succeeded—partially succeeded, actually. By way of explanation, he talked about the seductive nature of the therapeutic relationship, but as he did he saw Kathy stiffen.

The lady at the next table continued to pretend to read, not taking her eyes from the print, but she didn't turn the page once.

When he had finished, Kathy was silent.

"Well," she said after a painfully long pause, "maybe you're right. Maybe you would have reacted differently. But I don't know what you could have done."

She looked away, clearly uncomfortable. Her voice lacked its normal warmth, though she was obviously trying to hide her reaction.

"Kathy?" he said. "Do you view my past with Ana as a threat to—to us?"

"No, of course not," she answered too quickly.

"It was my first year in practice. I was naïve and unprepared—"

"You don't have to explain it to me," she said, still not looking at him.

He thought the lady at the next table was going to fall out of her chair if she leaned in toward them any more.

"I want to explain," he said. "I feel I owe you—"

"You don't owe me anything," Kathy replied, studying her untouched cake.

"Please, Kathy, I really need you to understand."

"Look, can we just move on?" she said. "Can we talk about something else?"

"But I want to—"

"You don't get it, do you?" she said, looking directly at him. "It's in your past, and there's nothing either of us can do to change it—or my reaction to it. I think it's childish and petty, and I'm not proud of the way I feel, but for now I'm stuck with it. So let's just move on, okay?"

He saw a pained expression he had never seen before in her face. It cut him to know that he was the cause of it.

"Okay," he said. "We'll move on."

They tried to talk about other things, but the air between them was strained now, her discontent hanging over them like a fog. After a few desultory attempts at conversation, she finished her coffee in one swallow and stood up.

"I'm tired—it's been a long week."

His heart gave a single quick thump. "You want to go back to my place?"

"I think I'll stay at Arlene's place tonight, if you don't mind."

Arlene was her friend in Murray Hill who traveled constantly and was rarely home. They had gone to school together, and Kathy had keys to her apartment.

"Okay," he said.

She bit her lip. "I just need some time."

"Sure," he said. "Whatever."

"I'll call you tomorrow," she said. Shouldering her bag, she snaked her way through the tables and down the stairs to the main floor. Her watched her black curls bounce as she walked through the stacks of books, hoping she would look back at him before leaving the store, but she didn't.

He stared out the window for a while, watching people stroll west along Eighty-second Street on their way to Riverside Park. A thin boy of about nine rode his bike next to his mother, who carried shopping bags in either hand, laughing at something her son was saying. He thought of his own mother and wondered if she had ever taken that kind of delight in him. He wished he could hear what the boy was saying, wished he had the secret to making women happy. He had no luck on the genetic front there, he thought bitterly. His father had done nothing but break his mother's heart— all their hearts, for that matter.

He was about to get up from his table when he felt a hand touch his shoulder, and turned to see the lady with the cloth bag standing next to him.

"She loves you, you know," she said. Her accent was British, refined and educated.

"What?" he replied, taken off guard.

"I know it's none of my business, of course, but you can see it in every move she makes. She's in love with you. She didn't leave because she doesn't care about you—she left because she cares too much."

"Oh," was all he could say.

"You'll see I'm right," the woman continued. "I know about these things. I can always read strangers. It's a gift, I suppose—and a curse. My Henry used to say that I should be a psychologist or something like that, but it's not something you can study." She shrugged. "It's—"

"A gift, I know."

"You do?"

He hesitated. This was surely the oddest conversation he had ever had with a stranger.

"I'm just saying that I understand what you're saying—" he said, but she interrupted him.

"I *knew* it!" she crowed, her face breaking into a broad smile. "You have it, too. I had a feeling about you, but I wasn't sure." She patted him on the shoulder. "Use it well—that's the only advice I can give you."

"Look—" he began, but she shook her head.

"No need to say anything more. I understand perfectly. But mark my words, will you? She loves you. She'll come around, but you have to be patient. Don't try to understand her reaction, because she doesn't even understand it herself. She just has to work her way out of it over time, but it will happen." She smiled at him fondly, like an indulgent aunt. "I hope the two of you are very happy together. I have a feeling you will be."

"That's very kind of you, but—" he started, but once again she cut him off.

"I know, I know—I'm being terribly pushy, and terribly forward. My dear Henry would always tell me to keep my nose out of other's people's affairs. 'Beryl,' he would say, 'people have better things to do than to listen to you go on about your gift.' But, you see, sometimes people need to hear these things—sometimes all that's needed is to know someone cares about you. And I'm telling you, young man, that girl cares about you. What you do with that information is your business."

And with that, she bent down and picked up her bag, slung it over her shoulder, and downed the rest of her coffee in one gulp.

"Nice meeting you," she said, with a final pat on his shoulder. "Best of luck to you." And she lumbered out of the café, moving between the tables with surprising agility for someone of her girth.

Lee wanted to say something, but he had no idea what it might be. He was too astonished to speak, and just watched as she made her way down the stairs and out the front door of the bookstore.

Her words echoed in his head. *Sometimes all that's needed is to know someone cares about you.* He wondered who, if anyone, cared about the man they were pursuing.

CHAPTER FORTY-SEVEN

The Jack Hammer was loud and crowded, smelling of stale beer and semen. Smoke swirled from dozens of cigarettes, sucked upward toward the bare blue lightbulbs hanging from the low ceiling. The sight that greeted Elena Krieger was like a Brueghel painting of hell. Writhing bodies twisted and snaked around each other on the dance floor, glistening with sweat and hormones, oozing desire into the close, fetid air. Into this atmosphere she strolled, her feather boa wrapped nonchalantly around her elegant neck. She tried to walk with a bored, world-weary saunter, but her left hand clutching the tiny leather purse hanging from her shoulder and the tightness around her eyes gave her away. Much as she tried to pretend otherwise, she was new to this scene.

She picked her way across the room, sidestepping the cluster of bodies, hugging the wall until she reached the bar. She slid onto a stool and surveyed the people around her. At the far end of the bar, a pair of young thugs with tattooed biceps had their tongues down each other's throats while their hands caressed each other's crotches. Elena swallowed hard and took a deep breath. She had been prepared for a raw scene, but this was a rough crowd—she fought back a creeping panic and fear that she might, for once, be out of her depth. Her forehead tingled as she forced her face to remain expressionless, calling on her acting training to keep her cool.

"Hey there—what are you drinking?"

She turned to see a strapping young man standing next to her. He leered at her, his eyes cloudy with booze and, she thought, drugs. He wore a white muscle shirt over ironed blue jeans, and a leather thong necklace with a single seashell hung around his bronzed neck. He was a good-looking blond with sensual, pouty lips and deep-set blue eyes—in fact, he reminded her of a cruder version of Captain Morton. His voice was high and light, with a pronounced outer-borough accent—Queens, maybe—but no trace of a lisp. There was nothing remotely feminine about him—on the street, she thought, he could pass for straight. She just hoped she could pass for a tranny—this would be her first test.

"I'll have what you're having," she said in her deepest voice, which was half an octave lower than his. She made no attempt to cover her German accent—she hoped it would be a turn-on to some of these guys.

"Good choice," he said, and signaled the bartender without taking his eyes off her. "I never seen you here before. This your first time?"

"Yes," she said as he handed her a sweating bottle of Brooklyn Brown.

"Bottoms up," he said, clinking bottles with her.

"Here's to anything else that comes up," she said.

He laughed and took a drink, wiping his mouth with a bare, muscular forearm. "So, where are you from? Austria or someplace?"

"Germany, actually."

He laughed again and took another drink.

"That's cool, that's cool. They got places like this over there?"

"Oh, sure, plenty—in Berlin," she guessed. She had never been to Berlin.

"Cool," he said, gulping down some more beer.

Even in the dim light, she could see that his eyes were bloodshot, the pupils contracted, and there was a noticeable tremor in his hands. She considered what drugs he might be on, and guessed cocaine—and maybe something else as well. She swallowed some beer and looked around the room. Elena didn't like drugs—she had seen too many people flip out on them.

"So what's a nice girl like you doing in a place like this?" he asked, draining the remainder of his beer in one long swallow. He tossed the bottle into a trash can behind the bar and flicked his hand toward the bartender, a gigantic black man with a shaved head, a tiny gold earring, and a swirl of colorful tattoos on his powerful arms. Elena wondered if they were prison tattoos. He wore an expression of grim stoicism as he tended to his increasingly rowdy clientele.

"Thanks," her companion said with a grin when the stony-faced bartender placed another round in front of him. Ignoring the young man's attempt to ingratiate himself, he collected the money and tip without making eye contact.

"By the way, my name's Matthew," the young man said, holding out his hand. "You can call me Matt—everyone does."

"Hi, Matt," Elena said, shaking his hand, which was warm and dry and unexpectedly grainy. She guessed maybe he did manual labor of some kind, based on the coarseness of his skin—she could see calluses on the palms of both hands. He looked at her expectantly, head cocked to one side, and she suddenly realized she had forgotten to come up with an alias.

"I'm . . . Lenny," she said, thinking fast.

"Lenny," he answered. "Like in *Of Mice and Men*?"

"Or I *was* Lenny, before," she continued. "Now I'm—Lottie."

"Hey, I like that!" he chuckled. "Lottie Lenny, like Lotte Lenya. I love her—not as much as my ex-boyfriend, though. He has all her records."

"Yes," she agreed. "She is good, isn't she?" But she was trying to figure out why a man with rough calluses on his hands would be familiar with John Steinbeck and Lotte Lenya.

"Drink up," he said, sliding the second bottle toward her.

She gulped down the rest of her beer, tossed the bottle into the container behind the bar, and lifted the sweating bottle of Brooklyn Brown in a toast.

"Here's to meeting new friends."

"I'll drink to that," he said, taking a swig and wiping his mouth with the back of his hand. "So, Lottie, what do you like to do for fun?"

"Oh, that depends on who I'm doing it with," she answered, batting her false eyelashes at him. The trick was to overdo it enough so that she didn't look like a woman, but like a man trying to pass as a woman. The key was overstatement—but not too much so that it veered into camp.

"Are you—a full-service playmate?" he asked, with a glance at her crotch.

She understood what he meant. He was expecting her to have a penis, as an actual transvestite would. She had chosen the miniskirt to avoid the issue—it effectively covered her crotch area. This was the moment of truth, where she had to convince him of the lie.

"What do you suppose?" she said, pressing her well-muscled thigh against his.

"Hmm, let's see," he replied, reaching out a hand to grab her crotch.

She turned away, and deftly grasping him by the wrist, she placed it on her chest. "You'll just have to wait and see," she said. "Meanwhile, try this."

"Hey, these are good," he answered, squeezing her breast. "Where did you get them done?"

"That's a secret," she responded. Guiding his hand to her face, she placed two fingers inside her mouth and sucked on them.

He closed his eyes and moaned, letting his head loll back. "Mmm, baby, you're a red-hot mama."

"You haven't seen anything," she answered, but at that moment her left ear exploded with pain, and everything went dark.

When she came to she was lying on the floor of the bar, looking up at Matt. He was struggling with a tall, thin woman—no, a tranny—with long, dark hair (a wig?), a tight black jumpsuit, and wicked stiletto heels. A few of the other patrons at the bar were looking at them, but the dancing on the dance floor continued as if nothing had happened.

"Hey, baby, what are you doing?" Matt was saying, holding tightly onto her wrists as the transvestite tried to claw his face with her long crimson nails.

"You—pig—how—*could*—you?" she responded, out of breath from the effort of struggling.

"Hey, we was just flirting," Matt said, still grasping her arms tightly.

"You call that *just flirting*?" the tranny hissed. Wrenching one hand free, she swiped at his face, nails clawing the air. But he ducked and pulled away from her, releasing his hold on her other arm.

"Whoa! You're too intense for me, baby," he said. Holding his hands up in surrender, he backed away from her. It was only then he seemed to notice Elena lying where she was on the floor. "Hey, sorry about that," he said, reaching down to help her up.

The tranny in the stilettos roared and lunged toward him. Matt raised his hands once again and continued to back away, keeping his eyes on his adversary as he sidled toward the door. Eyes blazing, she followed, her lean body coiled like a lioness about to spring, teetering on her stilettos. Elena noticed she moved with surprisingly agility on such high, thin heels.

Elena was about to pick herself up off the floor when she felt a strong hand seize her by the shoulder and lift her to her feet. She turned to see the bartender towering over her. Up close, he looked huge—easily six and a half feet tall, at least 250 pounds of muscle. He moved with the oiled grace of a ballet dancer.

"You okay?" he asked, his stern face softening as he wiped the grime from his hands. The floor was filthy, and Elena shuddered at the thought of the disgusting organisms now crawling over her skin. Her one weakness was an intense squeamishness regarding germs and dirt—a fear she had never shared with anyone. Excessive cleanliness was a stereotypical German trait, so she kept her phobia to herself.

Now, however, she had to fight panic as she brushed the dirt from her clothing. "Don't you have a bouncer in this place?" she asked the bartender.

"Yeah—me," he said. "Violet's a newcomer," he added with a glance in her direction. There was no sight of her or Matt—they had already been swallowed up in the perspiring press of bodies. "She'll get over it," he continued. "She and Matt were an item last week, but he's always on the lookout for fresh talent. Tough titties, but that's the way it goes." He lit a cigarette and held out the pack. "Want one?"

Elena stared at it. She hadn't smoked a cigarette in over ten years, since before she left Germany. It was all the rage in the Hamburg cafés—when she was a young actress she took up the habit to appear more sophisticated, even smoking one during a song in her nightclub act. But then her favorite uncle got throat cancer and she gave it up overnight.

"Sure, why not?" she said. Her hands trembled as she plucked a long, thin white cigarette from its cellophane wrapper. Holding it under her nose, she slid it slowly from one end to the other, inhaling deeply. The smell of raw tobacco brought back memories of her Hamburg days with unexpected vividness. Suddenly she was lounging against a shiny grand piano in a shimmery gold lamé dress, slit all the way up her thigh, a cigarette in one hand, a microphone in the other, crooning cabaret songs to an audience sitting in the darkness on the other side of the spotlight.

She slid the cigarette between her lips and leaned forward as the bartender held up a silver lighter and flicked the flame into life. She sucked in the smoke, held it in her lungs for a moment, and exhaled. Then she coughed violently, her head spinning as she grabbed his arm to steady herself.

"Been a while?" he said.

"Yeah," she acknowledged. When the coughing subsided she took another drag, this time not taking in so much smoke. Her head continued to spin, but she managed not to cough. As the nicotine flowed through her bloodstream, she felt her body relax. *Some things you never forget.*

She looked at the bartender, who was headed back to his post behind the bar. An impatient-looking man in tight black pants was waving a fistful of dollar bills at him.

"Hey," she called out to him. "What's your name?"

He glanced back at her as he ducked under the counter.

"Everyone calls me Diesel."

She thought that was a strange name, but she just nodded. "I'm Lottie."

"Pleased to meet you, Lottie."

"And you." She gazed at him with admiration. Now here was a man you'd want on your side in a tight spot, she thought. Calm, intelligent, and so powerful looking that she guessed he could take on three men at once without flinching.

"I'll have another beer, please," she said.

He pulled out a bottle and snapped off the cap in one fluid motion.

"It's on the house," he said, smiling for the first time that night.

CHAPTER FORTY-EIGHT

By the time Elena left the Jack Hammer it was after three a.m. The party was by no means wrapping up inside, but she had had enough. Her eyes were burning from the cigarette smoke, and her mouth felt like sandpaper. She had downed more beer in this one evening than she was used to drinking in a week—not because she didn't enjoy alcohol, but because maintaining a figure like hers took discipline.

She had her admirers at the bar. Several young men bought her drinks, but after the encounter with Matt's jealous girlfriend, they seemed wary of getting too close to her. She kept her eye out for Matt or his girl—Diesel said her name was Violet—but they had faded into the evening, along with Elena's makeup. Whatever mascara she hadn't sweated off had gathered in cakes at the tips of her eyelashes. Her lipstick had long since been rubbed away, and her hair had wilted from the heat and humidity.

Yellow cabs streamed up Sixth Avenue, all taken. She stood on the corner for a while, then headed for the subway in her pointed heels, her feet protesting at every step. She felt light-headed and bone tired, and was looking forward to a long, hot bath before crawling into bed.

She was aware there was plenty of drug use in the bathrooms—people would disappear in groups of two or three and come back with red eyes, wiping their running noses. She heard the sound of sniffing coming from one of the stalls during her own trip to the restroom, and on the dance floor people smoked weed almost as much as cigarettes. Still, she wasn't here on a drug bust. It was a more serious mission, and she would just have to overlook the illegal narcotics. The last thing she wanted to do was call attention to herself in a way that made anyone suspicious. She planned on returning again later in the week—maybe even tomorrow night, if she could stand it.

The walk to the subway felt endless. It couldn't have been more than a quarter of a mile, but with each step her feet cried out with pain. She longed to tear off her spiked heels and walk barefoot. The streets were fairly quiet, and she could even hear the wind rustling the leaves of the trees in the little pocket park on Sixth Avenue.

As she approached the entrance to the IRT on Waverly Place, she saw a black limousine with Jersey plates pull up to the curb. The automatic window slid down smoothly on the driver's side, and a young man leaned out.

"Need a lift?"

"Thank God!" she answered, grateful for her good luck. The private car service would no doubt cost twice what a cab would be, but Elena didn't care. The subway ride would have been long and ugly, and she was willing to pay triple fare just to get home.

When he asked her politely where she was headed and offered her a bottle of Evian water, she vowed to give him an extra-large tip. The automatic window whooshed back up as she settled back into the plush seat. Sipping the bottled water, she stared out at the buildings rushing by as the car glided uptown.

CHAPTER FORTY-NINE

Lee Campbell awoke drenched in sweat, his injured arm throbbing.

Fumbling for the bottle of water he kept on the bedside table, he tried to shake himself out of the dream's spell. He took a long drink and shivered. The room was cool, but the chill in his body was deeper. In his dream, he had *known* the killer's mind, imagined that he *was* him. That was all he could remember—but the feeling of being that deranged, obsessed person was still strong—so strong, in fact, that he would have trouble shaking it off.

He looked at the clock next to the bed. The red numbers read 3:00 A.M. *The dead hour.*

He tried to conjure up an image of the killer's face, but couldn't. In the dream, he had *been* the killer, felt his rage—but had never seen his face. Trying to shake the dream from his mind, he summoned all his willpower, threw off the blankets, and heaved himself out of bed.

He felt the evil fist of depression tightening its grip on him. All he wanted to do was burrow under the covers until it passed—or until night fell again, wrapping its comforting blanket of darkness around the city. The knowledge that he must get up in a few hours and face the day only made things worse, adding anxiety to the already unbearable bleakness in his soul. It was as if all the color and sweetness had been sucked out of him while he slept. Kathy was across town at Arlene's, and he didn't want to obsess about whether she would call him.

He rose from bed and tiptoed to the window. He looked through the back window of his apartment at the little garden below. The window faced uptown, and he thought of Kathy, sleeping peacefully (or was she?) a mile or so north of him. All around him, the city slept. A lyric from Puccini's *Turandot* scrolled through his mind: *Nessun dorma. No one sleeps tonight.*

There would be no more sleep for him tonight.

CHAPTER FIFTY

"What do you mean she's 'disappeared'?" Chuck Morton bellowed at his sergeant, who stood clinging to the knob of his office door as if it were a life raft. It was Monday morning, and he had arrived at the station house to find Ruggles waiting for him, white-faced and terrified.

"I haven't been able to reach her, sir," Ruggles replied. "I've left messages on her cell phone and her landline, but there's no response. And that's just not like her, sir—she usually calls back within half an hour or so."

Morton reached out and wrapped his hand around the glass butterfly paperweight on his desk, squeezing it until his knuckles turned white.

"What are you suggesting, Sergeant? That she's gone AWOL? That she's fled the country?"

"No, sir. I—I'm terribly afraid something's happened to her." Ruggles's ruddy complexion deepened; he looked frightened. His pale blue eyes were wide, and beads of sweat prickled on his forehead.

"Huh!" Chuck snorted. "Things don't 'happen' to Elena Krieger—not from what I hear."

"I just can't think of any other explanation, sir. It's not like her to—"

"You already said that," Chuck snapped. He knew he was being harsh on his sergeant, but he found the man's devotion to Krieger irritating. The woman was trouble. He had known that when she was forced on him, and now she was proving it. "Look," he said, his voice softer. "Let's not panic until we know more, all right? Keep trying to reach her, and let me know when you—"

The phone on his desk bleated. He grabbed the receiver.

"Morton here."

As Ruggles watched, his captain's expression changed from irritated to concerned to grim. He didn't say much, but Ruggles knew from his face that it was bad news—very bad news.

"Thanks for letting me know," Morton said, replacing the receiver. He looked away, then back at his sergeant. When Ruggles saw his captain's expression, he felt his stomach slide down to his shoes.

When Morton spoke, the words hit Ruggles like a bullet to the heart.

"They found Krieger's purse."

There was no need to elaborate—the phrase had a shattering clarity. Ruggles felt his knees go weak.

"Where?"

Morton looked down at his shoes. "In the Village."

"He got to her, didn't he?"

Again, there was no need to explain—they both knew who "he" was.

"I don't know, Sergeant." Morton sounded angry—weary but angry.

Suddenly Ruggles felt his vision narrowing, and the sight

of his commander was replaced by a swiftly descending blackness.

"Excuse me, sir," Sergeant Ruggles said stiffly, and fled the room without looking back.

CHAPTER FIFTY-ONE

At ten o'clock, Lee's phone rang. It was Kathy, and she sounded terrible.

"Can you meet me? I need to see you."

"Where are you?"

"The Life Café. How ironic," she added with a laugh that turned into a sob.

"What's wrong?"

"I'll tell you when you get here."

"I'll be right there," he said.

Kathy was sitting at a table in the corner when Lee arrived, staring out the window. Her eyes were swollen and puffy, rimmed with red, and her face wore an expression Lee had never seen on her before: she looked forlorn. When she saw him she looked up and smiled, but it was a mournful smile, and her mouth trembled at the edges.

"What is it?" Lee said, kissing her gently on the cheek. Her skin tasted salty. "What happened?" he asked, taking a chair across from her.

Kathy sucked in a long, slow breath, and gazed across the room at the thin fingers of sunlight snaking through the maze of lace curtains.

"My roommate in Philly called my cell phone this morning. My cat died in the night."

"Oh, no—I'm so sorry. Had he been sick?"

"Not really—but he was very old."

"How old?"

"I don't even know—he was a rescue cat. It's odd," she said. "He was there, and now he's not. It feels impossible that his consciousness could disappear so abruptly, and so—finally. I have this strange lingering feeling of his presence, as though he's still around in some way." She let out a deep sigh, heavy with unshed tears. "I don't mean anything mystical about it, but there is something profound about it—almost as if he's left an energy footprint of some kind."

"When my grandmother died, I saw women on the street who reminded me of her for weeks afterward," Lee said. He looked away, afraid she might ask him about his sister, but to his relief, she didn't.

The waitress appeared, a sweet, moonfaced young thing with clanking goth jewelry and a purple streak in her short black hair. Lee ordered a coffee—the coffee at the Life Café was strong and dark and good.

"It's weird," Kathy said, absently wrapping her paper straw cover around her index finger like a white ring. "Ever since she called, all I can think of is him, slinking into the bedroom, or padding into the kitchen to demand food. Except that he's not there at all."

"Maybe there is some kind of an energy footprint—who knows?" Lee said. "There are still so many things we don't understand yet."

"I never thought absence itself could have such a strong . . . presence."

Lee tried to push from his mind those awful days and nights of thinking about Laura, of picturing her last hours, her last moments, the recurring nightmares of seeing her dead body—but only in his dreams. He never had the chance to mourn her properly, because there was never a definitive moment when anyone could say that she was dead—though he knew in his heart that she was. In those days every young woman reminded him of his sister, and he resented them for being alive when she wasn't.

"At least I didn't have to make the decision to—you know," she said.

"Oh," he said. "I had to do that for my dog."

"What was that like?"

"It caught me off guard. I wasn't prepared for how difficult that decision would be, even when it was inevitable. It was uncomfortable and somehow it felt *wrong* to have that kind of power over another living creature. And then I was shocked by how irrevocable it was. Afterward I had the impulse to take it all back, to reverse my decision and bring him back to life—as if that were possible."

She smiled wanly. "I should know as well as anyone how irreversible death is, but when it's someone—something?— so close to my heart, part of me doesn't understand how that could be." She looked at him with that rueful little half-smile he found so endearing. "Does that make any sense at all?"

"Of course," he replied, saying the words she needed to hear. "Sure it does."

"I don't know how people do it for members of their family," she said, shaking her head. "If it's that hard to do for a dog, I can't imagine—oh, God, I'm sorry," she said, her face reddening. "I didn't mean to—I mean, I didn't mean to be insensitive."

He put his hand on hers. "We've all suffered losses, and we all have to grapple with death at some point."

"It's just hard for me right now, coming on top of the work I'm doing at the site. It's too much death—too much loss."

"That must be so hard for you," he said.

She bit her lower lip and stared at her coffee cup. "I don't know how much longer I can do this work. I'm used to identifying bodies, but . . . so many. The enormity of it. I keep thinking it will get better, but it's only getting worse."

"Maybe you should talk to someone about it."

"You mean like a professional?"

"Yeah."

"I'm no good at that." She stirred her cold coffee. "The other day there was a pocketbook next to one of the . . . victims. A little red purse, and in it there was a rabbit's foot keychain, like the kind I had when I was a kid. I started wondering if she had children, and if one of them had given her the keychain. . . ." She pulled air into her lungs, shuddering as she did.

Lee's cell phone rang.

"Excuse me," he said, rising from the table. He hated talking on his cell phone in public, especially restaurants. He saw the call was from Chuck and ducked outside to answer it.

He stood against the wall of the café, underneath the black and yellow awning. Across the street in Tompkins Square Park, some kids were playing basketball, shouting and grunting as they lunged for the ball. A couple of young mothers were pushing strollers up Avenue B, laughing as they exchanged stories. A rumpled elderly man was walking an equally disheveled looking terrier. It all looked so *normal*.

He flipped open his phone. "Hello?"

"It's me. I got some bad news," Morton said.

"What?"

"It's Krieger. I think he's got her."

He ceased to hear the sounds of the basketball game across the street, to feel the breeze on his face or smell the exhaust fumes from the M8 bus as it rumbled past. His entire world narrowed to the cell phone in his hand and the voice at the other end.

"*What?*"

"She sent an e-mail last night that we only just saw a few minutes ago. It seems she went out without any backup—to the seediest damn tranny bar in the Village. They found her purse this morning."

"Christ. Where was it?"

"On Sixth Avenue, Midtown."

"And no one saw him?"

"We can't find anyone who did so far. Or if they did, they're not talking."

"Jesus, Chuck—"

"I *know*!" Chuck said. He sounded exhausted and exasperated—and dangerously close to exploding. Chuck could be pushed beyond most people's limits—but when he did finally blow, Lee knew from experience, you had better watch out.

He felt a tug on his sleeve and turned around to see Kathy standing there.

"I'm sorry, but I have to go," he said to Chuck. "I'll call you back in two minutes."

He turned back to face her.

"What is it?" she said when she saw his expression.

"Krieger's missing."

Over on the basketball court, a young man missed a jump shot and cursed.

"Son of a bitch!"

The words floated across the street, and Lee registered them as appropriate to his situation.

Son of a bitch, he thought. *Son of a bitch.*

CHAPTER FIFTY-TWO

Depressed as Lee Campbell had been in recent years, Chuck Morton looked even worse. His normally ruddy face was pale as a bedsheet. Lines Lee had never noticed before crisscrossed his forehead like errant railroad tracks, and his blue eyes were rimmed with red.

If Elena Krieger had fallen victim to the killer, it would be worse than a tragedy—it was nothing less than a disaster. The death of a cop in the line of duty—any cop—always received lavish amounts of media attention in New York, which could be as claustrophobic as a fishbowl when it came to the relationship between the press and the police. But Krieger—that was as bad as it got. A woman, a foreigner, and an undercover agent—and a glamorous, beautiful woman to boot—working on a high-profile case of a serial offender. It was sure to set off a media frenzy. In a city weary with the aftermath of the greatest tragedy in its long history, a story like this would serve as a welcome distraction.

All of this had occurred to Lee on his way up on the subway, and he knew that Chuck Morton realized it, too. And it was Morton who would have to answer for it all—to the media, to the police brass, and most painfully, to every cop underneath him.

The door swung open, and Butts strode into the room, banging it closed behind him. He alone seemed energized by what had happened—not glad, by any means, but at least he didn't look depressed and defeated. In fact, he looked angry.

"Okay," he said, without bothering to say hello, "what happened?"

Chuck gave them the short version, at least as much as he knew. Krieger had gone to the infamous Jack Hammer on Friday night, and had disappeared sometime between 2 and 3 A.M.

"*The Jack Hammer?*" Butts exploded. "She went to the goddamn *Jack Hammer?*"

"You didn't have any luck there," Chuck pointed out. "She evidently thought she could do better."

Butts snorted. "For Christ's sake! It's a rough place, even with backup! Good God, who did she think she was—Wonder Woman?"

"Something like that, I guess," Lee said.

"I *knew* that woman was trouble," Butts muttered.

"That's enough, Detective," Chuck said wearily. "Calm down, will you?"

"Oh, sure, I'll calm down," Butts replied, biting viciously on the end of an unlit cigar, decapitating it. Lee hadn't seen him indulge in his cigar habit for a while—maybe it was an indication of how stressed he was.

"The question is, what are we gonna do about it?" he continued, flinging himself into the nearest chair.

"The first thing is to get straight exactly what we're going to tell the media," Chuck replied.

"Yeah, that'll be a real circus," Butts muttered. "Can't wait for that."

Lee looked at Chuck. Butts had made the mistake of not reading the warning signs of his mounting rage. Morton was naturally even tempered, and could take a lot—until he blew. And when he blew, look out. Lee had seen the signs—the gradual tightening of his voice, the tension in his shoulders, the flush spreading upward from the back of his neck.

Morton exploded, crashing his fist down on the desk with such force that Butts jumped backward, letting out a little yelp.

"You know, Detective, it would be nice to just wave a wand and make it all go away!" he bellowed, his face the color of raspberry pudding. "But that's not going to happen, so why don't you adjust your *attitude*?"

Butts stared at him, blinking rapidly, then fell back into his chair.

"Sorry," he said. "You're right." He shoved the cigar back into his pocket. "What do we know?"

"We know she left the bar around two," Chuck said, with a glance out the window, where a lone pigeon was scraping the sill with its beak in search of scraps.

"And that's the last time she was seen?" Lee asked.

"Yeah."

The door opened, and Sergeant Ruggles entered. As bad as Chuck Morton looked, the usually buoyant Ruggles looked even worse. He shuffled into the room like a sleep-walker and listlessly tossed some papers onto Morton's desk. He avoided looking at any of them. If Lee had any doubt before, it was clear to him now that Ruggles was in love with Krieger. And he probably blamed Chuck Morton for her disappearance.

Chuck picked up one of the papers from his desk and thrust it at Lee. "This was sent via the NYPD website this morning."

Lee took it and read it.

I guess I shouldn't be poking my nose where it doesn't belong. Bad, bad girl.

"Any chance of a trace?"

Morton shook his head. "It was sent from an Internet café in Chinatown. Paid for in cash—right, Ruggles?"

"Yes, sir," he replied in a leaden monotone, as if all the joy had been squeezed from his vocal cords. "The Chinese man running the place spoke almost no English."

There was a knock on the door.

"Yes?" Morton said.

When the door opened, Lee was startled to see the person who sauntered gracefully into the room, as much at home as if he owned the place.

There, standing in the office of the commander of the Bronx Major Cases Unit, was Diesel himself. As usual, he was dressed all in black, which seemed an odd choice for an August day. Yet he looked as cool and comfortable as he had last winter when Lee met him in the bar at McHale's.

"Hello," he said, taking them all in with a sweep of his massive head.

"Ah, yes, Mr.—" Chuck fumbled among the papers Ruggles had left on his desk.

"Just Diesel, if you don't mind," he answered, calm and dignified as always.

"Diesel, then. This is Detective Leonard Butts, Homicide."

"How ya doin'?" Butts said, as Diesel gave him a polite nod.

"And Sergeant Ruggles," Chuck said with a nod at his desk sergeant.

"How do you do?" Diesel bowed slightly, though he

would have had to kneel to close the height gap between him and the diminutive sergeant.

"How d'you do, sir?" Ruggles replied, still visibly distracted. "Please excuse me, but I must get back . . ." He abandoned the thought midsentence, and left the room without looking at any of them.

Chuck continued the introductions. "And this is—"

"Dr. Campbell and I are already acquainted," Diesel replied.

Chuck's eyebrows shot up, and his mouth fell open. "Really?" He looked at Lee, who nodded.

"We have—or rather, had—a mutual friend."

"I'm very sorry about your friend's death," Chuck said. "I wonder if we could get to the case at hand?"

"By all means," Diesel replied, sitting in one of the scarred captain's chairs opposite Chuck's desk.

Chuck picked up a memo from his desk and glanced at it. "It says here that you were the bartender at the Jack Hammer the night Detective Krieger went there."

"That is correct."

"And so you wanted to come here to tell us what what you saw."

"Again, correct."

"Wait a minute," Butts interrupted. "How did you know she—"

Lee started to speak, but Diesel held up a hand.

"I understand your concern, Detective. Her disappearance has not yet been made public."

"Yeah," Butts said. "So how did you—"

"You have sources, do you not, Detective?"

"Of course."

"Is it fair to say that some of them are not always on the straight and narrow?"

"Well, 'course. I mean, you can't always choose who you

get information from, as long as the source is tellin' the truth."

Diesel gave a single nod of his majestic head.

"Let's just say that I too have 'sources,' and they are not always the most savory of characters."

Lee stared at him. Diesel was full of surprises. For one thing, Lee had no idea that he was a bartender at the Jack Hammer; Diesel had told him less than a week ago that he and Rhino were working as hospital orderlies. He decided not to mention any of this, but wait and see where the conversation led.

Butts too was looking at him, though it was more of a glare. He was looking less than enchanted by the evasive response. Lee knew the little detective hated witnesses who hid anything, and Butts was already beginning to show signs of irritation. The corner of his left eye was twitching, and he was tearing at a loose fingernail with his teeth.

"Okay, okay," Chuck intervened. "Can you swear to us that you aren't hiding anything that might have a bearing on solving this case?"

Diesel replied without hesitation. "On my mother's grave, if you wish."

Butts opened his mouth to say something, but Chuck cut him off.

"That won't be necessary, Mr.—Diesel. Just tell us what you saw that night, if you would."

Diesel cleared his throat and intertwined his muscular fingers, leaning forward in his chair, his powerful shoulders straining against the material of his shirt.

"It was approximately nine o'clock when Detective Krieger showed up at the bar."

"Did you know who she was?" Chuck asked.

"No, but I knew she wasn't a transvestite."

Chuck frowned. "Really? How?"

"Her Adam's apple was too small. It was possible she was a post-op transsexual, but I was pretty sure she wasn't."

"Because—?"

"Her hands. The surgeons do remarkable things these days, but they can't change the size of a man's hands. She had the hands of a woman."

Chuck leaned back on the edge of his desk and crossed his arms, his face impassive, but Lee could tell he was impressed. Lee was pretty impressed himself. Diesel's composure and sangfroid made him an ideal witness—in fact, Lee thought, he'd make a damn good cop. He glanced at Butts, who was still frowning, chewing on his index finger as though it were his next meal.

"So you noticed her when she came in?" Chuck prompted.

Diesel smiled. "It was hard *not* to notice her. Apart from the fact that she was a good-looking woman, she was dressed to attract attention."

He went on to describe the outfit she was wearing in such detail that Lee wondered if Diesel knew more than he was letting on.

"I also knew she was a cop," he added.

Butts frowned. "Really? How's that?"

"My father was in the force. When you grow up around cops, you can spot them a mile away."

"'Zat so?" Butts said, crossing his arms. "What precinct was he?"

"The Ninth," Diesel answered without blinking. "Back when it was rough."

"Okay," Chuck interrupted. "So did Detective Krieger have admirers?"

"She did." He went on to describe the entire scene with Matt and Violet, giving every detail of the encounter, including introducing himself to Krieger.

Chuck smiled ruefully when he heard the undercover name Krieger had given herself. "Lottie . . . like Lotte Lenya."

"That's what Matt said," Diesel replied.

"Interesting," Lee mused. "A working-class guy who knows who Lotte Lenya is."

"Not unusual in that world," Diesel said. "Maybe not quite the icon Judy Garland is, but—"

"I get it," Butts said. Finished chewing on the fingers of his right hand, he had started on the left one. "A fag hag. She was in that Bond film, wasn't she?"

"*From Russia With Love,*" Diesel replied.

"Yeah," Butts said. "With the knives in her shoes! I remember that scene where she—"

"Okay," Chuck said impatiently. "Can we get on with it?'

"So you said both Matt and Violet are regulars?" Lee asked. "How long have they been coming there?"

"I've only been there a month," Diesel admitted. "I have a day job," he said to Chuck, "but I'm moonlighting for some extra cash."

"Okay," Chuck said. "So they've both been coming there for at least a month, then?'

"Actually, Violet only showed up a couple of weeks ago. Never saw her there before that."

"Okay, what we'd like to do is get a list of the credit card receipts, so—"

Diesel shook his head. "It's a cash-only business. It's just too crazy in there to be dealing with credit card machines and receipts. Sorry," he added, seeing the disappointment on Chuck's face.

"I think we should go there this weekend," Lee said.

Butts stared at him.

"Chances are a lot of the same people will be there, and we can interview as many as possible."

"He's right," Chuck said. "We wanted to try to keep a lot of the details out of the media, but—"

"Good luck with that," Diesel remarked dryly.

"Yeah, I know," Chuck agreed. "But as far as the Jack Hammer is concerned, the fewer of the patrons who make the connection that she was there working the case, the better."

"But some of them are sure to see her picture in the paper."

"I don't see how we can avoid that. But we won't tell the media she was there working undercover. That should buy us some time to conduct a few interviews."

"As soon as you start questioning people, some of them are bound to put two and two together."

"But until then, the fewer people who know, the better."

Diesel scratched behind his right ear, the one with the tiny gold earring.

"It's not like he doesn't know you're after him."

"Yeah," Butts said, "but the less he knows about what we know, the better."

"And what *do* you know?" Diesel asked.

"I'm afraid that's classified," Butts shot back with satisfaction.

Diesel shrugged. "I'm just trying to help, Detective."

Butts didn't say anything, but as far as Lee was concerned, they could use all the help they could get.

CHAPTER FIFTY-THREE

After Diesel left, they talked about what should be released to the media and when. It didn't take them long to agree to leave out the fact that Krieger was working with them on the case—though some people would certainly draw that conclusion. Apart from that, they decided to give out as much information as possible, encouraging other patrons of the Jack Hammer that night to come forward. Diesel had promised to do what he could from his end, but he wasn't scheduled to work until the weekend, and he knew his customers only by their first names—or so he said. Lee believed him, but he could tell Butts wasn't entirely persuaded.

Chuck leaned back to stretch his spine, groaning as his stiff muscles protested. "Is there anything you can add to his profile?" he asked Lee.

Lee poured himself some more coffee. Awake since before dawn, he was flagging, and needed the caffeine. "I still think he's reliving some kind of childhood trauma, something very specific."

"All right," Chuck said. "So how can that help us?"

"If we can identify how he was damaged, we'll be that

much closer," Lee said, taking a sip of coffee. It was strong and startling—like Krieger, he thought.

"So how do we do that?" Butts asked.

"Let's start with the signature aspects of each crime. What do they all have in common besides water?"

"He leaves notes," Butts said.

Lee took another gulp of coffee, feeling the caffeine trickle into his bloodstream. "What do they tell us?"

"He's punishing the victims," Chuck answered.

"Right," Lee said. "So there's a motive of retribution, of punishment."

Chuck rubbed his eyes. "Punishment for what, though?"

"Good question."

Butts pulled a long string of red licorice from his pocket. It was limp and covered with lint. He brushed off the lint and chewed on it, a contented expression on his cratered face. In response to a glance from Chuck, he said, "Stomach's been actin' up. The wife says this will help. She's into all this natural stuff."

"What else do we have to go on?" Chuck asked.

"Well, later he starts doin' the eyeball thing," Butts remarked.

"Yes, but *why*? What does that mean?" said Chuck.

"It has something to do with watching," Lee replied. "Being looked at."

"Who would have been watching him like that?" Butts asked.

"The most obvious answer would be a parent," Chuck suggested, picking up the glass paperweight on his desk and shifting it from one hand to the other.

"His dad, maybe?" said Butts. "Maybe he disapproved of the whole cross-dressing thing."

"Or his mother . . . but how would that fit with the water?" Chuck asked.

"I have an idea," Lee said. He turned to Chuck, who was slumped in his chair, the glass paperweight dangling from his right hand. "Can I borrow your computer?"

Morton rose from his chair and waved a hand toward it wearily. "Go ahead."

Lee sat down at the computer. Butts followed him, still chewing on the piece of licorice.

"What are you lookin' for?"

"Drownings—twenty years ago, in the tristate area."

"How come?"

"I think he may have had a trauma when he was still very young, involving water—probably a drowning."

Butts bit off a piece of licorice. "That seems like a long shot."

"I know. And that's even assuming it was reported."

The detective frowned and pulled up a chair next to him. "Why wouldn't it be reported?"

"If she was drowned by someone who knew her, it could have been covered up."

"Like her husband, you mean," Chuck said, perching on the edge of his desk.

"Exactly," Lee answered. "He could have done it and gotten away with it—said she went off with another man, that kind of thing."

"But if the kid saw it happen, he would know," Butts pointed out.

"Right," said Lee. "That kind of thing is bad enough when it's accidental. But if it was murder, and if his father told him to keep quiet, he would be replaying it over and over in his mind."

Chuck put down the paperweight, stood up, and paced in

front of the window. He looked animated for the first time all day. "So the reason he cuts out the eyes—"

"He doesn't want her looking at him," Lee finished for him.

"The way his mother did," Butts said.

"Right," Lee agreed, still typing. He studied the screen, frowning. "This search is too general. We'd have to comb through every newspaper from that time period."

"What about missing-person cases?" Butts suggested.

"That's a good idea," said Chuck. "If he covered up her death, someone could have still reported her as missing."

Lee typed some more, then shook his head. "It's still too general, even assuming he grew up around here. It's possible that he moved to this area at some point."

Butts shook his head as if trying to dispel the image from his mind. "Jeez. You gotta be one sick bastard to put your kid through somethin' like that."

"Not only that," said Lee, "but you are guaranteeing your kid will be—"

"One sick bastard."

"You know, this whole process kinda reminds me of bridge," Butts said, chewing on his licorice thoughtfully.

"How so?"

"Well, the wife has been playing lately, you know."

"Yeah, so you said," Chuck remarked impatiently.

"So when she opens with one no trump, for example, it's a code."

"Right—she's telling her partner she has a certain number of points, and asking for information back," said Lee.

"Yeah. So her partner answers in code, too—which she has to interpret. It all depends on whether he's a risky bidder or not. If he says two spades and he's a risk taker, it could mean one thing, but if he's a conservative player, it could mean something else."

"And that difference can make or break the hand," Lee observed. "You miss just one trick and you go down."

"Exactly. So part of the game of bidding depends on knowing your partner's personality, their strengths and weaknesses, and being able to guess what they mean by their bid."

Chuck stared at him. "So?"

"So this guy is talkin' to us in code—and it's our job to figure out what he's saying."

Lee gazed out the window as the soft pink light of early evening settled over the city, bathing the buildings in a strangely beautiful glow. It was in such contrast to the conversation in the rapidly darkening room. A shiver started at the back of his neck and radiated outward. He wished that the only thing at stake were a card game, but if they continued in their failure to decode the messages the killer was leaving behind, another victim would fall to his implacable rage.

CHAPTER FIFTY-FOUR

Caleb looked around the coffee shop. It was a clean, well-lighted place, but he couldn't imagine Hemingway spending five minutes in it. The décor was black and white, from the checkerboard floor tiles to the sleek counter. Everything was hard, reflective surfaces, shiny as the hair of the pubescent rich girls who were gathered there. School would start in a week or so, and there they were, freshly tanned from their summer in the Hamptons or the south of France.

They wore short flared skirts over bony-kneed coltish legs, but they also wore a smart, close-fitting self-assurance, a thick coating of self-esteem, smooth and sleek as their bouncy, well-cared-for hair. They moved among the short, squat members of the waitstaff as if they owned the restaurant—which, in a way, they did. Their parents were the monied classes of the Upper East Side, the highest average income bracket of any zip code in the country. Never mind Beverly Hills 90210, with its crude new money—these people were the true aristocracy, and their daughters knew it.

Caleb looked at the little sluts and imagined their parents roaming their roomy, multimillion-dollar apartments in their tailored Armani suits and Gucci loafers, pausing to deposit checks from wealthy clients or check on their blue-chip stocks before making lunch reservations at La Giraffe or Chanterelle. They owned the grand brownstone buildings they lived in and shopped in the expensive, exclusive boutiques of Madison Avenue. The immigrants from Ecuador, Mexico, or Peru who shined their silverware and washed their sheets came and went at their pleasure.

Caleb stirred another spoonful of sugar into his coffee. He hated these girls, living in the cocoon of comfort and care available only to the very rich. He watched a couple of them talking, slouched around one table, laughing as they flipped their long, shiny hair off a shoulder, delicately fingering their tiny designer backpacks.

They were disgusting, with their inbred complacency—that aura of self-satisfaction they had swallowed with their mother's milk, confidence absorbed through the placental fluid. These girls might not know who they were yet, but they *thought* they did.

Caleb watched as a short, pug-faced Dominican busboy cleared the table, his face set in that deliberate expression of disinterest he had seen on so many workers. He wondered what the Dominicans and Guatemalans thought of these girls. Did they resent their financial, social, and genetic superiority, or were they just grateful to be in America, working for minimum wage while waiting on these princesses of privilege? He was always amazed at the goodwill and cheerful humor of New York restaurant workers.

One of the girls, a coltish brunette in a pink sweater, bumped his table, then, catching his eye, giggled and whispered something to her friends. She looked at him out of the corner of her eye, so aware of her superiority it took his breath away. Caleb stirred his coffee and took a sip. *She is clearly a bad girl, and bad girls deserve to be punished.*

Caleb adjusted his stockings and straightened his wig. The disguise was a good one—no one had even glanced at him twice on the subway. He smiled as he smoothed his green tweed skirt. It was expensive and well cut—his mother would have looked good in it.

CHAPTER FIFTY-FIVE

Caroline Benton waved good-bye to her girlfriends and sauntered out into the gentle atmosphere of the late summer evening. The sun was sinking into a salmon-pink sunset, the air soft as a caress.

Pausing to wipe a few drops of moisture from her downy upper lip, she stood at the bus stop, rocking back and forth on her heels. Never mind trying to get a cab this time of day, in this neighborhood—you might as well wish for a unicorn to ride home. She unzipped her Prada shoulder bag and dug around inside. The bag was lemon yellow, the leather buttery and soft, and it cost seven hundred dollars, which she thought was a bargain—though her father had rolled his eyes when he saw the bill on his Visa card. God, she thought, he could be so *retarded* sometimes, considering what he spent on that single-malt Scotch of his.

Her fingers found what she was looking for, the pack of Marlboro Lights at the bottom of the bag. She wanted a cigarette very badly, but was afraid her stepmother would smell it on her clothes and hair—that woman had a nose like a bloodhound. Caroline didn't see why she should have to obey her, anyway. It's not like she was her real mother or anything.

She squinted and peered down Madison Avenue, as if that would make the bus come faster. She looked around. She was the only one at the bus stop, so maybe it would be okay to have a cigarette after all. She could run right up to her room when she got home, claiming she had homework to do, and her stepmother would never be the wiser.

As she was fiddling around in her bag for a lighter, a black limousine rolled up to the bus stop. It was a Lincoln Town Car, polished to a gleaming shine. Even the whitewall tires looked clean. The electric window slid down, and a young man leaned out. He was wearing a gray wool cap with a black leather brim—like the kind of hat you might see a cab driver wearing in an old movie on AMC or TCM, she thought.

"You the one who called for a car service?"

Caroline shook her head.

He held up a clipboard. "I got the address here—says I'm to meet a young lady in front of this coffee shop."

She looked back at the restaurant. No one was standing outside waiting to be picked up.

"Any idea who it might be?" he said. "One of your friends, maybe?"

In the back of her mind, she wondered briefly how he knew she had friends in the restaurant, but the thought never made its way into her conscious brain. Something else registered only vaguely in her pretty head: though it was August, he was wearing black leather gloves.

"I don't think so," she said.

"Okay," he said, and started to roll the window back up.

She glanced down the avenue—there was no bus in sight

as far as she could see. Yellow cabs zoomed by, all of them filled with passengers.

"Wait a minute!" she called to him.

He lowered the window again.

"Yes?" He smiled. He had a pleasant face—not handsome, but pleasant. The kind of face you would forget as soon as you saw it.

"I'd like a lift home, if you're free."

"Sure—hop in."

She slung her bag over her back and opened the door to the limo, inhaling the aroma of oiled leather seats. The cigarette could wait, she thought—now she just wanted to get home.

"Where to?" he said.

She told him.

"How much?"

He turned around and grinned.

"For you, no charge."

She smiled and leaned back into the soft, yielding embrace of expensive leather. She stretched out her tanned legs and regarded the polished toenails poking out from her Versace sandals with satisfaction. It was good to be young and pretty and rich on the Upper East Side of Manhattan.

"Help yourself to water," he said, and she saw a row of Poland Spring bottles tucked neatly into the pocket behind the front seat.

She reached for one and opened it, drinking greedily. It was a hot day, and she was thirsty. If she had noticed it tasted a little funny, or if that the seal had already been broken, she might have survived. But by the time the black Town Car turned toward the East River, she was already losing consciousness. She barely felt the car come to a stop after pulling into the cul-de-sac amid the block of warehouses on East Seventy-seventh Street. The last thing she saw before her young life ended was a pair of gloved hands moving toward her pretty white throat.

CHAPTER FIFTY-SIX

Lee was at home later that day when the phone rang. It was Kathy, and he knew immediately from her voice that something was wrong. She hadn't spent the night with him on Saturday either, and he thought she had already gone back to Philadelphia.

"I need to see you."

"Is it about your cat?"

"No, it's—I need to see you in person."

"You're still in town?"

"Yes. I leave for Philly later today."

"Why don't you come here?"

There was a pause, and in that single window of silence, despair crept into the room and nestled quietly beside him, warming itself in the fire of his passion.

"Can we meet somewhere else?"

"Sure."

"I'm still at Arlene's place in Murray Hill. Can you meet me at the Waterfront?"

The Waterfront was a friendly neighborhood joint on Second Avenue with a nautical theme, a long narrow room with dark wood floors and pictures of sailing boats on the walls. The elaborate mahogany bar sported a great selection of microbrewery beers, and the menu selections included ostrich burgers and rabbit stew. Lee had been going there for years, and when he took Kathy, she had loved the place as much as he did.

"I'll be there in fifteen minutes," he said.

He hailed a cab and was there in twelve.

Kathy was sitting at a square wooden table farthest from the bar, where the regular customers were perched on their barstools, shrouded in a blue haze of cigarette smoke. Lee's father had smoked, and he hated being around smoking of any kind.

She looked nervous, and the smile she gave him was fleeting, flitting across her face in the space of a second. He bent down to kiss her, but felt her stiffen.

He sat across from her, resting his elbows on the wooden surface, deeply scarred with the carved initials of previous patrons. In front of him the phrase *Kilroy was here* was written in large block letters.

"What are you drinking?" he said, glancing at the glass in front of her.

"Scotch," she answered. She seemed to be avoiding looking at him.

"Want another one?"

She nodded and drained her glass in a single swallow. *Bad sign*, he thought—normally she wasn't much of a drinker.

"Okay, I'll be right back."

He threaded his way through after-work crowd. They looked to be mostly office workers, men with their ties undone and suit jackets over their shoulders, the women at the bar slipping off their pumps to wiggle their toes under the bar stools. Everyone was in a festive mood. Even though it was Monday, the place was crowded. Waves of laughter crested and fell among the various groups; people flirted and gossiped, leaning into one another and then suddenly throwing their heads back to laugh at the punch line of a joke.

He ordered two Scotches, carrying them back to the table carefully through the crowd to avoid spilling them. She accepted the drink and took a large swallow. She put down the glass and looked at her hands, which were fidgeting with the drink straw, twisting it into tight knots.

"Okay," he said, his stomach slowly filling with dread, "what did you want to talk about?"

"This is really hard," she said, looking away.

"Waiting to hear it is harder—just say it."

"Okay." She looked up at him. In the rosy rays of the setting sun, her eyes were the color of caramel cream. A single lock of curly black hair fell over her forehead, and Lee's stomach went hollow. He forced himself to look away.

The words, when they came, hit him like a body blow.

"I think we should have some time apart."

"All right," he said calmly, though what he wanted was to yell and scream as loud as he could. "Why couldn't you tell me this over the phone?"

"Because it's not the kind of thing you say over the phone."

"Okay."

"I . . . I'm having trouble sleeping—"

"Me, too, but we both know it'll take a while—"

She raised a hand to stop him.

"Just hear me out, please?"

He nodded, miserable, and took a large gulp of Scotch. The peaty burn slid down his throat, bringing with it the welcome promise of numbness.

She studied her hands, which were trembling. "Lately it feels like when we're together you're not really . . . *there*."

"Okay," he said, forcing an evenness of tone he did not feel. He wished he were a better actor.

"I know this case has a personal element for you—"

His head felt like a parade of ants had invaded his brain. *What about the red dress?*

"*All* cases are personal for me," he said.

"I already thought about that, and it doesn't help. Maybe it should, but it doesn't. But what's worse is I don't feel *I'm* quite there either. The job I'm doing, the body identifications . . ." She looked away, her lips compressed. "At the end of the day all I want is to crawl into bed." She looked back again—not at him, but at her hands, gripping the glass of Scotch, the skin around her fingernails white. "And in less than two weeks is the—"

"I thought of that," he said quickly, knowing what she was going to say. It would be the first anniversary of the attack.

"Maybe I'm an emotional coward," she said, "but I've been around some of the families, and what they're going through. . . . Jesus." She took a long drink of Scotch. "When I lost my mother I thought I would never get through it."

"But you did."

"But I don't want to feel that pain ever again."

"To *live* is to feel pain, Kathy—you can't protect yourself forever, for Christ's sake!"

"There's another thing," she said, looking into her Scotch glass as if it held all the answers. "I don't feel like I can talk to you about it, because of your—your—"

"My depression." He knew she didn't like to say the word.

"Yes. I don't want to be the cause of an episode, and . . . it sounds really shitty to say it, but I don't want to have to deal with it right now. I have enough on my hands just doing my job."

"I understand," he said.

"No," she said, "I don't think you do. I'm not like you—I'm not good at putting things into words. I'm a scientist, and we're not good at that kind of thing. I just don't have room for a relationship right now—not with you, anyway."

The last phrase stopped his breathing for a moment. *Not with you, anyway.*

"I see," he said, his voice tight.

"Don't be angry," she said.

"What the hell do you expect me to be?"

"I'm not saying this is forever. I just need some time—"

"Fine," he said. "I thought we had something, but I guess I was wrong."

"Don't be a drama queen, for God's sake—"

"When couples have problems, they're supposed to work them out together."

"I've never been very good at that. I've always worked things out on my own. Maybe it's because I lost my mother young, and I didn't have a female role model."

They had joked about this from the first—how she was the "boy" in the relationship and he was the "girl." But now it felt like a stolid, ugly wall between them. The sun had dipped behind the Manhattan skyline, and the only lighting in the room came from wall sconces and the occasional standing lamp. Kathy's eyes had again changed color; now they were the shade of dark mahogany, like the burnished wood on the beautiful old bar.

"There's something else I want to tell you," she said.

"I'm listening."

"I'm . . . going into therapy."

"Well, good. It's probably what you need right now."

"But I'm scared and anxious and afraid I'll end up . . . like you."

"Look, Kathy," he said. "Everyone's different. Just because you're going into therapy, it doesn't mean you'll become clinically depressed. There are some hard truths in everyone's life. It may take courage to face them, and it'll be painful, sure—but that doesn't mean you'll end up like me."

"I hate the way that sounded—I'm sorry."

"And another thing. My sister, my only sibling, was murdered, probably by some psychopathic creep, and I can't even talk to my mother about it. So unless there's something about your family you haven't told me, I don't think you have that much to worry about." He was aware of the anger in his voice, but he didn't care. She wasn't the only one with issues, he thought bitterly.

A silence descended upon them. They had run out of words; anything else they might say to each other would only compound the hurt. It suddenly felt as if there were a frozen tundra between them, instead of a scarred wooden table in a crowded bar.

They finished their drinks and walked without speaking out into the gathering twilight. A brisk wind was blowing in from the East River, and as they faced the setting sun, it occurred to him this might be the last time he ever saw her.

She stood on the curb, waiting to snag one of the yellow cabs hurtling down Second Avenue. She turned back to him as if about to say something, just as a cab came grinding to a halt in front of them, brakes screeching.

"I'll call you," she called to him as she climbed in, closing the door behind her. With a gun of its engine and a squeal of tire rubber, the cab turned west and sped off across town.

Walking home through the darkening city, Lee replayed

the evening in his head. He watched the couples, arms linked, strolling in stride with one another, heels clacking crisply on the pavement. Just a few days ago he and Kathy had been one of those couples, and now he was headed home alone, while she caught a train back to Philadelphia.

He knew she was afraid; they were both afraid. And that's what frightened him most of all.

CHAPTER FIFTY-SEVEN

Drip, drip, drip . . .

Elena Krieger groaned as she fought her way into consciousness. It was cold here, so cold. . . . She opened her eyes, but there was little light in the room. She blinked rapidly and peered into the darkness, trying to make out the shape and size of the chamber where she was imprisoned.

Drip, drip, drip . . .

She struggled to move her limbs, but realized she was bound and gagged, her hands tied securely to her feet.

Drip, drip . . . drip.

The sound was maddening—more than the ropes binding her limbs or the rag wound tightly around her mouth. She struggled some more, but only succeeded in getting rope burns, tiring herself out in the process. She was thirsty, so thirsty.

Drip, drip . . . drip.

She inhaled the musty odor of dirt and damp stones and realized she was in a basement. As her eyes adjusted to the dim light, she could see a row of dusty jars on a shelf just above her. Yes— it was someone's basement, she thought, and this was the canning shelf. For some reason, the thought cheered her. Whoever owned this basement, it was someone who canned. Like her aunt in Düsseldorf, who lovingly boiled and strained fresh berries each summer to make quarts and quarts of fresh jelly: red currant, strawberry, or black raspberry—her favorite. Her tear glands began to thicken, and she could feel her eyes swelling up.

Not now, she scolded herself. *Gott im Himmel! Was kann ich jetzt tun?* She reverted to thinking in German, as she did in times of stress.

She tried to remember how she got here . . . the last thing she could recall was getting into the limo with the polite young driver. He had offered her a bottle of water—that was it! He had drugged her! Even now, her shame at being captured was almost as great as her fear. This kind of thing had never happened to her—not Hildegard Elena Krieger von Boehm, in whose veins ran the blood of her ancestors, great German warriors whose blond manes and chilling battle cries sent a stab of fear into the hearts of their opponents.

She had no doubt who her captor was—it was *him*, the man she had been hunting—but now she was in his power. Another more disquieting thought came to her. He hadn't killed her yet—but why not? What did he have in mind for her? She tried not to think about it, but fear wound itself around her intestines like a serpent, making her breath come in short bursts. She tried to calm herself by mouthing a bedtime prayer from her childhood, one her mother had taught her in her native Bavarian dialect. *Lieber Gott, mach mich fromm, dass ich kann in Himmel komm.* A beseechment to God to make her pious so she would go to Heaven when she died. Right now, the prayer seemed chillingly appropriate. A single tear slid slowly down her left cheek, dripping onto the cold stone floor, and Elena Krieger realized to her shame that she was crying.

She heard footsteps on the floor above her, and the sound

of a door opening. She struggled to move, but it was no use. There was a rustling sound; then a yellow band of light washed across the floor. He had turned on a light, perhaps at the top of the stairs. She held her breath at the sound of the footsteps coming down stone steps—he was coming! There was the sound of something falling, then a muffled curse. He had dropped something—a flashlight, perhaps, or something more sinister?

The heavy wooden door opposite her was flung open, and a figure stood silhouetted in the hall light from behind. Elena blinked, trying to make out his face.

"Hi there," he said in a surprisingly mild voice. He took a step into the room and clicked on the overhead light, giving her a clearer view of his face. She hadn't gotten a good look at the limo driver from the night before, but she was certain it was him. He had a delicate face, not handsome, but . . . pretty. Yes, that was it; he was pretty. She felt she had seen him somewhere else, too, but couldn't think where. He leaned over and removed the gag.

"What do you want from me?" she rasped, her voice tight and dry.

"I've come to make you a bit more comfortable," he said, holding a bottle of water out to her.

She gazed at the bottle longingly, saliva gathering in her mouth. She shook her head. She was so thirsty, but she couldn't take the chance.

"Don't worry—it's not drugged," he said, smiling. "I don't need to drug you anymore."

She didn't reply.

"Look," he said, holding it close to her face, "the seal isn't broken. Tell you what—I'll take a drink myself first, okay?" He unscrewed the lid and took a long swallow, then offered her the bottle.

She was so thirsty; her throat burned.

"Come on," he said, placing the mouth of the bottle to her lips. She leaned forward and drank, sucking greedily at the sweet, clear liquid, until the bottle was empty.

"There now, that wasn't so hard, was it?" he said. "I'm really not such a bad guy—you'll see."

"Are you going to kill me?"

He studied her, as if considering the question for the first time.

"Not right now, anyway," he said. "I like you. Of course, not as much as Matt liked you, but then Matt is a whore."

Matt . . . Matt? Where had she heard that name before? And then it came to her: Matt was the young man she had been flirting with in the bar. She looked at her captor again, and it suddenly became clear to her. He was the young tranny who had attacked Matt for flirting with her! *So,* she thought, *the killer is a transvestite.*

"Frankly, I don't know what I'm going to do with you," he said. "I wasn't even planning to capture you, but I was on my way home, driving up Sixth Avenue, and—well, there you were. It felt like fate was calling the shots."

"I'm a cop," she said.

He gazed at her with pity in his eyes.

"Oh, that's too bad. Now I really *will* have to kill you."

He took a step toward her.

A black mist began to descend over Krieger's eyes, but she fought the growing panic. "No—*wait!*"

He stopped and looked at her. "What?"

"If they find my body, you're dead."

He laughed softly. "I've evaded them so far. What makes you think you're so special?"

"No, you don't understand," she rasped, trying not to let the fear seep into her voice. "Right now they have a small task force looking for you. The minute you kill a cop they'll call in—"

"—the National Guard?" He gave a dismissive snort. "I don't think so."

"Everyone and anyone they can spare. They will hunt you down—and if they can, they'll kill you on the spot."

A narrowing at the corner of his eyes expressed the tiniest seed of doubt. Hope blossomed in her chest, and she fought to remain calm.

"And if they don't manage to kill you right away, do you know what they do to cop killers in jail?"

He tried bravado, but it sounded hollow. "Reward them, I would think."

She tried a short laugh, but it came out equally fake. "Oh, not the other prisoners—I mean the guards. They rape you, first separately and then together. And then they—"

There was a muffled scuffling sound upstairs, as though an animal was clawing at the basement door. His head snapped toward the sound; then he turned back to Krieger.

"I'll deal with you later."

Turning sharply, he left the room and bounded up the stairs two at a time. She could hear his shoes on the creaky boards.

Left alone in the dark, Elena Krieger's whole body began to tremble violently. She took a deep breath and began again. *Lieber Gott, mach mich fromm. . . .*

CHAPTER FIFTY-EIGHT

"Her name is Carolyn Benton, and she is—*was*—sixteen years old."

Chuck Morton tossed a folder of crime-scene photos onto the desk and glowered at the other three men in the room. He looked angry and exhausted and fed up. But then, they all were, Lee thought, looking at his friend. Morton was fishing around in his desk drawer for some thumbtacks to put the photos up on the bulletin board with all the other pictures of the victims, their poor dead bodies mute testimony to the impotence and helplessness everyone in the room felt. While most people were home having dinner, here they were, stuck in the cramped office once again.

Things could hardly be worse, in Lee's view. A serial killer was still at large, he and Kathy weren't speaking, and Krieger was missing. Poor brave, foolish Krieger—while he couldn't say he liked her, exactly, he had come to respect her as a formidable presence. He suspected she had more integrity than she was given credit for.

And now this. He looked at the pictures of Carolyn Benton spread out on the desk. The photo of her dead body bore little resemblance to the one of her with her family, all lined up in front of a grand marble fireplace. They wore expensive-looking matching Christmas sweaters—thick, creamy Irish wool with red and green trim. Her father wore a cheery Santa hat with a big red tassel. Her mother was petite and athletic-looking, with the kind of midwinter tan that didn't come from a tanning salon, but from a Caribbean cruise—probably on their own private yacht. Her brother was clean-cut and handsome and, Lee guessed, a couple of years older than Carolyn, probably a freshman at Yale or Duke or some other school where money and pedigree mattered as much as grade point average.

Lee held up the family Christmas photo. "Where did you get this one?"

Chuck ran a hand over his stiff blond crew cut and looked down at his shoes. "The family brought it with them when they ID'd the body this morning. Said they wanted us to know what she really looked like."

Lee could understand why. In the crime-scene photo, Carolyn lay on the banks of the East River, where she had been found floating a few hours ago. Her eyes had been removed, and this time the note had been found not attached to her body, but in her mouth—as with the others, neatly wrapped in a Ziploc bag.

Sergeant Ruggles studied the picture and looked nervously at his boss. After Krieger's disappearance he begged to join the task force officially, and Chuck had relented, removing him from desk duty for the duration of the investigation.

"And I'll tell you something else," Morton said, his pale face reddening. "The family has already released the same picture to the media. They're even talking about giving interviews—the victim's 'bereaved loved ones' and all that."

"Do they really think that's going to help catch this guy?" Butts said with disgust. "Or are they just publicity hogs?"

"Who knows?" Chuck answered. "But if we can't keep control of what the media does and doesn't know we're in even deeper than before."

"That's all we need," Butts grumbled. "A game of tug-of-war with the media."

Lee had his own personal struggle to wage, and had no desire to inflict it upon anyone else. He could feel the familiar claw of depression tugging at him, trying to pull him downward into its evil embrace. He was determined to keep it at bay at least until the investigation was over. The possibility of that being anytime soon felt very remote right now.

"What about this note?" he asked.

Chuck handed him the printout copy, with the familiar block-letter handwriting.

I guess I'm not all that bad after all. What I am is
a naughty girl – a very naughty girl.

"Okay," Chuck said to him, "Let's go over what we know about him already, and if there's anything you can add, this is the time."

Lee felt a sense of accusation behind his words, but just nodded.

"You know," Butts remarked, "the water may be part of his signature, but it sure as hell helps eliminate evidence."

"Yeah," Chuck agreed. "That's what I was thinking."

Lee summoned his dwindling wits, grabbed a Magic Marker, and wrote on the easel next to the bulletin board.

UNSUB
White Male
Mid twenties to early thirties

Butts scratched his ear. "Okay, I get the gender, but how do you figure the age?"

"The crimes are too sophisticated for a teenager, so he's at least in his twenties. The fantasy is well developed and elaborate, so he thought about this for a long time before his first kill. Therefore, he could be as old as his early thirties."

Ruggles frowned. "Excuse me, sir, but why couldn't he be older?"

"It's not impossible, especially if he was in jail for unrelated crimes for a period of time—but my guess is that's not the case. He's clever and he's careful. I'm not saying he hasn't broken the law before—I just don't think he's been caught yet."

"Why do you think he's white?" Butts asked.

"Two reasons. For one thing, most serial offenders are. But more importantly, all of the victims are white. He kills cross-gender, but it's unlikely that he would also kill cross-racially. If he were black, or even Hispanic, we would expect some of the victims to be as well."

Chuck grunted and folded his arms. "All right—continue."

Lee turned back to the board and wrote:

Mobile – job? Upper East Side/Bronx

"I think I catch your drift, sir, if you don't mind my saying so," Ruggles offered.

"Yes, Ruggles?" Chuck said.

"Well, it's the killings, sir—they're all spread out, which indicates that he is quite, uh, able to get around, you know. And I expect that his job could give him such mobility, as well as familiarity with the Upper East Side and the Bronx. Is that what you meant, sir?" he asked Lee.

"You have the makings of a first-class profiler, Sergeant," he replied, and Ruggles's rather prominent ears turned scarlet.

"Okay, okay," Butts grumbled irritably. "So he gets around. What else?"

Lee turned and wrote:

> Somewhat literate/educated
> Gender issues

"We know about the gender issues," Chuck said, "but just how literate do you think he is?"

"That's a good question. Krieger said the notes indicated he was trying to make an impression. He might be an overachiever trying to impress us with how intellectual he is. There was that reference to *Hamlet* in the note found on Ana, but it was clumsily done."

Butts shook his head. "Good God. It's not enough that he's leadin' us on by the nose—now he wants us to admire his learning on top of it?"

"We're his audience," Lee pointed out. "We've probably given him more attention in the past few weeks than he's had in his whole life."

"I see, sir—that makes sense to me," Ruggles said.

Butts glared at him. "So basically he's enjoying all this?" the detective said with disgust.

"On one level, absolutely. But people who know him will notice his behavior changing—maybe he's losing weight, or becoming forgetful. He might be short of temper or preoccupied, or acting odd in other ways."

He turned and wrote on the board in capital letters, underlining the words twice.

WATER TRAUMA

"You said that before," Chuck commented. "That he had some kind of trauma around water early in life. Any ideas what that could be?"

"Someone close to him might have drowned, sir," Ruggles offered.

"We already thought of that," Butts said in a bored voice. Lee turned and wrote.

EYES – Watching?

"What about the eyes?" said Butts.

"I think it's related. I think his trauma with water also involved being observed, maybe by women."

"The first victim whose eyes he removed was male, sir," Ruggles suggested.

"Good point," Lee said. "So probably it isn't gender specific, but could just be his signature evolving." Underneath the last entry he wrote:

ORGANIZED

"That's self-explanatory," said Chuck. "But how does it help us?"

"He's methodical and thorough. He probably drives a late-model car, well maintained. His appearance will be neat and not call attention to itself."

"What about visiting the bodies, sir? Might he do that?" Ruggles asked. "I remember how the Green River Killer used to do that, and that's how they caught him."

"It's possible," Lee said. "If they are there long enough without being discovered—but we've hardly given him time. They've usually been discovered within a day or two at the most."

"I take your point, sir," Ruggles said.

"The water motif means more to him than it did with the Green River Killer," Lee mused.

"Right," Chuck agreed. "The Green River Killer just used the water to dispose of his victims, but with this guy you think there's a deeper meaning there."

"There's one more thing," Lee said. "I don't know if it'll help us find him, but it's likely there was a precipitating stressor before his first victim. Something in his life that changed—probably for the worse."

"A breakup, a job loss, something like that?" Butts suggested.

"Could be—but I think we should keep our minds open. The important thing is not the event itself, but his reaction to it. Whatever it was, it pushed him over the edge, and caused him to start killing."

"All right," said Chuck, looking at his watch. "I don't know about the rest of you, but I need some caffeine."

He scooped some coffee into the Krups grinder and pushed the button. Lee watched as the beans tumbled over each other as the blades shredded and ground them to dust. The loud clattering assaulted his sleep-deprived system and made his ears ring. He looked at the others. Butts was staring at the coffee grinder with a blank expression, Ruggles was fiddling with the photos on the bulletin board, and Chuck was leaning wearily on the edge of his desk, pouring water into the coffeemaker.

It was going to be a long night.

CHAPTER FIFTY-NINE

Later that night, shortly after arriving home, Lee heard a rapid, timid rapping on his door. When he opened it he was stunned to find Charlotte Perkins standing there, rain dripping from her soaked garments. She wore a long woolen cloak with a hood, but it was no match for tonight's downpour. Her matted hair hung in damp strands around her face, and she was shivering.

"The lady who lives downstairs let me into the building," she said apologetically.

"Come in, please," he said, taking her sopping wet coat and hanging it on the coatrack to dry. "How did you find me?"

"You left your card with my brother when you were at our house." She looked around the apartment while rubbing her hands together.

"Can I get you something hot to drink?"

"Y-yes, p-please," she said, her teeth chattering.

He put the kettle on and came back to the living room. She was seated on the ottoman in front of the couch, her thin arms wrapped around her body. Whereas Ana Watkins had sauntered in and taken possession of the place as if she owned it, Charlotte Perkins was an uncomfortable visitor, trying to take up as little space as possible.

"Would you like some dry clothes?" he asked.

She looked up at him gratefully. "Do you have some?"

"Yes—my, uh, girlfriend keeps some clothes here I think you could wear."

Was Kathy still his girlfriend? She hadn't called to ask for her clothes back yet, at least. He thought of giving Charlotte something of his, but that felt like too intimate a gesture for this virginal woman in her prim lace-up boots and long skirt. He suffered a brief pang of guilt at offering Kathy's clothes, but brushed it aside. Charlotte Perkins was at least half a foot taller than Kathy, but had the rail-thin build of a fashion model, and he thought she would be able to slip into one of Kathy's dresses easily.

He ducked into the bedroom and returned with the most conservative things he could find in the closet—a long flowered skirt and a long-sleeved black oxford shirt. He handed them to Charlotte and pointed the way to the bathroom.

When she came out he had hot tea waiting. He was right—Kathy's clothes did fit, up to a point. Charlotte's long arms protruded from the shirtsleeves, which came down just past her elbows. He took her wet clothes down to the laundry room to put in the dryer, and when he returned she was perched on the edge of the sofa sipping Earl Grey (he didn't care for it much, but something told him that she would). He asked her why she had come.

She clutched her cup in her hands and hunched over her knees. Once again Lee was reminded of a tall, thin bird—an egret, perhaps, or a heron. Her wet hair was plastered to her head, and made her deep-set, luminous eyes appear even larger. He handed her a fresh bath towel for her hair and sat across from her on the leather hassock.

"You must excuse me, but this is very difficult," she said,

running the towel over her hair. He couldn't help notice how it curled around her face when damp, and looked rather fetching. In spite of her maidenly ways, she was quite an attractive woman.

He cleared his throat to push the thought from his mind. "Take your time." His words belied the sharp stab of anticipation in his stomach. He did not want to scare her off by appearing too eager.

Her gray eyes roamed the room as if searching for an escape. "I'm afraid my brother has been less than honest with you."

"Oh?" His attempt to sound disinterested failed, so he tried leaning back in his chair to conceal his impatience. But she wasn't paying much attention to him; she was too caught up in her own struggle.

"Yes. I—well, this is so hard. Forgive me. I am quite beside myself today."

"Of course," he said. "Can I get you some more tea?"

"Yes, that would be nice," she replied, hastily gulping down the rest in her cup.

He took her mug to the kitchen to refill it, and when he returned she was standing at the window, gazing out. As he entered the room she turned abruptly and blurted out the words as though she were afraid they might choke her.

"My brother and I are living as husband and wife."

The force of her confession made him take a step backward. Some tea sloshed out of the mug onto the floor, but neither of them made a move to wipe it up.

He tried to formulate a response to her words, but everything that came to him seemed grossly inappropriate or inadequate.

She rescued him by continuing. "No doubt you think we are very wicked."

"No," he said. "I don't. But—"

"We *are* very wicked," she said. "Or at least that's what I think. But my brother . . . " She waved her hand as if dismissing the very idea of him. "To my brother it is all very natural, you see—even foreordained."

"I don't understand," he said, still holding her tea in his outstretched hand. Something about her stopped him from crossing the remaining stretch of floor between them. He put the tea on the sideboard.

She paced in front of the window. For some reason the thought went through his head that she was a moving target, in case anyone outside tried to take a shot at her. He slipped behind her and closed the curtains.

"You have no doubt noticed that our attire is somewhat—antiquated."

"It did occur to me."

"There is a reason for that. It is not whim or fancy, or eccentricity, as you may have thought. It is because my brother believes that we are the reincarnation of a husband and wife who lived over a hundred years ago," she said, wringing her hands. "And since our souls are essentially theirs, it is not only right but necessary that we live as husband and wife."

"Who are they?"

She waved her hand again. "That is not important right now."

"I see. How long has he had this . . . notion?"

"For the past fifteen years. Ever since he received the Gift."

"What gift?"

"The Gift of Second Sight—the ability to see through the mists of time."

"I see. And what do you think about all this?"

"I don't know *what* to think. I have always believed my brother to be the wisest and most honorable of men, but now . . ."

"Has something happened to change your mind?"

She shook her whole body, as if trying to cast off her worries. "I told you before that I had no contact with my brother's patients."

"Yes."

"I was being less than honest. In fact, I tend to his appointment book and often admit patients for their visits."

"Why did you lie to us?"

"Because he told me to."

"Why?"

She looked at him, her eyes anguished.

"I don't *know*—when I asked him, he told me to mind my own business."

"And why would he do that?"

She bit her lip until a small pinpoint of blood appeared—she was clearly struggling with her conscience.

"Because," she said, the words wrenching themselves out of her, "I am certain he was having . . . relations . . . with one of his patients."

"I see. And who was it?"

But even before she spoke, Lee knew the answer.

"Ana Watkins."

CHAPTER SIXTY

Patiently you wait for me to come home to you—with such care I've collected you, my only true friends, beautiful and pure in your shiny glass bowl.

Caleb opened the door softly so as not to disturb his father. His treasure was tucked away carefully in his coat pocket, wrapped in plastic to keep it pure until he could add it to his collection. He closed the door behind him and tiptoed across the living room to the back bedroom. His keys rattled as he took them from his pocket—his hands were trembling a little. Sliding the key into the lock, he gave a quick twist and pushed. The door slid open on its oiled hinges, revealing his sanctuary, his secret lair, his holiest of holies.

He took a step into the room and closed the door behind him. It would not do to let his father wander in here, so he kept the door locked at all times. No one must come in here—this room was for him and his treasures only, so he could admire them at his leisure. It was his little secret.

He pulled the tightly wrapped parcel from his coat pocket and carefully undid the rubber band around the plastic bag. Holding his hand out flat, he slid the contents of the bag onto his bare palm, shivering at the feel of them—soft and smooth and wet as eels. He examined them—each pair was different, and the more he collected the more he came to appreciate the subtle variations—the singular shades of blue, or brown, or—his favorite—hazel.

He looked at the pair in his hand. They were blue, but not a deep ocean blue—more of an aquamarine blue, with a greenish tinge to them. They were on the large side, and if he looked closely enough he could see tiny flecks of gold at the edges of the irises. Yes, these were nice, very nice—definitely a worthy specimen to keep the others company.

He sighed with pleasure. Carefully he lifted the lid of the glass jar on the middle shelf of the bookcase and added his trophies to the ones floating in the jar. *Come to me, my pretty ones, my little jewels, my windows to the soul.* They stared out at him—perhaps they were severed now from their souls, or maybe—just maybe—the souls lived behind them still.

He heard his father coughing in the other room—a bitter, grating sound. He replaced the lid on the jar and slid it back into the bookshelf. He would go to his father now, safe in the knowledge that he had yet another secret to keep from him.

CHAPTER SIXTY-ONE

"Oh, Dr. Campbell, do you think my brother is capable of—of murder?"

Charlotte Perkins stood in front of the French window overlooking the street, her damp hair plastered to her head, awkward in ill-fitting clothes, hands hanging at her sides in surrender.

"What do you think?" Lee said.

"Until now I would have said no, but then I would not have thought him capable of desecrating the doctor–patient relationship either. To say nothing of the . . . union . . . between us." She looked at Lee with pleading eyes. "Before you judge us too harshly, let me tell you that there was never any question of our having children. Of course, now we are too old, but it was never a possibility in the first place."

Lee didn't ask for details.

"So you see, what we did—who we were—caused no harm to anyone else."

"What about you? Did it cause harm to you?"

She drew her sweater tighter around her shoulders. "I used to believe everything my brother told me, but now . . ." Her voice trailed off, as if she couldn't bear to continue the thought.

"Why do you believe your brother was . . . intimate with Ana Watkins?"

"You may perhaps think me foolish," she said. "But I had my suspicions for some time. Then one day I lingered outside the office during one of her sessions, and I heard—" She paused to blink back tears. "I heard sounds that could only mean one thing. Later, I was standing outside in the hall when she came out. She caught my eye, and gave a triumphant little smile, as if to say, *'See, he's mine now.'* I hated her then, and I hate her still."

"If you hate her, then why come to me to help catch her killer?"

"Because if you don't find him, other women will die. And I could never live with that on my conscience."

"Even if the killer turns out to be your brother?"

"Yes."

"Do you hate him, too?"

"I tried to hate him—oh, how I tried! But I couldn't. It seems I am incapable of hating him—weak, pathetic creature that I am."

"You are neither weak nor pathetic, Miss Perkins," Lee said. "In fact, you are very determined and brave, coming here through a storm like this to tell me something that is obviously so difficult for you to talk about."

In response, she walked over to the piano, its shiny wood gleaming in the lamplight, and touched the keyboard lightly. Her back to him, she said, "There's something else I should tell you."

"What's that?"

"I wrote the threatening note Ana received in the mail."

"You? But the magazine was found at her house."

"Yes—because I left it there. After she died I wanted the police to think she had written it herself."

"How did her prints get on it?"

For the first time since she arrived, Charlotte Perkins smiled—a sly, prideful smile. "I saw her reading that same magazine in the waiting room—that's why I chose it when I made my note."

"You would make a very good criminal, Miss Perkins," Lee said.

"But I only did it to scare her! I wanted her to stay away from my brother, not only for my sake, but for her own."

"Did it occur to you that you could be arrested and prosecuted for your actions?"

"There is something else I doubt my brother told you," she said, ignoring the question.

"What's that?"

"He sees patients at a public clinic in the city twice a month. He doesn't want people to know because it hurts his pride that he can't make his living entirely from private practice."

"Where is this clinic?"

"It's the mental health outpatient clinic at St. Vincent's."

At the sound of the words, Lee's mind momentarily froze.

"What is it?" she said. "Is something wrong?"

"Oh, no," he said.

"You know of it?"

"Yes."

He knew of it more than he was willing to tell her. He had spent a week there as a patient following his sister's disappearance, suffering from a clinical depression so severe that he was considered a suicide risk.

"Do you think one of his patients there could be violent?"

"Possibly. But I thought I ought to tell you, in any case."

She looked at him with an anxious expression, her thin lips compressed, worry lines crisscrossing her forehead like railroad tracks at a busy junction.

"I'll look into it. Can I ask you something?"

"Yes, of course."

"There was an entry in Ana's diary about confronting someone. Do you think that could have referred to your brother?"

She bit her lip again. "I suppose so. One day a few weeks after I realized they were . . . together . . . I heard what sounded like an argument in his office, and when she came out after her session, I could see she had been crying."

"So you think she might have wanted to break it off with him?"

"Perhaps. It was a violation of the doctor–patient relationship, after all."

Lee thought about how he had nearly violated that relationship himself, and a thin shiver sliced its way up his spine. He put a hand on Charlotte's shoulder and was surprised when she reacted by leaning into him. He stepped away and coughed to cover his own reaction. "Thank you for everything you've told me."

"What happens now?" she said.

"Does your brother know where you are?"

"No. He thinks I'm at the hospital all day."

"Do you have someone there to cover for you in case he calls?"

She smiled sadly. "He won't. He never calls me at work. He doesn't care for the telephone—he likes to point out that when we were first 'alive,' it had not yet been invented."

"Does anyone besides you and your brother know of your . . . relationship?"

"I used to think no one did. But now I am not so sure. I

think it's entirely possible that Ana Watkins knew—based on that smile she gave me when she left his office that day."

"So you think he may have killed her to silence her?"

She rose and began to pace the room.

"Oh, Dr. Campbell, I don't know what to think! I pray that is not the case—I pray it with all my heart and soul!"

"Clearly you can't return home. You're not safe there."

"Oh, but I must. If I don't, he'll suspect something, and then who knows what he'll do?"

"You can't. I don't care if he suspects or not."

She startled him by taking his hands in hers. To his surprise, her hands were warm and soft.

"Dr. Campbell, you must let me play this game out as I see fit."

"If you insist on returning, at least let me put a police guard on your house."

She laughed for the first time since he had known her. It was an odd, strangled chortle, the laugh of someone unfamiliar with joy.

"My brother is very observant. He would sniff out a police presence immediately."

"I can't let you—"

"You can't stop me," she said. "And now, if I might request my clothes back again, I must be on my way."

He thought wildly of holding on to her clothes as a way of preventing her from leaving, but he knew it was useless. She would leave anyway, and when she turned up in a stranger's clothes, her brother wold be even more suspicious. He went to the laundry room to fetch her clothes. When she was dressed again, she pulled on her curiously old-fashioned boots and threw her cloak around her shoulders.

"At least let me give you an umbrella," he said, looking out the window at the rain, which, though no longer torrential, was still falling.

"I will have to leave it on the bus," she said. "He will see at once that it isn't mine."

"Fine—leave it on the bus. I'm sure someone will find it useful," he said, handing her his sturdiest umbrella.

"Thank you," she said, pulling the hood over her head.

"No, thank *you*. You've helped us enormously. Wait!" he said, getting an idea. "Do you have a cell phone?"

She shook her head. "My brother—"

"Take mine." Grabbing it from the hall table, he pressed it into her hand.

"I don't—"

"Have you ever used one?"

"Yes, at the hospital—"

"All right. Now, here's my home number," he said, showing her the entry in the contact list, "and here is Detective Butts's cell number. I want you to call either or both of us if you find yourself in any kind of trouble."

She turned her eyes up to him, and with the soft yellow hall light shining on her sharp, earnest face, she looked quite pretty.

"All right—thank you." She hesitated, looking down at the phone clutched in her hand. "At the very least Martin knows more about Ana Watkins than he is admitting. I'll see what I can find out."

"You've done quite enough, Miss Perkins. Please promise me you won't put yourself in jeopardy."

"I can only promise to do my best. The rest is in God's hands."

"If you can't think of your own safety, then think of how I would feel if anything happened to you."

"Very well," she said with a little smile that, on anyone else, would have been flirtatious.

And with that she slipped out into the night. As the door

closed behind her, he was reminded of the night Ana left in much the same way—and of the terrible fate she met. He looked out the window at her retreating form, watching her sidestep the puddles forming on the sidewalk as she hurried down the street toward Third Avenue.

CHAPTER SIXTY-TWO

The house was dark and quiet when Charlotte pushed open the front door and crept into the foyer. The rain had stopped, but she could hear the slow, steady drip of water from the eaves, residue of the evening's downpour. She removed her cloak and hung it from the bentwood coatrack in the hall, then unlaced her soft leather ankle boots, which were wet and muddy. Martin hated finding stains on the lush Oriental carpets. It wasn't a long walk from the bus stop, but in the dark she couldn't avoid the puddles lying in wait for her among the cracks in the sidewalks. She propped her boots on the bottom of the rack and tiptoed along the side of the long maroon runner rug leading from the foyer through the front hall. She shivered a little as she dug her bare toes into the deep, plush wool—it felt so good after sitting on the bus for two hours in damp clothes.

She tiptoed up the stairs and toward her room at the end of the long, narrow hall, silent as a cat, sliding her feet along the carpet to avoid tripping in the dark. She crept along the edge of the carpet, avoiding the center, where she knew the floorboards creaked underfoot. This was not the first time she had snuck home at night, hoping to avoid waking her brother. She had to pass his room in order to get to hers, so it was important to be extra quiet.

As she tiptoed down the hallway, she ran her hand along the wall for balance, tracing the familiar pattern of the textured wallpaper with her fingers. As she approached her brother's bedroom, her fingers touched something wet and sticky. It was too dark to see what it was; it felt like someone had spilled pudding on the wall. She made a mental note to wipe it off in the morning—Martin had no doubt spilled it himself, but would hold her responsible and expect her to clean it up.

The house was eerily silent, she thought as she passed her brother's room. She noticed the door was ajar, which struck her as odd. A shaft of moonlight sliced through the crack in the door, the long, pale blade of light falling across her path. Normally Martin kept it closed at night—maybe he had left it open because she was working late at the hospital. That is what she planned to tell him to explain why she was out so late tonight. With the practice of one used to deceiving, she had her story ready: one of her patients had gone into labor. It was a difficult birth, and she had stayed at the woman's side half the night. Of course, he could easily check up on her—he had done so before—so she would have to coach her colleagues to cover for her. But that shouldn't prove too difficult; they had done it in the past. Most of the women she worked with thought Martin was a tyrant and a cad, and couldn't understand why she let her brother boss her around so much.

But they didn't understand—no one did, really. He had a power over her she could not explain, deeper than blood, shared history, or even sex. There was something preternatural about it, a bond that she had tried hard to break, but never with success. He was her Mesmer, her Rasputin, her Houdini.

When she reached her bedroom she slipped inside and closed the door quietly behind her. She lit an oil lamp—Martin made concessions to the modern world, but electricity was not one of them—and went to her dressing table. Sitting in front of the graceful beveled mirror, she leaned over and felt underneath the table for what she knew was hiding there. Her fingers closed on the familiar object; carefully she withdrew the ornately carved wooden box, placing it in front of her. Her hands trembled a little as she opened it and took out the amber-colored bottle. She shook it gently to disperse the reddish-brown liquid inside, then used the attached eyedropper to measure out a small amount, which she placed on her tongue. The droplets sparkled like gold in the warm light of the gas lamp. One, two, three drops—her body began to relax the moment she tasted the familiar bitterness. She felt the liquid slide down the back of her throat and let her head fall back. A thin sigh of pleasure escaped her lean body.

She studied the label on the bottle for a moment before putting it away. The handmade lettering was old fashioned and carefully wrought; she was proud of her work. Too bad she could not share it with Martin. Her job at the hospital gave her access to the raw materials; the rest of the work was hers. After a few hours of pouring through herbalist texts and chemists' textbooks for measurements and formulas, the rest was not hard.

She put the bottle back in its hiding place and opened a window—the room suddenly felt unbearably stuffy—then lay down on her four-poster canopy bed. The laudanum went to work quickly—the alcohol in the homemade tincture made certain of that. Her head began to fill with a pleasant cotton-wool sensation, and she stared up at the ceiling, studying the water stain that always reminded her of a unicorn. . . . Her mind relaxed more and more as she slid further from consciousness, wrapped in the welcoming arms of a drug-induced sleep. She floated through opium-flavored dreams in which she danced in a grand ballroom with that handsome Dr. Campbell while her brother watched from the sidelines, his face purple with fury.

She jerked into consciousness abruptly, her skin tingling, shivering from the cool evening air. She wasn't sure what had awakened her—was it an unfamiliar sound or smell, or the curtains billowing out in the sudden gust of wind blowing in through the open window? Whatever it was, she was certain something had changed in the atmosphere of the room—something was different.

She sat up, her head swimming in a blur of opium. The drug dragged at her body as she rose from the bed; the air itself seemed encased in a blue haze. She was not frightened or even startled when the door to her bedroom opened and the tall, slim figure in white entered the room. In her drug-induced fog, she was unable to make out the face, even though she squinted hard at it. She realized all at once that it was a spirit. So her brother's prophecies had come to pass, and she was at long last able to communicate with the dead! She had long chided herself for being unable to sense, as he did, that they were both the embodiment of long-departed souls. He alone seemed to have access to the "world beyond the veil," as he called it. But now, she thought joyfully, the veil was at last lifting for her! She too would know the mysteries that, until now, she had sensed only vaguely.

She approached the shape lurking deep in the shadows of her room, her arms outstretched as if to embrace it. The figure shrank back, and she was afraid it would leave. She tried to speak to it, to call it back, but the laudanum had thickened her tongue, and her attempt at speech came out as a guttural grunt.

The sound of her voice seemed to startle the spirit, and

he—she could see clearly now it was a man—gave a little gasp.

She tried to tell him not to be afraid, but it came out as, "Doan bay fried."

Now he was standing less than a yard away, and she reached out a hand to him. To her surprise, the spirit grabbed her wrist, and she was startled to find that, for a ghost, his grip was very firm indeed, the fingers quite strong. His skin was surprisingly warm. She wasn't sure what she expected, but not this.

She tried to wrest her hand free, but, with one quick pull, her visitor drew her body close to his, wrapping his long arms around her. She had an impulse to surrender, to swoon in the firmness of his embrace, but another, more primal impulse took over, and she resisted, trying to wrench free. But the laudanum had turned her muscles to rubber, and her effort was pathetically ineffective. It was like struggling in a hangman's noose—any attempt to free herself only served to tighten his grip.

She fought against the effect of the drug, but it was no use. Her head was hopelessly fuzzy, and she only vaguely felt the sharp prick in her arm. She twisted around to see what had caused it, and was surprised to see her captor holding a syringe in his free hand. She tried to figure out what possible use a ghost could have with a syringe, but her sight was already beginning to dim as he lifted her up and carried her from the room.

CHAPTER SIXTY-THREE

As soon as Charlotte left, Lee could feel the cloud of depression, which he had been staving off by sheer willpower, begin to descend. It blanketed him from above, but also blossomed within, like an evil vine whose tendrils crept into his brain, his heart, his soul. He looked out the window. A steady rain was falling over the city, sending its soothing sound into the nooks and crannies of the jumbled hodgepodge of low buildings that is the East Village. Normally, Lee would have found it calming, but he couldn't stop thinking about Kathy.

Thinking about Kathy led to thoughts about his sister, which led to thoughts about the three thousand souls whose bodies had been reduced to rubble, ashes, and bone fragments on the southern tip of the island he called home. The sense of loss compounded upon itself, and he didn't know whether to feel anger or sadness at the whole terrible waste. He tried to push these thoughts from his weakening brain, but it was like pushing a stone uphill, a Sisyphean task.

There was only one thing that could help right now: strenuous exercise. If he went for a run, it might give him enough endorphins at least for the time being. He went to the bedroom closet, extracted his running shoes from under a bag of laundry, pulled on a pair of sweatpants, and threw on a plastic Windbreaker. In spite of the rain, he headed down the steps, determined to run until he was worn out.

He ran west, through the darkened streets of the West Village, to the embankment along the Hudson. The river was stormy, the waves slapping against the wooden piers jutting out into its murky water, as he jogged north along the embankment. He was the only one foolish enough to be out on a night like this, but he liked the solitude, the darkness, and the rain stinging his face, hard as little diamond bullets. The abundance of physical sensations stimulated his brain so much that it couldn't hold on to the feeling of depression, and he could feel it releasing from his body like water circling a drain.

He ran harder, pounding his feet against the pavement, sending water splashing in all directions—the weeks of rain had created puddles that didn't have time to drain before the next downpour. As he ran, odd phrases ran through his brain. *Past lives, past lives. . . .* Ahead of him the *Intrepid* loomed, silent and imposing in its permanent mooring, its great gray bulkhead dark against the night sky. The aircraft carrier was now a military museum, and drew scores of tourists all year round. *Too bad it couldn't protect us when terror and death rained down from the sky.*

He turned and headed back south, toward the hole in the earth that once was the pair of proud towers anchoring the bottom of the island. *Past lives, past lives. . . .* He felt a visceral sense of the souls who had perished when those towers came crashing down. On nights like this it was almost as though they were there with him, keeping him company as he hurtled through the storm, squinting against the hard little pellets of rain.

Past lives, past lives . . . that was all they had now, these people, their lives past, gone in an instant, victims of crazed religious fanatics. He thought about what Kathy had said about her job. The effects of the tragedy were still rippling outward, like a stone thrown in a pond. He wondered where it would all stop. He hadn't realized until she told him how hard her job was, how emotionally taxing. On the one hand, he felt bad for her, and on the other, he resented her for using it as an excuse to pull away from him.

He thought about Martin Perkins as he ran: Was he a crazed religious fanatic? It was hard to tell. Certainly he was eccentric, but was he dangerous? Lee might not have the answer to that until it was too late. He thought about what Charlotte had revealed to him tonight. It was odd, but in some ways the news didn't surprise him at all. Martin Perkins was so odd that it would be strange if he didn't have some behavioral skeletons in his closet. He didn't envy poor Charlotte. He wasn't sure if incest between consenting adults was a crime in New Jersey or not, but it certainly was creepy.

He arrived back at his apartment soaking wet, his hand throbbing, the bandages on his arm beginning to peel off in sodden strands—but not depressed. In fact, he felt an almost giddy sense of possibilities. He knew it was just the chemicals firing in his brain, but the relief was so great he felt like crying. Kathy had broken up with him, the killer was still at large, and Krieger was still missing, but somehow the future unfurled itself before him like a flag, rippling through his endorphin-drenched brain.

He looked at the phone machine on the desk, which was blinking, its amber light winking at him like an evil red eye. He peeled off his Windbreaker; crossing the room in four steps, he pressed the button.

The flat, dry voice sent a chill through the entire room.

"I was wondering when you would start tapping this

phone line. Fat lot of good it will do you. So let's keep it short: What about the red dress?"

Lee stood staring at the machine as it whirred into rewind, completely unaware of the steady dripping of his wet clothing onto the expensive Persian carpet his mother had given him.

CHAPTER SIXTY-FOUR

When he reported the call into the wiretapping switchboard, the answer was predictable: It came from a pay phone somewhere deep in Queens.

"You want us to send a car over?" the bored-sounding woman at the switchboard asked. There was a faint scratching sound in the background, as if she were filing her nails.

"No, thanks—he'll be long gone," Lee answered, and hung up.

He threw himself on the couch without removing his sopping clothes and stared at the ceiling, running possibilities through his mind. Finally, disgusted with the whole situation, he got up and took a shower. Afterward, he felt clean but not cleansed; the sound of that voice on his answering machine made him feel soiled. He wandered into the bathroom, broke a Xanax in two, and swallowed half. Then, just to be sure, he gulped down the other half as well.

He lay back down on the couch, a pillow over his head, as a welcome drowsiness settled over his limbs. He surrendered gladly, sinking into a deep slumber. He slipped through a series of dreams, shifting imagery of places and people he knew, until he found himself in a deep pool of water. He was in the middle of a mountain lake, treading water, the bottom far beneath him, the water itself crystalline and clear, the sun sparkling off its surface. He didn't know how he had gotten there, but decided to swim back to the shore. As he got closer, he saw a woman lying facedown, half in and half out of the water. He swam faster, and when he reached her, he turned her over, and saw that it was Ana Watkins. She was warm, but she didn't appear to be breathing, so he began giving her mouth-to-mouth resuscitation. As he did, her body began to dissolve in his arms, and he was holding a rotting corpse.

He awoke with a start to the sound of loud knocking. Leaping from the couch, he made his way to the front door, but before he got there, he heard a deep voice.

"It's me—Diesel!"

He opened the door to find Diesel standing in the hallway, draped in a dark oilcloth poncho, like a great black bird. Next to him stood Detective Butts, looking like a drowned walrus. His wet hair was plastered to his head so that his large ears protruded even more alarmingly; his bulbous nose dripped onto the straw doormat.

Lee stared at the unlikely pair. "What you doing here?"

"You gonna let us in or what?" Butts demanded.

He let them in and gave them towels to dry off. Outside, he could tell it was morning, which meant he had slept through the night, though the day was so dark he had no idea what time it was.

"What time is it?" he asked Butts.

"It's after ten," Butts replied, briskly toweling off what was left of his hair.

"So what's going on?"

In response, Butts handed him his cell phone. The text message read *pls help*, and the call was from Lee's cell number.

"I called back, but it bounced straight to voice mail," Butts said. "Then I called your number here and got a busy signal, so I called Diesel. He couldn't reach you either, so I got in the car and drove over."

"And picked me up on the way," Diesel added.

Lee groaned. He had forgotten to call Butts to tell him about giving his cell phone to Charlotte. He quickly explained the situation, then used Butts's cell to call his own. Again it bounced straight to his voice mail.

"My car's outside," Butts said.

"Let's go."

"I'm coming with you," Diesel said.

"That's not—" Butts began, but Diesel interrupted.

"I'm coming *with you*."

The detective looked at Lee, who shrugged.

"The more the merrier," Butts said, opening the apartment door.

Within ten minutes they were barreling down Varick Street, and within twenty had cleared the Holland Tunnel. Butts's car was a massive blue Ford, a rattling old gas guzzler the size of a small boat.

They used Butts's phone to call the Jersey police in Lambertville, the nearest station to Stockton. A patrol car was dispatched to the Perkins place. Repeated calls to Lee's cell had gone straight to voice mail—it was possible the battery had run down. He wished he had thought to give Charlotte the phone charger. Numerous calls to Perkins's office number were picked up by his voice mail recording.

"Nice wheels," Lee remarked as they swung onto Route 78. He was doing his best to keep his mind off what they might find when they reached Stockton.

"Don't knock it till you've tried it," Butts muttered, gnawing on a thumbnail. He always seemed to have something in his mouth—cigars, doughnuts, candy. Failing that, his finger would do. "I wanted to get a smaller car, but the wife was attached to old Blue Bertha, so we kept it. Now I've gotten kinda attached, you know?"

"Doesn't it eat up gas?" Diesel asked from the backseat.

"Not as much as you'd think," Butts said. "It does okay on the highway. The trick is to keep it tuned up and all. One of my sons works for a mechanic, so we get a family rate."

"Hey," Lee said suddenly. "Why did both of you show up at my place?" He craned his neck to look at Diesel in the backseat. He was so enormous that even in this roomy old car he looked cramped. "Have you added law enforcement to your other gigs?"

"No—I was on my way to see you when I ran into Detective Butts."

"What for?"

"I just thought you might need my help."

This wasn't the first time Diesel had turned up at an opportune moment—he seemed to have a nose for trouble.

"One thing surprises me," Butts remarked as they reached the turnoff for Route 202 South. "I wouldn't think that—uh, Charlotte—would know how to do a text message, y'know?"

"That's true," Lee said. "She did tell me she used a cell phone at the hospital where she works. She must have learned how to do it there."

"What do you think the chances are Krieger's still alive?" Butts asked as he steered the big car onto the exit ramp.

"Based on how quickly he's killed the others, not very good," Lee said grimly.

At that moment Butts's own cell phone rang. It was the patrol cop calling from the Perkins house to report that he was sitting in his car outside the place, but it all was quiet inside the house. There had been no answer when he knocked on the door, and no sign of life in the house. There was a car parked outside, however, and when he ran a check on the plates it came up as belonging to Martin Perkins.

Lee didn't know if that was good news or bad, but he asked the officer if he could possibly wait until they arrived to go in, and he said he would try.

Butts didn't need any help finding the way to Stockton—they'd traveled it enough times by now. As they zigzagged down the winding road that led to the town's main street, Lee's stomach twisted with anticipation. He had zoomed down this road so many times on his bike, flying along with the wind rushing in his ears—and now he was driving down it in search of a murderer.

The big car rattled down the modest main street, past Errico's Market, the gas station and liquor store, and the little clump of restaurants around the Stockton Inn. The rain had stopped, and the street was quiet. A couple of kids were playing Hula-hoop on their front lawn, and a young mother was pushing her baby in a stroller on the way to the grocery store. The sun had come out, and the street was bathed in a golden glow. It looked as though nothing could ever be wrong on such a street on such a summer's day. The air of normalcy wasn't convincing. Though he hoped he was wrong, Lee had a bad feeling as they approached the Perkins place.

The police cruiser sat in front of the house. A couple of small boys had stopped by on their bikes to talk to the officer behind the wheel. As soon as he saw Butts pull up, he got out of the car and strode over to greet them. To Lee's surprise, it was Officer Lars Anderson, the young cop they had met at Ana Watkins's house.

"Hi there," he said. "I heard it was you two and volunteered to come on over. You think we have probable cause to go in?"

Lee showed him the text message on Butts's cell phone

and explained that, in all likelihood, it came from Charlotte Perkins.

"That's good enough for me," Anderson replied, and led the way up the steps to the front porch. He paused and glanced at Diesel, then back at Butts.

"Undercover," Butts said in a confidential tone, and the trooper nodded.

A round of knocking also brought no response, so Anderson whipped a towel out of his car's trunk, wrapped it around his arm, and broke the bottom pane of glass on the door with one deft punch.

"Looks like you've done that a few times before," Butts remarked as he reached around to unlatch the lock from the inside.

"That's why I keep a towel in the trunk," Anderson replied. "You never know when it'll come in handy."

They followed him into the front hall, which was dark and deserted.

"Anybody home?" Anderson called out, but was met with silence.

They walked through to the living room, where everything looked to be in order. The piano keys gleamed ivory white in the morning sun. There was no sign of life in the first-floor parlor, the kitchen, or the butler's pantry to the side of the kitchen. On the other side of the kitchen was an office that evidently served as a consulting room as well. It contained a couch and several armchairs, as well as a desk and built-in bookcase.

When they had secured the first floor, they proceeded upstairs. The two small bedrooms in what must have originally been the servants' wing were clear, but as they approached the master bedroom, they saw the blood. There were crimson fingerprints on the wall, as well as high-velocity splatter in all directions; some blood had even landed on the windowsill on the other side of the corridor. It was clear that someone had been viciously attacked in this hallway. The four of them stopped walking, and Officer Anderson put a finger to his lips. There was no need for silence, though; it was clear from the heavy stillness of the air that the violence had occurred hours ago. A trail of blood led into the master bedroom, apparently ending behind the slightly open door.

Lee's heart beat wildly as Anderson and Butts drew their revolvers. Butts waved to Anderson to indicate that he should continue down the hall to make sure the far bedroom was clear. The young cop nodded and crept down the hall, holding his gun stiffly in front of him.

Moments later, he emerged from the room and called, "All clear."

Holding his revolver in both hand, Butts pushed open the door to the master bedroom with his foot.

"Stay here," he called over his shoulder as he went in. There was no need—Lee had no desire to enter what was obviously a crime scene. Through the open door, he and Diesel could see into the room—and Lee felt a shiver of relief when he saw the dead body on the floor. The sight that greeted them, disturbing as it was, was not Charlotte Perkins. His relief was followed by shame and disgust—shame at having been relieved, and disgust at what lay before them. Though his worst fears had not been realized, the murder scene was not a pretty sight.

Martin Perkins lay on his back, arms and legs akimbo, his head smashed in by what looked to be a series of blows from a heavy blunt object. Though his face was bloody and disfigured, his eyes had not been removed, and there was no sign of a suicide note. There were, however, signs of frenetic rage and overkill. The expensive-looking carpet he was lying on had soaked up a tremendous amount of blood—no doubt the blood loss alone would have been enough to kill him. It was hard to tell how many times he had been hit, but it was clear that the amount of force used was far in excess of what was needed.

Vines, twigs, and leaves had been piled on top of his body, some arranged in such a way that they looked as if they were growing out of his mouth and ears.

"Okay, Doc," Butts said, looking at Lee. "What's with all the foliage? What does it mean?"

All at once, Lee realized saw the connection.

"He's the Green Man," he said. "His killer is mocking the whole idea of it, by turning Perkins into one after killing him."

"Oh, yeah," Butts said, bending down to examine the body. "I think you're right."

What Lee wasn't prepared for was the smell. The odor of blood—so much blood—was unlike anything he had experienced. It seemed to penetrate a part of his brain, causing an aversion, a deep-seated feeling of distress that he thought must be genetic, ancestral. Ancient hominids, coming across this terrible and terrifying smell, must have taken flight immediately, knowing instinctively that death lurked around the corner. But he couldn't flee, much as he wanted to. He continued to stare at the body until he heard Officer Anderson come up behind him.

"Jesus," Anderson said softly, and Lee realized this was his first murder scene. He looked at Butts for help, and the burly detective took charge at once. He beckoned them all to stay out of the room; putting his gun back in its holster, he proceeded to investigate the crime scene.

Butts was in his element. Lee watched with admiration as the detective examined the body without touching anything, then managed to move around the room without transferring any of the blood to his shoes or in any other way compromising the evidence.

After a few minutes he joined the rest of them in the hall.

"No sign of the murder weapon," he said, "though from the shape of the blows I'd say it was somethin' long and narrow—a cane, or a thick stick of some kind. No sign of defensive wounds—looks like he wasn't expecting this attack. You got CSIs on duty around here?" he asked Anderson.

"Uh, in Trenton—that's the nearest city," the young officer replied, obviously shaken.

"Then I suggest you call it in ASAP," Butts said. Looking down at Perkins, he shook his head. "Whoever did this wasn't looking to make a statement," he said. "He just wanted Perkins dead."

Looking at the body sprawled on the floor in front of them, Lee had to agree. If ever he had seen a rage-driven homicide, this was it. Whoever had killed Martin Perkins was now spinning dangerously out of control.

CHAPTER SIXTY-FIVE

"What now?" Diesel asked as the three of them stood looking at the body while Officer Anderson reported the murder to his station house, which would then call the crime unit in Trenton. Butts had already called Chuck Morton to inform him, though there was little he could do at this point.

"I think whoever did this has Charlotte Perkins," Lee said.

"Unless *she* did this," Butts remarked.

Lee had to admit that wasn't completely unrealistic. She obviously had great resentment against her brother, with good reason—and it wouldn't be the first time a victim of domestic abuse snapped and murdered her abuser. Lee wasn't sure their relationship fit the legal definition of abuse, but he didn't like what he'd heard from her. And so now Perkins was dead—*Serves him right*, he thought uncharitably—but where was Charlotte? And even more puzzling, assuming she was still alive, where was Krieger?

"You think a—a *woman* could have done this?" Officer Anderson said, with a naïveté that was touching.

Butts frowned at him. "Kid, one thing you learn when

you've been a cop as long as I have is that *anyone* can do anything to anybody."

Anderson's pale eyes widened. "But—I mean, wouldn't it take a lot of force to deliver blows like this?"

"Yeah," Butts said. "But when a person's angry enough, you'd be surprised how strong they are."

"I don't think Charlotte did this," Lee said, looking at the body. "She wasn't angry—she was frightened."

"Okay," Butts replied. "But I'd sure like to know where she is."

"So would I," Lee agreed. "Let's have a look at his patient files. Perkins is dead now—we don't need a warrant," he added in response to Officer Anderson's inquiring look.

"Yeah—yeah, I guess you're right," the young policeman agreed. "Where do you suppose they'd be?"

"Well, I kept mine in a filing cabinet in my office," Lee answered.

"So all we gotta to do is go back to his office," Butts remarked, leading the way back downstairs to the consulting room at the back of the house.

The room's proximity to the kitchen made Lee guess it was originally a maid's bedroom. Though not as large as the upstairs bedrooms, it was a decent size, as elegantly furnished as the rest of the house, and with the same obsessive sense of order. The books were lined up on the built-in bookcase so that the spines were exactly even, and on the desk, not a thing was out of place. Lee's office was full of mismatched pens, pencils of different lengths and various stages of working order, all tossed in with dried-up Magic Markers and paper clips. Perkins's desk had two pewter mugs (antique, no doubt): one for pens, and one for pencils. All the pencils were exactly the same length, sharpened to perfect points, a circle of tiny spears jabbing toward the ceiling.

"Jeez," Butts said, looking around. "Was this guy anal or *what*?"

"I wonder if his underwear is alphabetized," Diesel remarked, and Officer Anderson giggled nervously.

"Yes, it does appear he had a case of OCD," he said.

"Try not to touch anything," Butts admonished Anderson as he ran a finger over the shiny surface of a table, apparently amazed at the lack of dust. The young cop jumped as though he'd been stung, and gave another nervous laugh.

"Yeah, right," he said, and pulled a pair of rubber gloves from his uniform pocket.

"Got any more of those?" Butts asked.

"Uh, no—sorry," Anderson said.

"Go into the kitchen and see if you can find more rubber gloves," Butts instructed him. "Surgical would be best, but kitchen gloves are okay."

"You think that's necessary?" Lee asked.

"The whole house is a crime scene," Butts replied. "We have to avoid destroying evidence of any kind, and that includes prints, trace evidence, that kind of thing." He regarded Diesel, chewing on his lip. "You shouldn't be in here at all. You said your dad was a cop?"

"Yes, he was," Diesel replied, crossing his powerful arms over his chest.

"Okay, tell you what," Butts said. "Why don't you go out and stand guard and make sure no one gets into the house? And when the boys from Trenton arrive, you can explain things to them, okay?"

"You don't have to treat me as though I'm ten," Diesel replied, frowning. "I can just sit in the car."

"No, no—it'd be really helpful," Butts said earnestly. "I don't want the locals getting too curious, y'know?"

"Very well," Diesel said. Drawing himself up with a dignified scowl, he left the room.

Officer Anderson appeared with a box of surgical gloves, holding them out to Butts with the pride of a child who has done a very clever thing. "Will these do?" he said eagerly. "I found these under the sink—a whole box of them!"

"Fine," Butts said, taking the box and handing a pair to Lee, while he put on another himself.

Officer Anderson looked disappointed, as if he had expected a pat on the back, or perhaps a lollipop.

Butts started looking through desk drawers, while Lee went to the wooden filing cabinet next to the desk. Starting at the top, he slid open the heavy oak drawer, and studied the folders inside. The top drawer was mainly about finances: the tabs, perfectly organized—and alphabetized—read, BANKING, followed by BILLS, PAID, and BILLS, UNPAID, and so on.

Meanwhile, Officer Anderson roamed the room restlessly, not touching anything, looking out of place and apprehensive.

"Any luck?" Butts grunted as he rifled through desk drawers, which Lee thought he was doing with unnecessarily vigor.

"Not yet," he said, closing the top drawer and moving on to the middle one. There he hit pay dirt: the first tab proclaimed, PATIENT FILES, in neat capital letters. "Got it," he said, pulling a stack of manila folders from the cabinet.

"Good," Butts said, slamming closed the desk drawer.

Lee handed Butts half the folders and kept the rest. He estimated there were about forty or so, one for each patient; Perkins appeared to have quite a thriving practice. Of course, some of the folders were possibly of past patients, though he imagined someone like Perkins would create separate file drawers for past and present patients. There was no sign of a computer—another indication of Perkins's avoidance of modern technology.

Ana Watkins's file was in the stack of folders Lee kept. He started by looking at it—perhaps there was a clue hidden in it. Perkins kept impeccable notes, all handwritten. The file was organized in chronological order, with notes for each session on a separate page, all in blue ink, the handwriting obsessively neat and precise, but oddly ornate. Lee started with the most recent sessions first.

> *Patient believes she is being followed. Paranoia? Cannot dismiss the possibility of attention-seeking behavior, consistent with borderline narcissist personality. Patient seems genuinely concerned, however—she produced a threatening note she claimed she received. Urged her to resume exploration of past life; patient seems resistant this week, for some reason. She may be about to consult another therapist, which could be very damaging at this point in her treatment.*

"Got anything so far?" Butts asked.

"Not really. How about you?"

"Naw—just a bunch of neurotics so far; no one that looks threatening. A lotta people whining about their mothers. What are you reading?"

"I'm reading Ana's file, hoping to see some clues to who might have killed her. So far I haven't seen anything I didn't already know about her."

"Well, keep lookin'," Butts said. "I still think it's possible the UNSUB is one of his patients."

"I do, too," Lee agreed, especially now that Perkins seemed to be eliminated as the killer—or was he? "Hey," he said suddenly, "how likely it is that Perkins could still be the UNSUB?"

Butts frowned. "Doesn't that seem like too much of a coincidence? He's the killer, but then he's found murdered?"

"Yeah. I was just wondering what you thought."

"What I think is that the same guy who did Perkins did everyone else, and has got Charlotte—and if we're lucky, Krieger, too. If we're really lucky, his name is somewhere among these papers."

"Right," Lee said, and went back to perusing the patient files.

Then one file in particular caught Lee's eye. The patient's name was Eric McNamara. He was in his late twenties, worked as a chauffeur, and owned his own limousine, which he garaged somewhere in the Bronx. He also took care of an infirm and elderly father. But what really caught Lee's attention was the mention of an unnamed tragedy in his past, one that Dr. Perkins could not seem to get to the bottom of, but which, it was hinted, was something involving water. There was only one reference to gender issues. After a session two weeks ago, Perkins had written

Cross-dressing fantasies. Investigate further.

There were plenty of other patients who had cross-dressing fantasies, but Eric was the right age and matched other aspects of the profile. Throughout Eric's file, as with most of the patients, there were mentions of a past-life identity. Here, though, Perkins was more specific, referring to a person by the name of Caleb, whose soul he believed Eric had inhabited in a previous life. The man named Caleb was a troubled spirit, and had died tragically by water—though the file wasn't specific on exactly how.

"Hey, look at this," Lee said to Butts, handing him the folder. Officer Anderson, who had been wandering aimlessly around the room, looked on with interest, like a dog waiting for a scrap of food or affection.

Butts glanced at it and handed it back at Lee. "Caleb . . . wasn't that one of the names on Ana's pottery receipts?"

"You're right!" Lee said. "You commented what an old-fashioned name it was."

"You think this could be the guy?"

"Look at the similarities to the profile. The age is right, there's the cross-dressing thing—and look at this." He pointed out the section where Perkins had written:

> *Childhood trauma . . . patient unwilling to speak of it. Tragedy so disturbing he has blocked it from memory, or at least will not speak of it. Drowning? Someone he loved, perhaps?*

Butts looked at Lee. "Curiouser and curiouser," he said softly. "Too bad the good doctor had to die for us to find this."

Finally Officer Anderson could stand it no longer. "Find what?" he cried impatiently, twitching all over with excitement. "Did you find the killer?"

"Maybe," Lee said.

Anderson lunged eagerly across the room to have a look. In his haste, his foot caught the edge of the Persian carpet, and he tripped, falling forward.

"Hey—watch it! Don't contaminate evi—" Butts yelled, but stopped in midsentence, staring at the edge of carpet where Anderson's foot had caught. The corner of the rug had been pulled from the floor, exposing it. "Wait just a minute," Butts said as the trooper got to his feet, leaning over to straighten the carpet.

"What is it?" asked Lee.

"I dunno, but there's something funny about that floor," Butts replied.

Lee looked at the section of the floor Anderson had just exposed. The smooth pattern of floorboard was interrupted by something at that spot. He walked over to inspect it more closely. There appeared to be a small round handle, the kind you could hook your thumb through to open—*a hidden compartment*. He looked at Butts, who smiled.

"Are you thinking what I'm thinking?" Lee said.

"What is it?" Anderson almost yelped. "Is something hidden down there?"

"The good doctor had somethin' he didn't want anyone else to see," the detective said. He kneeled, his knees cracking like walnuts, and inserted a stubby thumb through the handle. There was a click, and the door slid smoothly open.

They all gazed down at the opening. It was a small recessed compartment underneath the floorboards, about a yard square on all sides, and a couple of feet deep. It contained a video camera, a stack of tapes, and a VCR.

"Bingo," Butts said softly.

Lee had a cold, hollow feeling in his stomach. What other secrets did the eccentric Martin Perkins keep hidden from the world—including his sister?

Butts lifted the tapes out carefully with his gloved hands. They were all neatly labeled, each with a different name on them. Two of the tapes were of particular interest: one of them said ANA, and the other CALEB.

"Well, whaddya waitin' for?" Butts scolded Officer Anderson, who stood staring at their discovery. "Plug in the video recorder so we can see these damn things!"

"Which one should we start with?" Lee said when the machine was ready to go.

"I'm really curious about this Caleb character," Butts said. "Why don't we start with him?"

Anderson hit the play button, and they gathered around the machine like teenagers at their first porn film, with a combination of excitement and uneasiness.

The camera was focused on the couch in the corner of Perkins's office. After a moment, a young man entered the frame and lay on the couch. Dr. Perkins was not in sight, but his voice came through the camera's microphone.

"Are you comfortable?"

The young man nodded.

"Good," said Perkins, and began to lead his patient through a series of imagery Lee recognized immediately as standard suggestions intended to induce hypnosis.

"He's hypnotizing the kid!" Butts whispered, as if he didn't want to disturb the other movie patrons around him. "Right, Doc?" he asked Lee.

"That's right," Lee said.

"Very well," Perkins was saying, "go ahead, let yourself go—and when you're ready, let Caleb come through."

"Jesus," Officer Anderson whispered. "This is weird."

The young man twisted and fidgeted on the couch, his eyes still closed; then he became still. He appeared to be sleeping.

"Caleb?" Dr. Perkins said. "Are you there?"

"I'm here," the young man said in a firm, clear voice. His eyes were still closed.

"Do you know who I am?" Perkins asked.

"You're . . . my father."

"Holy shit," whispered Butts. "He's got the kid involved in this whole past-lives crap."

"Are you a good son?" Perkins asked.

"Yes, father."

"And what do good sons do?"

"What their fathers tell them to do."

Perkins's disembodied voice was calm, as if he had just asked the boy to pick up some groceries. "Do bad girls have to die?"

"Yes, father."

"And who has been a very bad girl?"

"Ana has."

"You mean your sister?"

"Yes, father."

Butts hit the pause button.

"Holy crap!" he said, droplets of sweat gathering on his pockmarked face. "If Perkins has this kid convinced Ana is his sister in some past life, and he's his father, that makes Charlotte—"

"His mother." Lee finished for him.

"So Perkins convinces him to kill Ana—why?"

"Maybe so she won't rat him out to the authorities about their affair," Lee reasoned. "Her diary did suggest she was going to confront someone, which fits in with what Charlotte told me."

"But then why would this Caleb guy kill Dr. Perkins?" Officer Anderson said.

"Jealousy," Butts answered. "Oldest motive in the book. He finds out somehow that Perkins was sleeping with Ana—"

"Maybe Charlotte told him!" Anderson suggested, making no attempt to hide his excitement.

"So if he's abducted Charlotte," Lee continued, "in his mind—"

This time Butts finished for him. "He's kidnapping his mother."

CHAPTER SIXTY-SIX

Caleb's real identity was indeed Eric McNamara, and according to his file, he lived in Sergeantsville, one of the tiny hamlets nestled amid the rolling farmland of Hunterdon County, to the northeast of Stockton.

"Well, what are we waitin' for?" Butts said. "Let's go!"

They went outside to get Diesel, who was still standing guard by the front door, leaving Officer Anderson to deal with the CSI team just arriving from Trenton. The young policeman gazed out wistfully from the porch as the three of them climbed into the old Ford. Butts cranked up the engine, and they sped off in a cloud of blue smoke.

The hills of Hunterdon County were not ideal for the enormous rattrap of a car, especially not at the speed Butts was driving. Lee avoided looking at the speedometer, but held his breath each time they bounded up the crest of a blind hill or careened around a sharp curve. Lee glanced at the backseat to see how their passenger was taking it. He was irritated to see Diesel looking calmly out the window, his powerful hands folded in his lap, taking in the scenery as though they were on a leisurely Sunday drive instead of pursuing a murder suspect.

They had tried calling Lee's cell phone periodically, with no luck. It went straight to voice mail, indicating that either the phone was turned off or the battery was dead.

Butts gunned the engine up a steep hill, zooming past stone houses with freshly painted wood fences and elaborately landscaped properties. This was where the moneyed classes moved when they retired—those who had too much class to move to Boca or Orlando, and enough money to winter in Florida and spend summers here. "What do you reckon the chances are he'll be there?"

"Probably not very good," Lee said. There was no question of calling ahead—the worst thing they could do was alert a suspect ahead of time. The only thing they could do was go there and hope to find him.

But Lee figured he was too smart to be anywhere near home, if he had in fact kidnapped Charlotte, and especially if he had murdered Perkins. The attack did show signs of frenzy and overkill, but the killer had been clever at hiding his tracks so far, and Lee thought it likely he had regained his wits soon after killing Perkins. He had enough presence of mind to take the murder weapon with him.

Of course, there was still a chance Charlotte had killed her brother and made a run for it, but he didn't think so. He couldn't see her sending a text message asking for help, then picking up a heavy object and wielding it with enough force to do the kind of damage they had seen. And he definitely didn't see her taking Krieger in a fair fight.

They found the house at the end of a narrow street a mile or so from the center of the little town, which consisted of an upscale restaurant and a few shops. There was no car in the driveway, and no sign of life in the house. Butts parked at the end of the drive, and the three of them got out of the car quietly.

"Why don't you stay here and be lookout?" Butts told Diesel as he and Lee started up the dirt driveway.

Lee was sorry leave him behind—if there was a struggle, the powerful Diesel would be more useful than either the pudgy little detective or himself. But they were in delicate legal territory; he and Butts were employees of the NYPD, and Diesel wasn't.

The house was an 1860s farmhouse, and like many others in the area, it had been modernized, with wings added on over the years. The property was well maintained, with a vegetable garden out back and a rose trellis over an old well that looked as if it was still in use. A fresh coat of white paint on the porch gave the place a cheery, inviting look—though their arrival would be anything but welcome.

On one of the porch columns, next to the front steps, was a sculpture of a Green Man. It was different from both the one at Perkins's house and the one Ana Watkins owned. Made of plaster, it was larger and even more fierce-looking, and a few actual leaves and twigs had been shoved behind it, so that it looked like they were growing out of its head. Lee tugged on the detective's sleeve and pointed to it. Butts turned to look, nodded, then drew his revolver and mounted the porch steps, which creaked from age and damp weather.

The front door was open from the inside; only the screen door stood between them and the front hallway. He strode to the front door and yanked the rope attached to the clanger on the old-fashioned dinner bell hanging next to the front door. Its hollow report sent a chill through Lee's body. *Ask not for whom the bell tolls. . . .*

"Police—open up!" Butts called out, holding his gun close to his body, the barrel pointing upward. There was no answer. Peering through the screen door, Lee could see no movement inside the house. He strained to hear something—anything—but there was no furtive shuffling, no scurrying footsteps of a fugitive on the lam.

"Police! If you're in there, open up!" Butts called again, but he was met once again with silence. He looked at Lee and ran a hand through his thinning hair. "No warrant—we're on shaky ground here. I don't see a judge buyin' probable cause. I think we're stuck."

They stood contemplating their options as a swarm of gnats lazily circled the far end of the porch. A gentle breeze brought the scent of honeysuckle wafting in from the garden, mixed with the tart green smell of tomato vines and geraniums. In the woods, cicadas began their metallic descending scale, signaling the end of summer.

A faint sound from within the house broke the stillness. It was a gentle rustling, as though a mouse or some other small animal was trying to burrow into a nest and hide. It seemed to come from the other end of the front hall. Lee pressed his face against the screen door and peered down the dark corridor.

"Hey, be careful!" Butts whispered fiercely behind him, but Lee remained where he was, trying to make out the dim figure advancing down the hall toward them. His instincts told him the person, whoever it was, held no threat for them.

"Hello?" he called. The form stopped moving, then crumpled to the floor. He looked at Butts, but the detective's hand was already on the screen doorknob.

"Now we got probable cause," the detective said, pushing the door open.

Lee followed Butts into the house. They reached the end of the hall in three or four steps. In front of them was the emaciated figure of a man. He had collapsed onto the floor next to the stairs and was clutching at the banister, trying to heave his wasted body to his feet. With his other hand he clutched wildly at the air, as though trying to reach out for their assistance. He sawed the air frantically, like a broken antenna trying to find a signal.

They reached down and gently helped him to his feet, though the spindly legs appeared unable to support the weight of even his meager body. One on either side of him, they helped him to a chair, setting him down gingerly. He looked elderly, perhaps seventy or so, though it was hard to tell; in his condition, he could have been twenty years younger. Lee figured that he was probably Eric McNamara's father.

"I'm Detective Butts with the NYPD," Butts said gently. "And this is Dr. Lee Campbell. Can you tell us where your son is?"

The old man opened his mouth to speak, but all that came out were pitiful, strangled sounds.

At that moment Lee realized he had no tongue.

"Jesus Christ," Butts muttered, running a hand over his face. "Jesus goddamn Christ."

"Mr. McNamara?" Lee said. "Are you Mr. McNamara?"

He nodded frantically, clutching Lee's hand in his claw-like grip. His skin felt loose, and it was as thin as rice paper.

"Do you know where your son is?"

The old man shook his head violently, trying again to speak, producing more pathetic gurgling noises.

"He lives here with you?" Lee asked.

Mr. McNamara nodded, taking Lee's hand in both of his, babbling incoherently. Lee felt his stomach lurch, and turned to Butts for help.

"Do you mind if we have a look around?" Butts asked.

The old man shook his head, and made a disturbing attempt at a smile, displaying pink gums with a smattering of teeth.

"Are you hungry?" Lee said.

McNamara nodded, tightening his grip on Lee's hand.

"You go ahead and start looking around," Lee said to Butts. "I'm going to get him something to eat."

"Let Diesel do it," Butts said. "You and me need to case this place as soon as possible."

Lee called Diesel in from the yard and gave him the task of escorting Mr. McNamara to the kitchen for some food. Diesel said very little, but from the look on his usually impassive face, Lee could tell he was shocked and disturbed by the sight of the old man. He led McNamara gently off to the kitchen, talking to him soothingly, as Lee and Butts headed upstairs.

"It's gotta be him," Butts muttered as he lumbered up the steps after Lee. "Otherwise it's just too goddamn weird."

Lee agreed, but didn't say anything as they reached the first floor landing. He turned right, and Butts followed him to the first room on the left. There was a lock on the outside, but it had been broken off, the nails ripped out of the wood, which was old and riddled with termites. It was clear someone had been locked inside that room, but had broken out. Lee and Butts exchanged a look.

"Jesus," Butts said. "He kept his dad locked up."

Inside the room was a single bed, a bureau, and a bookcase. It was not uncomfortably furnished—there was a red eiderdown quilt on the bed, and a hand-crocheted wall hanging of a rocking chair, over which were the words *Home Sweet Home*.

They continued down the hall to the next room. Pushing open the door, Lee entered a small room with candles on every surface—the bureau, the bookshelves, the small table under the window.

But it was the glass jar on the bookcase that drew his eyes. Hesitating, he approached it. As he got closer, he realized—without question—they had found their UNSUB.

The jar was full of eyeballs floating in a liquid he assumed was formaldehyde.

He looked at Butts. For once, the detective was speechless. He stared at the jar, then looked back at Lee, his face slack.

They had their killer's identity. Now all they had to do is find him.

CHAPTER SIXTY-SEVEN

Caleb found what he wanted in the back of the little grocery store, and went up to the counter to pay for his two large bottles of Poland Spring water. You could never have too much water with you in the woods—he knew that from long experience. The woman behind the desk had a comforting look. Her face fell into itself, the skin deflated, her plump cheeks puckered in soft, round folds like a baked apple left in the oven too long. The sight of her full, matronly bosom seemed an invitation to lay his weary head on it. Looking at her, he yearned to nestle within those warm folds of femininity forever.

"That will be five ninety-five," she said, smiling at him.

He handed her a twenty, inhaling her scent as she took his money and counted out the change. Even the smell of her was comforting. It made him think of things baking: the aroma of vanilla, cinnamon, and cloves rose gently from within the billowy sleeves of her paisley blouse. It brought to mind warm, toasty kitchens at Christmastime, with racks of grinning gingerbread men hardening gently as steam rose and condensed into droplets on windowpanes.

He wondered if his mother had smelled like that, but it

was so long ago he couldn't remember. He wanted to say something to the woman, but when she gave him the change, her fingers brushed his palm, and he felt the heat rise to his forehead. He averted his eyes, mumbled his thanks, and fled the store.

She wouldn't have smiled so sweetly at him if she had known what secrets he hid in his sinful breast. He hurried out to his car, where Charlotte lay waiting for him. He would take her to his secret place, to the sacred waters, where they would meet their fate together. And then, at last, his transformation would be complete: He would become the Green Man.

CHAPTER SIXTY-EIGHT

A search of the house confirmed that Eric McNamara was gone. The only occupant of the house was the old man, and it looked as though he had been alone for some time. It was amazing that he had summoned enough strength to break out of his room—he was fortunate that the house was old and some of the wood was rotting. Diesel went out to search the barn, while Butts called for Social Services to come get Mr. McNamara.

Diesel's search of the grounds turned up nothing, so they had to assume Eric had gone somewhere with Charlotte. Whether she was dead or alive was something Lee didn't want to speculate on; they could only hope she was still alive. As for Krieger, he was beginning to lose hope that she would ever be found alive.

The first thing they did was call both the New York and Jersey state police to put out an APB. Their geographic profiling of the victims turned out to be right. Sure enough, Eric owned his own car, but was part of a conglomerate of limos operating out of Fleet Car Service, located in Riverdale— just a few blocks away from Spuyten Duyvil. It was easy enough to get the car's plate number; they just had to hope it was in time.

"Who knows which way he went?" Butts said. "Let's call Pennsylvania, too."

That made sense. They were so close to the border, and he might have decided to flee west with Charlotte. There was no telling where he had gone—or whether he had taken Krieger with him as well. They gathered in the kitchen to decide their next step.

"Do you think the old guy knows anything?" Diesel asked. He had made a peanut butter sandwich for Mr. McNamara, who sat at the white-painted kitchen table gobbling it down, smacking his lips, taking large gulps of cold milk in between bites. Eating for him was a messy business, given his physical limitations; Lee tried not to watch. The old man kept looking up at the three of them, as if afraid they might leave him.

Butts leaned down and spoke loudly and slowly to the old man, as though he were an imbecile.

"Do – You – Know – Where – Your – Son – Went?"

The old man narrowed his eyes and chewed his sandwich, spewing bits of bread in every direction.

Butts straightened up and stretched his back. "You think he knows anything about Krieger?" he asked Lee.

"Ask him."

Butts leaned down, his face closer to the old man's ear. "Did – You – See – A – Tall – Redhead? With – A – German – Accent?" he shouted.

McNamara stared at him.

"The kid keeps him locked in his room," Diesel said with disgust. "He probably doesn't know a thing."

"Eric probably went somewhere he feels comfortable,"

Lee said. "Somewhere near water. But that could be anywhere."

He leaned against the kitchen counter and gazed at a framed photograph on the opposite wall of a waterfall. It was a romantic picture, the water cascading gracefully down a series of ledges, smooth and white as clouds in a summer sky. In the foreground, a young man smiled at the camera, shielding his eyes from the bright sunlight. He took a step toward the picture, to see if there was a caption, but there was none. He turned to Mr. McNamara.

"Is this your son?"

The old man nodded, his mouth full of sandwich.

"Do you know where this is?"

Another nod, in between slurps of milk.

"Does he go there often?"

Mr. McNamara began gesticulating and making strangled attempts at speech. Then his eyes lit up, and he pointed at his glass of milk.

"What's he doin'?" Butts asked.

The old man leapt from his chair, yanked open the refrigerator, grabbed a stick of butter, and held it out triumphantly. The consumption of food had apparently energized him. He pointed to the butter, then back at the glass of milk.

"Butter—milk?" said Diesel.

"Buttermilk!" Lee cried. "Buttermilk Falls!" He seized Mr. McNamara by the shoulders. "The photo—it's Buttermilk Falls?"

The old man opened his mouth and made a sound that was his version of a laugh, though it was more like the mooing of a dyspeptic cow.

"What's Buttermilk Falls?" Butts said. "You know the place?"

"It's up the Delaware, near the Water Gap," Lee said. "It's

a county park with hiking trails. I went there once or twice as a teenager." What he didn't say was that his first trip there was with his father.

"You think he took her there?" Butts asked, frowning.

"I think it's very possible," Lee replied.

"Yeah, but why drag her all the way up there?"

"There's been a progression in his killing—from a bathtub to the East River to Spuyten Duyvil, each location has been successively more dangerous and turbulent."

Mr. McNamara began nodding vigorously, making strained yelping sounds.

"You think he went there?" Butts asked him.

The old man nodded some more, looking at each of them, his face earnest.

"Did he tell you he was going there?" Lee asked.

McNamara hesitated, then grabbed a pencil from a canister on the shelf and wrote on his napkin. *I saw his hiking map!*

"You heard the man," said Butts.

"He wouldn't be trying to protect his son, would he?" Diesel asked.

"When he's been lockin' him up for God knows how long?" Butts replied. "C'mon—let's go!"

As they started out through the dining room, Lee thought he heard something—a faint scratching sound, like a mouse in the woodwork. He turned to Butts.

"You hear that?"

Butts listened. "Naw, I don't hear anything."

But Lee heard it again—a rustling, like a small animal burrowing inside the walls. "There it is again," he said. "I think it's coming from—from there." He pointed to one of the paneled dining room walls. A sudden loud clattering came from somewhere behind the walls, like the sound of cans being overturned.

Lee stepped closer to the wall and ran a hand over the wood, which was coated in peeling blue and white paint. He moved along the wall, pressing and tapping on the panels one by one. When he reached the end of the wall, he noticed the last panel sounded different—more hollow, somehow. Then he saw the floor—it had a deep scratch in the shape of a half-moon. He realized all at once that what he was looking at was not a wall, but a door.

His heart jackhammered against his chest as he pushed against the panel where it met the wall—and it gave way. A narrow stone staircase snaked down to a hidden basement— perhaps originally built as a hideout from the Indians who roamed these lands in the nineteenth century when the house was built.

He turned to Butts and motioned him over, a finger to his lips. The detective pulled his gun from its holster and crept toward the stairs.

"Shouldn't you call for backup?" Lee whispered, but Butts shook his head and started down the steps. Lee followed, searching for a light switch, but found none.

There, at the bottom of the stairs, they found her. Bound, gagged, and exhausted, Elena Krieger sat on the cold stone floor, crumpled amid a pile of overturned paint cans. When they removed the gag, she shivered so violently she could barely speak.

"Did he hurt you?" Butts said, dispensing with the formalities of greeting.

"N-no, I'm okay," she said through clattering teeth, but she didn't look okay. She tried to rise, but her legs failed her and she collapsed into their arms.

"Easy, easy," Lee said, removing his light jacket to wrap it around her shoulders.

They called for Diesel, who scooped her up in his powerful arms and carried her up the steps as though she were a child.

"Now," Butts said, turning to Lee. "That waterfall in the picture—can you get us there?"

"I think so. Do you have a map of Jersey in your car?"

"Of course," Butts replied. "Never go anywhere without it."

"Good. We'll start off on the River Road."

"What are we waitin' for?" Butts said, fishing out his car keys.

"What if we're wrong?" Diesel asked, Krieger still in his arms.

"We'd better pray we're not," Lee answered as the three of them hurried out toward the car. Mr. McNamara followed close behind, braying like a mournful donkey. Lee was getting used to his vocalizations, and understood this was his way of saying *Don't leave me.*

"Don't worry, Mr. McNamara," he called over his shoulder. "Someone is on their way to take care of you."

The Social Services ambulance was waiting outside, and they handed Krieger over to them to be whisked away, protesting, along with Mr. McNamara. Ignoring the stares of the social workers, they climbed into the old Ford and headed west on County Road 604. The car rattled through the old covered bridge that used to enchant Laura as a child—she always dreamed of living in the little green cottage next to it and being, as she called it, The Bridge Keeper. Lee would tease her, saying that a covered bridge didn't need a keeper, but she always insisted that it did, and that would be her job.

When they reached the Delaware they took the River Road north, following the river until County 519 cut away from the shoreline. They took that all the way into Sussex

County, at which time Lee unfolded the state map and studied it carefully. The entire western section of the county was a great swath of parkland known as Stokes State Forest. Right in the middle of it was Wallpack Center—and just below it, Buttermilk Falls.

"Okay," he said, "got it. Just follow Wallpack Road."

The forest was dotted with lakes and creeks connecting them, and in the middle, where three streams met, was the Falls.

"Okay," Lee said as they traveled north on Route 206. "Any minute now—there! Turn left on Struble Road."

They did, following that to an intersection with a cemetery, where they turned left again. If Butts and Diesel thought the cemetery was a bad omen, they didn't say anything. The trailhead was just up the road on their left. Parked in the lot across the road was a black limousine with a New Jersey license plate.

"Looks like we were right," Butts said as he swung the big Ford in next to it. He drew his revolver before cautiously opening his driver's side door, but there didn't appear to be anyone in the limo. They all got out of the car and tried looking in, but the windows, were heavily tinted, and they couldn't see anything.

"I'm gonna call it in to the local cops," Butts said, taking out his cell phone. "Shit," he said, after stabbing at the buttons for a minute. "No damn signal."

"Should we break in?" Diesel asked.

"As an officer of the law, I wouldn't do something like that without a search warrant," Butts remarked, "but if a private citizen were to do that while I wasn't looking, I would have no way of stopping him."

He proceeded to stare off toward the woods. Diesel whipped a long thin wire out of his pocket, inserted it into the passenger side keyhole, and within seconds, had the door open, leaving no scratch marks.

"Jesus," Butts said with undisguised admiration. "How did you *do* that?"

"Practice," Diesel said, peering into the front of the van.

There was nothing especially remarkable about the car. Other than the gray tinted windows, which were rather sinister, it appeared to be an ordinary limousine, much like any other. The interior was clean and swept, devoid of clutter. There were two paper Oren's coffee cups in the holder up front, and a couple of granola bars on the passenger side seat. In the back, a khaki sleeping bag was laid out on the seat.

"So that's probably where he kept her," Butts remarked, looking at it. He was very careful not to touch anything, maybe so he could deny having participated in the break-in if it ever came up in court. Cops had to be very careful about these things—without probable cause, a search like this could completely sabotage a case once it came to trial. Lee had seen it happen on more than one occasion, and figured Butts had seen it even more.

Diesel wasn't so delicate he climbed inside the limo and sniffed around a bit.

"Don't touch anything," Butts instructed. "They might be dusting for prints later."

Diesel nodded. He took a Kleenex from his pocket, and put it between his fingers before picking up the corner of the sleeping bag. He turned it over and looked underneath, revealing a roll of duct tape. He climbed out and dusted off his hands.

"I don't see any blood—but he probably used the duct tape to help subdue her. Well," he said, "shall we go up the trail?"

"Yeah," Butts said. "Let's go."

They crossed the road to the trailhead, where a wooden sign stood at the entrance.

Buttermilk Falls Trail

2 MI. TO FALLS

Lee looked at Butts. "It's very steep. You up to it?"

The detective snorted. "Get on with it, for Christ's sake."

With Lee leading the way, the three of them started up the trail as a brisk wind whipped the tree branches, and the sky began to darken. Within minutes they heard the patter of raindrops on the canopy of leaves above them. Soon the droplets began to thicken, piercing the cover of the forest and falling upon their faces and shoulders, quickly soaking through their clothing.

"Great, just great," Butts muttered as he trudged behind Lee. "That's all we needed."

CHAPTER SIXTY-NINE

Charlotte was tired . . . so very tired. She just wanted it all to end. Trudging up the hill in front of her captor, she stumbled on the rocky trail, her head still fuzzy from the laudanum and whatever he had injected her with. Every time she lost her footing, he poked her with his hiking stick and commanded her to move along. She tried hard not to trip, but she was so tired, and it was so difficult walking with her hands bound in front of her. She didn't know where he was taking her and hardly cared. She just wanted to lie down among the leaves and bushes and go back to sleep.

After falling into his arms in her room the previous night, she had slept a dreamless, drugged sleep, regaining consciousness in a moving vehicle. She was aware that it was now daytime. The light hurt her eyes, even though the windows were tinted, blocking out much of the brightness. After a few moments she realized she was in the back of a limo, lying on a sleeping bag. The glass partition separating her from the driver was closed, but she could see the back of his head from where she lay. When she tried to move, she realized her hands were bound in front of her with duct tape. But the cell phone Lee Campbell had given her was still in her pocket, and she managed to dig her hand in and get out the phone.

Even though her brother didn't like modern technology, she found it fascinating and had often watched her friends at the hospital send text messages. She was afraid to speak lest her abductor would hear her, so she typed out a hurried text message and pretended to be unconscious again. Her heart was thumping wildly in her chest, and her head was pounding. She could feel the blood coursing through her temples. But she was aware that this experience was something Martin would have disapproved of, and, in spite of her fear, was filled with a thrilling sense of adventure.

The limo was barreling along a winding road, and as there was a fair amount of road noise, he didn't hear her moving around in the back. After a while she struggled to sit up, clutching the back of the passenger seat to pull herself erect. She could make out the back of his head, and it looked familiar somehow. . . .

Now, struggling up the trail to God only knew where, she tried to figure out why this young man had abducted her, and why her brother hadn't come to rescue her. It didn't make sense—but then, nothing lately made much sense. Above them, the sky darkened, threatening rain. The worse the weather was, she thought, the fewer the chances that they would meet other hikers on the trail, reducing the likelihood of her being rescued. And now, of course, she knew her captor's identity.

His voice came from behind her, cutting the stillness of the summer air.

"It's time for a break. You can sit and rest here."

She stopped walking and lowered herself down on a clump of moss in front of a thick old oak tree. She could hear the rustling of woodland creatures in the bushes, and noticed the air smelled of mint. There was probably some growing wild nearby. She leaned against the oak tree, its jagged bark digging into her back. Still, it was a friendly feeling—she had always liked trees, and found them comforting. A pair of squirrels chattered and scolded them from the branches above. How nice it must be to be a squirrel, she thought, able to climb trees so nimbly and easily. She looked up at them—they jerked their bushy gray tails irritably, their restless little bodies twitching, ever watchful.

She looked up at her captor. He remained on his feet, standing over her, vigilant, peering down the trail behind them, as if afraid they were being followed. His hand holding the walking stick twitched, and he was sweating.

"Where are you taking me?" she asked.

His answer was brusque and businesslike. "To the sacred waters." His voice gave nothing away, but she thought she saw a flicker of vulnerability pass over his face. She decided to take advantage of it—it might be her only chance.

"Why, Eric?" she said softly. "Why are you taking me all the way up here?"

He avoided looking at her. "Because it's my sacred place. This must be done in my most sacred place. We must go to our fate together—then our transformation will be complete."

"What transformation, Eric? What are you talking about?"

He still refused to look at her. "My name is Caleb."

"Is that what Martin told you?"

His face reddened, and he tightened his grip on the hiking stick. "I don't *care* what he told me—he lied to me."

"About what, Eri—Caleb? What did he lie about?"

He kicked at a pebble, sending it sliding and bouncing down the trail. "Everything."

"Like what?"

"He told me my mother would come back—that her spirit would be reborn in another person."

She tried to figure out what this meant. Her brother never spoke with her about his patients. She made their appointments, and let them into the waiting room, and occasionally brought them tea, but that was all. She knew little or nothing about their lives, their hopes, their disappointments—or why they were in therapy.

And Eric was a relatively new patient—he had been seeing Martin less than a year. She had seen him in the waiting room, spoken with him once or twice on the phone, but that was all. She knew next to nothing about him. She decided to take a stab in the dark.

"You miss her very much, don't you?" she said.

His face began to soften, and then it was as though a dark filter passed across his features, hardening his countenance into something stony and heartless and cruel.

"She was—*a whore*," he rasped, spitting out the words as if they burned his tongue.

"But—you loved her, didn't you?" she cried desperately. The air itself seemed to turn colder, as a chill wind blew up out of nowhere, scattering dry leaves in little gusts. They seemed to scurry from it in terror, as if they shared her sense of alarm. A few drops of rain spattered against the leaves, flattening them, cutting off their escape. A hollow, panicked feeling gnawed at the pit of her stomach.

"Miss her?" he said, his voice flat and mocking. "I *hate* her. I hate *you*."

A thin cruel smile turned up the corners of his mouth, and she knew she was lost.

CHAPTER SEVENTY

"Good God," Detective Butts said, wiping sweat and rain from his forehead. "I thought there weren't any goddamn mountains in Jersey."

They had been hiking for close to an hour. The rain had let up for the time being, but there were sinister rumbles of thunder in the distance. Lee's side was aching, and he felt as if he could feel each of the seventeen stitches in his arm.

"We must be near the top," Diesel commented. "I'm pretty sure we've gone nearly two miles."

"I think you're right," Lee agreed. "Shouldn't be too much longer."

"We'd better be there soon, or someone's gonna have hell to pay," Butts muttered. "Oh, *Jesus*!" he gasped suddenly, doubling over and clutching his side.

"What's wrong?" said Lee, dropping down beside him.

"Nothin'—got a—stitch in—my side," Butts groaned, holding the right side of his abdomen.

"Can you stand?" Lee asked.

"I'll—try," Butts answered, straightening up, but he immediately bent over again. "Sorry—no use—you go on without me. I'll catch up."

Lee looked at Diesel, who raised an eyebrow. "We need to get there as soon as possible," he said.

"Okay," Lee agreed. "We'll go on without you. You sure you'll be okay?"

"Yeah," Butts said, lowering himself next to a boulder on the side of the trail. "Too—many—goddamn doughnuts."

In a lighter moment, this would have been funny, but now all Lee felt was a pressing need to get up the trail. They left Butts leaning against the boulder and continued their climb. Lee didn't mention the fact that his own side had been throbbing for the last mile and a half.

When they had been going for a good fifteen minutes, well out of earshot, Diesel said, "Maybe now he'll back off on the sugar and fat and hit the gym more often."

"I wouldn't bet on it," Lee panted.

As he said the words, he heard the sound of running water.

"Hear that?" he asked.

"Yeah," Diesel said. "We're not far now."

They clambered on in silence for a while, and then they saw it through the trees—the water tumbling and gurgling gracefully over the rocks, as if it didn't have a care in the world. High above the falls was a wooden viewing platform. Standing on the platform were two people. It was hard to make out their features at this distance, but there could be no doubt that the people on the platform were Eric McNamara and Charlotte Perkins.

Diesel clutched at Lee's arm. "What'll we do?"

"He hasn't seen us yet," Lee said. "We need to get closer without being spotted."

"Perhaps one of us could serve as a decoy or distraction while the other one sneaks up on him?"

"Good idea," Lee said. "Do you want to be the decoy?"

"All right," Diesel agreed, "since you know the trail."

Lee didn't want to point out that it had been many years since he hiked these woods, but he didn't want to put Diesel in danger, and he thought it was riskier to approach someone like Eric from behind than to stand talking with him at a distance.

"Okay," he said. "Don't get too close—he might have a gun. Keep yourself covered at all times."

"Right."

He looked back down the trail for any sign of Butts, but saw nothing. He left the trail and bushwhacked through the woods, veering to the south, so that he would come up on the platform from the back. The foliage was dense once he left the path, and he scrambled up the hill, pushing branches and leaves out of his way.

The roaring of the falls made it hard to hear anything else, but he hoped Diesel was occupying Eric's attention. He pushed onward. Sweat was trickling into his eyes, and he paid no heed to the branches and twigs whipping him across the face. Twice he stumbled on the rocky ground and was brought to his knees by vines wrapping themselves around his ankles. Still, he pressed on, until he could see through the trees that he was above the viewing platform.

He clambered back to the trail, scurrying down the hill toward the place in the falls where they had seen the viewing platform. He cleared the underbrush only yards away from the platform, just in time to see the figure standing on it extend his arm. He saw the glint of metal, and the unmistakable flash of a firearm. Far on the trail below, he watched horrified as Diesel fell to the ground, clutching his side.

There was a roaring in Lee's ears as his body filled with fury. All of the rage of the past months gathered within him, propelling him forward, just as a tremendous clap of thunder sounded overhead.

He heaved himself up the few steps at the rear of the platform before his quarry had time to turn around—the combined sound of the roaring falls and the thunder made anyone standing on the platform effectively deaf. He saw the combination of alarm and relief in Charlotte Perkins's eyes as he threw himself at Eric McNamara, aiming at his knees in a rugby tackle. The young man turned around just as Lee lunged, bringing him down hard on the cedar planks of the floor. The gun went clattering across the platform, coming to rest against a cedar support timber in the far corner. Charlotte lay sprawled in the opposite corner, stunned and dazed.

To his surprise, McNamara was strong, and he was quick. In a flash, he had thrown Lee off and was diving for the gun, scrambling on his hands and knees across the wooden boards as fast as he could. Lee grabbed his ankle and pulled with all his might, flames of pain shooting through his injured hand. McNamara responded by twisting his body around and kicking him in the face. Lee felt his nose thicken with blood as he lunged at his foe, reaching him just as his fingers closed on the handle of the gun. Lee grabbed him by the wrist, surprised once again by the wiry strength in that body, as his enemy writhed and twisted like a serpent beneath him.

McNamara wrenched his hand free, and Lee felt a swift, hard blow on the back of his head, delivered by the barrel of a gun, followed by a hard kick to his ribs. He heard a cracking sound, felt something give inside him, and sank to the floor with a groan. He looked up, his vision blurry, just as a streak of lightning ripped through the sky. McNamara stood over him, the gun aimed at his head. Meanwhile, Charlotte Perkins had risen shakily to her feet. McNamara was unaware of her, smiling down at Lee as he took aim. Charlotte had a thick cudgel in her hand—it looked like a hiking stick. Backlit by the stark white streak of lightning, her damp hair streaming in the wind behind her, she raised the cudgel over her head, her usually mild features distorted by fury.

She struck, and McNamara went down, crumpling to his knees as another clap of thunder shook the heavens. Lee struggled to get up, but pain seared his torso, and he collapsed again with a groan. Charlotte Perkins tore the gun from McNamara's limp hand. Incredibly, he was still conscious, and struggled unsteadily to his feet as Charlotte aimed the gun at his chest.

He leaned against the platform railing for support. "Give—me—the gun, Charlotte," he commanded groggily.

Her face rigid with rage, she aimed the revolver at McNamara's chest. "You killed my brother," she said in a flat voice, all the more terrible because of its utter lack of emotion.

"He—lied—to me," McNamara said, gazing with dazed eyes at the barrel of the gun. "He promised me—"

"I don't *care* what he promised!" she hissed. "You killed him, and now you're going to pay!"

"No!" Lee gasped, but it was too late. The gun barrel blazed, a brief yellow flash against the darkening sky. He didn't know if it was thunder or the sound of the gunshot ringing in his ears. McNamara looked at Charlotte with shock and surprise as a bright red flower of blood blossomed on his chest. Then, teetering on unsteady feet, he let go of the platform and plunged through the opening in the railing, onto the rushing waterfalls below. Lee watched in horror as his body hit the rocks. Tossed by the torrential flood of water, it was quickly washed downstream, bobbing and twisting, caught in the pulsating current, as another resounding clap of thunder sounded, shaking the skies with its fury.

Lee remained conscious long enough to see a jagged streak of lightning slash across the sky, and then everything went black.

CHAPTER SEVENTY-ONE

Forty-eight hours later Lee sat at a table in the front window of McSorley's, waiting for Detective Leonard Butts to show up. In front of him was a pair of cold mugs of beer—one for him and one for the detective. You couldn't order just one mug of beer at McSorley's. They were always served two at a time, and you had two choices: light or dark. Lee had ordered one of each. The room was quiet, and sunlight streamed in through the big picture window, falling on the businessmen and women who had slipped in for a late lunch.

The events of two days ago still had an unreal, dreamlike quality. He vaguely remembered Butts lumbering up the platform stairs and taking the gun away from Charlotte, who, after shooting Eric McNamara, was meek as a kitten. He recalled the search for McNamara's body, which they finally found at the bottom of the falls, lodged behind some rocks. A few sticks and leaves had become trapped by his body on their way downstream, so that he resembled a grotesque version of a Green Man. There was a sheathed hunting knife in his pocket, and no one had any doubt about what he intended to use that for.

Lee also remembered—and wished he didn't—the slow, painful descent back down the trail. He was in worse shape than Diesel, who had suffered a flesh wound to his side—whereas, as it turned out, Lee had three broken ribs and smashed nose cartilage. Somehow the four of them made it down the hill. Butts had driven them to the emergency room in the nearest town, grumbling all the way that he should have been there, and that he would now start a program of diet and exercise, and so forth.

Lee took a long, deep swallow of beer and looked around the room. He liked the atmosphere here. True to its origins as a bar for working-class Irish men, McSorley's sported a thick layer of sawdust on the floor. An even thicker layer of dust covered the musical instruments, knickknacks, paintings, and photographs occupying every spare inch of wall. There was always a smell of onions in the air—he liked to order the cheese and crackers and onions, which were served "on the house" to the nineteenth-century working-class customers.

The bell over the door tinkled, and in strode Detective Butts, carrying a leather gym bag. He nodded to the waiter—a big, burly Irishman, probably an ex-cop—as the man slung half a dozen beers onto one of the thick oak tables, as though he were wielding billy clubs instead of beer mugs.

Butts lowered himself into the chair next to Lee with a groan, putting the satchel on the floor next to him. "Just came from the gym," he said with a rueful but triumphant smile. "Bench presses and abs today."

"Do you think you're tackling this fitness thing a little too vigorously?" Lee asked, sliding a beer across the table toward him.

Butts looked at the mug of beer. "I shouldn't," he said,

patting his generous girth. "Aw, what the hell," he shrugged, lifting the glass to his lips. "You only live once, right?"

Drinking deeply, he set the mug down with a satisfied clunk.

The waiter appeared again, wiping his hands on the long white apron tucked into his pants.

"Ready for another round, then, are ya?" His accent was pure County Cork.

"Yeah," Butts said. "This one's on me."

The mugs were small, and needed refilling often, but that meant the beer was always cold and fresh. They drank again, and Lee settled back into his chair, the edges of the room softened by alcohol.

"Okay," Butts said. "So I have answers to some loose ends you were asking about."

"Right."

"Turns out that Baldy was someone he picked up at the Jack Hammer. When I showed pics of him around the place, some of the guys remembered seein' him on more than one occasion."

"So the pickup went bad in some way, and—"

"—and Baldy was history. He must have got as far as the guy's apartment, but what happened next I guess we'll never know."

"What about the doctor—the anesthesiologist?"

Butts took a long swig of beer and wiped his mouth.

"Far as I can make out, poor guy was at the wrong place at the wrong time. I found a pickup request at Fleet Limos that McNamara responded to at Roosevelt Hospital. Somethin' must have gone down in that limousine—maybe a proposition gone wrong, I dunno. Whatever happened, it got McNamara mad enough to off the doc."

He took another swallow of beer. "Tox screens came back positive for GHB on all the vics. In some cases they drank the stuff, but with a couple it looks like he injected them with it." Butts traced one of the deep groves in the dark wood of the table with his finger. "I, uh—I watched some more of the videotapes, too."

"Yeah?"

"That is some weird shit, let me tell you."

"Like what?"

"Well, Perkins has this Caleb guy convinced that in his past life he killed his mother, see? I think it was some twisted notion of therapy, to try and get the truth of what happened to the kid in childhood. It was somethin' involving his mother, I know that much."

"So when he took Charlotte to the waterfall, he was going to reenact that event in his 'past life'?"

"Somethin' like that, yeah—by that time he was so whacked who knows what was goin' through his head?"

"How is Charlotte doing?" Lee asked.

"She's out at Rikers. How do you think someone like her would be at a place like that?"

Lee looked down at the round oak table, heavily scarred by initials carved into its surface by over a century and a half of patrons.

"She shouldn't have shot him," he said. What he didn't say was that if Caleb had lived, it would have been a chance to study him, leading to potentially valuable insights into his mind and motives.

Butts waved a hand dismissively. "She'll get off easy. I can't imagine a jury alive that wouldn't have sympathy for her after what happened."

"I guess you're right."

"How's Diesel—he okay?"

"He's back at work already. I think he's enjoying the fuss everyone's making over him—big hero, you know, taking a bullet and all that."

Butts looked down and pushed his beer mug away. "Yeah, about that. Look, I'm sorry—"

"Don't say another word about it. It's a tough hike for anyone, and you just happened to get a stitch in your side. It could happen to anybody."

"Well, it happened to *me*, so I'm hittin' the gym from now on. I'm tellin' you, Doc, I'm a new man—you just wait and see!"

Lee smiled. "Okay. I'll wait and see."

"How 'bout you? How're you doin'?"

"Oh, fine. I'm a little beat up, but I'll live."

"Yeah." Butts paused and looked out the window at the pedestrians striding along East Seventh Street, so full of purpose and energy. "Any follow-up on the phone calls—the ones about the dress?"

"No. I don't know who was making them. It wasn't Mc-Namara. Chuck still has my line tapped, of course."

"How about . . . have you talked to . . . her?"

"No. I'm going to call her."

"Okay," Butts said. "Be sure you do. You two got somethin', I'm tellin' you. You be sure to call her."

Lee nodded and took another swig of beer. It slid down his throat, cold and bitter, rich with the promise of the serenity of forgetfulness. Gazing at the amber liquid, he longed to sink into its River Lethe for a long, deep sleep.

CHAPTER SEVENTY-TWO

Barefoot, Lee padded into the kitchen and stared at the phone hanging on the wall next to the refrigerator. It was the old-fashioned kind—the receiver was attached to the phone with a cord—but he liked it. It was there when he moved into the apartment, and he liked its cherry-red color. It seemed to be waiting patiently for him to make up his mind.

He circled the room like a bird dog on a scent three times before finally picking up the receiver from its cradle. He dialed her number, hung up before the first ring, then dialed again. He almost hung up again, but forced himself to wait for at least three rings. He prayed he would get her answering machine, but she picked up after the third ring.

"Hi," he said, trying to sound as casual as possible. *Don't want too much, don't be too needy.*

"Hi."

He wondered if Kathy felt as neutral as she sounded, or if she was deliberately flattening her voice.

"How are you?"

"I'm doing okay. How about you? I hear you got a little beat up."

Was she really okay? Or was she hiding her desperate need for him with a deliberately dispassionate tone, feeling him out before committing to anything herself?

"I'm okay." *Liar, liar, pants on fire.* He took a deep breath, and felt a sharp stab from his injured ribs. *Okay, fine—tell her the truth.* "I miss you."

Time stretched out like pulled taffy in the pause that followed.

"Congratulations on solving the case."

Congratulations. Could she sound any more impersonal?

But all he said was, "Thanks."

Another pause. He twisted the phone cord around his finger and shifted his weight to the other foot. He regretted using the kitchen phone rather than the portable in the living room. All he wanted to do was flee, rather than stand here and wait for her next response.

"I miss you too, you know."

Caught off guard, he wasn't sure how to answer.

"Okay," he said, feeling immediately it was a lame response.

"It's not that I don't care about you."

"Okay," he repeated. What were you supposed to say to something like that? *And what's with the double negatives?* he thought irritably.

"Look," she said, "the last thing I want is to hurt you."

Too late for that.

He summoned his courage. If the truth wasn't good enough, then to hell with the whole thing.

"Look," he said, "relationships are hard—they just are. And we've both been through a lot lately. But we can handle it one of two ways. We can get over it separately, or we can work on getting through it together. Either way, we'll probably survive. But if we do it together, we have a chance to grow closer rather than farther apart."

Another pause, and then she said, "I'm so . . . angry."

"I know. I am, too."

"Sometimes I just want to scream. Other times I feel like I could . . . kill someone."

"Me, too."

"I hate feeling that way."

"As long as we both feel that way, we might as well feel it together."

She gave a little laugh, and he felt a dam break inside him. Relief flooded through his veins like rushing water.

"Wise guy, eh?" she said.

"Whaddya gonna do about, ya crazy dame?"

"Think you're a big shot, huh? Why, I oughta—"

"Just try it—you'll be sorry, see?"

She laughed again; it sounded like water tumbling over rocks. "I'll be in New York tomorrow. I'll see you for dinner, but on one condition."

"Name it."

"I'm buying."

"Now who's being funny? My city, I'm buying. You can pay when I come to Philly."

"See you at Keens, then."

"Hey—that place is expensive!"

"Yeah, and you just said you're buying."

"But—"

"Eight o'clock—don't be late. I'll be the one behind the enormous seafood appetizer platter and single-malt Scotch."

He hung up and looked around the kitchen as the golden light of late August filtered in through the French lace curtains his mother had snapped up at an estate sale in Frenchtown. He watched as the sun snaked in through the lace, landing in splashes of gold on the kitchen counter, a lattice of light. It was the color of hope and of the future.

All at once, he felt like laughing.

Don't miss the next C. E. Lawrence thriller from Pinnacle, coming Fall 2011!

More Books From Your Favorite Thriller Authors